PREY

ALSO BY MICHAEL CRICHTON

Fiction

The Andromeda Strain

The Terminal Man

The Great Train Robbery

Eaters of the Dead

Congo

Sphere

Jurassic Park

Rising Sun

Disclosure

The Lost World

Airframe

Timeline

Nonfiction

Five Patients

Jasper Johns

Electronic Life

Travels

MICHAEL CRICHTON

PREY

HarperCollins*Publishers*

HarperCollins*Publishers*
77–85 Fulham Palace Road,
Hammersmith, London W6 8JB

www.**fire**and**water**.com

Published by HarperCollins*Publishers* 2002
1 3 5 7 9 8 6 4 2

A catalogue record for this book
is available from the British Library

ISBN 0 00 715379 1
ISBN 0 00 715380 5 (trade pbk)

Printed and bound in Great Britain by
Clays Ltd, St Ives plc

Within fifty to a hundred years, a new class of organisms is likely to emerge. These organisms will be artificial in the sense that they will originally be designed by humans. However, they will reproduce, and will "evolve" into something other than their original form; they will be "alive" under any reasonable definition of the word. These organisms will evolve in a fundamentally different manner. . . . The pace . . . will be extremely rapid. . . . The impact on humanity and the biosphere could be enormous, larger than the industrial revolution, nuclear weapons, or environmental pollution. We must take steps now to shape the emergence of artificial organisms. . . .

— *Doyne Farmer and Alletta Belin, 1992*

There are many people, including myself, who are quite queasy about the consequences of this technology for the future.

— *K. Eric Drexler, 1992*

INTRODUCTION

Artificial Evolution in the
Twenty-first Century

The notion that the world around us is continuously evolving is a plat-
itude; we rarely grasp its full implications. We do not ordinarily think, for
example, of an epidemic disease changing its character as the epidemic
spreads. Nor do we think of evolution in plants and animals as occurring
in a matter of days or weeks, though it does. And we do not ordinarily
imagine the green world around us as a scene of constant, sophisticated
chemical warfare, with plants producing pesticides in response to attack,
and insects developing resistance. But that is what happens, too.

If we were to grasp the true nature of nature—if we could comprehend
the real meaning of evolution—then we would envision a world in which
every living plant, insect, and animal species is changing at every instant,
in response to every other living plant, insect, and animal. Whole populations of organisms are rising and falling, shifting and changing. This restless and perpetual change, as inexorable and unstoppable as the waves and
tides, implies a world in which all human actions necessarily have uncertain effects. The total system we call the biosphere is so complicated that
we cannot know in advance the consequences of anything that we do.[1]

That is why even our most enlightened past efforts have had undesirable outcomes—either because we did not understand enough, or

---

1. This uncertainty is characteristic of all complex systems, including man-made
systems. After the U.S. stock market dropped 22 percent in one day in October 1987,
new rules were implemented to prevent such precipitate declines. But there was no
way to know in advance whether the rules would increase stability, or make things
worse. According to John L. Casti, "Imposition of the rules was simply a calculated
risk on the part of the governors of the Exchange." See Casti's very readable
Would-be Worlds, New York: Wiley, 1997, p. 80 ff.

because the ever-changing world responded to our actions in unexpected ways. From this standpoint, the history of environmental protection is as discouraging as the history of environmental pollution. Anyone who is willing to argue, for example, that the industrial policy of clear-cutting forests is more damaging than the ecological policy of fire suppression ignores the fact that both policies have been carried out with utter conviction, and both have altered the virgin forest irrevocably. Both provide ample evidence of the obstinate egotism that is a hallmark of human interaction with the environment.

The fact that the biosphere responds unpredictably to our actions is not an argument for inaction. It is, however, a powerful argument for caution, and for adopting a tentative attitude toward all we believe, and all we do. Unfortunately, our species has demonstrated a striking lack of caution in the past. It is hard to imagine that we will behave differently in the future.

We think we know what we are doing. We have always thought so. We never seem to acknowledge that we have been wrong in the past, and so might be wrong in the future. Instead, each generation writes off earlier errors as the result of bad thinking by less able minds—and then confidently embarks on fresh errors of its own.

We are one of only three species on our planet that can claim to be self-aware,[2] yet self-delusion may be a more significant characteristic of our kind.

Sometime in the twenty-first century, our self-deluded recklessness will collide with our growing technological power. One area where this will occur is in the meeting point of nanotechnology, biotechnology, and computer technology. What all three have in common is the ability to release self-replicating entities into the environment.

---

2. The only animals for which self-awareness has been convincingly demonstrated are human beings, chimpanzees, and orangutans. Contrary to widespread belief, claims for other animals such as dolphins and monkeys have not been unambiguously proven.

We have lived for some years with the first of these self-replicating entities, computer viruses. And we are beginning to have some practical experience with the problems of biotechnology. The recent report that modified maize genes now appear in native maize in Mexico—despite laws against it, and efforts to prevent it—is just the start of what we may expect to be a long and difficult journey to control our technology. At the same time, long-standing beliefs about the fundamental safety of biotechnology—views promoted by the great majority of biologists since the 1970s—now appear less secure. The unintended creation of a devastatingly lethal virus by Australian researchers in 2001 has caused many to rethink old assumptions.[3] Clearly we will not be as casual about this technology in the future as we have been in the past.

Nanotechnology is the newest of these three technologies, and in some ways the most radical. It is the quest to build man-made machinery of extremely small size, on the order of 100 nanometers, or a hundred billionths of a meter. Such machines would be about 1,000 times smaller than the diameter of a human hair. Pundits predict these tiny machines will provide everything from miniaturized computer components to new cancer treatments to new weapons of war.

As a concept, nanotechnology dates back to a 1959 speech by Richard Feynman called "There's Plenty of Room at the Bottom."[4] Forty years later, the field is still very much in its infancy, despite relentless media hype. Yet practical advances are now being made, and funding has increased dramatically. Major corporations such as IBM, Fujitsu, and Intel are pouring money into research. The U.S. government has spent $1 billion on nanotechnology in the last two years.

Meanwhile, nanotechniques are already being used to make sun-screens, stain-resistant fabrics, and composite materials in cars. Soon they will be used to make computers and storage devices of extremely small size.

---

3. Jackson, R. J., A. J. Ramsay, C. D. Christensen, S. Beaton, D. F. Hall, and I. A. Ramshaw. 2001. "Expression of Mouse Interleukin-4 by a Recombinant Ectromelia Virus Suppresses Cytolytic Lymphocyte Responses and Overcomes Genetic Resistance to Mousepox." *Journal of Virology* 75: 1205–1210.

4. Feynman, R. P., "There's Plenty of Room at the Bottom." *Eng. and Sci.* 23 (1960), p. 22.

And some of the long-anticipated "miracle" products have started to appear as well. In 2002 one company was manufacturing self-cleaning window glass; another made a nanocrystal wound dressing with antibiotic and anti-inflammatory properties.

At the moment nanotechnology is primarily a materials technology, but its potential goes far beyond that. For decades there has been speculation about self-reproducing machines. In 1980 a NASA paper discussed several methods by which such machines could be made. Ten years ago, two knowledgeable scientists took the matter seriously:

> Within fifty to a hundred years, a new class of organisms is likely to emerge. These organisms will be artificial in the sense that they will originally be designed by humans. However, they will reproduce, and will "evolve" into something other than their original form; they will be "alive" under any reasonable definition of the word. . . . The pace of evolutionary change will be extremely rapid. . . . The impact on humanity and the biosphere could be enormous, larger than the industrial revolution, nuclear weapons, or environmental pollution. We must take steps now to shape the emergence of artificial organisms. . . .[5]

And the chief proponent of nanotechnology, K. Eric Drexler, expressed related concerns:

> There are many people, including myself, who are quite queasy about the consequences of this technology for the future. We are talking about changing so many things that the risk of society handling it poorly through lack of preparation is very large.[6]

Even by the most optimistic (or dire) predictions, such organisms are probably decades into our future. We may hope that by the time

5. Farmer, J. Doyne, and Alletta d'A. Belin, "Artificial Life: The Coming Evolution" in *Artificial Life II*, edited by C. G. Langton, C. Taylor, J. D. Farmer, and S. Rasmussen. Santa Fe Institute Studies in the Sciences of Complexity, Proc. Vol. X, Redwood City, Calif.: Addison-Wesley, 1992, p. 815.

6. K. Eric Drexler, "Introduction to Nanotechnology," in *Prospects in Nanotechnology: Toward Molecular Manufacturing (Proceedings of the First General Conference on Nanotechnology: Development, Applications and Opportunities)*, edited by Markus Krummenacker and James Lewis, New York: Wiley & Sons, 1995, p. 21.

they emerge, we will have settled upon international controls for self-reproducing technologies. We can expect such controls to be stringently enforced; already we have learned to treat computer virus–makers with a severity unthinkable twenty years ago. We've learned to put hackers in jail. Errant biotechnologists will soon join them.

But of course, it is always possible that we will not establish controls. Or that someone will manage to create artificial, self-reproducing organisms far sooner than anyone expected. If so, it is difficult to anticipate what the consequences might be. That is the subject of the present novel.

Michael Crichton
LOS ANGELES, 2002

PREY

It's midnight now. The house is dark. I am not sure how this will turn out. The kids are all desperately sick, throwing up. I can hear my son and daughter retching in separate bathrooms. I went in to check on them a few minutes ago, to see what was coming up. I'm worried about the baby, but I had to make her sick, too. It was her only hope.

I think I'm okay, at least for the moment. But of course the odds aren't good: most of the people involved in this business are already dead. And there are so many things I can't know for sure.

The facility is destroyed, but I don't know if we did it in time.

I'm waiting for Mae. She went to the lab in Palo Alto twelve hours ago. I hope she succeeded. I hope she made them understand how desperate the situation is. I expected to hear from the lab but so far there has been no word.

I have ringing in my ears, which is a bad sign. And I feel a vibrating in my chest and abdomen. The baby is spitting up, not really vomiting. I am feeling dizzy. I hope I don't lose consciousness. The kids need me, especially the little one. They're frightened. I don't blame them.

I am, too.

Sitting here in the dark, it's hard to believe that a week ago my biggest problem was finding a job. It seems almost laughable now.

But then, things never turn out the way you think they will.

HOME

DAY 1
10:04 A.M.

Things never turn out the way you think they will.

I never intended to become a househusband. Stay-at-home husband. Full-time dad, whatever you want to call it—there is no good term for it. But that's what I had become in the last six months. Now I was in Crate & Barrel in downtown San Jose, picking up some extra glasses, and while I was there I noticed they had a good selection of placemats. We needed more placemats; the woven oval ones that Julia had bought a year ago were getting pretty worn, and the weave was crusted with baby food. The trouble was, they were woven, so you couldn't wash them. So I stopped at the display to see if they had any placemats that might be good, and I found some pale blue ones that were nice, and I got some white napkins. And then some yellow placemats caught my eye, because they looked really bright and appealing, so I got those, too. They didn't have six on the shelf, and I thought we'd better have six, so I asked the salesgirl to look in the back and see if they had more. While she was gone I put the placemat on the table, and put a white dish on it, and then I put a yellow napkin next to it. The setting looked very cheerful, and I began to think maybe I should get eight instead of six. That was when my cell phone rang.

It was Julia. "Hi, hon."

"Hi, Julia. How's it going?" I said. I could hear machinery in the background, a steady chugging. Probably the vacuum pump for the electron microscope. They had several scanning electron microscopes at her laboratory.

She said, "What're you doing?"

"Buying placemats, actually."

"Where?"

"Crate and Barrel."

She laughed. "You the only guy there?"

"No . . ."

"Oh, well, that's good," she said. I could tell Julia was completely uninterested in this conversation. Something else was on her mind. "Listen, I wanted to tell you, Jack, I'm really sorry, but it's going to be a late night again."

"Uh-huh . . ." The salesgirl came back, carrying more yellow mats. Still holding the phone to my ear, I beckoned her over. I held up three fingers, and she put down three more mats. To Julia, I said, "Is everything all right?"

"Yeah, it's just crazy like normal. We're broadcasting a demo by satellite today to the VCs in Asia and Europe, and we're having trouble with the satellite hookup at this end because the video truck they sent—oh, you don't want to know . . . anyway, we're going to be delayed two hours, hon. Maybe more. I won't get back until eight at the earliest. Can you feed the kids and put them to bed?"

"No problem," I said. And it wasn't. I was used to it. Lately, Julia had been working very long hours. Most nights she didn't get home until the children were asleep. Xymos Technology, the company she worked for, was trying to raise another round of venture capital—twenty million dollars—and there was a lot of pressure. Especially since Xymos was developing technology in what the company called "molecular manufacturing," but which most people called nanotechnology. Nano wasn't popular with the VCs—the venture capitalists—these days. Too many VCs had been burned in the last ten years with products that were supposedly just around the corner, but then never made it out of the lab. The VCs considered nano to be all promise, no products.

Not that Julia needed to be told that; she'd worked for two VC firms

herself. Originally trained as a child psychologist, she ended up as someone who specialized in "technology incubation," helping fledgling technology companies get started. (She used to joke she was still doing child
psychology.) Eventually, she'd stopped advising firms and joined one of
them full-time. She was now a vice president at Xymos.

Julia said Xymos had made several breakthroughs, and was far ahead
of others in the field. She said they were just days away from a prototype
commercial product. But I took what she said with a grain of salt.

"Listen, Jack, I want to warn you," she said, in a guilty voice, "that
Eric is going to be upset."

"Why?"

"Well . . . I told him I would come to the game."

"Julia, why? We talked about making promises like this. There's no
way you can make that game. It's at three o'clock. Why'd you tell him
you would?"

"I thought I could make it."

I sighed. It was, I told myself, a sign of her caring. "Okay. Don't
worry, honey. I'll handle it."

"Thanks. Oh, and Jack? The placemats? Whatever you do, just don't
get yellow, okay?"

And she hung up.

I made spaghetti for dinner because there was never an argument about
spaghetti. By eight o'clock, the two little ones were asleep, and Nicole
was finishing her homework. She was twelve, and had to be in bed by ten
o'clock, though she didn't like any of her friends to know that.

The littlest one, Amanda, was just nine months. She was starting to
crawl everywhere, and to stand up holding on to things. Eric was eight;
he was a soccer kid, and liked to play all the time, when he wasn't dressing up as a knight and chasing his older sister around the house with his
plastic sword.

Nicole was in a modest phase of her life; Eric liked nothing better than
to grab her bra and go running around the house, shouting, "Nicky wears

a bra-a! Nicky wears a bra-a!" while Nicole, too dignified to pursue him, gritted her teeth and yelled, "Dad? He's doing it again! Dad!" And I would have to go chase Eric and tell him not to touch his sister's things.

This was what my life had become. At first, after I lost the job at MediaTronics, it was interesting to deal with sibling rivalry. And often, it seemed, not that different from what my job had been.

At MediaTronics I had run a program division, riding herd over a group of talented young computer programmers. At forty, I was too old to work as a programmer myself anymore; writing code is a young person's job. So I managed the team, and it was a full-time job; like most Silicon Valley programmers, my team seemed to live in a perpetual crisis of crashed Porsches, infidelities, bad love affairs, parental hassles, and drug reactions, all superimposed on a forced-march work schedule with all-night marathons fueled by cases of Diet Coke and Sun chips.

But the work was exciting, in a cutting-edge field. We wrote what are called distributed parallel processing or agent-based programs. These programs model biological processes by creating virtual agents inside the computer and then letting the agents interact to solve real-world problems. It sounds strange, but it works fine. For example, one of our programs imitated ant foraging—how ants find the shortest path to food—to route traffic through a big telephone network. Other programs mimicked the behavior of termites, swarming bees, and stalking lions.

It was fun, and I would probably still be there if I hadn't taken on some additional responsibilities. In my last few months there, I'd been put in charge of security, replacing an outside tech consultant who'd had the job for two years but had failed to detect the theft of company source code, until it turned up in a program being marketed out of Taiwan. Actually, it was my division's source code—software for distributed processing. That was the code that had been stolen.

We knew it was the same code, because the Easter eggs hadn't been touched. Programmers always insert Easter eggs into their code, little nuggets that don't serve any useful purpose and are just put there for fun. The Taiwanese company hadn't changed any of them; they used our code wholesale. So the keystrokes Alt-Shift-M-9 would open up a window giving the date of one of our programmers' marriage. Clear theft.

Of course we sued, but Don Gross, the head of the company, wanted to make sure it didn't happen again. So he put me in charge of security, and I was angry enough about the theft to take the job. It was only part-time; I still ran the division. The first thing I did as security officer was to monitor workstation use. It was pretty straightforward; these days, eighty percent of companies monitor what their workers do at terminals. They do it by video, or they do it by recording keystrokes, or by scanning email for certain keywords . . . all sorts of procedures out there.

Don Gross was a tough guy, an ex-Marine who had never lost his military manner. When I told him about the new system, he said, "But you're not monitoring my terminal, right?" Of course not, I said. In fact, I'd set up the programs to monitor every computer in the company, his included. And that was how I discovered, two weeks later, that Don was having an affair with a girl in accounting, and had authorized her to have a company car. I went to him and said that based on emails relating to Jean in accounting, it appeared that someone unknown was having an affair with her, and that she might be getting perks she wasn't entitled to. I said I didn't know who the person was, but if they kept using email, I'd soon find out.

I figured Don would take the hint, and he did. But now he just sent incriminating email from his home, never realizing that everything went through the company server and I was getting it all. That's how I learned he was "discounting" software to foreign distributors, and taking large "consultant fees" into an account in the Cayman Islands. This was clearly illegal, and I couldn't overlook it. I consulted my attorney, Gary Marder, who advised me to quit.

"Quit?" I said.

"Yeah. Of course."

"Why?"

"Who cares why? You got a better offer elsewhere. You've got some health problems. Or some family issues. Trouble at home. Just get out of there. Quit."

"Wait a minute," I said. "You think *I* should quit because *he's* breaking the law? Is that your advice to me?"

"No," Gary said. "As your attorney, my advice is that if you are aware of any illegal activity you have a duty to report it. But as your friend, my advice is to keep your mouth shut and get out of there fast."

"Seems kind of cowardly. I think I have to notify the investors."

Gary sighed. He put his hand on my shoulder. "Jack," he said, "the investors can look out for themselves. You get the fuck out of there."

I didn't think that was right. I had been annoyed when my code had been stolen. Now I found myself wondering if it actually had been stolen. Maybe it had been sold. We were a privately held company, and I told one of the board members.

It turned out he was in on it. I was fired the next day for gross negligence and misconduct. Litigation was threatened; I had to sign a raft of NDAs in order to get my severance package. My attorney handled the paperwork for me, sighing with every new document.

At the end, we went outside into the milky sunshine. I said, "Well, at least that's over."

He turned and looked at me. "Why do you say that?" he said.

Because of course it wasn't over. In some mysterious way, I had become a marked man. My qualifications were excellent and I worked in a hot field. But when I went on job interviews I could tell they weren't interested. Worse, they were uncomfortable. Silicon Valley covers a big area, but it's a small place. Word gets out. Eventually I found myself talking to an interviewer I knew slightly, Ted Landow. I'd coached his kid in Little League baseball the year before. When the interview was over, I said to him, "What have you heard about me?"

He shook his head. "Nothing, Jack."

I said, "Ted, I've been on ten interviews in ten days. Tell me."

"There's nothing to tell."

"Ted."

He shuffled through his papers, looking down at them, not at me. He sighed. "Jack Forman. Troublemaker. Not cooperative. Belligerent. Hotheaded. Not a team player." He hesitated, then said, "And supposedly you were involved in some kind of dealings. They won't say what, but some kind of shady dealings. You were on the take."

"*I* was on the take?" I said. I felt a flood of anger, and started to say more, until I realized I was probably looking hotheaded and belligerent. So I shut up, and thanked him.

As I was leaving, he said, "Jack, do yourself a favor. Give it a while. Things change fast in the Valley. Your résumé is strong and your skill set is outstanding. Wait until . . ." He shrugged.

"A couple of months?"

"I'd say four. Maybe five."

Somehow I knew he was right. After that, I stopped trying so hard. I began to hear rumors that MediaTronics was going belly up, and there might be indictments. I smelled vindication ahead, but in the meantime there was nothing to do but wait.

The strangeness of not going to work in the morning slowly faded. Julia was working longer hours at her job, and the kids were demanding; if I was in the house they turned to me, instead of our housekeeper, Maria. I started taking them to school, picking them up, driving them to the doctor, the orthodontist, soccer practice. The first few dinners I cooked were disastrous, but I got better.

And before I knew it, I was buying placemats and looking at table settings in Crate & Barrel. And it all seemed perfectly normal.

Julia got home around nine-thirty. I was watching the Giants game on TV, not really paying attention. She came in and kissed me on the back of my neck. She said, "They all asleep?"

"Except Nicole. She's still doing homework."

"Jeez, isn't it late for her to be up?"

"No, hon," I said. "We agreed. This year she gets to stay up until ten, remember?"

Julia shrugged, as if she didn't remember. And maybe she didn't. We had undergone a sort of inversion of roles; she had always been more knowledgeable about the kids, but now I was. Sometimes Julia felt uncomfortable with that, experiencing it somehow as a loss of power.

"How's the little one?"

"Her cold is better. Just sniffles. She's eating more."

I walked with Julia to the bedrooms. She went into the baby's room, bent over the crib, and kissed the sleeping child tenderly. Watching her, I thought there was something about a mother's caring that a father could never match. Julia had some connection to the kids that I never would. Or at least a different connection. She listened to the baby's soft breathing, and said, "Yes, she's better."

Then she went into Eric's room, took the Game Boy off the bed covers, gave me a frown. I shrugged, faintly irritated; I knew Eric played with his Game Boy when he was supposed to be going to sleep, but I was busy getting the baby down at that time, and I overlooked it. I thought Julia should be more understanding.

Then she went into Nicole's room. Nicole was on her laptop, but shut the lid when her mother walked in. "Hi, Mom."

"You're up late."

"No, Mom . . ."

"You're supposed to be doing homework."

"I did it."

"Then why aren't you in bed?"

"Because—"

"I don't want you spending all night talking to your friends on the computer."

"Mom . . ." she said, in a pained voice.

"You see them every day at school, that should be enough."

"Mom . . ."

"Don't look at your father. We already know he'll do whatever you want. I'm talking to you, now."

She sighed. "I know, Mom."

This kind of interaction was increasingly common between Nicole and Julia. I guess it was normal at this age, but I thought I'd step in. Julia was tired, and when she was tired she got rigid and controlling. I put my arm around her shoulder and said, "It's late for everybody. Want a cup of tea?"

"Jack, don't interfere."

"I'm not, I just—"

"Yes, you are. I'm talking to Nicole and you're interfering, the way you always do."

"Honey, we all agreed she could stay up until ten, I don't know what this—"

"But if she's finished her homework, she should go to bed."

"That wasn't the deal."

"I don't want her spending all day and night on the computer."

"She's not, Julia."

At that point, Nicole burst into tears, and jumped to her feet crying, "You always criticize me! I *hate* you!" She ran into the bathroom and slammed the door. That woke the baby, who started to cry.

Julia turned to me and said, "If you would *please* just let me handle this myself, Jack."

And I said, "You're right. I'm sorry. You're right."

In truth, that wasn't what I thought at all. More and more, I regarded this as my house, and my kids. She was barging into *my* house, late at night, when I'd gotten everything quiet, the way I liked it, the way it should be. And she was raising a fuss.

I didn't think she was right at all. I thought she was wrong.

And in the last few weeks I'd noticed that incidents like this had become more frequent. At first, I thought Julia felt guilty about being away so much. Then I thought she was reasserting her authority, trying to regain control of a household that had fallen into my hands. Then I thought it was because she was tired, or under so much pressure at work.

But lately I felt I was making excuses for her behavior. I started to have the feeling Julia had changed. She was different, somehow, tenser, tougher.

The baby was howling. I picked her up from the crib, hugged her, cooed at her, and simultaneously stuck a finger down the back of the diaper to see if it was wet. It was. I put her down on her back on top of the dresser, and she howled again until I shook her favorite rattle, and put it in her hand. She was silent then, allowing me to change her without much kicking.

"I'll do that," Julia said, coming in.

"It's okay."

"I woke her up, it's only right I do it."

"Really honey, it's fine."

Julia put her hand on my shoulder, kissed the back of my neck. "I'm sorry I'm such a jerk. I'm really tired. I don't know what came over me. Let me change the baby, I never get to see her."

"Okay," I said. I stepped aside, and she moved in.

"Hi, Poopsie-doopsie," she said, chucking the baby under the chin. "How's my little Winkie-dinkie?" All this attention made the baby drop the rattle, and then she started to cry, and to twist away on the table. Julia didn't notice the missing rattle caused the crying; instead she made soothing sounds and struggled to put on the new diaper, but the baby's twisting and kicking made it hard. "Amanda, stop it!"

I said, "She does that now." And it was true, Amanda was in the stage where she actively resisted a diaper change. And she could kick pretty hard.

"Well, she should stop. Stop!"

The baby cried louder, tried to turn away. One of the adhesive tabs pulled off. The diaper slid down. Amanda was now rolling toward the edge of the dresser. Julia pulled her back roughly. Amanda never stopped kicking.

"God damn it, I said stop!" Julia said, and smacked the baby on the leg. The baby just cried harder, kicked harder. "Amanda! Stop it! Stop it!" She slapped her again. *"Stop it! Stop it!"*

For a moment I didn't react. I was stunned. I didn't know what to do. The baby's legs were bright red. Julia was still hitting her. "Honey . . ." I said, leaning in, "let's not—"

Julia exploded. "Why do you always fucking interfere?" she yelled, slamming her hand down on the dresser. "What is your fucking problem?"

And she stomped off, leaving the room.

I let out a long breath, and picked the baby up. Amanda howled inconsolably, as much in confusion as in pain. I figured I would need to give her a bottle to get her to sleep again. I stroked her back until she settled down a little. Then I got her diaper on, and brought her into the kitchen while I heated a bottle. The lights were low, just the fluorescents over the counter.

Julia was sitting at the table, drinking beer out of a bottle, staring into space. "When are you going to get a job?" she said.

"I'm trying."

"Really? I don't think you're trying at all. When was your last interview?"

"Last week," I said.

She grunted. "I wish you'd hurry up and get one," she said, "because this is driving me crazy."

I swallowed anger. "I know. It's hard for everybody," I said. It was late at night, and I didn't want to argue anymore. But I was watching her out of the corner of my eye.

At thirty-six, Julia was a strikingly pretty woman, petite, with dark hair and dark eyes, upturned nose, and the kind of personality that people called bubbly or sparkling. Unlike many tech executives, she was attractive and approachable. She made friends easily, and had a good sense of humor. Years back, when we first had Nicole, Julia would come home with hilarious accounts of the foibles of her VC partners. We used to sit at this same kitchen table and laugh until I felt physically sick, while little Nicole would tug at her arm and say, "What's the funny, Mom? What's the funny?" because she wanted to be in on the joke. Of course we could never explain it to her, but Julia always seemed to have a new "Knock knock" joke for Nicole, so she could join in the laughter, too. Julia had a real gift for seeing the humorous side of life. She was famous for her equanimity; she almost never lost her temper.

Right now, of course, she was furious. Not even willing to look at me. Sitting in the dark at the round kitchen table, one leg crossed over the other, kicking impatiently while she stared into space. As I looked at her, I had the feeling that her appearance had changed, somehow. Of course she had lost weight recently, part of the strain of the job. A certain softness in her face was gone; her cheekbones protruded more; her chin seemed sharper. It made her look harder, but in a way more glamorous.

Her clothes were different, too. Julia was wearing a dark skirt and a white blouse, sort of standard business attire. But the skirt was tighter than usual. And her kicking foot made me notice she was wearing slingback high heels. What she used to call fuck-me shoes. The kind of shoes she would never wear to work.

And then I realized that everything about her was different—her manner, her appearance, her mood, everything—and in a flash of insight I knew why: *my wife was having an affair.*

The water on the stove began to steam, and I pulled out the bottle, tested it on my forearm. It had gotten too hot, and I would have to wait a minute for it to cool. The baby started to cry, and I bounced her a little on my shoulder, while I walked her around the room.

Julia never looked at me. She just kept swinging her foot, and staring into space.

I had read somewhere that this was a syndrome. The husband's out of work, his masculine appeal declines, his wife no longer respects him, and she wanders. I had read that in *Glamour* or *Redbook* or one of those magazines around the house that I glanced through while waiting for the washing machine to finish its cycle, or the microwave to thaw the hamburger.

But now I was flooded with confused feelings. Was it really true? Was I just tired, making up bad stories in my mind? After all, what difference did it make if she was wearing tighter skirts and different shoes? Fashions changed. People felt different on different days. And just because she was sometimes angry, did that really mean she was having an affair? Of course it didn't. I was probably just feeling inadequate, unattractive. These were probably my insecurities coming out. My thoughts went on in this vein for a while.

But for some reason, I couldn't talk myself out of it. I was *sure* it was true. I had lived with this woman for more than twelve years. I knew she was different, and I knew why. I could sense the presence of someone else, an outside person, some intruder in our relationship. I felt it with a conviction that surprised me. I felt it in my bones, like an ache.

I had to turn away.

*   *   *

The baby took the bottle, gurgling happily. In the darkened kitchen, she stared up at my face with that peculiar fixed stare that babies have. It was sort of soothing, watching her. After a while she closed her eyes, and then her mouth went slack. I put her on my shoulder and burped her as I carried her back into her bedroom. Most parents pat their babies too hard, trying to get a burp. It's better to just rub the flat of your hand up their back, and sometimes just along the spine with two fingers. She gave a soft belch, and relaxed.

I set her down in the crib, and I turned out the night-light. Now the only light in the room came from the aquarium, bubbling green-blue in the corner. A plastic diver trudged along the bottom, trailing bubbles.

As I turned to go, I saw Julia silhouetted in the doorway, dark hair backlit. She had been watching me. I couldn't read her expression. She stalked forward. I tensed. She put her arms around me and rested her head on my chest.

"Please forgive me," she said. "I'm a real jerk. You're doing a wonderful job. I'm just jealous, that's all." My shoulder was wet with her tears.

"I understand," I said, holding her. "It's okay."

I waited to see if my body relaxed, but it didn't. I was suspicious and alert. I had a bad feeling about her, and it wasn't going away.

She came out of the shower into the bedroom, toweling her short hair dry. I was sitting on the bed, trying to watch the rest of the game. It occurred to me that she never used to take showers at night. Julia always took a shower in the morning before work. Now, I realized, she often came home and went straight to the shower before coming out to say hello to the kids.

My body was still tense. I flicked the TV off. I said, "How was the demo?"

"The what?"

"The demo. Didn't you have a demo today?"

"Oh," she said. "Oh, yes. We did. It went fine, when we finally got it going. The VCs in Germany couldn't stay for all of it because of the time change, but—listen, do you want to see it?"

"What do you mean?"

"I have a dub of it. Want to see it?"

I was surprised. I shrugged. "Okay, sure."

"I'd really like to know what you think, Jack." I detected a patronizing tone. My wife was including me in her work. Making me feel a part of her life. I watched as she opened her briefcase and took out a DVD. She stuck it in the player, and came back to sit with me on the bed.

"What were you demoing?" I said.

"The new medical imaging technology," she said. "It's really slick, if I say so myself." She snuggled up, tucking herself into my shoulder. All very cozy, just like old times. I still felt uneasy, but I put my arm around her.

"By the way," I said, "how come you take showers at night now, instead of in the morning?"

"I don't know," she said. "Do I? I guess I do. It just seems easier, honey. Mornings are so rushed, and I've been getting those conference calls from Europe, they take so much time—okay, here we go," she said, pointing to the screen. I saw black-and-white scramble, and then the image resolved.

The tape showed Julia in a large laboratory that was fitted out like an operating room. A man lay on his back on the gurney, an IV in his arm, an anesthesiologist standing by. Above the table was a round flat metal plate about six feet in diameter, which could be raised and lowered, but was now raised. There were video monitors all around. And in the foreground, peering at a monitor, was Julia. There was a video technician by her side.

"This is terrible," she was saying, pointing to the monitor. "What's all the interference?"

"We think it's the air purifiers. They're causing it."

"Well, this is unacceptable."

"Really?"

"Yes, really."

"What do you want us to do?"

"I want you to fix it," Julia said.

"Then we have to boost power, and you have—"

"I don't care," she said. "I can't show the VCs an image of this quality. They've seen better pictures from Mars. Fix it."

Beside me on the bed, Julia said, "I didn't know they recorded all this. This is before the demo. You can fast forward."

I pushed the remote. The picture scrambled. I waited a few seconds, and played it again.

Same scene. Julia still in the foreground. Carol, her assistant, whispering to her.

"Okay, but then what do I tell him?"

"Tell him no."

"But he wants to get started."

"I understand. But the transmission isn't for an hour. Tell him no."

On the bed, Julia said to me, "Mad Dog was our experimental subject. He was very restless. Impatient to get started."

On the screen, the assistant lowered her voice. "I think he's nervous, Julia. I would be, too, with a couple of million of those things crawling around inside my body—"

"It's not a couple of million, and they're not crawling," Julia said. "Anyway, they're his invention."

"Even so."

"Isn't that an anesthesiologist over there?"

"No, just a cardiologist."

"Well, maybe the cardiologist can give him something for his nervousness."

"They already did. An injection."

On the bed beside me, Julia said, "Fast forward, Jack." I did. The picture jumped ahead. "Okay, here."

I saw Julia standing at the monitor again, with the technician beside her. "That's acceptable," onscreen Julia was saying, pointing to the image. "Not great, but acceptable. Now, show me the STM."

"The what?"

"The STM. The electron microscope. Show me the image from that."

The technician looked confused. "Uh . . . Nobody told us about any electron microscope."

"For God's sake, read the damn storyboards!"

The technician blinked. "It's on the storyboards?"

"Did you *look* at the storyboards?"

"I'm sorry, I guess I must have missed it."

"There's no time now to be sorry. Fix it!"

"You don't have to shout."

"Yes I do! I have to shout, because I'm surrounded by idiots!" She waved her hands in the air. "I'm about to go online and talk to eleven billion dollars of venture capital in five countries and show them submicroscopic technology, except *I* don't have a microscope feed, so *they* can't see the technology!"

On the bed, Julia said, "I kind of lost it with this guy. It was so frustrating. We had a clock counting down to the satellite time, which was booked and locked. We couldn't change it. We had to make the time, and this guy was a dimbus. But eventually we got it working. Fast forward."

The screen showed a static card, which read:

A Private Demonstration of
Advanced Medical Imaging
by
Xymos Technology
Mountain View, CA
World Leader in Molecular Manufacturing

Then, on the screen, Julia appeared, standing in front of the gurney and the medical apparatus. She'd brushed her hair and tucked in her blouse.

"Hello to all of you," she said, smiling at the camera. "I'm Julia Forman of Xymos Technology, and we're about to demonstrate a revolutionary medical imaging procedure just developed here. Our subject, Peter Morris, is lying behind me on the table. In a few moments, we're going to look inside his heart and blood vessels with an ease and accuracy never before possible."

She began walking around the table, talking as she went.

"Unlike cardiac catheterization, our procedure is one hundred per-cent safe. And unlike catheterization, we can look everywhere in the body, at every sort of vessel, no matter how large or small. We'll see inside his aorta, the largest artery of the body. But we'll also look inside the alveoli of his lungs, and the tiny capillaries of his fingertips. We can do all this because the camera we put inside his vessels is smaller than a red blood cell. Quite a bit smaller, actually.

"Xymos microfabrication technology can now produce these minia-turized cameras, and produce them in quantity—cheaply, quickly. It would take a thousand of them just to make a dot the size of a pencil point. We can fabricate a kilogram of these cameras in an hour.

"I'm sure you are all skeptical. We're well aware that nanotechnology has made promises it couldn't deliver. As you know, the problem has been that scientists could design molecular-scale devices, but they couldn't manufacture them. But Xymos has solved that problem."

It suddenly hit me, what she was saying. *"What?"* I said, sitting up in bed. "Are you kidding?" If it was true, it was an extraordinary develop-ment, a genuine technological breakthrough, and it meant—

"It's true," Julia said quietly. "We're manufacturing in Nevada." She smiled, enjoying my astonishment.

Onscreen, Julia was saying, "I have one of our Xymos cameras under the electron microscope, here"—she pointed to the screen—"so you can see it in comparison to the red blood cell alongside it."

The image changed to black-and-white. I saw a fine probe push what looked like a tiny squid into position on a titanium field. It was a bullet-nosed lump with streaming filaments at the rear. It was a tenth of the size of the red blood cell, which in the vacuum of the scanning electron microscope was a wrinkled oval, like a gray raisin.

"Our camera is one ten-billionth of an inch in length. As you see, it is shaped like a squid," Julia said. "Imaging takes place in the nose. Microtubules in the tail provide stabilization, like the tail of a kite. But they can also lash actively, and provide locomotion. Jerry, if we can turn the camera to see the nose . . . Okay, there. Thank you. Now, from the front, you see that indentation in the center? That is the miniature gallium arsenide photon detector, acting as a retina, and the surrounding banded area—sort of like a radial tire—is bioluminescent, and lights the area ahead. Within the nose itself you may be able to just make out a rather complex series of twisted molecules. That is our patented ATP cascade. You can think of it as a primitive brain, which controls the behavior of the camera—very limited behavior, true, but enough for our purposes."

I heard a hiss of static, and a cough. The screen image opened a small window in the corner, and now showed Fritz Leidermeyer, in Germany. The investor shifted his enormous bulk. "I'm sorry, Ms. Forman. Tell me please where is the lens?"

"There is no lens."

"How can you have a camera with no lens?"

"I'll explain that as we go," she said.

Watching, I said, "It must be a camera obscura."

"Right," she said, nodding.

Camera obscura—Latin for "dark room"—was the oldest imaging device known. The Romans had found that if you made a small hole in the wall of a dark room, an upside-down image of the exterior appeared on the opposite wall. That was because light coming through any small aperture was focused, as if by a lens. It was the same principle as a kid's pinhole camera. It was why ever since Roman times, image-recording devices were called cameras. But in this case—

"What makes the aperture?" I said. "Is there a pinhole?"

"I thought you knew," she said. "You're responsible for that part."

"Me?"

"Yes. Xymos licensed some agent-based algorithms that your team wrote."

"No, I didn't know. Which algorithms?"

"To control a particle network."

"Your cameras are networked? All those little cameras communicate with each other?"

"Yes," she said. "They're a swarm, actually." She was still smiling, amused by my reactions.

"A swarm." I was thinking it over, trying to understand what she was telling me. Certainly my team had written a number of programs to control swarms of agents. Those programs were modeled on behavior of bees. The programs had many useful characteristics. Because swarms were composed of many agents, the swarm could respond to the environment in a robust way. Faced with new and unexpected conditions, the swarm programs didn't crash; they just sort of flowed around the obstacles, and kept going.

But our programs worked by creating virtual agents inside the computer. Julia had created real agents in the real world. At first I didn't see how our programs could be adapted to what she was doing.

"We use them for structure," she said. "The program makes the swarm structure."

Of course. It was obvious that a single molecular camera was inadequate to register any sort of image. Therefore, the image must be a composite of millions of cameras, operating simultaneously. But the cameras would also have to be arranged in space in some orderly structure, probably a sphere. That was where the programming came in. But that in turn meant that Xymos must be generating the equivalent of—

"You're making an eye."

"Kind of. Yes."

"But where's the light source?"

"The bioluminescent perimeter."

"That's not enough light."

"It is. Watch."

Meanwhile, the onscreen Julia was turning smoothly, pointing to the intravenous line behind her. She lifted a syringe out of a nearby ice bucket. The barrel appeared to be filled with water. "This syringe," she said, "contains approximately twenty million cameras in isotonic saline suspension. At the moment they exist as particles. But once they are injected into the bloodstream, their temperature will increase, and they will soon flock together, and form a meta-shape. Just like a flock of birds forms a V-shape."

"What kind of a shape?" one of the VCs asked.

"A sphere," she said. "With a small opening at one end. You might think of it as the equivalent of a blastula in embryology. But in effect the particles form an eye. And the image from that eye will be a composite of millions of photon detectors. Just as the human eye creates an image from its rods and cone cells."

She turned to a monitor that showed an animation loop, repeated over and over again. The cameras entered the bloodstream as an untidy, disorganized mass, a kind of buzzing cloud within the blood. Immediately the blood flow flattened the cloud into an elongated streak. But within seconds, the streak began to coalesce into a spherical shape. That shape became more defined, until eventually it appeared almost solid.

"If this reminds you of an actual eye, there's a reason. Here at Xymos we are explicitly imitating organic morphology," Julia said. "Because we are designing with organic molecules, we are aware that courtesy of millions of years of evolution, the world around us has a stockpile of molecular arrangements that work. So we use them."

"You don't want to reinvent the wheel?" someone said.

"Exactly. Or the eyeball."

She gave a signal, and the flat antenna was lowered until it was just inches above the waiting subject.

"This antenna will power the camera, and pick up the transmitted image," she said. "The image can of course be digitally stored, intensified, manipulated, or anything else that you might do with digital data. Now, if there are no other questions, we can begin."

She fitted the syringe with a needle, and stuck it into a rubber stopper in the IV line.

"Mark time."

"Zero point zero."

"Here we go."

She pushed the plunger down quickly. "As you see, I'm doing it fast," she said. "There's nothing delicate about our procedure. You can't hurt anything. If the microturbulence generated by the flow through the needle rips the tubules from a few thousand cameras, it doesn't matter. We have millions more. Plenty to do the job." She withdrew the needle.

"Okay? Generally we have to wait about ten seconds for the shape to form, and then we should begin getting an image . . . Ah, looks like something is coming now . . . And here it is."

The scene showed the camera moving forward at considerable speed through what looked like an asteroid field. Except the asteroids were red cells, bouncy purplish bags moving in a clear, slightly yellowish liquid. An occasional much larger white cell shot forward, filled the screen for a moment, then was gone. What I was seeing looked more like a video game than a medical image.

"Julia," I said, "this is pretty amazing."

Beside me, Julia snuggled closer and smiled. "I thought you might be impressed."

Onscreen, Julia was saying, "We've entered a vein, so the red cells are not oxygenated. Right now our camera is moving toward the heart. You'll see the vessels enlarging as we move up the venous system . . . Yes, now we are approaching the heart . . . You can see the pulsations in the bloodstream that result from the ventricular contractions . . ."

It was true, I could see the camera pause, then move forward, then pause. She had an audio feed of the beating heart. On the table, the subject lay motionless, with the flat antenna just over his body.

"We're coming to the right atrium, and we should see the mitral valve. We activate the flagella to slow the camera. There the valve is now. We are in the heart." I saw the red flaps, like a mouth opening and closing, and then the camera shot through, into the ventricle, and out again.

"Now we are going to the lungs, where you will see what no one has ever witnessed before. The oxygenation of the cells."

As I watched, the blood vessel narrowed swiftly, and then the cells plumped up, and popped brilliantly red, one after another. It was extremely quick; in less than a second, they were all red.

"The red cells have now been oxygenated," Julia said, "and we are on our way back to the heart."

I turned to Julia in the bed. "This is really fantastic stuff," I said.

But her eyes were closed, and she was breathing gently.

"Julia?"

She was asleep.

Julia had always tended to fall asleep while watching TV. Falling asleep during your own presentation was reasonable enough; after all, she'd already seen it. And it was pretty late. I was tired myself. I decided I could watch the rest of the demo another time. It seemed pretty lengthy for a demo, anyhow. How long had I been watching so far? When I turned to switch off the TV, I looked down at the time code running at the bottom of the image. Numbers were spinning, ticking off hundredths of a second. Other numbers to the left, not spinning. I frowned. One of them was the date. I hadn't noticed it before, because it was in international format, with the year first, the day, and the month. It read 02.21.09.

September 21.

Yesterday.

She'd recorded this demo yesterday, not today.

I turned off the TV, and turned off the bedside light. I lay down on the pillow and tried to sleep.

DAY 2
9:02 A.M.

We needed skim milk, Toastie-Os, Pop-Tarts, Jell-O, dishwasher detergent—and something else, but I couldn't read my own writing. I stood in the supermarket aisle at nine o'clock in the morning, puzzling over my notes. A voice said, "Hey, Jack. How's it hanging?"

I looked up to see Ricky Morse, one of the division heads at Xymos.

"Hey, Ricky. How are you?" I shook his hand, genuinely glad to see him. I was always glad to see Ricky. Tanned, with blond crewcut hair and a big grin, he could easily be taken for a surfer were it not for his Source-Forge 3.1 T-shirt. Ricky was only a few years younger than I was, but he had an air of perpetual youthfulness. I'd given him his first job, right out of college, and he'd rapidly moved into management. With his cheerful personality and upbeat manner, Ricky made an ideal project manager, even though he tended to underplay problems, and give management unrealistic expectations about when a project would be finished.

According to Julia, that had sometimes caused trouble at Xymos; Ricky tended to make promises he couldn't keep. And sometimes he didn't quite tell the truth. But he was so cheerful and appealing that everyone always forgave him. At least, I always did, when he worked for me. I had become quite fond of him, and thought of him almost as a younger brother. I'd recommended him for his job at Xymos.

Ricky was pushing a shopping cart filled with disposable diapers in big plastic bundles; he had a young baby at home, too. I asked him why he was shopping and not at the office.

"Mary's got the flu, and the maid's in Guatemala. So I told her I'd pick up some things."

"I see you've got Huggies," I said. "I always get Pampers, myself."

"I find Huggies absorb more," he said. "And Pampers are too tight. They pinch the baby's leg."

"But Pampers have a layer that takes moisture away, and keeps the bottom dry," I said. "I have fewer rashes with Pampers."

"Whenever I use them, the adhesive tabs tend to pull off. And with a big load, it tends to leak out the leg, which makes extra work for me. I don't know, I just find Huggies are higher quality."

A woman glanced at us as she pushed past with her shopping cart. We started to laugh, thinking we must sound like we were in a commercial.

Ricky said loudly, "So hey, how about those Giants?" to the woman's back as she continued down the aisle.

"Fuckin' A, are they great or what?" I said, scratching myself.

We laughed, then pushed our carts down the aisle together. Ricky said, "Want to know the truth? Mary likes Huggies, and that's the end of the conversation."

"I know that one," I said.

Ricky looked at my cart, and said, "I see you buy organic skim milk . . ."

"Stop it," I said. "How are things at the office?"

"You know, they're pretty damn good," he said. "The technology's coming along nicely, if I say so myself. We demoed for the money guys the other day, and it went well."

"Julia's doing okay?" I said, as casually as I could.

"Yeah, she's doing great. Far as I know," Ricky said.

I glanced at him. Was he suddenly reserved? Was his face set, the muscles controlled? Was he concealing something? I couldn't tell.

"Actually, I rarely see her," Ricky said. "She's not around much these days."

"I don't see much of her either," I said.

"Yeah, she's spending a lot of time out at the fab complex. That's where the action is now." Ricky glanced quickly at me. "You know, because of the new fabrication processes."

The Xymos fab building had been completed in record time, considering how complex it was. The fabrication building was where they assembled molecules from individual atoms. Sticking the molecule fragments together like Lego blocks. Much of this work was carried out in a vacuum, and required extremely strong magnetic fields. So the fab building had tremendous pump assemblies, and powerful chillers to cool the magnets. But according to Julia, a lot of the technology was specific to that building; nothing like it had ever been built before.

I said, "It's amazing they got the building up so fast."

"Well, we kept the pressure on. Molecular Dynamics is breathing down our necks. We've got our fab up and running, and we've got patent applications by the truckload. But those guys at MolDyne and NanoTech can't be far behind us. A few months. Maybe six months, if we're lucky."

"So you're doing molecular assembly at the plant now?" I said.

"You got it, Jack. Full-bore molecular assembly. We have been for a few weeks now."

"I didn't know Julia was interested in that stuff." With her background in psychology, I'd always regarded Julia as a people person.

"She's taken a real interest in the technology, I can tell you. Also, they're doing a lot of programming up there, too," he said. "You know. Iterative cycles as they refine the manufacturing."

I nodded. "What kind of programming?" I said.

"Distributed processing. Multi-agent nets. That's how we keep the individual units coordinated, working together."

"This is all to make the medical camera?"

"Yes." He paused. "Among other things." He glanced at me uneasily, as if he might be breaking his confidentiality agreement.

"You don't have to say," I said.

"No, no," he said quickly. "Jeez, you and I go way back, Jack." He slapped me on the shoulder. "And you got a spouse in management. I mean, what the hell." But he still looked uneasy. His face didn't match his words. And his eyes slid away from me when he said the word "spouse."

The conversation was coming to an end, and I felt filled with tension, the kind of awkward tension when you think another guy knows something and isn't telling you—because he's embarrassed, because he doesn't know how to put it, because he doesn't want to get involved, because it's too dangerous even to mention, because he thinks it's your job to figure it out for yourself. Especially when it's something about your wife. Like she's screwing around. He's looking at you like you're the walking wounded, it's night of the living dead, but he won't tell you. In my experience, guys never tell other guys when they know something about their wives. But women always tell other women, if they know of a husband's infidelity.

That's just how it is.

But I was feeling so tense I wanted to—

"Hey, look at the time," Ricky said, giving me a big grin. "I'm late, Mary'll kill me, I've got to run. She's already annoyed because I have to spend the next few days at the fab facility. So I'll be out of town while the maid's gone . . ." He shrugged. "You know how it is."

"Yeah, I do. Good luck."

"Hey, man. Take care."

We shook hands. Murmured another good-bye. Ricky rolled his cart around the corner of the aisle, and was gone.

Sometimes you can't think about painful things, you can't make your mind focus on them. Your brain just slips away, no thank you, let's change the subject. That was happening to me now. I couldn't think about Julia, so I started thinking about what Ricky had told me about their fabrication plant. And I decided it probably made sense, even though it went against the conventional wisdom about nanotechnology.

There was a long-standing fantasy among nanotechnologists that once somebody figured out how to manufacture at the atomic level, it would be like running the four-minute mile. Everybody would do it, unleashing a flood of wonderful molecular creations rolling off assembly lines all around the world. In a matter of days, human life would be changed by this marvelous new technology. As soon as somebody figured out how to do it.

But of course that would never happen. The very idea was absurd. Because in essence, molecular manufacturing wasn't so different from computer manufacturing or flow-valve manufacturing or automobile manufacturing or any other kind of manufacturing. It took a while to get it right. In fact, assembling atoms to make a new molecule was closely analogous to compiling a computer program from individual lines of code. And computer code never compiled, the first time out. The programmers always had to go back and fix the lines. And even after it was compiled, a computer program never *ever* worked right the first time. Or the second time. Or the hundredth time. It had to be debugged, and debugged again, and again. And again.

I always believed it would be the same with these manufactured molecules—they'd have to be debugged again and again before they worked right. And if Xymos wanted "flocks" of molecules working together, they'd also have to debug the way the molecules communicated with each other, however limited that communication was. Because once the molecules communicated, you had a primitive network. To organize it, you'd probably program a distributed net. Of the kind I had been developing at MediaTronics.

So I could perfectly well imagine them doing programming along with the manufacturing. But I couldn't see Julia hanging around while they did it. The fab facility was far from the Xymos headquarters. It was literally in the middle of nowhere—out in the desert near Tonopah, Nevada. And Julia didn't like to be in the middle of nowhere.

I was sitting in the pediatrician's waiting room because the baby was due for her next round of immunizations. There were four mothers in the room, bouncing sick kids on their laps while the older children played on the floor. The mothers all talked to each other and studiously ignored me.

I was getting used to this. A guy at home, a guy in a setting like the pediatrician's office, was an unusual thing. But it also meant that something was wrong. There was probably something wrong with the guy, he couldn't get a job, maybe he was fired for alcoholism or drugs, maybe he was a bum. Whatever the reason, it wasn't normal for a man to be in the pediatrician's office in the middle of the day. So the other mothers pretended I wasn't there.

Except they shot me the occasional worried glance, as if I might be sneaking up on them to rape them while their backs were turned. Even the nurse, Gloria, seemed suspicious. She glanced at the baby in my arms—who wasn't crying, and was hardly sniffling. "What *seems* to be the problem?"

I said we were here for immunizations.

"She's been here before?"

Yes, she had been coming to the doctor since she was born.

"Are you related?"

Yes, I was the father.

Eventually we were ushered in. The doctor shook hands with me, was very friendly, never asked why I was there instead of my wife or the housekeeper. He gave two injections. Amanda howled. I bounced her on my shoulder, comforted her.

"She may have a little swelling, a little local redness. Call me if it's not gone in forty-eight hours."

Then I was back in the waiting room, trying to get out my credit card to pay the bill while the baby cried. And that was when Julia called.

"Hi. What're you doing?" She must have heard the baby screaming.

"Paying the pediatrician."

"Bad time?"

"Kind of . . ."

"Okay, listen, I just wanted to say I have an early night—finally!—so I'll be home for dinner. What do you say I pick up on my way home?"

"That'd be great," I said.

Eric's soccer practice ran late. It was getting dark on the field. The coach always ran practice late. I paced the sidelines, trying to decide whether to complain. It was so hard to know when you were coddling your kid, and when you were legitimately protecting them. Nicole called on her cell to say that her play rehearsal was over, and why hadn't I picked her up? Where was I? I said I was still with Eric and asked if she could catch a ride with anybody.

"Dad . . ." she said, exasperated. You'd think I had asked her to crawl home.

"Hey, I'm stuck."

Very sarcastic: "Whatever."

"Watch that tone, young lady."

But a few minutes later, soccer was abruptly canceled. A big green maintenance truck pulled onto the field, and two men came out wearing masks and big rubber gloves, with spray cans on their backs. They were going to spray weed killer or something, and everybody had to stay off the field overnight.

I called Nicole back and said we would pick her up.

"When?"

"We're on our way now."

"From the little creep's practice?"

"Come on, Nic."

"Why does he always come first?"

"He doesn't always come first."

"Yes he *does*. He's a little creep."

"Nicole . . ."

"Sor-ry."

"See you in a few minutes." I clicked off. Kids are more advanced these days. The teenage years now start at eleven.

By five-thirty the kids were home, raiding the fridge. Nicole was eating a big chunk of string cheese. I told her to stop; it would ruin her dinner. Then I went back to setting the table.

"When *is* dinner?"

"Soon. Mom's bringing it home."

"Uh-huh." She disappeared for a few minutes, and then she came back. "She says she's sorry she didn't call, but she's going to be late."

"What?" I was pouring water into the glasses on the table.

"She's sorry she didn't call but she's going to be late. I just talked to her."

"Jesus." It was irritating. I tried never to show my irritation around the kids, but sometimes it slipped out. I sighed. "Okay."

"I'm really hungry now, Dad."

"Get your brother and get into the car," I said. "We're going to the drive-in."

Later that night, as I was carrying the baby to bed, my elbow brushed against a photograph on the living-room bookshelf. It clattered to the floor; I stooped to pick it up. It was a picture of Julia and Eric in Sun Valley when he was four. They were both in snowsuits; Julia was helping him learn to ski, and smiling radiantly. Next to it was a photo of Julia and me on our eleventh wedding anniversary in Kona; I was in a loud Hawaiian shirt and she had colorful leis around her neck, and we were kissing at sunset. That was a great trip; in fact, we were pretty sure Amanda was conceived there. I remember Julia came home from work one day and said, "Honey, remember how you said mai-tais were dangerous?" I said, "Yes . . ." And she said, "Well, let me put it this way. It's a girl," and I was so startled the soda I was drinking went up my nose, and we both started to laugh.

Then a picture of Julia making cupcakes with Nicole, who was so young she sat on the kitchen counter and her legs didn't reach the edge. She couldn't have been more than a year and a half old. Nicole was frowning with concentration as she wielded a huge spoon of dough, making a fine mess while Julia tried not to laugh.

And a photo of us hiking in Colorado, Julia holding the hand of six-year-old Nicole while I carried Eric on my shoulders, my shirt collar dark with sweat—or worse, if I remembered that day right. Eric must have been about two; he was still in diapers. I remember he thought it was fun to cover my eyes while I carried him on the trail.

The hiking photo had slipped inside its frame so it stood at an angle. I tapped the frame to try and straighten it, but it didn't move. I noticed that several of the other pictures were faded, or the emulsion was sticking to the glass. No one had bothered to take care of these pictures. The baby snuffled in my arms, rubbing her eyes with her fists. It was time for bed. I put the pictures back on the shelf. They were old images from another, happier time. From another life. They seemed to have nothing to do with me, anymore. Everything was different now.

The world was different now.

I left the table set for dinner that night, a silent rebuke. Julia saw it when she got home around ten. "I'm sorry, hon."

"I know you were busy," I said.

"I was. Please forgive me?"

"I do," I said.

"You're the best." She blew me a kiss, from across the room. "I'm going to take a shower," she said. And she headed off down the hallway. I watched her go.

On the way down the hall, she looked into the baby's room, and then darted in. A moment later, I heard her cooing and the baby gurgling. I got out of my chair, and walked down the hall after her.

In the darkened nursery, she was holding the baby up, nuzzling her nose.

I said, "Julia . . . you woke her up."

"No I didn't, she was awake. Weren't you, little honey-bunny? You were awake, weren't you, Poopsie-doopsie?"

The baby rubbed her eyes with tiny fists, and yawned. She certainly appeared to have been awakened.

Julia turned to me in the darkness. "I didn't. Really. I didn't wake her up. Why are you looking at me that way?"

"What way?"

"You know what way. That accusing way."

"I'm not accusing you of anything."

The baby started to whimper and then to cry. Julia touched her diaper. "I think she's wet," she said, and handed her to me as she walked out of the room. "You do it, Mr. Perfect."

*　　*　　*

Now there was tension between us. After I changed the baby and put her back to bed, I heard Julia come out of the shower, banging a door. Whenever Julia started banging doors, it was a sign for me to come and mollify her. But I didn't feel like it tonight. I was annoyed she'd awakened the baby, and I was annoyed by her unreliability, saying she'd be home early and never calling to say she wouldn't. I was scared that she had become so unreliable because she was distracted by a new love. Or she just didn't care about her family anymore. I didn't know what to do about all this, but I didn't feel like smoothing the tension between us.

I just let her bang the doors. She slammed her sliding closet-door so hard the wood cracked. She swore. That was another sign I was supposed to come running.

I went back to the living room, and sat down. I picked up the book I was reading, and stared at the page. I tried to concentrate but of course I couldn't. I was angry and I listened to her bang around in the bedroom. If she kept it up, she'd wake Eric and then I would have to deal with her. I hoped it wouldn't go that far.

Eventually the noise stopped. She had probably gotten into bed. If so, she would soon be asleep. Julia could go to sleep when we were fighting. I never could; I stayed up, pacing and angry, trying to settle myself down.

When I finally came to bed, Julia was fast asleep. I slipped between the covers, and rolled over on my side, away from her.

It was one o'clock in the morning when the baby began to scream. I groped for the light, knocked over the alarm clock, which turned the clock radio on, blaring rock and roll. I swore, fumbled in the dark, finally got the bedside light on, turned the radio off.

The baby was still screaming.

"What's the matter with her?" Julia said sleepily.

"I don't know." I got out of bed, shaking my head, trying to wake up. I went into the nursery and flicked on the light. The room seemed very bright, the clown wallpaper very yellow and burning. Out of nowhere, I thought: why doesn't she want yellow placemats when she painted the whole nursery yellow?

The baby was standing up in her crib, holding on to the rails and howling, her mouth wide open, her breath coming in jagged gasps. Tears were running down her cheeks. I held my arms out to her and she reached for me, and I comforted her. I thought it must be a nightmare. I comforted her, rocked her gently.

She continued to scream, unrelenting. Maybe something was hurting her, maybe something in her diaper. I checked her body. That was when I saw an angry red rash on her belly, extending in welts around to her back, and up toward her neck.

Julia came in. "Can't you stop it?" she said.

I said, "There's something wrong," and I showed her the rash.

"Has she got a fever?"

I touched Amanda's head. She was sweaty and hot, but that could be from the crying. The rest of her body felt cool. "I don't know. I don't think so."

I could see the rash on her thighs now. Was it on her thighs a moment before? I almost thought I was seeing it spread before my eyes. If it was possible, the baby screamed even louder.

"Jesus," Julia said. "I'll call the doctor."

"Yeah, do." By now I had the baby on her back—she screamed more—and I was looking carefully at her entire body. The rash was spreading, there was no doubt about it. And she seemed to be in terrible pain, screaming bloody murder.

"I'm sorry, honey, I'm sorry . . ." I said.

Definitely spreading.

Julia came back and said she left word for the doctor. I said, "I'm not going to wait. I'm taking her to the emergency room."

"Do you really think that's necessary?" she said.

I didn't answer her, I just went into the bedroom to put on my clothes.

Julia said, "Do you want me to come with you?"

"No, stay with the kids," I said.

"You sure?"

"Yes."

"Okay," she said. She wandered back to the bedroom. I reached for my car keys.

The baby continued to scream.

"I realize it's uncomfortable," the intern was saying. "But I don't think it's safe to sedate her." We were in a curtained cubicle in the emergency room. The intern was bent over my screaming daughter, looking in her ears with his instrument. By now Amanda's entire body was bright, angry red. She looked as if she had been parboiled.

I felt scared. I'd never heard of anything like this before, a baby turning bright red and screaming constantly. I didn't trust this intern, who seemed far too young to be competent. He couldn't be experienced; he didn't even look as if he shaved yet. I was jittery, shifting my weight from one foot to the other. I was beginning to feel slightly crazy, because my daughter had never stopped screaming once in the last hour. It was wearing me down. The intern ignored it. I didn't know how he could.

"She has no fever," he said, making notes in a chart, "but in a child this age that doesn't mean anything. Under a year, they may not run fevers at all, even with severe infections."

"Is that what this is?" I said. "An infection?"

"I don't know. I'm presuming a virus because of that rash. But we should have the preliminary blood work back in—ah, good." A passing nurse handed him a slip of paper. "Uhh . . . hmmm . . ." He paused. "Well . . ."

"Well what?" I said, shifting my weight anxiously.

He was shaking his head as he stared at the paper. He didn't answer.

"Well *what*?"

"It's not an infection," he said. "White cells counts all normal, protein fractions normal. She's got no immune mobilization at all."

"What does that mean?"

He was very calm, standing there, frowning and thinking. I wondered if perhaps he was just dumb. The best people weren't going into medicine anymore, not with the HMOs running everything. This kid might be one of the new breed of dumb doctor.

"We have to widen the diagnostic net," he said. "I'm going to order a surgical consult, a neurological consult, we have a dermo coming, we have infectious coming. That'll mean a lot of people to talk to you about your daughter, asking the same questions over again, but—"

"That's okay," I said. "I don't mind. Just . . . what do you think is wrong with her?"

"I don't know, Mr. Forman. If it's not infectious, we look for other reasons for this skin response. She hasn't traveled out of the country?"

"No." I shook my head.

"No recent exposures to heavy metals or toxins?"

"Like what?"

"Dump sites, industrial plants, chemical exposure . . ."

"No, no."

"Can you think of anything at all that might have caused this reaction?"

"No, nothing . . . wait, she had vaccinations yesterday."

"What vaccinations?"

"I don't know, whatever she gets for her age . . ."

"You don't know what vaccinations?" he said. His notebook was open, his pen poised over the page.

"No, for Christ's sake," I said irritably, "I don't know what vaccinations. Every time she goes there, she gets another shot. You're the goddamned doctor—"

"That's okay, Mr. Forman," he said soothingly. "I know it's stressful. If you just tell me the name of your pediatrician, I'll call him, how is that?"

I nodded. I wiped my hand across my forehead. I was sweating. I spelled the pediatrician's name for him while he wrote it down in his notebook. I tried to calm down. I tried to think clearly.

And all the time, my baby just screamed.

* * *

Half an hour later, she went into convulsions.

They started while one of the white-coated consultants was bent over her, examining her. Her little body wrenched and twisted. She made retching sounds as if she was trying to vomit. Her legs jerked spastically. She began to wheeze. Her eyes rolled up into her head.

I don't remember what I said or did then, but a big orderly the size of a football player came in and pushed me to one side of the cubicle and held my arms. I looked past his huge shoulder as six people clustered around my daughter; a nurse wearing a Bart Simpson T-shirt was sticking a needle into her forehead. I began to shout and struggle. The orderly was yelling, "Scowvane, scowvane, scowvane," over and over. Finally I realized he was saying "Scalp vein." He explained it was just to start an IV, that the baby had become dehydrated. That was why she was convulsing. I heard talk of electrolytes, magnesium, potassium.

Anyway, the convulsions stopped in a few seconds. But she continued to scream.

I called Julia. She was awake. "How is she?"

"The same."

"Still crying? Is that her?"

"Yes." She could hear Amanda in the background.

"Oh God." She groaned. "What are they saying it is?"

"They don't know yet."

"Oh, the poor baby."

"There have been about fifty doctors in here to look at her."

"Is there anything I can do?"

"I don't think so."

"Okay. Let me know."

"Okay."

"I'm not sleeping."

"Okay."

*   *   *

Shortly before dawn the huddled consultants announced that she either had an intestinal obstruction or a brain tumor, they couldn't decide which, and they ordered an MRI. The sky was beginning to lighten when she was finally wheeled to the imaging room. The big white machine stood in the center of the room. The nurse told me it would calm the baby if I helped her prepare her, and she took the needle out of her scalp because there couldn't be any metal during the MRI reading. Blood squirted down Amanda's face, into her eye. The nurse wiped it away.

Now Amanda was strapped onto the white board that rolled into the depths of the machine. My daughter was staring up at the MRI in terror, still screaming. The nurse told me I could wait in the next room with the technician. I went into a room with a glass window that looked in on the MRI machine.

The technician was foreign, dark. "How old is she? Is it a she?"

"Yes, she. Nine months."

"Quite a set of lungs on her."

"Yes."

"Here we go." He was fiddling at his knobs and dials, hardly looking at my daughter.

Amanda was completely inside the machine. Her sobs sounded tinny over the microphone. The technician flicked a switch and the pump began to chatter; it made a lot of noise. But I could still hear my daughter screaming.

And then, abruptly, she stopped.

She was completely silent.

"Uh-oh," I said. I looked at the technician and the nurse. Their faces registered shock. We all thought the same thing, that something terrible had happened. My heart began to pound. The technician hastily shut down the pumps and we hurried back into the room.

My daughter was lying there, still strapped down, breathing heavily, but apparently fine. She blinked her eyes slowly, as if dazed. Already her skin was noticeably a lighter shade of pink, with patches of normal color. The rash was fading right before our eyes.

"I'll be damned," the technician said.

*　　*　　*

Back in the emergency room, they wouldn't let Amanda go home. The surgeons still thought she had a tumor or a bowel emergency, and they wanted to keep her in the hospital for observation. But the rash continued to clear steadily. Over the next hour, the pink color faded, and vanished.

No one could understand what had happened, and the doctors were uneasy. The scalp vein IV was back in on the other side of her forehead. But Amanda took a bottle of formula, guzzling it down hungrily while I held her. She was staring up at me with her usual hypnotic feeding stare. She really seemed to be fine. She fell asleep in my arms.

I sat there for another hour, then began to make noises about how I had to get back to my kids, I had to get them to school. And not long afterward, the doctors announced another victory for modern medicine and sent me home with her. Amanda slept soundly all the way, and didn't wake when I got her out of her car seat. The night sky was turning gray when I carried her up the driveway and into the house.

DAY 3
6:07 A.M.

The house was silent. The kids were still asleep. I found Julia standing in the dining room, looking out the window at the backyard. The sprinklers were on, hissing and clicking. Julia held a cup of coffee and stared out the window, unmoving.

I said, "We're back."

She turned. "She's okay?"

I held out the baby to her. "Seems to be."

"Thank God," she said, "I was so worried, Jack." But she didn't approach Amanda, and didn't touch her. "I was *so* worried."

Her voice was strange, distant. She didn't really sound worried, she sounded formal, like someone reciting the rituals of another culture that they didn't really understand. She took a sip from her coffee mug.

"I couldn't sleep all night," she said. "I was so worried. I felt awful. God." Her eyes flicked to my face, then away. She looked guilty.

"Want to hold her?"

"I, uh . . ." Julia shook her head, and nodded to the coffee cup in her hand. "Not right now," she said. "I have to check the sprinklers. They're overwatering my roses." And she walked into the backyard.

I watched her go out in the back and stand looking at the sprinklers. She glanced back at me, then made a show of checking the timer box on the wall. She opened the lid and looked inside. I didn't get it. The gardeners had adjusted the sprinkler timers just last week. Maybe they hadn't done it right.

Amanda snuffled in my arms. I took her into the nursery to change her, and put her back in bed.

When I returned, I saw Julia in the kitchen, talking on her cell phone. This was another new habit of hers. She didn't use the house phone much anymore; she used her cell. When I had asked her about it, she'd said it was just easier because she was calling long distance a lot, and the company paid her cellular bills.

I slowed my approach, and walked on the carpet. I heard her say, "Yes, damn it, of course I do, but we have to be careful now . . ."

She looked up and saw me coming. Her tone immediately changed. "Okay, uh . . . look, Carol, I think we can handle that with a phone call to Frankfurt. Follow up with a fax, and let me know how he responds, all right?" And she snapped the phone shut. I came into the kitchen.

"Jack, I hate to leave before the kids are up, but . . ."

"You've got to go?"

"I'm afraid so. Something's come up at work."

I glanced at my watch. It was a quarter after six. "Okay."

She said, "So, will you, uh . . . the kids . . ."

"Sure, I'll handle everything."

"Thanks. I'll call you later."

And she was gone.

I was so tired I wasn't thinking clearly. The baby was still asleep, and with luck she'd sleep several hours more. My housekeeper, Maria, came in at six-thirty and put out the breakfast bowls. The kids ate and I drove them to school. I was trying hard to stay awake. I yawned.

Eric was sitting on the front seat next to me. He yawned, too.

"Sleepy today?"

He nodded. "Those men kept waking me up," he said.

"What men?"

"The men that came in the house last night."

"What men?" I said.

"The vacuum men," he said. "They vacuumed everything. And they vacuumed up the ghost."

From the backseat, Nicole snickered. "The *ghost* . . ."

I said, "I think you were dreaming, son." Lately Eric had been having vivid nightmares that often woke him in the night. I was pretty sure it was because Nicole let him watch horror movies with her, knowing they would upset him. Nicole was at the age where her favorite movies featured masked killers who murdered teenagers after they had had sex. It was the old formula: you have sex, you die. But it wasn't appropriate for Eric. I'd spoken to her many times about letting him see them.

"No, Dad, it wasn't a dream," Eric said, yawning again. "The men were there. A whole bunch of them."

"Uh-huh. And what was the ghost?"

"He was a ghost. All silver and shimmery, except he didn't have a face."

"Uh-huh." By now we were pulling up at the school, and Nicole was saying I had to pick her up at 4:15 instead of 3:45 because she had a chorus rehearsal after class, and Eric was saying he wasn't going to his pediatrician appointment if he had to get a shot. I repeated the timeless mantra of all parents: "We'll see."

The two kids piled out of the car, dragging their backpacks behind them. They both had backpacks that weighed about twenty pounds. I never got used to this. Kids didn't have huge backpacks when I was their age. We didn't have backpacks at all. Now it seemed all the kids had them. You saw little second-graders bent over like sherpas, dragging themselves through the school doors under the weight of their packs. Some of the kids had their packs on rollers, hauling them like luggage at the airport. I didn't understand any of this. The world was becoming digital; everything was smaller and lighter. But kids at school lugged more weight than ever.

A couple of months ago, at a parents' meeting, I'd asked about it. And the principal said, "Yes, it's a big problem. We're all concerned." And then changed the subject.

I didn't get that, either. If they were all concerned, why didn't they do something about it? But of course that's human nature. Nobody does anything until it's too late. We put the stoplight at the intersection *after* the kid is killed.

I drove home again, through sluggish morning traffic. I was thinking I might get a couple of hours of sleep. It was the only thing on my mind.

Maria woke me up around eleven, shaking my shoulder insistently. "Mr. Forman. Mr. Forman."

I was groggy. "What is it?"

"The baby."

I was immediately awake. "What about her?"

"You see the baby, Mr. Forman. She all . . ." She made a gesture, rubbing her shoulder and arm.

"She's all what?"

"You see the baby, Mr. Forman."

I staggered out of bed, and went into the nursery. Amanda was standing up in her crib, holding on to the railing. She was bouncing and smiling happily. Everything seemed normal, except for the fact that her entire body was a uniform purple-blue color. Like a big bruise.

"Oh, Jesus," I said.

I couldn't take another episode at the hospital, I couldn't take more white-coated doctors who didn't tell you anything, I couldn't take being scared all over again. I was still drained from the night before. The thought that there was something wrong with my daughter wrenched my stomach. I went over to Amanda, who gurgled with pleasure, smiling up at me. She stretched one hand toward me, grasping air, her signal for me to pick her up.

So I picked her up. She seemed fine, immediately grabbing my hair and trying to pull off my glasses, the way she always did. I felt relieved, even though I could now see her skin better. It looked bruised—it was the color of a bruise—except it was absolutely uniform everywhere on her body. Amanda looked like she'd been dipped in dye. The evenness of the color was alarming.

I decided I had to call the doctor in the emergency room, after all. I fished in my pocket for his card, while Amanda tried to grab my glasses.

I dialed one-handed. I could do pretty much everything one-handed. I got right through; he sounded surprised.

"Oh," he said. "I was just about to call you. How is your daughter feeling?"

"Well, she seems to feel fine," I said, jerking my head back so Amanda couldn't get my glasses. She was giggling; it was a game, now. "She's fine," I said, "but the thing is—"

"Has she by any chance had bruising?"

"Yes," I said. "As a matter of fact, she has. That's why I was calling you."

"The bruising is all over her body? Uniformly?"

"Yes," I said. "Pretty much. Why do you ask?"

"Well," the doctor said, "all her lab work has come back, and it's all normal. Completely normal. Healthy child. The only thing we're still waiting on is the MRI report, but the MRI's broken down. They say it'll be a few days."

I couldn't keep ducking and weaving; I put Amanda back in her crib while I talked. She didn't like that, of course, and scrunched up her face, preparing to cry. I gave her her Cookie Monster toy, and she sat down and played with that. I knew Cookie Monster was good for about five minutes.

"Anyway," the doctor was saying, "I'm glad to hear she's doing well."

I said that I was glad, too.

There was a pause. The doctor coughed.

"Mr. Forman, I noticed on your hospital admissions form you said your occupation was software engineer."

"That's right."

"Does that mean you are involved with manufacturing?"

"No. I do program development."

"And where do you do that work?"

"In the Valley."

"You don't work in a factory, for example?"

"No. I work in an office."

"I see." A pause. "May I ask where?"

"Actually, at the moment, I'm unemployed."

"I see. All right. How long has that been?"

"Six months."

"I see." A short pause. "Well, okay, I just wanted to clear that up."

I said, "Why?"

"I'm sorry?"

"Why are you asking me those questions?"

"Oh. They're on the form."

"What form?" I said. "I filled out all the forms at the hospital."

"This is another form," he said. "It's an OHS inquiry. Office of Health and Safety."

I said, "What's this all about?"

"There's been another case reported," he said, "that's very similar to your daughter's."

"Where?"

"Sacramento General."

"When?"

"Five days ago. But it's a completely different situation. This case involved a forty-two-year-old naturalist sleeping out in the Sierras, some wildflower expert. There was a particular kind of flower or something. Anyway, he was hospitalized in Sacramento. And he had the same clinical course as your daughter—sudden unexplained onset, no fever, painful erythematous reaction."

"And an MRI stopped it?"

"I don't know if he had an MRI," he said. "But apparently this syndrome—whatever it is—is self-limited. Very sudden onset, and very abrupt termination."

"He's okay now? The naturalist?"

"He's fine. A couple of days of bruising, and nothing more."

"Good," I said. "I'm glad to hear it."

"I thought you'd want to know," he said. Then he said he might be calling me again, with some more questions, and would that be all right? I said he could call whenever he wanted. He asked me to call if there was any change in Amanda, and I said I would, and I hung up.

*　　*　　*

Amanda had abandoned Cookie Monster, and was standing in the crib, holding on to the railing with one hand and reaching for me with the other, her little fingers clutching air.

I picked her up—and in an instant she had my glasses off. I grabbed for them as she squealed with pleasure. "Amanda . . ." But too late; she threw them on the floor.

I blinked.

I don't see well without my glasses. These were wire-frames, hard to see now. I got down on my hands and knees, still holding the baby, and swept my hand across the floor in circles, hoping to touch glass. I didn't. I squinted, edged forward, swept my hand again. Still nothing. Then I saw a glint of light underneath the crib. I set the baby down and crawled under the crib, retrieved the glasses, and put them on. In the process I banged my head on the crib, dropped down low again.

And I found myself staring at the electrical outlet on the wall underneath the crib. A small plastic box was plugged into the outlet. I pulled it out and looked at it. It was a two-inch cube, a surge suppressor by the look of it, an ordinary commercial product, made in Thailand. The input/output voltages were molded into the plastic. A white label ran across the bottom, reading PROP. SSVT, with a bar code. It was one of those stickers that companies put on their inventory.

I turned the cube over in my hand. Where had this come from? I'd been in charge of the house for the last six months. I knew what was where. And certainly Amanda didn't need a surge suppressor in her room. You only needed that for sensitive electronic equipment, like computers.

I got to my feet, and looked around the room to see what else was different. To my surprise, I realized that everything was different—but just slightly different. Amanda's night-light had Winnie-the-Pooh characters printed on the shade. I always kept Tigger facing toward her crib, because Tigger was her favorite. Now, Eeyore faced the crib. Amanda's changing pad was stained in one corner; I always kept the stain bottom left. Now it was top right. I kept her diaper-rash ointments on the counter to the left, just out of her reach. Now they were too close; she could grab them. And there was more—

The maid came in behind me. "Maria," I said, "did you clean this room?"

"No, Mr. Forman."

"But the room is different," I said.

She looked around, and shrugged. "No, Mr. Forman. The same."

"No, no," I insisted. "It's different. Look." I pointed to the lampshade, the changing cloth. "Different."

She shrugged again. "Okay, Mr. Forman." I read confusion in her face. Either she didn't follow what I was saying, or she thought I was crazy. And I probably did look a little crazy, a grown man obsessing about a Winnie-the-Pooh lampshade.

I showed her the cube in my hand. "Have you seen this before?"

She shook her head. "No."

"It was under the crib."

"I don't know, Mr. Forman." She inspected it, turning it in her hand. She shrugged, and gave it back to me. She acted casual, but her eyes were watchful. I began to feel uncomfortable.

"Okay, Maria," I said. "Never mind."

She bent over to scoop up the baby. "I feed her now."

"Yes, okay."

I left the room, feeling odd.

Just for the hell of it, I looked up "SSVT" on the Net. I got links to the Sri Siva Vishnu Temple, the Waffen-SS Training School at Konitz, Nazi Regalia for sale, Subsystems Sample Display Technology, South Shore Vocational-Technical School, Optical VariTemp Cryostat Systems, Solid Surfacing Veneer Tiles for home floors, a band called SlingshotVenus, the Swiss Shooting Federation—and it went downhill from there.

I turned away from the computer.

I stared out the window.

Maria had given me a shopping list, the items scrawled in her difficult hand. I really should get the shopping done before I picked up the kids. But I didn't move. There were times when the relentless pace of life at home seemed to defeat me, to leave me feeling washed out and hollow. At those times I just had to sit for a few hours.

I didn't want to move. Not right now.

I wondered if Julia was going to call me tonight, and I wondered if she would have a different excuse. I wondered what I would do if she walked in one of these days, and announced she was in love with someone else. I wondered what I would do if I still didn't have a job by then.

I wondered when I would get a job again. I turned the little surge suppressor over in my hand idly, as my mind drifted.

Right outside my window was a large coral tree, with thick leaves and a green trunk. We had planted it as a much smaller tree not long after we moved into the house. Of course the tree guys did it, but we were all out there. Nicole had her plastic shovel and bucket. Eric was crawling around on the lawn in his diapers. Julia had charmed the workmen into staying late to finish the job. After they had all gone I kissed her, and brushed dirt from her nose. She said, "One day it'll cover our whole house."

But as it turned out, it didn't. One of the branches had broken off in a storm, so it grew a little lopsided. Coral is soft wood; the branches break easily. It never grew to cover the house.

But my memory was vivid; staring out the window, I saw all of us again, out on the lawn. But it was just a memory. And I was very afraid it didn't fit anymore.

After working for years with multi-agent systems, you begin to see life in terms of those programs.

Basically, you can think of a multi-agent environment as something like a chessboard, and the agents like chess pieces. The agents interact on the board to attain a goal, just the way the chess pieces move to win a game. The difference is that nobody is moving the agents. They interact on their own to produce the outcome.

If you design the agents to have memory, they can know things about their environment. They remember where they've been on the board, and what happened there. They can go back to certain places, with certain expectations. Eventually, programmers say the agents have beliefs about their environment, and that they are acting on those beliefs. That's not literally true, of course, but it might as well be true. It looks that way.

But what's interesting is that over time, some agents develop mistaken beliefs. Whether from a motivation conflict, or some other reason, they start acting inappropriately. The environment has changed but they don't seem to know it. They repeat outmoded patterns. Their behavior no longer reflects the reality of the chessboard. It's as if they're stuck in the past.

In evolutionary programs, those agents get killed off. They have no children. In other multi-agent programs, they just get bypassed, pushed to the periphery while the main thrust of agents moves on. Some programs have a "grim reaper" module that sifts them out from time to time, and pulls them off the board.

But the point is, they're stuck in their own past. Sometimes they pull themselves together, and get back on track. Sometimes they don't.

Thoughts like these made me very uneasy. I shifted in my chair, glanced at the clock. With a sense of relief, I saw it was time to go pick up the kids.

Eric did his homework in the car while we waited for Nicole to finish her play rehearsal. She came out in a bad mood; she had thought she was in line for a lead role, but instead the drama teacher had cast her in the chorus. "Only two lines!" she said, slamming the car door. "You want to know what I say? I say, 'Look, here comes John now.' And in the second act, I say, 'That sounds pretty serious.' Two lines!" She sat back and closed her eyes. "I don't understand *what* Mr. Blakey's *problem* is!"

"Maybe he thinks you suck," Eric said.

"Rat turd!" She smacked him on the head. "Monkey butt!"

"That's enough," I said, as I started the car. "Seat belts."

"Little stink-brain dimrod, he doesn't know anything," Nicole said, buckling her belt.

"I said, that's enough."

"I know that you stink," Eric said. "Pee-yew."

"That's enough, Eric."

"Yeah, Eric, listen to your father, and shut up."

"Nicole . . ." I shot her a glance in the rearview mirror.

"Sor-ry."

She looked on the verge of tears. I said to her, "Honey, I'm really sorry you didn't get the part you wanted. I know you wanted it badly, and it must be very disappointing."

"No. I don't care."

"Well, I'm sorry."

"Really, Dad, I don't care. It's in the past. I'm moving on." And then a moment later, "You know who got it? That little suckup Katie Richards! Mr. Blakey is *just a dick*!" And before I could say anything, she burst into tears, sobbing loudly and histrionically. Eric looked over at me, and rolled his eyes.

I drove home, making a mental note to speak to Nicole about her language after dinner, when she had calmed down.

I was chopping green beans so they would fit in the steamer when Eric came and stood in the kitchen doorway. "Hey Dad, where's my MP3?"

"I have no idea." I could never get used to the idea that I was supposed to know where every one of their personal possessions was. Eric's Game Boy, his baseball glove, Nicole's tank tops, her bracelet . . .

"Well, I can't find it." Eric remained standing in the doorway, not coming any closer, in case I made him help set the table.

"Have you looked?"

"Everywhere, Dad."

"Uh-huh. You looked in your room?"

"All over."

"Family room?"

"Everywhere."

"In the car? Maybe you left it in the car."

"I didn't, Dad."

"You leave it in your locker at school?"

"We don't have lockers, we have cubbies."

"You look in the pockets of your jacket?"

"Dad. Come on. I did all that. I need it."

"Since you've already looked everywhere, I won't be able to find it either, will I?"

"Dad. Would you please just help me?"

The pot roast had another half hour to go. I put down the knife and went into Eric's room. I looked in all the usual places, the back of his closet where clothes were kicked into a heap (I would have to talk to Maria about that), under the bed, behind the bed table, in the bottom drawer in the bathroom, and under the piles of stuff on his desk. Eric was right. It wasn't in his room. We headed toward the family room. I glanced in at the baby's room as I passed by. And I saw it immediately. It was on the shelf beside the changing table, right alongside the tubes of baby ointment. Eric grabbed it. "Hey, thanks Dad!" And he scampered off.

There was no point in asking why it was in the baby's room. I went back to the kitchen and resumed chopping my green beans. Almost immediately:

"Daa-ad!"

"What?" I called.

"It doesn't work!"

"Don't shout."

He came back to the kitchen, looking sulky. "She broke it."

"Who broke it?"

"Amanda. She drooled on it or something, and she broke it. It's not fair."

"You check the battery?"

He gave me a pitying look. " 'Course, Dad. I told you, she broke it! It's not fair!"

I doubted his MP3 player was broken. These things were solid-state devices, no moving parts. And it was too large for the baby to handle. I dumped the green beans on the steamer tray, and held out my hand. "Give it to me."

We went into the garage and I got out my toolbox. Eric watched my every move. I had a full set of the small tools you need for computers and electronic devices. I worked quickly. Four Phillips head screws, and the back cover came off in my hand. I found myself staring at the green circuit board. It was covered by a fine layer of grayish dust, like lint from a clothes dryer, that obscured all the electronic components. I suspected that Eric had slid into home plate with this thing in his pocket. That was probably why it didn't work. But I looked along the edge of the plastic and saw a rubber gasket where the back fitted against the device. They'd made this thing airtight . . . as they should.

I blew the dust away, so I could see better. I was hoping to see a loose battery connection, or a memory chip that had popped up from heat, anyway something that would be easy to fix. I squinted at the chips, trying to read the writing. The writing on one chip was obscured, because there seemed to be some kind of—

I paused.

"What is it?" Eric said, watching me.

"Hand me that magnifying glass."

Eric gave me a big glass, and I swung my high-intensity lamp low, and bent over the chip, examining it closely. The reason I couldn't read the writing was that the surface of the chip had been corroded. The whole chip was etched in rivulets, a miniature river delta. I understood now where the dust had come from. It was the disintegrated remains of the chip.

"Can you fix it, Dad?" Eric said. "Can you?"

What could have caused this? The rest of the motherboard seemed fine. The controller chip was untouched. Only the memory chip was damaged. I wasn't a hardware guy, but I knew enough to do basic computer repairs. I could install hard drives, add memory, things like that. I'd handled memory chips before, and I'd never seen anything like this. All I could think was that it was a faulty chip. These MP3 players were probably built with the cheapest components available.

"Dad? Can you fix it?"

"No," I said. "It needs another chip. I'll get you one tomorrow."

"'Cause she slimed it, right?"

"No. I think it's just a faulty chip."

"Dad. It was fine for a whole year. She slimed it. It's not fair!"

As if on cue, the baby started crying. I left the MP3 player on the garage table, and went back inside the house. I looked at my watch. I would just have time to change Amanda's diaper, and mix her cereal for dinner, before the pot roast came out.

By nine, the younger kids were asleep, and the house was quiet except for Nicole's voice, saying, "*That* sounds pretty serious. That *sounds* pretty serious. That sounds . . . *pretty serious*." She was standing in front of the bathroom mirror, staring at herself and reciting her lines.

I'd gotten voice mail from Julia saying she'd be back by eight, but she hadn't made it. I wasn't about to call and check up on her. Anyway, I was tired, too tired to work up the energy to worry about her. I'd picked up a lot of tricks in the last months—mostly involving liberal use of tinfoil so I didn't have to clean so much—but even so, after I did the cooking, set the table, fed the kids, played airplane to get the baby to eat her cereal, cleared the table, wiped down the high chair, put the baby to bed, and then cleaned up the kitchen, I was tired. Especially since the baby kept spitting out the cereal, and Eric kept insisting all through dinner that it wasn't fair, he wanted chicken fingers instead of the roast.

I flopped down on the bed, and flicked on the TV.

There was only static, and then I realized the DVD player was still turned on, interrupting the cable transmission. I hit the remote button, and the disc in the machine began to play. It was Julia's demo, from several days before.

The camera moved through the bloodstream, and into the heart. Again, I saw that the liquid of blood was almost colorless, with bouncing red cells. Julia was speaking. On the table, the subject lay with the antenna above his body.

"We're coming out of the ventricle, and you see the aorta ahead . . . And now we will go through the arterial system . . ."

She turned to face the camera.

"The images you have seen are fleeting, but we can allow the camera to cycle through for as much as half an hour, and we can build up highly detailed composites of anything we want to see. We can even pause the camera, using a strong magnetic field. When we are finished, we simply shunt the blood through an intravenous loop surrounded by a strong magnetic field, removing the particles, and then send the patient home."

The video image came back to Julia. "This Xymos technology is safe, reliable, and extremely easy to use. It does not require highly trained personnel; it can be administered by an IV nurse or a medical technician. In the United States alone, a million people die each year from vascular disease. More than thirty million have diagnosed cardiovascular disease. Commercial prospects for this imaging technology are very strong. Because it is painless, simple, and safe, it will replace other imaging techniques such as CAT scans and angiography and will become the standard procedure. We will market the nanotech cameras, the antenna, and monitor systems. Our per-test cost will be only twenty dollars. This is in contrast to certain gene technologies that currently charge two to three thousand dollars a test. But at a mere twenty dollars, we expect worldwide revenues to exceed four hundred million dollars in the first year. And once the procedure is established, those figures will triple. We are talking about a technology that generates one point two billion dollars a year. Now if there are questions . . ."

I yawned, and flicked the TV off. It was impressive, and her argument was compelling. In fact, I couldn't understand why Xymos was having trouble getting their next round of funding. For investors, this should be a slam dunk.

But then, she probably wasn't having trouble. She was probably just using the funding crisis as an excuse to stay late every night. For her own reasons.

I turned out the light. Lying in bed, staring at the ceiling in the dark, I began to see fleeting images. Julia's thigh, over another man's leg. Julia's back arched. Julia breathing heavily, her muscles tensed. Her arm reaching up to push against the headboard. I found I couldn't stop the images.

I got out of bed, and went to check the kids. Nicole was still up, emailing her friends. I told her it was time for lights out. Eric had kicked off his covers. I pulled them back up. The baby was still purple, but she slept soundly, her breathing gentle and regular.

I got back into bed. I willed myself to go to sleep, to think of something else. I tossed and turned, adjusted the pillow, got up for a glass of milk and cookies. Eventually, finally, I fell into a restless sleep.

And I had a very strange dream.

Sometime during the night, I rolled over to see Julia standing by the bed, undressing. She was moving slowly, as if tired or very dreamy, unbuttoning her blouse. She was turned away from me, but I could see her face in the mirror. She looked beautiful, almost regal. Her features looked more chiseled than I remembered, though perhaps it was just the light.

My eyes were half-closed. She hadn't noticed I was awake. She continued to slowly unbutton her blouse. Her lips were moving, as if she were whispering something, or praying. Her eyes seemed vacant, lost in thought.

Then as I watched, her lips turned dark red, and then black. She didn't seem to notice. The blackness flowed away from her mouth across her cheeks and over her lower face, and onto her neck. I held my breath. I felt great danger. The blackness now flowed in a sheet down her body until she was entirely covered, as if with a cloak. Only the upper half of her face remained exposed. Her features were composed; in fact she seemed oblivious, just staring into space, dark lips silently moving. Watching her, I felt a chill that ran deep into my bones. Then a moment later the black sheet slid to the floor and vanished.

Julia, normal again, finished removing her blouse, and walked into the bathroom.

I wanted to get up and follow her, but I found I could not move. A heavy fatigue held me down on the bed, immobilizing me. I was so exhausted I could hardly breathe. This oppressive sense of fatigue grew rapidly, and overwhelmed my consciousness. Losing all awareness, I felt my eyes close, and I slept.

DAY 4
6:40 A.M.

The next morning the dream was still fresh in my mind, vivid and disturbing. It felt utterly real, not like a dream at all.

Julia was already up. I got out of bed and walked around to where I had seen her the night before. I looked down at the rug, the bedside table, the creased sheets and pillow. There was nothing unusual, nothing out of order. No dark lines or marks anywhere.

I went into the bathroom and looked at her cosmetics, in a neat line on her side of the sink. Everything I saw was mundane. However disturbing my dream had been, it was still a dream.

But one part of it was true enough: Julia *was* looking more beautiful than ever. When I found her in the kitchen, pouring coffee, I saw that her face did indeed look more chiseled, more striking. Julia had always had a chubby face. Now it was lean, defined. She looked like a high-fashion model. Her body, too—now that I looked closely—appeared leaner, more muscular. She hadn't lost weight, she just looked trim, tight, energetic.

I said, "You look great."

She laughed. "I can't imagine why. I'm exhausted."

"What time did you get in?"

"About eleven. I hope I didn't wake you."

"No. But I had a weird dream."

"Oh yes?"

"Yes, it was—"

"Mommy! Mommy!" Eric burst into the kitchen. "It's not fair! Nicole won't get out of the bathroom. She's been in there for *an hour*. It's not fair!"

"Go use our bathroom."

"But I need my socks, Mommy. It's not fair."

This was a familiar problem. Eric had a couple of pairs of favorite socks that he wore day after day until they were black with grime. For some reason, the other socks in his drawer were not satisfactory. I could never get him to explain why. But putting on socks in the morning was a major problem with him.

"Eric," I said, "we talked about this, you're supposed to wear clean socks."

"But those are my good ones!"

"Eric. You have plenty of good socks."

"It's not fair, Dad. She's been in there an hour, I'm not kidding."

"Eric, go choose other socks."

"Dad . . ."

I just pointed my finger toward his bedroom.

"Shees." He walked off muttering about how it wasn't fair.

I turned back to Julia to resume our conversation. She was staring at me coldly. "You really don't get it, do you?"

"Get what?"

"He came in talking to me, and you just took over. You took over the whole thing."

Immediately, I realized she was right. "I'm sorry," I said.

"I don't get to see the children very much these days, Jack. I think I should be able to have my interaction without your taking control."

"I'm sorry. I handle this kind of thing all day, and I guess—"

"This really is a problem, Jack."

"I said I'm sorry."

"I know that's what you said, but I don't think you are sorry, because I don't see you doing anything to change your controlling behavior."

"Julia," I said. Now I was trying to control my temper. I took a breath. "You're right. I'm sorry it happened."

"You're just shutting me out," she said, "and you are keeping me from my children—"

"Julia, God damn it, *you're never here!*"

A frosty silence. Then:

"I certainly am here," she said. "Don't you dare say I am not."

"Wait a minute, wait a minute. When are you here? When was the last time you made it for dinner, Julia? Not last night, not the night before, not the night before that. Not all week, Julia. You are *not* here."

She glared at me. "I don't know what you're trying to do, Jack. I don't know what kind of game you are playing."

"I'm not playing any game. I'm asking you a question."

"I'm a good mother, and I balance a very demanding job, a *very* demanding job, and the needs of my family. And I get absolutely no help from you."

"What are you talking about?" I said, my voice rising still higher. I was starting to have a sense of unreality here.

"You undercut me, you sabotage me, you turn the children against me," she said. "I see what you're doing. Don't think I don't. You are not supportive of me at all. After all these years of marriage, I must say it's a lousy thing to do to your wife."

And she stalked out of the room, fists clenched. She was so angry, she didn't see that Nicole was standing back from the door, listening to the whole thing. And staring at me, as her mother swept past.

Now we were driving to school. "She's crazy, Dad."

"No, she's not."

"You know that she is. You're just pretending."

"Nicole, she's your mother," I said. "Your mother is not crazy. She's working very hard right now."

"That's what you said last week, after the fight."

"Well, it happens to be true."

"You guys didn't used to fight."

"There's a lot of stress right now."

Nicole snorted, crossed her arms, stared forward. "I don't know why you put up with her."

"And I don't know why you were listening to what is none of your business."

"Dad, why do you pull that crap with me?"

"Nicole . . ."

"Sor-ry. But why can't you have a real conversation, instead of defending her all the time? It's not normal, what she's doing. I *know* you think she's crazy."

"I don't," I said.

From the backseat, Eric whacked her on the back of the head. "You're the one who's crazy," he said.

"Shut up, butt breath."

"Shut up yourself, weasel puke."

"I don't want to hear any more from either of you," I said loudly. "I am not in the mood."

By then we were pulling into the turnaround in front of the school. The kids piled out. Nicole jumped out of the front seat, turned back to get her backpack, shot me a look, and was gone.

I didn't think Julia was crazy, but something had certainly changed, and as I replayed that morning's conversation in my head, I felt uneasy for other reasons. A lot of her comments sounded like she was building a case against me. Laying it out methodically, step by step.

You are shutting me out and keeping me away from my children.

I am here, you just don't notice.

I'm a good mother, I balance a very demanding job with the needs of my family.

You are not supportive of me at all. You undercut me, you sabotage me.

You are turning the children against me.

I could easily imagine her lawyer saying these things in court. And I knew why. According to a recent article I had read in *Redbook* magazine, "alienation of affection" was currently the trendy argument in court. The father is turning the children against the mother. Poisoning their little minds by word and deed. While the Mom is blameless as always.

Every father knew the legal system was hopelessly biased in favor of mothers. The courts gave lip service to equality, and then ruled a child needed its mother. Even if she was absent. Even if she smacked them around, or forgot to feed them. As long as she wasn't shooting up, or breaking their bones, she was a fit mother in the eyes of the court. And even if she *was* shooting up, a father might not win the case. One of my friends at MediaTronics had an ex-wife on heroin who'd been in and out of rehab for years. They'd finally divorced and had joint custody. She was supposedly clean but the kids said she wasn't. My friend was worried. He didn't want his ex driving the kids when she was loaded. He didn't want drug dealers around his kids. So he went to court to ask for full custody, and he lost. The judge said the wife was genuinely trying to overcome her addiction, and that children need their mother.

So that was the reality. And now it looked to me as if Julia was starting to lay out that case. It gave me the creeps.

About the time I had worked myself into a fine lather, my cell phone rang. It was Julia. She was calling to apologize.

"I'm really sorry. I said stupid things today. I didn't mean it."

"What?"

"Jack, I know you support me. Of course you do. I couldn't manage without you. You're doing a great job with the kids. I'm just not myself these days. It was stupid, Jack. I'm sorry I said those things."

When I got off the phone I thought, I wish I had recorded that.

I had a ten o'clock meeting with my headhunter, Annie Gerard. We met in the sunny courtyard of a coffee shop on Baker. We always met outside, so Annie could smoke. She had her laptop out and her wireless modem plugged in. A cigarette dangled from her lip, and she squinted in the smoke.

"Got anything?" I said, sitting down opposite her.

"Yeah, as a matter of fact I do. Two very good possibilities."

"Great," I said, stirring my latte. "Tell me."

"How about this? Chief research analyst for IBM, working on advanced distributed systems architecture."

"Right up my alley."

"I thought so, too. You're highly qualified for this one, Jack. You'd run a research lab of sixty people. Base pay two-fifty plus options going out five years plus royalties on anything developed in your lab."

"Sounds great. Where?"

"Armonk."

"New York?" I shook my head. "No way, Annie. What else?"

"Head of a team to design multi-agent systems for an insurance company that's doing data mining. It's an excellent opportunity, and—"

"Where?"

"Austin."

I sighed. "Annie. Julia's got a job she likes, she's very devoted to it, and she won't leave it now. My kids are in school, and—"

"People move all the time, Jack. They all have kids in school. Kids adapt."

"But with Julia . . ."

"Other people have working wives, too. They still move."

"I know, but the thing is with Julia . . ."

"Have you talked to her about it? Have you broached the subject?"

"Well, no, because I—"

"Jack." Annie stared at me over the laptop screen. "I think you better cut the crap. You're not in a position to be picky. You're starting to have a shelf-life problem."

"Shelf life," I said.

"That's right, Jack. You've been out of work six months now. That's a long time in high tech. Companies figure if it takes you that long to find a job, there must be something wrong with you. They don't know what, they just assume you've been rejected too many times, by too many other companies. Pretty soon, they won't even interview. Not in San

Jose, not in Armonk, not in Austin, not in Cambridge. The boat's sailed. Are you hearing me? Am I getting through here?"

"Yes, but—"

"No buts, Jack. You've got to talk to your wife. You've got to figure out a way to get yourself off the shelf."

"But I can't leave the Valley. I have to stay here."

"Here is not so good." She flipped the screen up again. "Whenever I bring up your name, I keep getting—listen, what's going on at Media-Tronics, anyway? Is Don Gross going to be indicted?"

"I don't know."

"I've been hearing that rumor for months now, but it never seems to happen. For your sake, I hope it happens soon."

"I don't get it," I said. "I'm perfectly positioned in a hot field, multi-agent distributed processing, and—"

"Hot?" she said, squinting at me. "Distributed processing's not hot, Jack. It's fucking *radioactive*. Everybody in the Valley figures that the breakthroughs in artificial life are going to come from distributed processing."

"They are," I said, nodding.

In the last few years, artificial life had replaced artificial intelligence as a long-term computing goal. The idea was to write programs that had the attributes of living creatures—the ability to adapt, cooperate, learn, adjust to change. Many of those qualities were especially important in robotics, and they were starting to be realized with distributed processing.

Distributed processing meant that you divided your work among several processors, or among a network of virtual agents that you created in the computer. There were several basic ways this was done. One way was to create a large population of fairly dumb agents that worked together to accomplish a goal—just like a colony of ants worked together to accomplish a goal. My own team had done a lot of that work.

Another method was to make a so-called neural network that mimicked the network of neurons in the human brain. It turned out that even simple neural nets had surprising power. These networks could learn. They could build on past experience. We'd done some of that, too.

A third technique was to create virtual genes in the computer, and let them evolve in a virtual world until some goal was attained.

And there were several other procedures, as well. Taken together, these procedures represented a huge change from the older notions of artificial intelligence, or AI. In the old days, programmers tried to write rules to cover every situation. For example, they tried to teach computers that if someone bought something at a store, they had to pay before leaving. But this commonsense knowledge proved extremely difficult to program. The computer would make mistakes. New rules would be added to avoid the mistakes. Then more mistakes, and more rules. Eventually the programs were gigantic, millions of lines of code, and they began to fail out of sheer complexity. They were too large to debug. You couldn't figure out where the errors were coming from.

So it began to seem as if rule-based AI was never going to work. Lots of people made dire predictions about the end of artificial intelligence. The eighties were a good time for English professors who believed that computers would never match human intelligence.

But distributed networks of agents offered an entirely new approach. And the programming philosophy was new, too. The old rules-based programming was "top down." The system as a whole was given rules of behavior.

But the new programming was "bottom up." The program defined the behavior of individual agents at the lowest structural level. But the behavior of the system as a whole was not defined. Instead, the behavior of the system emerged, the result of hundreds of small interactions occurring at a lower level.

Because the system was not programmed, it could produce surprising results. Results never anticipated by the programmers. That was why they could seem "lifelike." And that was why the field was so hot, because—

"Jack."

Annie was tapping my hand. I blinked.

"Jack, did you hear anything I just said to you?"

"Sorry."

"I don't have your full attention," she said. She blew cigarette smoke in my face. "Yes, you're right, you're in a hot field. But that's all the more reason to worry about shelf life. It's not like you're an electrical engineer specializing in optical-drive mechanisms. Hot fields move fast. Six months can make or break a company."

"I know."

"You're at risk, Jack."

"I understand."

"So. Will you talk to your wife? Please?"

"Yes."

"Okay," she said. "Make sure you do. Because otherwise, I can't help you." She flicked her burning cigarette into the remains of my latte. It sizzled and died. She snapped her laptop shut, got up, and left.

I put a call in to Julia, but didn't get her. I left voice mail. I knew it was a waste of time even to bring up moving to her. She'd certainly say no— especially if she had a new boyfriend. But Annie was right, I was in trouble. I had to do something. I had to ask.

I sat at my desk at home, turning the SSVT box in my hands, trying to think what to do. I had another hour and a half before I picked up the kids. I really wanted to talk to Julia. I decided to call Julia again through the company switchboard, to see if they could track her down.

"Xymos Technology."

"Julia Forman, please."

"Please hold." Some classical music, then another voice. "Ms. Forman's office."

I recognized Carol, her assistant. "Carol, it's Jack."

"Oh, hi, Mr. Forman. How are you?"

"I'm fine, thanks."

"Are you looking for Julia?"

"Yes, I am."

"She's in Nevada for the day, at the fab plant. Shall I try to connect you there?"

"Yes, please."

"One moment."

I was put on hold. For quite a while.

"Mr. Forman, she's in a meeting for the next hour. I expect her to call back when it breaks up. Do you want her to call you?"

"Yes, please."

"Do you want me to tell her anything?"

"No," I said. "Just ask her to call."

"Okay, Mr. Forman."

I hung up, stared into space, turning the SSVT box. *She's in Nevada for the day.* Julia had said nothing to me about going to Nevada. I replayed the conversation with Carol in my mind. Had Carol sounded uncomfortable? Was she covering? I couldn't be sure. I couldn't be sure of anything now. I stared out the window and as I watched, the sprinklers kicked on, shooting up cones of spray all over the lawn. It was right in the heat of midday, the wrong time to water. It wasn't supposed to happen. The sprinklers had been fixed just the other day.

I began to feel depressed, staring at the water. It seemed like everything was wrong. I had no job, my wife was absent, the kids were a pain, I felt constantly inadequate dealing with them—and now the fucking sprinklers weren't working right. They were going to burn out the fucking lawn.

And then the baby began to cry.

I waited for Julia to call, but she never did. I cut up chicken breasts into strips (the trick is to keep them cold, almost frozen) for dinner, because chicken fingers were another meal they never argued about. I got out rice to boil. I looked at the carrots in the fridge and decided that even though they were a little old, I'd still use them tonight.

I cut my finger while I was chopping the carrots. It wasn't a big cut but it bled a lot, and the Band-Aid didn't stop the bleeding. It kept bleeding through the pad, so I kept putting on new Band-Aids. It was frustrating.

Dinner was late and the kids were cranky. Eric complained loudly that my chicken fingers were gross, that McDonald's were *way* better, and why couldn't we have those? Nicole tried out various line readings for her play, while Eric mimicked her under his breath. The baby spit up every mouthful of her cereal until I stopped and mixed it with some mashed banana. After that, she ate steadily. I don't know why I never thought to do that before. Amanda was getting older, and she didn't want the bland stuff anymore.

Eric had left his homework at school; I told him to call his friends for the assignment, but he wouldn't. Nicole was online for an hour with her friends; I kept popping into her room and telling her to get off the computer until her homework was done, and she'd say, "In just a minute, Dad." The baby fussed, and it took a long time for me to get her down.

I went back into Nicole's room and said, "*Now*, damn it!" Nicole began to cry. Eric came in to gloat. I asked him why he wasn't in bed. He saw the look on my face, and scampered away. Sobbing, Nicole said I should apologize to her. I said she should have done what I told her to do twice before. She went into the bathroom and slammed the door.

From his room, Eric yelled, "I can't sleep with all that racket!"

I yelled back, "One more word and no television for a week!"

"Not fair!"

I went into the bedroom and turned on the TV to watch the rest of the game. After half an hour, I checked on the kids. The baby was sleeping peacefully. Eric was asleep, all his covers thrown off. I pulled them back on him. Nicole was studying. When she saw me, she apologized. I gave her a hug.

I went back into the bedroom, and watched the game for about ten minutes before I fell asleep.

DAY 5
7:10 A.M.

When I awoke in the morning, I saw that Julia's side of the bed was still made up, her pillow uncreased. She hadn't come home last night at all. I checked the telephone messages; there were none. Eric wandered in, and saw the bed. "Where's Mom?"

"I don't know, son."

"Did she leave already?"

"I guess so . . ."

He stared at me, and then at the unmade bed. And he walked out of the room. He wasn't going to deal with it.

But I was beginning to think I had to. Maybe I should even talk to a lawyer. Except in my mind, there was something irrevocable about talking to a lawyer. If the trouble was that serious, it was probably fatal. I didn't want to believe my marriage was over, so I wanted to postpone seeing a lawyer.

That was when I decided to call my sister in San Diego. Ellen is a clinical psychologist, she has a practice in La Jolla. It was early enough that I figured she hadn't gone to the office yet; she answered the phone at home. She sounded surprised I had called. I love my sister but we are very different. Anyway, I told her briefly about the things I'd been suspecting about Julia, and why.

"You're saying Julia didn't come home and she didn't call?"

"Right."

"Did you call her?"

"Not yet."

"How come?"

"I don't know."

"Maybe she was in an accident, maybe she's hurt . . ."

"I don't think so."

"Why not?"

"You always hear if there's an accident. There's no accident."

"You sound upset, Jack."

"I don't know. Maybe."

My sister was silent for a moment. Then she said, "Jack, you've got a problem. Why aren't you doing something?"

"Like what?"

"Like see a marriage counselor. Or a lawyer."

"Oh, jeez."

"Don't you think you should?" she asked.

"I don't know. No. Not yet."

"Jack. She didn't come home last night and she didn't bother to call. When this woman drops a hint, she uses a bombsight. How much clearer do you need it to be?"

"I don't know."

"You're saying 'I don't know' a lot. Are you aware of that?"

"I guess so."

A pause. "Jack, are you all right?"

"I don't know."

"Do you want me to come up for a couple of days? Because I can, no problem. I was supposed to go out of town with my boyfriend, but his company just got bought. So I'm available, if you want me to come up."

"No. It's okay."

"You sure? I'm worried about you."

"No, no," I said. "You don't have to worry."

"Are you depressed?"

"No. Why?"

"Sleeping okay? Exercising?"

"Fair. Not really exercising that much."

"Uh-huh. Do you have a job yet?"

"No."

"Prospects?"

"Not really. No."

"Jack," she said. "You have to see a lawyer."

"Maybe in a while."

"Jack. What's the matter with you? This is what you've told me. Your wife is acting cold and angry toward you. She's lying to you. She's acting strange with the kids. She doesn't seem to care about her family. She's angry and absent a lot. It's getting worse. You think she's involved with someone else. Last night, she doesn't even show up or call. And you're just going to let this go without doing anything?"

"I don't know what to do."

"I told you. See a lawyer."

"You think so?"

"You're damn right I think so."

"I don't know . . ."

She sighed, a long exasperated hiss. "Jack. Look. I know you're a little passive at times, but—"

"I'm not passive," I said. And I added, "I hate it when you shrink me."

"Your wife is screwing around on you, you think she's building a case to take the kids away from you, and you're just letting it happen. I'd say that's passive."

"What am I supposed to do?"

"I told you." Another exasperated sigh. "Okay. I'm taking a couple of days and coming up to see you."

"Ellen—"

"Don't argue. I'm coming. You can tell Julia I'm going to help out with the kids. I'll be up there this afternoon."

"But—"

"Don't argue."

And she got off the phone.

*　　　*　　　*

I'm not passive. I'm thoughtful. Ellen's very energetic, her personality's perfect for a psychologist, because she loves to tell people what to do. Frankly, I think she's pushy. And she thinks I'm passive.

This is Ellen's idea about me. That I went to Stanford in the late seventies, and studied population biology—a purely academic field, with no practical application, no jobs except in universities. In those days population biology was being revolutionized by field studies of animals, and by advances in genetic screening. Both required computer analysis, using advanced mathematical algorithms. I couldn't find the kind of programs I needed for my research, so I began to write them myself. And I slid sideways into computer science—another geeky, purely academic field.

But my graduation just happened to coincide with the rise of Silicon Valley and the personal-computer explosion. Low-number employees at startup companies were making a fortune in the eighties, and I did pretty well at the first one I worked for. I met Julia, and we got married, had kids. Everything was smooth. We were both doing great, just by showing up for work. I got hired away by another company; more perks, bigger options. I just rode the advancing wave into the nineties. By then I wasn't programming anymore, I was supervising software development. And things just fell into place for me, without any real effort on my part. I just fell into my life. I never had to prove myself.

That's Ellen's idea of me. My idea is different. The companies of Silicon Valley are the most intensely competitive in the history of the planet. Everybody works a hundred hours a week. Everybody is racing against milestones. Everybody is cutting development cycles. The cycles were originally three years to a new product, a new version. Then it was two years. Then eighteen months. Now it was twelve months—a new version every year. If you figure beta debugging to golden master takes four months, then you have only eight months to do the actual work. Eight months to revise ten million lines of code, and make sure it all works right.

In short, Silicon Valley is no place for a passive person, and I'm not one. I hustled my ass off every minute of every day. I had to prove myself every day—or I'd be gone.

That was my idea about myself. I was sure I was right.

Ellen was right about one part, though. A strong streak of luck ran through my career. Because my original field of study had been biology, I had an advantage when computer programs began to explicitly mimic biological systems. In fact, there were programmers who shuttled back and forth between computer simulation and studies of animal groups in the wild, applying the lessons of one to the other.

But further, I had worked in population biology—the study of groups of living organisms. And computer science had evolved in the direction of massively parallel networked structures—the programming of populations of intelligent agents. A special kind of thinking was required to handle populations of agents, and I had been trained in that thinking for years.

So I was admirably suited to the trends of my field, and I made excellent progress as the fields emerged. I had been in the right place at the right time.

That much was true.

Agent-based programs that modeled biological populations were increasingly important in the real world. Like my own programs that mimicked ant foraging to control big communications networks. Or programs that mimicked division of labor among termite colonies to control thermostats in a skyscraper. And closely related were the programs that mimicked genetic selection, used for a wide range of applications. In one program, witnesses to a crime were shown nine faces and asked to choose which was most like the criminal, even if none really were; the program then showed them nine more faces, and asked them to choose again; and from many repeated generations the program slowly evolved a highly accurate composite picture of the face, far more accurate than any police artist could make. Witnesses never had to say what exactly they were responding to in each face; they just chose, and the program evolved.

And then there were the biotech companies, which had found they could not successfully engineer new proteins because the proteins tended to fold up weirdly. So now they used genetic selection to "evolve" the new proteins instead. All these procedures had become standard practice in a matter of just a few years. And they were increasingly powerful, increasingly important.

So, yes, I had been in the right place at the right time. But I wasn't passive, I was lucky.

I hadn't showered or shaved yet. I went in the bathroom, stripped off my T-shirt, and stared at myself in the mirror. I was startled to see how soft I looked around the gut. I hadn't realized. Of course I was forty, and the fact was, I hadn't been exercising as much lately. Not because I was depressed. I was busy with the kids, and tired a lot of the time. I just didn't feel like exercising, that was all.

I stared at my own reflection, and wondered if Ellen was right.

There's one problem with all psychological knowledge—nobody can apply it to themselves. People can be incredibly astute about the short-comings of their friends, spouses, children. But they have no insight into themselves at all. The same people who are coldly clear-eyed about the world around them have nothing but fantasies about themselves. Psychological knowledge doesn't work if you look in a mirror. This bizarre fact is, as far as I know, unexplained.

Personally, I always thought there was a clue from computer programming, in a procedure called recursion. Recursion means making the program loop back on itself, to use its own information to do things over and over until it gets a result. You use recursion for certain data-sorting algorithms and things like that. But it's got to be done carefully, or you risk having the machine fall into what is called an infinite regress. It's the programming equivalent of those funhouse mirrors that reflect mirrors, and mirrors, ever smaller and smaller, stretching away to infinity. The program keeps going, repeating and repeating, but nothing happens. The machine hangs.

I always figured something similar must happen when people turn their psychological insight-apparatus on themselves. The brain hangs. The thought process goes and goes, but it doesn't get anywhere. It must be something like that, because we know that people can think about themselves indefinitely. Some people think of little else. Yet people never seem to change as a result of their intensive introspection. They never understand themselves better. It's very rare to find genuine self-knowledge.

It's almost as if you need someone else to tell you who you are, or to hold up the mirror for you. Which, if you think about it, is very weird.

Or maybe it's not.

There's an old question in artificial intelligence about whether a program can ever be aware of itself. Most programmers will say it was impossible. People have tried to do it, and failed.

But there's a more fundamental version of the question, a philosophical question about whether any machine can understand its own workings. Some people say that's impossible, too. The machine can't know itself for the same reason you can't bite your own teeth. And it certainly seems to be impossible: the human brain is the most complicated structure in the known universe, but brains still know very little about themselves.

For the last thirty years, such questions have been fun to kick around with a beer on Friday afternoons after work. They were never taken seriously. But lately these philosophical questions have taken on new importance because there has been rapid progress in reproducing certain brain functions. Not the entire brain, just certain functions. For example, before I was fired, my development team was using multi-agent processing to enable computers to learn, to recognize patterns in data, to understand natural languages, to prioritize and switch tasks. What was important about the programs was that the machines literally learned. They got better at their jobs with experience. Which is more than some human beings can claim.

The phone rang. It was Ellen. "Did you call your lawyer?"

"Not yet. For Christ's sake."

"I'm on the 2:10 to San Jose. I'll see you around five at your house."

"Listen, Ellen, it really isn't necessary—"

"I know that. I'm just getting out of town. I need a break. See you soon, Jack." And she hung up.

So now she was handling me.

In any case, I figured there was no point in calling a lawyer today. I had too much to do. The dry cleaning had to be picked up, so I did that. There was a Starbucks across the street, and I went over to get a latte to take with me.

And there was Gary Marder, my attorney, with a very young blonde in low-cut jeans and crop top that left her belly exposed. They were nuzzling each other in the checkout line. She didn't look much older than a college student. I was embarrassed and was turning to leave when Gary saw me, and waved.

"Hey, Jack."

"Hi, Gary."

He held out his hand, and I shook it. He said, "Say hello to Melissa."

I said, "Hi, Melissa."

"Oh hi." She seemed vaguely annoyed at this interruption, although I couldn't be sure. She had that vacant look some young girls get around men. It occurred to me that she couldn't be more than six years older than Nicole. What was she doing with a guy like Gary?

"So. How's it going, Jack?" Gary said, slipping his arm around Melissa's bare waist.

"Okay," I said. "Pretty good."

"Yeah? That's good." But he was frowning at me.

"Well, uh, yeah . . ." I stood there, hesitating, feeling foolish in front of the girl. She clearly wanted me to leave. But I was thinking of what Ellen would say: *You ran into your lawyer and you didn't even ask him?*

So I said, "Gary, could I speak to you for a minute?"

"Of course." He gave the girl money to pay for the coffee, and we stepped to one side of the room.

I lowered my voice. "Listen, Gary," I said, "I think I need to see a divorce lawyer."

"Because what?"

"Because I think Julia is having an affair."

"You think? Or you know for a fact?"

"No. I don't know for sure."

"So you just suspect it?"

"Yes."

Gary sighed. He gave me a look.

I said, "And there's other things going on, too. She's starting to say that I am turning the kids against her."

"Alienation of affection," he said, nodding. "Legal cliché du jour. She makes these statements when?"

"When we have fights."

Another sigh. "Jack, couples say all kinds of shit when they fight. It doesn't necessarily mean anything."

"I think it does. I'm worried it does."

"This is upsetting you?"

"Yes."

"Have you seen a marriage counselor?"

"No."

"See one."

"Why?"

"Two reasons. First, because you should. You've been married to Julia a long time, and as far as I know it's been mostly good. And second, because you'll start to establish a record of trying to save the marriage, which contradicts a claim of alienation of affection."

"Yes, but—"

"If you're right that she is starting to build a case, then you have to be extremely careful, my friend. Alienation of affection is a tough argument to defend against. The kids are pissed at Mom, and she says you're behind it. How can you prove it's not true? You can't. Plus you've been home a lot, so it's easier to imagine that it might be true. The court will see you as dissatisfied, and possibly resentful of your working spouse." He held up his hand. "I know, I know none of that's true, Jack, but it's an easy argument to make, that's my point. And her attorney will make it. In your resentment, you turned the kids against her."

"That's bullshit."

"Of course. I know that." He slapped me on the shoulder. "So see a good counselor. If you need names, call my office and Barbara'll give you a couple of reputable ones."

I called Julia to tell her that Ellen was coming up for a few days. Of course, I didn't reach Julia, just her voice mail. I left a longish message, explaining what was happening. Then I went to do the shopping because with Ellen staying over, we'd need some extra supplies.

I was rolling my cart down the supermarket aisle when I got a call from the hospital. It was the beardless ER doctor again. He was calling to check on Amanda and I said her bruises were almost gone.

"That's good," he said. "Glad to hear it."

I said, "What about the MRI?"

The doctor said the MRI results were not relevant, because the machine had malfunctioned and had never examined Amanda. "In fact, we're worried about all the readings for the last few weeks," he said. "Because apparently the machine was slowly breaking down."

"How do you mean?"

"It was being corroded or something. All the memory chips were turning to powder."

I felt a chill, remembering Eric's MP3 player. "Why would that happen?" I said.

"The best guess is it's been corroded by some gas that escaped from the wall lines, probably during the night. Like chlorine gas, that'd do it. Except the thing is, only the memory chips were damaged. The other chips were fine."

Things were getting stranger by the minute. And they got stranger still a few minutes later, when Julia called all cheerful and upbeat, to announce that she was coming home in the afternoon and would be there in plenty of time for dinner.

"It'll be great to see Ellen," she said. "Why is she coming?"

"I think she just wanted to get out of town."

"Well, it'll be great for you to have her around for a few days. Some grown-up company."

"You bet," I said.

I waited for her to explain why she hadn't come home. But all she said was, "Hey, I got to run, Jack, I'll talk to you later—"

"Julia," I said. "Wait a minute."

"What?"

I hesitated, wondering how to put it. I said, "I was worried about you last night."

"You were? Why?"

"When you didn't come home."

"Honey, I called you. I got stuck out at the plant. Didn't you check your messages?"

"Yes . . ."

"And you didn't have a message from me?"

"No. I didn't."

"Well, I don't know what happened. I left you a message, Jack. I called the house first and got Maria, but she couldn't, you know, it was too complicated . . . So then I called your cell and I left you a message that I was stuck at the plant until today."

"Well, I didn't get it," I said, trying not to sound like I was pouting.

"Sorry about that, honey, but check your service. Anyway listen, I really have to go. See you tonight, okay? Kiss kiss."

And she hung up.

I pulled my cell phone out of my pocket and checked it. There was no message. I checked the phone log. There were no calls last night.

Julia hadn't called me. No one had called me.

I began to feel a sinking sensation, that descent into depression again.

I felt tired, I couldn't move. I stared at the produce on the supermarket shelves. I couldn't remember why I was there.

I had just about decided to leave the supermarket when my cell phone rang in my hand. I flipped it open. It was Tim Bergman, the guy who had taken over my job at MediaTronics. "Are you sitting down?" he said.

"No. Why?"

"I've got some pretty strange news. Brace yourself."

"Okay . . ."

"Don wants to call you."

Don Gross was the head of the company, the guy who had fired me. "What for?"

"He wants to hire you back."

"He wants *what*?"

"Yeah. I know. It's crazy. To hire you back."

"Why?" I said.

"We're having some problems with distributed systems that we've sold to customers."

"Which ones?"

"Well, PREDPREY."

"That's one of the old ones," I said. "Who sold that?" PREDPREY was a system we'd designed over a year ago. Like most of our programs, it had been based on biological models. PREDPREY was a goal-seeking program based on predator/prey dynamics. But it was extremely simple in its structure.

"Well, Xymos wanted something very simple," Tim said.

"You sold PREDPREY to Xymos?"

"Right. Licensed, actually. With a contract to support it. That's driving us crazy. "

"Why?"

"It isn't working right, apparently. Goal seeking has gone haywire. A lot of the time, the program seems to lose its goal."

"I'm not surprised," I said, "because we didn't specify reinforcers." Reinforcers were program weights that sustained the goals. The reason you needed them was that since the networked agents could learn, they might learn in a way that caused them to drift away from the goal. You needed a way to store the original goal so it didn't get lost. The fact was you could easily come to think of agent programs as children. The programs forgot things, lost things, dropped things.

It was all emergent behavior. It wasn't programmed, but it was the outcome of programming. And apparently it was happening to Xymos.

"Well," Tim said, "Don figures you were running the team when the program was originally written, so you're the guy to fix it. Plus, your wife is high up in Xymos management, so your joining the team will reassure their top people."

I wasn't sure that was true, but I didn't say anything.

"Anyway, that's the situation," Tim continued. "I'm calling you to ask if Don should call you. Because he doesn't want to get rejected."

I felt a burst of anger. *He doesn't want to get rejected.* "Tim," I said. "I can't go back to work there."

"Oh, you wouldn't be here. You'd be up at the Xymos fab plant."

"Oh yes? How would that work?"

"Don would hire you as an off-site consultant. Something like that."

"Uh-huh," I said, in my best noncommittal tone. Everything about this proposal sounded like a bad idea. The last thing I wanted to do was go back to work for that son of a bitch Don. And it was always a bad idea to return to a company after you'd been fired—for any reason, under any arrangement. Everybody knew that.

But on the other hand, if I agreed to work as a consultant, it would get rid of my shelf-life problem. And it would get me out of the house. It would accomplish a lot of things. After a pause, I said, "Listen, Tim, let me think about it."

"You want to call me back?"

"Okay. Yes."

"When will you call?" he said.

The tension in his voice was clear. I said, "You've got some urgency about this . . ."

"Yeah, well, some. Like I said, that contract's driving us crazy. We have five programmers from the original team practically living out at that Xymos plant. And they're not getting anywhere on this problem.

So if you're not going to help us, we have to look elsewhere, right away."

"Okay, I'll call you tomorrow," I said.

"Tomorrow morning?" he said, hinting.

"Okay," I said. "Yes, tomorrow morning."

Tim's call should have made me feel better about things, but it didn't. I took the baby to the park, and pushed her in the swing for a while. Amanda liked being pushed in the swing. She could do it for twenty or thirty minutes at a time, and always cried when I took her out. Later I sat on the concrete curb of the sandbox while she crawled around, and pulled herself up to standing on the concrete turtles and other playthings. One of the older toddlers knocked her over, but she didn't cry; she just got back up. She seemed to like being around the older kids.

I watched her, and thought about going back to work.

"Of course you told them yes," Ellen said to me. We were in the kitchen. She had just arrived, her black suitcase unpacked in the corner. Ellen looked exactly the same, still rail-thin, energetic, blond, hyper. My sister never seemed to age. She was drinking a cup of tea from teabags that she had brought with her. Special organic oolong tea from a special shop in San Francisco. That hadn't changed, either—Ellen had always been fussy about food, even as a kid. As an adult, she traveled around with her own teas, her own salad dressings, her own vitamins neatly arranged in little glassine packs.

"No, I didn't," I said. "I didn't tell them yes. I said I'd think about it."

"Think about it? Are you kidding? Jack, you *have* to go back to work. You know you do." She stared at me, appraising. "You're depressed."

"I'm not."

"You should have some of this tea," she said. "All that coffee is bad for your nerves."

"Tea has more caffeine than coffee."

"Jack. You *have* to go back to work."

"I know that, Ellen."

"And if it's a consulting job . . . wouldn't that be perfect? Solve all your problems?"

"I don't know," I said.

"Really? What don't you know."

"I don't know if I'm getting the full story," I said. "I mean, if Xymos is having all this trouble, how come Julia hasn't said anything about it to me?"

Ellen shook her head. "It sounds like Julia isn't saying much of anything to you these days." She stared at me. "So why didn't you accept right away?"

"I need to check around first."

"Check what, Jack?" Her tone conveyed disbelief. Ellen was acting like I had a psychological problem that needed to be fixed. My sister was starting to get to me, and we'd only been together a few minutes. My older sister, treating me like I was a kid again. I stood up. "Listen, Ellen," I said. "I've spent my life in this business, and I know how it works. There's two possible reasons Don wants me back. The first is the company's in a jam and they think I can help."

"That's what they said."

"Right. That's what they said. But the other possibility is that they've made an incredible mess of things and by now it can't be fixed—and they know it."

"So they want somebody to blame?"

"Right. They want a donkey to pin the tail on."

She frowned. I saw her hesitate. "Do you really think so?"

"I don't know, that's the point," I said. "But I have to find out."

"Which you will do by . . ."

"By making some calls. Maybe paying a surprise visit to the fab building tomorrow."

"Okay. That sounds right to me."

"I'm glad I have your approval." I couldn't keep the irritation out of my voice.

"Jack," she said. She got up and hugged me. "I'm just worried about you, that's all."

"I appreciate that," I said. "But you're not helping me."

"Okay. Then what can I do to help you?"

"Watch the kids, while I make some calls."

I figured I would first call Ricky Morse, the guy I'd seen in the supermarket buying Huggies. I had a long relationship with Ricky; he worked at Xymos and he was casual enough about information that he might tell me what was really going on there. The only problem was that Ricky was based in the Valley, and he'd already told me that the action was all at the fab building. But he was a place for me to start.

I called his office, but the receptionist said, "I'm sorry, Mr. Morse is not in the office."

"When is he expected back?"

"I really couldn't say. Do you want voice mail?"

I left Ricky a voice-mail message. Then I called his home number.

His wife answered. Mary was getting her Ph.D. in French history; I imagined her studying, bouncing the baby, with a book open on her lap. I said, "How are you, Mary?"

"I'm fine, Jack."

"How's the baby? Ricky tells me you never get diaper rash. I'm jealous." I tried to sound casual. Just a social call.

Mary laughed. "She's a good baby, and we didn't have colic, thank God. But Ricky hasn't been around for the rashes," she said. "We've had some."

I said, "Actually, I'm looking for Ricky. Is he there?"

"No, Jack. He's been gone all week. He's out at that fab plant in Nevada."

"Oh, right." I remembered now that Ricky had mentioned that, when we had met in the supermarket.

"Have you been out to that plant?" Mary said. I thought I detected an uneasy tone.

"No, I haven't, but—"

"Julia is there a lot, isn't she? What does she say about it?" Definitely worried.

"Well, not much. I gather they have new technology that's very hush-hush. Why?"

She hesitated. "Maybe it's my imagination . . ."

"What is?"

"Well, sometimes when Ricky calls, he sounds kind of weird to me."

"How?"

"I'm sure he's distracted and working hard, but he says some strange things. He doesn't always make a lot of sense. And he seems evasive. Like he's, I don't know, hiding something."

"Hiding something . . ."

She gave a self-deprecating laugh. "I even thought maybe he's having an affair. You know, that woman Mae Chang is out there, and he always liked her. She's so pretty."

Mae Chang used to work in my division at MediaTronics. "I hadn't heard she was at the fab plant."

"Yes. I think a lot of the people who used to work for you are there, now."

"Well," I said. "I don't think Ricky is having an affair, Mary. It's just not like him. And it's not like Mae."

"It's the quiet ones you have to watch out for," she said, apparently referring to Mae. "And I'm still nursing, so I haven't lost my weight yet, I mean, my thighs are as big as sides of beef."

"I don't think that—"

"They rub together when I walk. Squishy."

"Mary, I'm sure—"

"Is Julia okay, Jack? She's not acting weird?"

"No more than usual," I said, trying to make a joke. I was feeling bad as I said it. For days I had wished that people would level with me about Julia, but now that I had something to share with Mary, I wasn't going to level with her. I was going to keep my mouth shut. I said, "Julia's working hard, and she sometimes is a little odd."

"Does she say anything about a black cloud?"

"Uh . . . no."

"The new world? Being present for the birth of the new world order?"

That sounded like conspiracy talk to me. Like those people who worried about the Trilateral Commission and thought that the Rockefellers ran the world. "No, nothing like that."

"She mention a black cloak?"

I felt suddenly slowed down. Moving very slowly. "What?"

"The other night Ricky was talking about a black cloak, being covered in a black cloak. It was late, he was tired, he was sort of babbling."

"What did he say about the black cloak?"

"Nothing. Just that." She paused. "You think they're taking drugs out there?"

"I don't know," I said.

"You know, there's pressure, working around the clock, and nobody's sleeping much. I wonder about drugs."

"Let me call Ricky," I said.

Mary gave me his cell phone number, and I wrote it down. I was about to dial it when the door slammed, and I heard Eric say, "Hey, Mom! Who's that guy in the car with you?" I got up, and looked out the window at the driveway. Julia's BMW convertible was there, top down. I checked my watch. It was only 4:30.

I went out into the hall and saw Julia hugging Eric. She was saying, "It must have been sunlight on the windshield. There's nobody else in the car."

"Yes there was. I saw him."

"Oh yes?" She opened the front door. "Go look for yourself." Eric went out onto the lawn. Julia smiled at me. "He thinks someone was in the car."

Eric came back in, shrugging. "Oh well. Guess not."

"That's right, honey." Julia walked down the hall toward me. "Is Ellen here?"

"Just got here."

"Great. I'm going to take a shower, and we'll talk. Let's open some wine. What do you want to do about dinner?"

"I've got steaks ready."

"Great. Sounds great."

And with a cheerful wave, she went down the hallway.

It was a warm evening and we had dinner in the backyard. I put out the red-checkered tablecloth and grilled the steaks on the barbecue, wearing my chef's apron that said THE CHEF'S WORD IS LAW, and we had a sort of classic American family dinner.

Julia was charming and chatty, focusing her attention on my sister, talking about the kids, about school, about changes she wanted to make on the house. "That window has to come out," she said, pointing back at the kitchen, "and we'll put French doors in so it'll open to the outside. It'll be great." I was astonished by Julia's performance. Even the kids were staring at her. Julia mentioned how proud she was of Nicole's big part in the forthcoming school play. Nicole said, "Mom, I have a *bad* part."

"Oh, not really, honey," Julia said.

"Yes, I do. I just have two lines."

"Now honey, I'm sure you're—"

Eric piped up. " 'Look, here comes John now.' 'That sounds pretty serious.' "

"Shut up, weasel turd."

"She says 'em in the bathroom, over and over," Eric announced. "About a billion gazillion times."

Julia said, "Who's John?"

"Those are the lines in the play."

"Oh. Well, anyway, I'm sure you'll be wonderful. And our little Eric is making such progress in soccer, aren't you, hon?"

"It's over next week," Eric said, turning sulky. Julia hadn't made it to any of his games this fall.

"It's been so good for him," Julia said to Ellen. "Team sports build cooperation. Especially with boys, it helps with that competitiveness."

Ellen wasn't saying anything, just nodding and listening.

For this particular evening, Julia had insisted on feeding the baby, and had positioned the high chair beside her. But Amanda was accustomed to playing airplane at every mealtime. She was waiting for someone to move the spoon toward her, saying, "Rrrrrrr-owwwww . . . here comes the airplane . . . open the doors!" Since Julia wasn't doing that, Amanda kept her mouth tightly shut. Which was part of the game, too.

"Oh well. I guess she's not hungry," Julia said, with a shrug. "Did she just have a bottle, Jack?"

"No," I said. "She doesn't get one until after dinner."

"Well, I know *that*. I meant, before."

"No," I said. "Not before." I gestured toward Amanda. "Shall I try?"

"Sure." Julia handed me the spoon, and I sat beside Amanda and began to play airplane. "Rrrrr-owwww . . ." Amanda immediately grinned and opened her mouth.

"Jack's been wonderful with the kids, just wonderful," Julia said to Ellen.

"I think it's good for a man to experience home life," Ellen said.

"Oh, it is. It *is*. He's helped me a lot." She patted my knee. "You really have, Jack."

It was clear to me that Julia was too bright, too cheerful. She was keyed up, talking fast, and obviously trying to impress Ellen that she was in charge of her family. I could see that Ellen wasn't buying it. But Julia was so speedy, she didn't notice. I began to wonder if she were on drugs. Was that the reason for her strange behavior? Was she on amphetamines?

"And work," Julia continued, "is *so* incredible these days. Xymos is really making breakthroughs—the kind of breakthroughs people have been waiting for more than ten years to happen. But at last, it's happening."

"Like the black cloak?" I said, fishing.

Julia blinked. "The what?" She shook her head. "What're you talking about, hon?"

"A black cloak. Didn't you say something about a black cloak the other day?"

"No . . ." She shook her head. "I don't know what you mean." She turned back to Ellen. "Anyway, all this molecular technology has been much slower to come to market than we expected. But at last, it really is here."

"You seem very excited," Ellen said.

"I have to tell you, it's thrilling, Ellen." She lowered her voice. "And on top of it, we'll probably make a bundle."

"That'd be good," Ellen said. "But I guess you've had to put in long hours . . ."

"Not that long," Julia said. "All things considered, it hasn't been bad. Just the last week or so."

I saw Nicole's eyes widen. Eric was staring at his mother as he ate. But the kids didn't say anything. Neither did I.

"It's just a transition period," Julia continued. "All companies have these transitional periods."

"Of course," Ellen said.

The sun was going down. The air was cooler. The kids left the table. I got up and started to clear. Ellen was helping me. Julia kept talking, then said, "I'd love to stay, but I have something going on, and I have to get back to the office for a while."

If Ellen was surprised to hear this, she didn't show it. All she said was, "Long hours."

"Just during this transition." She turned to me. "Thanks for holding the fort, honey." At the door, she turned, blew me an air kiss. "Love, Jack."

And she left.

Ellen frowned, watching her go. "Just a *little* abrupt, wouldn't you say?"

I shrugged.

"Will she say good-bye to the kids?"

"Probably not."

"She'll just run right out the door?"

"Right."

Ellen shook her head. "Jack," she said, "I don't know if she's having an affair or not, but—what's she taking?"

"Nothing, as far as I know."

"She's on something. I'm certain of it. Would you say she's lost weight?"

"Yes. Some."

"And sleeping very little. And obviously speedy . . ." Ellen shook her head. "A lot of these hard-charging executives are on drugs."

"I don't know," I said.

She just looked at me.

I went back into my office to call Ricky, and from the office window I saw Julia backing her car down the driveway. I went to wave to her, but she was looking over her shoulder as she backed away. In the evening light I saw golden reflections on the windshield, streaking from the trees above. She had almost reached the street when I thought I saw someone sitting in the passenger seat beside her. It looked like a man.

I couldn't see his features clearly through the windshield, with the car moving down the drive. When Julia backed onto the street, her body blocked my view of the passenger. But it seemed as if Julia was talking to him, animatedly. Then she put the car in gear and leaned back in her seat, and for a moment I had a brief, clear look. The man was backlit, his face in shadow, and he must have been looking directly at her because I still couldn't make out any features, but from the way he was slouching I had the impression of someone young, maybe in his twenties, though I honestly couldn't be sure. It was just a glimpse. Then the BMW accelerated, and she drove off down the street.

I thought: the hell with this. I ran outside, and down the driveway. I reached the street just as Julia came to the stop sign to the end of the block, her brake lights flaring. She was probably fifty yards away, the street illuminated in low, slanting yellow light. It looked as if she was alone in the car, but I really couldn't see well. I felt a moment of relief, and of foolishness. There I was, standing in the street, for no good reason. My mind was playing tricks on me. There was nobody in the car.

Then, as Julia made the right turn, the guy popped up again, like he had been bent over, getting something from the glove compartment. And then the car was gone. And in an instant all my distress came flooding back, like a hot pain that spread across my chest and body. I felt short of breath, and a little dizzy.

There *was* somebody in the car.

I trudged back up the driveway, feeling churning emotions, not sure what to do next.

"You're not sure what to do next?" Ellen said. We were doing the pots and pans at the sink, the things that didn't go in the dishwasher. Ellen was drying, while I scrubbed. "You pick up the phone and call her."

"She's in the car."

"She has a car phone. Call her."

"Uh-huh," I said. "So how do I put it? Hey Julia, who's the guy in the car with you?" I shook my head. "That's going to be a tough conversation."

"Maybe so."

"That'll be a divorce, for sure."

She just stared at me. "You don't want a divorce, do you."

"Hell, no. I want to keep my family together."

"That may not be possible, Jack. It may not be your decision to make."

"None of this makes any sense," I said. "I mean the guy in the car, he was like a kid, somebody young."

"So?"

"That's not Julia's style."

"Oh?" Ellen's eyebrows went up. "He was probably in his twenties or early thirties. And anyway, are you so sure about Julia's style?"

"Well, I've lived with her for thirteen years."

She set down one of the pots with a bang. "Jack. I understand that all this must be hard to accept."

"It is, it is." In my mind, I kept replaying the car backing down the driveway, over and over. I was thinking that there was something strange about the other person in the car, something odd in his appearance. In my mind, I kept trying to see his face but I never could. The features were blurred by the windshield, by the light shifting as she backed down the drive . . . I couldn't see the eyes, or the cheekbones, or the mouth. In my memory, the whole face was dark and indistinct. I tried to explain that to her.

"It's not surprising."

"No?"

"No. It's called denial. Look Jack, the fact is, you have the evidence right in front of your eyes. You've *seen* it, Jack. Don't you think it's time you believed it?"

I knew she was right. "Yes," I said. "It's time."

The phone was ringing. My hands were up to the elbows in soap suds. I asked Ellen to get it, but one of the kids had already picked it up. I finished scrubbing the barbecue grill, handed it to Ellen to dry.

"Jack," Ellen said, "you have to start seeing things as they really are, and not as you want them to be."

"You're right," I said. "I'll call her."

At that moment Nicole came into the kitchen, looking pale.

"Dad? It's the police. They want to talk to you."

DAY 5
9:10 P.M.

Julia's convertible had gone off the road about five miles from the house. It had plunged fifty feet down a steep ravine, cutting a track through the sage and juniper bushes. Then it must have rolled, because now it lay at an angle, wheels facing upward. I could see only the underside of the car. The sun was almost down, and the ravine was dark. The three rescue ambulances on the road had their red lights flashing, and the rescue crews were already rappelling down on ropes. As I watched, portable floodlights were set up, bathing the wreck in a harsh blue glow. I heard the crackle of radios all around.

I stood up on the road with a motorcycle police officer. I had already asked to go down there, and was told I couldn't; I had to stay on the road. When I heard the radios, I said, "Is she hurt? Is my wife hurt?"

"We'll know in a minute." He was calm.

"What about the other guy?"

"Just a minute," he said. He had a headset in his helmet, because he just started talking in a low voice. It sounded like a lot of code words. I heard ". . . update a four-oh-two for seven-three-nine here . . ."

I stood at the edge, and looked down, trying to see. By now there were workers all around the car, and several hidden behind the upturned frame. A long time seemed to pass.

The cop said, "Your wife is unconscious but she's . . . She was wearing her seat belt, and stayed in the car. They think she's all right. Vital signs are stable. They say no spinal injuries but . . . she . . . sounds like she broke her arm."

"But she's all right?"

"They think so." Another pause while he listened. I heard him say, "I have the husband here, so let's eight-seven." When he turned back to me, he said, "Yes. She's coming around. She'll have to be checked for internal bleeding at the hospital. And she's got a broken arm. But they say she's all right. They're getting her on a stretcher now."

"Thank God," I said.

The policeman nodded. "This is a bad piece of road."

"This has happened before?"

He nodded. "Every few months. Not usually so lucky."

I flipped open my cell phone and called Ellen, told her to explain to the kids there was nothing to worry about, that Mom was going to be okay. "Especially Nicole," I said.

"I'll take care of it," Ellen promised me.

I flipped the phone shut and turned back to the cop. "What about the other guy?" I said.

"She's alone in the car."

"No," I said. "There was another guy with her."

He spoke on his headset, then turned back to me. "They say no. There's no sign of anyone else."

"Maybe he was thrown," I said.

"They're asking your wife now . . ." He listened a moment. "She says she was alone."

"You're kidding," I said.

He looked at me, shrugged. "That's what she says." In the flashing red lights of the ambulances, I couldn't read his expression. But his tone implied: another guy who doesn't know his own wife. I turned away, looked over the edge of the road.

One of the rescue vehicles had extended a steel arm with a winch that hung over the ravine. A cable was being lowered. I saw the workers, struggling for footing against the steep slope, as they attached a stretcher to the winch. I couldn't see Julia clearly on the stretcher, she was strapped down, covered in a silver space blanket. She started to rise, passing through the cone of blue light, then into darkness.

The cop said, "They're asking about drugs and medicines. Is your wife taking any drugs or medicines?"

"Not that I know of."

"How about alcohol? Was she drinking?"

"Wine at dinner. One or two glasses."

The cop turned away and spoke again, quietly in the darkness. After a pause, I heard him say, "That's affirmative."

The stretcher twisted slowly as it rose into the air. One of the workers, halfway up the slope, reached out to steady it. The stretcher continued upward.

I still couldn't see Julia clearly, until it reached the level of the road and the rescue workers swung it around, and unclipped it from the line. She was swollen; her left cheekbone was purple and the forehead above her left eye was purple as well. She must have hit her head pretty hard. She was breathing shallowly. I moved alongside the stretcher. She saw me and said, "Jack . . ." and tried to smile.

"Just take it easy," I said.

She gave a little cough. "Jack. It was an accident."

The medics were maneuvering around the motorcycle. I had to watch where I was going. "Of course it was."

"It's not what you think, Jack."

I said, "What is, Julia?" She seemed to be delirious. Her voice seemed to drift in and out.

"I know what you're thinking." Her hand gripped my arm. "Promise me you won't get involved in this, Jack."

I didn't say anything, I just walked with her.

She squeezed me harder. "Promise me you'll stay out of it."

"I promise," I said.

She relaxed then, dropping my arm. "This doesn't involve our family. The kids will be fine. You'll be fine. Just stay out, okay?"

"Okay," I said, just wanting to mollify her.

"Jack?"

"Yes, honey, I'm here."

By now we were approaching the nearest ambulance. The doors swung open. One of the rescue team said, "You related to her?"

"I'm her husband."

"You want to come?"

"Yes."

"Hop in."

I got into the ambulance first, then they slid the stretcher in, one of the rescue team got in and slammed the doors shut. We started down the road, siren moaning.

I was immediately moved aside by the two paramedics, working on her. One was recording notes on a handheld device and the other was starting a second IV in her other arm. They were worried about her blood pressure, which was dropping. That was a great cause for concern. During all this I couldn't really see Julia, but I heard her murmuring.

I tried to move forward, but the medics pushed me back. "Let us work, sir. Your wife's got injuries. We have to work."

For the rest of the way, I sat on a little jump seat and gripped a wall handle as the ambulance careened around curves. By now Julia was clearly delirious, babbling nonsense. I heard something about "the black clouds," that were "not black anymore." Then she shifted into a kind of lecture, talking about "adolescent rebellion." She mentioned Amanda by name, and Eric, asking if they were all right. She seemed agitated. The medics kept trying to reassure her. And finally she lapsed into repeating "I didn't do anything wrong, I didn't mean to do anything wrong" as the ambulance sped through the night.

Listening to her, I couldn't help but worry.

The examination suggested Julia's injuries might be more extensive than they first thought. There was a lot to rule out: possible pelvic fracture, possible hematoma, possible fracture of a cervical vertebra, left arm broken in two places and might need to be pinned. The doctors seemed most worried about her pelvis. They were handling her much more gingerly when they put her into intensive care.

But Julia was conscious, catching my eye and smiling at me from time to time, until she fell asleep. The doctors said there was nothing for me to do; they would wake her up every half hour during the night. They said that she would be in the hospital at least three days, probably a week.

They told me to get some rest. I left the hospital a little before midnight.

I took a taxi back to the crash site, to pick up my car. It was a cold night. The police cars and rescue ambulances were gone. In their place was a big flatbed tow truck, which was winching Julia's car up the hill. A skinny guy smoking a cigarette was running the winch.

"Nothing to see," he said to me. "Everybody's gone to the hospital."

I said it was my wife's car.

"Can't drive it," he said. He asked me for my insurance card. I got it out of my wallet and handed it to him. He said, "I heard your wife's okay."

"So far."

"You're a lucky guy." He jerked his thumb, pointing across the road. "Are they with you?"

Across the street a small white van was parked. The sides were bare, with no markings or company logo. But low on the front door I saw a serial number, in black. And underneath it said SSVT UNIT.

I said, "No, they're not with me."

"Been here an hour," he said. "Just sitting there."

I couldn't see anyone inside the van; the front windows were dark. I started across the street toward them. I heard the faint crackle of a radio. When I was about ten feet away the lights came on, the engine started, and the van roared past me, and drove down the highway.

As it passed, I had a glimpse of the driver. He was wearing a shiny suit of some kind, like silvery plastic, and a tight hood of the same material. I thought I saw some funny, silver apparatus hanging around his neck. It looked like a gas mask, except it was silver. But I wasn't sure.

As the car drove away, I noticed the rear bumper had two green stickers, each with a big X. That was the Xymos logo. But it was the license plate that really caught my eye. It was a Nevada plate.

That van had come from the fabrication plant, out in the desert.

I frowned. It was time for me to visit the fab plant, I thought.

I pulled out my cell phone, and dialed Tim Bergman. I told him I had reconsidered his offer and I would take the consulting job, after all.

"That's great," Tim said. "Don will be very happy."

"Great," I said. "How soon can I start?"

DESERT

DAY 6
7:12 A.M.

With the vibration of the helicopter, I must have dozed off for a few minutes. I awoke and yawned, hearing voices in my headphones. They were all men speaking:

"Well, what exactly is the problem?" A growling voice.

"Apparently, the plant released some material into the environment. It was an accident. Now, several dead animals have been found out in the desert. In the vicinity of the plant." A reasonable, organized voice.

"Who found them?" Growly.

"Couple of nosy environmentalists. They ignored the keep-out signs, snooped around the plant. They've complained to the company and are demanding to inspect the plant."

"Which we can't allow."

"No, no."

"How do we handle this?" said a timid voice.

"I say we minimize the amount of contamination released, and give data that show no untoward consequence is possible." Organized voice.

"Hell, I wouldn't play it that way," said growling voice. "We're better off flatly denying it. Nothing was released. I mean, what's the evidence anything was released?"

"Well, the dead animals. A coyote, some desert rats. Maybe a few birds."

"Hell, animals die in nature all the time. I mean, remember the business about those slashed cows? It was supposed to be aliens from UFOs that were slashing the cows. Finally turned out the cows were dying of natural causes, and it was decomposing gas in the carcasses that split them open. Remember that?"

"Vaguely."

Timid voice: "I'm not sure we can just deny—"

"Fuck yes, deny."

"Aren't there pictures? I think the environmentalists took pictures."

"Well, who cares? What will the pictures show, a dead coyote? Nobody is going to get worked up about a dead coyote. Trust me. Pilot? Pilot, where the fuck are we?"

I opened my eyes. I was sitting in the front of the helicopter, alongside the pilot. The helicopter was flying east, into the glare of low morning sun. Beneath my feet I saw mostly flat terrain, with low clumps of cactus, juniper, and the occasional scraggly Joshua tree.

The pilot was flying alongside the power-line towers that marched in single file across the desert, a steel army with outstretched arms. The towers cast long shadows in the morning light.

A heavyset man leaned forward from the backseat. He was wearing a suit and tie. "Pilot? Are we there yet?"

"We just crossed the Nevada line. Another ten minutes."

The heavyset man grunted and sat back. I'd met him when we took off, but I couldn't remember his name now. I glanced back at the three men, all in suits and ties, who were traveling with me. They were all PR consultants hired by Xymos. I could match their appearance to their voices. A slender, nervous man, twisting his hands. Then a middle-aged man with a briefcase on his lap. And the heavyset man, older and growly, obviously in charge.

"Why the hell did they put it in Nevada, anyway?"

"Fewer regulations, easier inspections. These days California is sticky about new industry. There was going to be a year's delay just for environmental-impact statements. And a far more difficult permitting process. So they came here."

Growly looked out the window at the desert. "What a shithole," he said. "I don't give a fuck what goes on out here, it's not a problem." He turned to me. "What do you do?"

"I'm a computer programmer."

"You covered by an NDA?" He meant, did I have a non-disclosure agreement that would prevent me from discussing what I had just heard.

"Yes," I said.

"You coming out to work at the plant?"

"To consult," I said. "Yes."

"Consulting's the way to go," he said, nodding as if I were an ally. "No responsibility. No liability. Just give your opinion, and watch them not take it."

With a crackle, the pilot's voice broke in over the headsets. "Xymos Molecular Manufacturing is dead ahead," he said. "You can just see it now."

Twenty miles in front of us, I saw an isolated cluster of low buildings silhouetted on the horizon. The PR people in the back all leaned forward.

"Is that it?" said Growly. "That's all it is?"

"It's bigger than it looks from here," the pilot said.

As the helicopter came closer, I could see that the buildings were interlocked, featureless concrete blocks, all whitewashed. The PR people were so pleased they almost burst into applause. "Hey, it's beautiful!"

"Looks like a fucking hospital."

"Great architecture."

"It'll photograph great."

I said, "Why will it photograph great?"

"Because it has no projections," the man with the briefcase said. "No antennas, no spikes, no things poking up. People are afraid of spikes and antennas. There are studies. But a building that's plain and square like this, and *white*—perfect color choice, associations to virginal, hospital, cure, pure—a building like this, they don't care."

"Those environmentalists are fucked," said Growly, with satisfaction. "They do medical research here, right?"

"Not exactly . . ."

"They will when I get through, trust me. Medical research is the way to go on this."

The pilot pointed out the different buildings as he circled them. "That first concrete block, that's power. Walkway to that low building, that's the residences. Next door, fab support, labs, whatever. And then the square windowless three-story one, that's the main fab building. They tell me it's a shell, it's got another building inside it. Then over to the right, that low flat shed, that's external storage and parking. Cars have to be under shade here, or the dashboards buckle. Get a first-degree burn if you touch your steering wheel."

I said, "And they have residences?"

The pilot nodded. "Yeah. Have to. Nearest motel is a hundred and sixty-one miles. Over near Reno."

"So how many people live in this facility?" Growly said.

"They can take twelve," the pilot said. "But they've generally got about five to eight. Doesn't take a lot to run the place. It's all automated, from what I hear."

"What else do you hear?"

"Not very damn much," the pilot said. "They're closed-mouthed about this place. I've never even been inside."

"Good," said Growly. "Let's make sure they keep it that way."

The pilot turned the stick in his hand. The helicopter banked, and started down.

I opened the plastic door in the bubble cockpit, and started to get out. It was like stepping into an oven. The blast of heat made me gasp.

"This is nothing!" the pilot shouted, over the whirr of the blades. "This is almost winter! Can't be more than a hundred and five!"

"Great," I said, inhaling hot air. I reached in the back for my overnight bag and my laptop. I'd stowed them under the seat of the timid man.

"I have to take a piss," said Growly, releasing his seat belt.

"Dave . . ." said the man with the briefcase, in a warning tone.

"Fuck, it's just for a minute."

"*Dave*—" an embarrassed glance toward me, then lowering his voice: "They said, *we don't get out of the helicopter*, remember?"

"Aw hell. I can't wait another hour. Anyway, what's the difference?" He gestured toward the surrounding desert. "There's nothing the fuck out here for a million miles."

"But, Dave—"

"You guys give me a pain. I'm going to pee, damn it." He hefted his bulk up, and moved toward the door.

I didn't hear the rest of their conversation because by then I had taken off my earphones. Growly was clambering out. I grabbed my bags, turned and moved away, crouched beneath the blades. They cast a flickering shadow on the pad. I came to the edge of the pad where the concrete ended abruptly in a dirt path that threaded among the clumps of cholla cactus toward the blocky white power building fifty yards away. There was no one to greet me—in fact, no one in sight at all.

Looking back, I saw Growly zip up his trousers and climb back into the helicopter. The pilot pulled the door shut and lifted off, waving to me as he rose into the air. I waved back, then ducked away from the swirl of spitting sand. The helicopter circled once and headed west. The sound faded.

The desert was silent except for the hum of the electrical power lines a few hundred yards away. The wind ruffled my shirt, flapped my trouser legs. I turned in a slow circle, wondering what to do now. And thinking about the words of the PR guy: *They said, we don't get out of the helicopter, remember?*

"Hey! Hey, you!"

I looked back. A door had cracked open in the white power block. A man's head stuck out. He shouted, "Are you Jack Forman?"

"Yes," I said.

"Well, what the hell you waiting for, an engraved invitation? Get inside, for Chrissake."

And he slammed the door shut again.

That was my welcome to the Xymos Fabrication Facility. Lugging my bags, I trudged down the dirt path toward the door.

Things never turn out the way you expect.

*　　　*　　　*

I stepped into a small room, with dark gray walls on three sides. The walls were some smooth material like Formica. It took my eyes a moment to adjust to the relative darkness. Then I saw that the fourth wall directly ahead of me was entirely glass, leading to a small compartment and a second glass wall. The glass walls were fitted with folding steel arms, ending in metal pressure pads. It looked a little bit like what you'd expect to see in a bank vault.

Beyond the second glass wall I could see a burly man in blue trousers and a blue work shirt, with the Xymos logo on the pocket. He was clearly the plant maintenance engineer. He gestured to me.

"It's an airlock. Door's automatic. Walk forward."

I did, and the nearest glass door hissed open. A red light came on. In the compartment ahead, I saw grillwork on floor, ceiling, and both walls. I hesitated.

"Looks like a fuckin' toaster, don't it?" the man said, grinning. He had some teeth missing. "But don't worry, it'll just blow you a little. Come ahead."

I stepped into the glass compartment, and set my bag on the ground.

"No, no. Pick the bag up."

I picked it up again. Immediately, the glass door behind me hissed shut, the steel arms unfolding smoothly. The pressure pads sealed with a thunk. I felt a slight discomfort in my ears as the airlock pressurized. The man in blue said, "You might want to close your eyes."

I closed my eyes and immediately felt chilling spray strike my face and body from all sides. My clothes were soaked. I smelled a stinging odor like acetone, or nail polish remover. I began to shiver; the liquid was really cold.

The first blast of air came from above my head, a roar that quickly built to hurricane intensity. I stiffened my body to steady myself. My clothes flapped and pressed flat against my body. The wind increased, threatening to tear the bag from my hand. Then the air stopped for a moment, and a second blast came upward from the floor. It was disorienting, but it only lasted a few moments. Then with a *whoosh* the vacuum pumps kicked in and I felt a slight ache in my ears as the pressure dropped, like an airplane descending. Then silence.

A voice said, "That's it. Come ahead."

I opened my eyes. The liquid they'd sprayed on me had evaporated; my clothes were dry. The doors hissed open before me. I stepped out and the man in blue looked at me quizzically. "Feel okay?"

"Yeah, I think so."

"No itching?"

"No . . ."

"Good. We had a few people who were allergic to the stuff. But we've got to do this routine, for the clean rooms."

I nodded. It was obviously a procedure to remove dust and other contaminants. The dousing fluid was highly volatile, evaporating at room temperature, drawing off microparticles on my body and clothes. The air jets and vacuum completed the scrub. The procedure would remove any loose particles on my body and suck them away.

"I'm Vince Reynolds," the man said, but he didn't hold out his hand. "You call me Vince. And you're Jack?"

I said I was.

"Okay, Jack," he said. "They're waiting for you, so let's get started. We got to take precautions, because this is an HMF, that's high magnetic field environment, greater than 33 Tesla, so . . ." He picked up a cardboard box. "Better lose your watch."

I put the watch in the box.

"And the belt."

I took my belt off, put it in the box.

"Any other jewelry? Bracelet? Necklace? Piercings? Decorative pins or medals? MedicAlert?"

"No."

"How about metal inside your body? Old injury, bullets, shrapnel? No? Any pins for broken arms or legs, hip or knee replacement? No? Artificial valves, artificial cartilage, vascular pumps or implants?"

I said I didn't have any of those things.

"Well, you're still young," he said. "Now how about in your bag?" He made me take everything out and spread it on a table, so he could rummage through it. I had plenty of metal in there: another belt with a metal buckle, nail clippers, a can of shaving cream, razor and blades, a pocket knife, blue jeans with metal rivets . . .

He took the knife and the belt but left the rest. "You can put your stuff back in the bag," he said. "Now, here's the deal. Your bag goes to the residence building, but no farther. Okay? There's an alarm at the residence door if you try to take any metal past there. But do me a favor and don't set it off, okay? 'Cause it shuts down the magnets as a safety procedure and it takes about two minutes to start 'em up again. Pisses the techs off, especially if they're fabbing at the time. Ruins all their hard work."

I said I would try to remember.

"The rest of your stuff stays right here." He nodded to the wall behind me; I saw a dozen small safes, each with an electronic keypad. "You set the combination and lock it up yourself." He turned aside so I could do that.

"I won't need a watch?"

He shook his head. "We'll get you a watch."

"What about a belt?"

"We'll get you a belt."

"And my laptop?" I said.

"It goes in the safe," he said. "Unless you want to scrub your hard drive with the magnetic field."

I put the laptop in with the rest of my stuff, and locked the door. I felt strangely stripped, like a man entering prison. "You don't want my shoelaces, too?" I said, making a joke.

"Nah. You keep those. So you can strangle yourself, if it turns out you need to."

"Why would I need to?"

"I really couldn't say." Vince shrugged. "But these guys working here? Let me tell you, they're all fucking crazy. They're making these teeny-weeny little things you can't see, pushing around molecules and shit, sticking 'em together. It's real tense and detailed work, and it makes them crazy. Every fucking one of 'em. Nutty as loons. Come this way."

We passed through another set of glass doors. But this time, there was no spray.

*   *   *

We entered the power plant. Beneath blue halogen lamps, I saw huge metal tubs ten feet high, and fat ceramic insulators thick as a man's leg. Everything hummed. I felt a distinct vibration in the floor. There were signs all around with jagged red lightning bolts saying WARNING: LETHAL ELECTRICAL CURRENTS!

"You use a lot of power here," I said.

"Enough for a small town," Vince said. He pointed to one of the signs. "Take those warnings seriously. We had problems with fires, a while back."

"Oh?"

"Yeah. Got a nest of rats in the building. Buggers kept getting fried. Literally. I hate the smell of burning rat fur, don't you?"

"Never had that experience," I said.

"Smells like what you'd think."

"Uh-huh," I said. "How did the rats get in?"

"Up through the toilet bowl." I must have looked surprised, because Vince said, "Oh, you don't know that? Rats do that all the time, it's just a short swim for them to get in. 'Course, if it happened while you were sitting, it'd be a nasty surprise." He gave a short laugh. "Problem was the contractor for the building didn't bury the leach field deep enough. Anyhow, rats got in. We've had a few accidents like that since I've been here."

"Is that right? What kind of accidents?"

He shrugged. "They tried to make these buildings perfect," he said. "Because they're working with such small-size things. But it's not a perfect world, Jack. Never has been. Never will be."

I said again, "What kind of accidents?"

By then we had come to the far door, with a keypad, and Vince punched in numbers quickly. The door clicked open. "All the doors are keyed the same. Oh six, oh four, oh two."

Vince pushed the door wide, and we stepped into a covered passageway connecting the power plant to the other buildings. It was stifling hot here, despite the roar of the air conditioner.

"Contractor," Vince explained. "Never balanced the air handlers right. We had 'em back five times to fix it, but this passage is always hot."

At the end of the corridor was another door, and Vince had me punch in the code myself. The door clicked open.

I faced another airlock: a wall of thick glass, with another wall a few feet beyond. And behind that second wall, I saw Ricky Morse in jeans and a T-shirt, grinning and waving cheerfully to me.

His T-shirt said, "Obey Me, I Am Root."

It was an inside joke. In the UNIX operating system, it meant the boss.

Over an intercom speaker, Ricky said, "I'll take it from here, Vince."

Vince waved. "No problem."

"You fix that positive pressure setting?"

"Did it an hour ago. Why?"

"It may not be holding in the main lab."

"I'll check it again," Vince said. "Maybe we got another leak some-where." He slapped me on the back, jerked his thumb toward the interior of the building. "Lots of luck in there." Then he turned and walked back the way he came.

"It's great to see you," Ricky said. "You know the code to get in?"

I said I did. He pointed to a keypad. I punched the numbers in. The glass wall slid sideways. I stepped into another narrow space about four feet wide, with metal grills on all four sides. The wall closed behind me.

A fierce blast of air shot up from the floor, puffing up my trouser legs, ruffling my clothing. Almost immediately it was followed by blasts of air coming from both sides, then from top, blowing down hard on my hair and shoulders. Then a *whoosh* of vacuum. The glass in front of me slid laterally. I smoothed down my hair and stepped out.

"Sorry about that." Ricky shook my hand vigorously. "But at least we don't have to wear bunny suits," he said. I noticed that he looked strong, healthy. The muscles in his forearms were defined.

I said, "You look good, Ricky. Working out?"

"Oh, you know. Not really."

"You're pretty cut," I said. I punched him on the shoulder.

He grinned. "Just tension on the job. Did Vince frighten you?"

"Not exactly . . ."

"He's a little strange," Ricky said. "Vince grew up alone out in the desert with his mother. She died when he was five. Body was pretty decomposed when they finally found her. Poor kid, he just didn't know what to do. I guess I'd be strange, too." Ricky gave a shrug. "But I'm glad you're here, Jack. I was afraid you wouldn't come." Despite Ricky's apparent good health, I was noticing now that he seemed nervous, edgy. He led me briskly down a short hallway. "So. How's Julia?"

"Broke her arm, and hit her head pretty badly. She's in the hospital for observation. But she's going to be all right."

"Good. That's good." He nodded quickly, continuing down a corridor. "Who's taking care of the kids?"

I told him that my sister was in town.

"Then you can stay awhile? A few days?"

I said, "I guess. If you need me that long." Ordinarily, software consultants don't spend a lot of time on-site. One day, maybe two. Not more than that.

Ricky glanced over his shoulder at me. "Did Julia, ah, explain to you about this place?"

"Not really, no."

"But you knew she was spending a lot of time here."

I said, "Oh sure. Yes."

"The last few weeks, she came out almost every day on the helicopter. Stayed over a couple of nights, too."

I said, "I didn't know she took such an interest in manufacturing."

Ricky seemed to hesitate a moment. Then he said, "Well, Jack, this is a whole new thing . . ." He frowned. "She really didn't tell you anything?"

"No. Not really. Why?"

He didn't answer.

He opened the far door and waved me through. "This is our residential module, where everybody sleeps and eats."

The air was cool after the passageway. The walls were the same smooth Formica material. I heard a low, continuous *whoosh* of air handlers.

A series of doors opened off the hallway. One of them had my name on it, written in marker on a piece of tape. Ricky opened the door. "Home sweet home, Jack."

The room was monastic—a small bed, a tiny desk just large enough to hold a workstation monitor and keyboard. Above the bed, a shelf for books and clothes. All the furniture had been coated with smooth-flowing white plastic laminate. There were no nooks or crannies to hold stray particles of dirt. There was no window in the room either, but a liquid-crystal screen showed a view of the desert outside.

There was a plastic watch and a belt with a plastic buckle on the bed. I put them on.

Ricky said, "Dump your gear, and I'll give you the tour."

Still keeping his brisk pace, he led me into a medium-size lounge with a couch and chairs around a coffee table, and a bulletin board on the wall. All the furniture here was the same flowing plastic laminate. "To the right is the kitchen and the rec room with TV, video games, so forth."

We entered the small kitchen. There were two people there, a man and a woman, eating sandwiches standing up. "I think you know these guys," Ricky said, grinning. And I did. They had been on my team at MediaTronics.

Rosie Castro was dark, thin, exotic-looking, and sarcastic; she wore baggy cargo shorts and a T-shirt tight across her large breasts, which read YOU WISH. Independent and rebellious, Rosie had been a Shake-spearean scholar at Harvard before she decided, in her words, that "Shakespeare is fucking *dead*. For fucking *centuries*. There is *nothing* new to say. What's the point?" She transferred to MIT, became a protégée of Robert Kim, working on natural language programming. It turned out she was brilliant at it. And these days natural language programs were starting to involve distributed processing. Because it turned out people evaluate a sentence in several ways simultaneously, while it is being spoken; they don't wait until it is finished but rather they form expectations of what is coming. That's a perfect situation for distributed processing, which can work on a problem at several points simultaneously.

I said, "Still wearing those T-shirts, Rosie." At MediaTronics, we'd had some trouble about the way she dressed.

"Hey. Keeps the boys awake," she said, shrugging.

"Actually, we ignore them." I turned to David Brooks, stiff, formal, obsessively neat, and almost bald at twenty-eight. He blinked behind thick glasses. "They're not that good, anyway," he said.

Rosie stuck her tongue out at him.

David was an engineer, and he had an engineer's bluntness and lack of social skills. He was also full of contradictions; although he fussed over every detail of his work and appearance, on weekends he raced a dirt bike, often coming back covered in mud. He shook my hand enthusiastically. "I'm very glad you're here, Jack."

I said, "Somebody's going to have to tell me why you're all so glad to see me."

Rosie said, "Well, it's because you know more about the multi-agent algorithms that—"

"I'm going to show him around first," Ricky said, interrupting. "Then we'll talk."

"Why?" Rosie said. "You want it to be a surprise?"

"Hell of a surprise," David said.

"No, not at all," Ricky said, giving them a hard look. "I just want Jack to have some background first. I want to go over that with him."

David looked at his watch. "Well, how much time do you think that will take? Because I figure we've got—"

"*I said, Let me show him around, for Christ's sake!*" Ricky was almost snarling. I was surprised; I'd never seen him lose his temper before. But apparently they had:

"Okay, okay, Ricky."

"Hey, you're the boss, Ricky."

"That's right, I am," Ricky said, still visibly angry. "And by the way, your break ended ten minutes ago. So let's get back to work." He looked into the adjoining game room. "Where are the others?"

"Fixing the perimeter sensors."

"You mean they're *outside*?"

"No, no. They're in the utility room. Bobby thinks there's a calibration problem with the sensor units."

"Great. Did anybody tell Vince?"

"No. It's software: Bobby's taking care of it."

It was at that point that my cell phone beeped. I was surprised, pulled it out of my pocket. I turned to the others. "Cell phones work?"

"Yeah," Ricky said, "we're wired here." He went back to his argument with David and Rosie.

I stepped into the corridor and got my messages. There was only one, from the hospital, about Julia. "We understand you are Ms. Forman's husband, and if you could call us please as soon as possible . . ." Then an extension for a Dr. Rana. I dialed back at once.

The switchboard put me through. "ICU."

I asked for Dr. Rana, and waited until he came on. I said, "This is Jack Forman. Julia Forman's husband."

"Oh yes, Mr. Forman." A pleasant, melodic voice. "Thank you for calling back. I understand you accompanied your wife to the hospital last night. Yes? Well then you know the seriousness of her injuries, or should I say her potential injuries. We really do feel that she needs to have a thorough workup for cervical fracture, and for subdural hematoma, and she needs a pelvic fracture workup as well."

"Yes," I said. "That's what I was told last night. Is there a problem?"

"Actually, there is. Your wife is refusing treatment."

"She is?"

"Last night, she allowed us to take X-rays and to set the fractures in her wrist. We've explained to her that X-rays are limited in what we can see, and that it is quite important for her to have an MRI, but she is refusing that."

I said, "Why?"

"She says she doesn't need it."

"Of course she needs it," I said.

"Yes, she does, Mr. Forman," Rana said. "I don't want to alarm you but the concern with pelvic fracture is massive hemorrhaging into the abdomen and, well, bleeding to death. It can happen very quickly, and—"

"What do you want me to do?"

"We'd like you to talk to her."

"Of course. Put her on."

"Unfortunately, she's gone for some additional X-rays just now. Is there a number where you can be reached? Your cell phone? All right. One other thing, Mr. Forman, we weren't able to take a psychiatric history from your wife . . ."

"Why is that?"

"She refuses to talk about it. I'm referring to drugs, any history of behavioral disorders, that kind of thing. Can you shed any light in that area?"

"I'll try . . ."

"I don't want to alarm you, but your wife has been, well, a bit on the irrational side. At times, almost delusional."

"She's been under a lot of stress lately," I said.

"Yes, I am sure that contributes," Dr. Rana said smoothly. "And she has suffered a severe head injury, which we need to investigate further. I don't want to alarm you, but frankly it was the opinion of the psychiatric consult that your wife was suffering from a bipolar disorder, or a drug disorder, or both."

"I see . . ."

"And of course such questions naturally arise in the context of a single-car automobile accident . . ."

He meant that the accident might be a suicide attempt. I didn't think that was likely. "I have no knowledge of my wife taking drugs," I said. "But I have been concerned about her behavior for, oh, a few weeks now."

Ricky came over, and stood by me impatiently. I put my hand over the phone. "It's about Julia." He nodded, and glanced at his watch. Raised his eyebrows. I thought it was pretty odd, that he would push me when I was talking to the hospital about my wife—and his immediate superior.

The doctor rambled on for a while, and I did my best to answer his questions, but the fact was I didn't have any information that could help him. He said he would have Julia call when she got back, and I said I would wait for the call. I flipped the phone closed.

Ricky said, "Okay, fine. Sorry to rush you, Jack, but . . . you know, I've got a lot to show you."

"Is there a time problem?" I said.

"I don't know. Maybe."

I started to ask what he meant by that, but he was already leading me forward, walking quickly. We left the residential area, passing through another glass door, and down another passageway.

This passage, I noticed, was tightly sealed. We walked along a glass walkway suspended above the floor. The glass had little perforations, and beneath was a series of vacuum ducts for suction. By now I was growing accustomed to the constant hiss of the air handlers.

Midway down the corridor was another pair of glass doors. We had to go through them one at a time. They parted as we went through, and closed behind us. Continuing on, I again had the distinct feeling of being in a prison, of going through a succession of barred gates, going deeper and deeper into something.

It might be all high-tech and shiny glass walls—but it was still a prison.

DAY 6
8:12 A.M.

We came into a large room marked UTILITY and beneath it, MOLSTOCK/FABSTOCK/FEEDSTOCK. The walls and ceiling were covered with the familiar smooth plastic laminate. Large laminated containers were stacked on the floor. Off to the right I saw a row of big stainless-steel kettles, sunk below ground with lots of piping and valves surrounding them, and coming up to the first-floor level. It looked exactly like a microbrewery, and I was about to ask Ricky about it when he said, "So there you are!"

Working at a junction box beneath a monitor screen were three more members of my old team. They looked slightly guilty as we came up, like kids caught with their hands in the cookie jar. Of course Bobby Lembeck was their leader. At thirty-five, Bobby now supervised more code than he wrote, but he could still write when he wanted to. As always, he was wearing faded jeans and a Ghost in the Shell T-shirt, his ubiquitous Walkman clamped to his waist.

Then there was Mae Chang, beautiful and delicate, about as different from Rosie Castro as any woman could be. Mae had worked as a field biologist in Sichuan studying the golden snub-nosed monkey before turning to programming in her mid-twenties. Her time in the field, as well as her natural inclination, led her to be almost silent. Mae said very little, moved almost soundlessly, and never raised her voice—but she never lost an argument, either. Like many field biologists, she had developed the uncanny ability to slip into the background, to become unnoticed, almost to vanish.

And finally Charley Davenport, grumpy, rumpled, and already overweight at thirty. Slow and lumbering, he looked as if he had slept in his clothes, and in fact he often did, after a marathon programming session. Charley had worked under John Holland in Chicago and Doyne Farmer at Los Alamos. He was an expert in genetic algorithms, the kind of programming that mimicked natural selection to hone answers. But he was an irritating personality—he hummed, he snorted, talked to himself, and farted with noisy abandon. The group only tolerated him because he was so talented.

"Does it really take three people to do this?" Ricky said, after I'd shaken hands all around.

"Yes," Bobby said, "it does take three people, El Rooto, because it's complicated."

"Why? And don't call me El Rooto."

"I obey, Mr. Root."

"Just get on with it . . ."

"Well," Bobby said, "I started to check the sensors after this morning's episode, and it looks to me like they're miscalibrated. But since nobody is going outside, the question is whether we're reading them wrong, or whether the sensors themselves are faulty, or just scaled wrong on the equipment in here. Mae knows these sensors, she's used them in China. I'm making code revisions now. And Charley is here because he won't go away and leave us alone."

"Shit, I have better things to do," Charley said. "But I wrote the algorithm that controls the sensors, and we need to optimize the sensor code after they're done. I'm just waiting until they stop screwing around. Then I'll optimize." He looked pointedly at Bobby. "None of these guys can optimize worth a damn."

Mae said, "Bobby can."

"Yeah, if you give him six months, maybe."

"Children, children," Ricky said. "Let's not make a scene in front of our guest."

I smiled blandly. The truth was, I hadn't been paying attention to what they were saying. I was just watching them. These were three of my best programmers—and when they had worked for me, they had been self-assured to the point of arrogance. But now I was struck by how nervous the group was. They were all on edge, bickering, jumpy. And thinking back, I realized that Rosie and David had been on edge, too.

Charley started humming in that irritating way of his.

"Oh, *Christ*," Bobby Lembeck said. "Would you tell him to shut up?"

Ricky said, "Charley, you know we've talked about the humming."

Charley continued to hum.

"Charley . . ."

Charley gave a long, theatrical sigh. He stopped humming.

"*Thank* you," Bobby said.

Charley rolled his eyes, and looked at the ceiling.

"All right," Ricky said. "Finish up quickly, and get back to your stations."

"Okay, fine."

"I want everybody in place as soon as possible."

"Okay," Bobby said.

"I'm serious. In your places."

"For Christ's sake, Ricky, okay, okay. Now will you stop talking and let us work?"

Leaving the group behind, Ricky took me across the floor to a small room. I said, "Ricky, these kids aren't the way they were when they worked for me."

"I know. Everybody's a little uptight right now."

"And why is that?"

"Because of what's going on here."

"And what *is* going on here?"

He stopped before a small cubicle on the other side of the room. "Julia couldn't tell you, because it was classified." He touched the door with a keycard.

I said, "Classified? Medical imaging is classified?"

The door latch clicked open, and we went inside. The door closed behind us. I saw a table, two chairs, a computer monitor and a keyboard. Ricky sat down, and immediately started typing.

"The medical imaging project was just an afterthought," he said, "a minor commercial application of the technology we are already developing."

"Uh-huh. Which is?"

"Military."

"Xymos is doing military work?"

"Yes. Under contract." He paused. "Two years ago, the Department of Defense realized from their experience in Bosnia that there was enormous value to robot aircraft that could fly overhead and transmit battlefield images in real time. The Pentagon knew that there would be more and more sophisticated uses for these flying cameras in future wars. You could use them to spot the locations of enemy troops, even when they were hidden in jungle or in buildings; you could use them to control laser-guided rocket fire, or to identify the location of friendly troops, and so on. Commanders on the ground could call up the images they wanted, in the spectra they wanted—visible, infrared, UV, whatever. Real-time imaging was going to be a very powerful tool in future warfare."

"Okay . . ."

"But obviously," Ricky said, "these robot cameras were vulnerable. You could shoot them down like pigeons. The Pentagon wanted a camera that couldn't be shot down. They imagined something very small, maybe the size of a dragonfly—a target too small to hit. But there were problems with power supply, with small control surfaces, and with resolution using such a small lens. They needed a bigger lens."

I nodded. "And so you thought of a swarm of nanocomponents."

"That's right." Ricky pointed to the screen, where a cluster of black spots wheeled and turned in the air, like birds. "A cloud of components would allow you to make a camera with as large a lens as you wanted. And it couldn't be shot down because a bullet would just pass through the cloud. Furthermore, you could disperse the cloud, the way a flock of birds disperses with a gunshot. Then the camera would be invisible until it re-formed again. So it seemed an ideal solution. The Pentagon gave us three years of DARPA funding."

"And?"

"We set out to make the camera. It was of course immediately obvious that we had a problem with distributed intelligence."

I was familiar with the problem. The nanoparticles in the cloud had to be endowed with a rudimentary intelligence, so that they could interact with each other to form a flock that wheeled in the air. Such coordinated activity might look pretty intelligent, but it occurred even when the individuals making up the flock were rather stupid. After all, birds and fish could do it, and they weren't the brightest creatures on the planet.

Most people watching a flock of birds or a school of fish assumed there was a leader, and that all the other animals followed the leader. That was because human beings, like most social mammals, had group leaders.

But birds and fish had no leaders. Their groups weren't organized that way. Careful study of flocking behavior—frame-by-frame video analysis—showed that, in fact, there was no leader. Birds and fish responded to a few simple stimuli among themselves, and the result was coordinated behavior. But nobody was controlling it. Nobody was leading it. Nobody was directing it.

Nor were individual birds genetically programmed for flocking behavior. Flocking was not hard-wired. There was nothing in the bird brain that said, "When thus-and-such happens, start flocking." On the contrary, flocking simply emerged within the group as a result of much simpler, low-level rules. Rules like, "Stay close to the birds nearest you, but don't bump into them." From those rules, the entire group flocked in smooth coordination.

Because flocking arose from low-level rules, it was called emergent behavior. The technical definition of emergent behavior was behavior that occurred in a group but was not programmed into any member of the group. Emergent behavior could occur in any population, including a computer population. Or a robot population. Or a nanoswarm.

I said to Ricky, "Your problem was emergent behavior in the swarm?"

"Exactly."

"It was unpredictable?"

"To put it mildly."

In recent decades, this notion of emergent group behavior had caused a minor revolution in computer science. What that meant for programmers was that you could lay down rules of behavior for individual agents, but not for the agents acting together.

Individual agents—whether programming modules, or processors, or as in this case, actual micro-robots—could be programmed to cooperate under certain circumstances, and to compete under other circumstances. They could be given goals. They could be instructed to pursue their goals with single-minded intensity, or to be available to help other agents. But the result of these interactions could not be programmed. It just emerged, with often surprising outcomes.

In a way this was very exciting. For the first time, a program could produce results that absolutely could not be predicted by the programmer. These programs behaved more like living organisms than man-made automatons. That excited programmers—but it frustrated them, too.

Because the program's emergent behavior was erratic. Sometimes competing agents fought to a standstill, and the program failed to accomplish anything. Sometimes agents were so influenced by one another that they lost track of their goal, and did something else instead. In that sense the program was very childlike—unpredictable and easily distracted. As one programmer put it, "Trying to program distributed intelligence is like telling a five-year-old kid to go to his room and change his clothes. He may do that, but he is equally likely to do something else and never return."

Because these programs behaved in a lifelike way, programmers began to draw analogies to the behavior of real organisms in the real world. In fact, they began to model the behavior of actual organisms as a way to get some control over program outcomes.

So you had programmers studying ant swarming, or termite mounding, or bee dancing, in order to write programs to control airplane landing schedules, or package routing, or language translation. These programs often worked beautifully, but they could still go awry, particularly if circumstances changed drastically. Then they would lose their goals.

That was why I began, five years ago, to model predator-prey relationships as a way to keep goals fixed. Because hungry predators weren't distracted. Circumstances might force them to improvise their methods; and they might try many times before they succeeded—but they didn't lose track of their goal.

So I became an expert in predator-prey relationships. I knew about packs of hyenas, African hunting dogs, stalking lionesses, and attacking columns of army ants. My team had studied the literature from the field biologists, and we had generalized those findings into a program module called PREDPREY, which could be used to control any system of agents and make its behavior purposeful. To make the program seek a goal.

Looking at Ricky's screen, the coordinated units moving smoothly as they turned through the air, I said, "You used PREDPREY to program your individual units?"

"Right. We used those rules."

"Well, the behavior looks pretty good to me," I said, watching the screen. "Why is there a problem?"

"We're not sure."

"What does that mean?"

"It means we know there's a problem, but we're not sure what's causing it. Whether the problem is programming—or something else."

"Something else? Like what?" I frowned. "I don't get it, Ricky. This is just a cluster of microbots. You can make it do what you want. If the programming's not right, you adjust it. What don't I understand?"

Ricky looked at me uneasily. He pushed his chair away from the table and stood. "Let me show you how we manufacture these agents," he said. "Then you'll understand the situation better."

Having watched Julia's demo tape, I was immensely curious to see what he showed me next. Because many people I respected thought molecular manufacturing was impossible. One of the major theoretical objections was the time it would take to build a working molecule. To work at all, the nanoassembly line would have to be far more efficient than anything previously known in human manufacturing. Basically, all manmade assembly lines ran at roughly the same speed: they could add one part per second. An automobile, for example, had a few thousand parts. You could build a car in a matter of hours. A commercial aircraft had six million parts, and took several months to build.

But a typical manufactured molecule consisted of 10^{25} parts. That was 10,000,000,000,000,000,000,000,000 parts. As a practical matter, this number was unimaginably large. The human brain couldn't comprehend it. But calculations showed that even if you could assemble at the rate of *a million parts* per second, the time to complete one molecule would still be 3,000 trillion years—longer than the known age of the universe. And that was a problem. It was known as the build-time problem.

I said to Ricky, "If you're doing industrial manufacturing . . ."

"We are."

"Then you must have solved the build-time problem."

"We have."

"How?"

"Just wait."

Most scientists assumed this problem would be solved by building from larger subunits, molecular fragments consisting of billions of atoms. That would cut the assembly time down to a couple of years. Then, with partial self-assembly, you might get the time down to several hours, perhaps even one hour. But even with further refinements, it remained a theoretical challenge to produce commercial quantities of product. Because the goal was not to manufacture a single molecule in an hour. The goal was to manufacture several pounds of molecules in an hour.

No one had ever figured out how to do that.

We passed a couple of laboratories, including one that looked like a standard microbiology lab, or a genetics lab. I saw Mae standing in that lab, puttering around. I started to ask Ricky why he had a microbiology lab here, but he brushed my question aside. He was impatient now, in a hurry. I saw him glance at his watch. Directly ahead was a final glass air-lock. Stenciled on the glass door was MICROFABRICATION. Ricky waved me in. "One at a time," he said. "That's all the system allows."

I stepped in. The doors hissed shut behind me, the pressure pads again thunking shut. Another blast of air: from below, from the sides, from above. By now I was getting used to it. The second door opened, and I walked forward down another short corridor, opening into a large room beyond. I saw bright, shining white light—so bright it hurt my eyes.

Ricky came after me, talking as we walked, but I don't remember what he said. I couldn't focus on his words. I just stared. Because by now I was inside the main fab building—a huge windowless space, like a giant hangar three stories high. And within this hangar stood a structure of immense complexity that seemed to hang in midair, glowing like a jewel.

DAY 6
9:12 A.M.

At first, it was hard to understand what I was seeing—it looked like an enormous glowing octopus rising above me, with glinting, faceted arms extending outward in all directions, throwing complex reflections and bands of color onto the outer walls. Except this octopus had multiple layers of arms. One layer was low, just a foot above the floor. A second was at chest-level; the third and fourth layers were higher, above my head. And they all glowed, sparkled brilliantly.

I blinked, dazzled. I began to make out the details. The octopus was contained within an irregular three-story framework built entirely of modular glass cubes. Floors, walls, ceilings, staircases—everything was cubes. But the arrangement was haphazard, as if someone had dumped a mound of giant transparent sugar cubes in the center of the room. Within this cluster of cubes the arms of the octopus snaked off in all directions. The whole thing was held up by a web of black anodized struts and connectors, but they were obscured by the reflections, which is why the octopus seemed to hang in midair.

Ricky grinned. "Convergent assembly. The architecture is fractal. Neat, huh?"

I nodded slowly. I was seeing more details. What I had seen as an octopus was actually a branching tree structure. A central square conduit ran vertically through the center of the room, with smaller pipes branching off on all sides. From these branches, even smaller pipes branched off in turn, and smaller ones still. The smallest of the pipes were pencil-thin. Everything gleamed as if it were mirrored.

"Why is it so bright?"

"The glass has diamondoid coating," he said. "At the molecular level, glass is like Swiss cheese, full of holes. And of course it's a liquid, so atoms just pass right through it."

"So you coat the glass."

"Right. Have to."

Within this shining forest of branching glass, David and Rosie moved, making notes, adjusting valves, consulting handheld computers. I understood that I was looking at a massively parallel assembly line. Small fragments of molecules were introduced into the smallest pipes, and atoms were added to them. When that was finished, they moved into the next largest pipes, where more atoms were added. In this way, molecules moved progressively toward the center of the structure, until assembly was completed, and they were discharged into the central pipe.

"Exactly right," Ricky said. "This is just the same as an automobile assembly line, except that it's on a molecular scale. Molecules start at the ends, and come down the line to the center. We stick on a protein sequence here, a methyl group there, just the way they stick doors and wheels on a car. At the end of the line, off rolls a new, custom-made molecular structure. Built to our specifications."

"And the different arms?"

"Make different molecules. That's why the arms look different." In several places, the octopus arm passed through a steel tunnel reinforced with heavy bolts, for vacuum ducting. In other places, a cube was covered with quilted silver insulation, and I saw liquid nitrogen tanks nearby; extremely low temperatures were generated in that section.

"Those're our cryogenic rooms," Ricky said. "We don't go very low, maybe -70 Centigrade, max. Come on, I'll show you." He led me through the complex, following glass walkways that threaded among the arms. In some places, a short staircase enabled us to step over the lowest arms.

Ricky chatted continuously about technical details: vacuum-jacketed hoses, metal phase separators, globe check valves. When we reached the insulated cube, he opened the heavy door to reveal a small room, with a second room adjacent. It looked like a pair of meat lockers. Small glass windows were set in each door. At the moment, everything was at room temperature. "You can have two different temps here," he said. "Run one from the other, if you want, but it's usually automated."

Ricky led me back outside, glancing at his watch as he did so. I said, "Are we late for an appointment?"

"What? No, no. Nothing like that." Nearby two cubes were actually solid metal rooms, with thick electrical cables running inside. I said, "Those your magnet rooms?"

"That's right," Ricky said. "We've got pulsed field magnets generating 33 Tesla in the core. That's something like a million times the magnetic field of the earth."

With a grunt, he pushed open the steel door to the nearest magnet room. I saw a large doughnut-shaped object, about six feet in diameter, with a hole in the center about an inch wide. The doughnut was completely encased in tubing and plastic insulation. Heavy steel bolts running from top to bottom held the jacketing in place.

"Lot of cooling for this puppy, I can tell you. And a lot of power: fifteen kilovolts. Takes a full-minute load time for the capacitors. And of course we can only pulse it. If we turned it on continuously, it'd explode—ripped apart by the field it generates." He pointed to the base of the magnet, where there was a round push button at knee level. "That's the safety cutoff there," he said. "Just in case. Hit it with your knee if your hands are full."

I said, "So you use high magnetic fields to do part of your assemb—"

But Ricky had already turned and headed out the door, again glancing at his watch. I hurried after him.

"Ricky . . ."

"I have more to show you," he said. "We're getting to the end."

"Ricky, this is all very impressive," I said, gesturing to the glowing arms. "But most of your assembly line is running at room temperature—no vacuum, no cryo, no mag field."

"Right. No special conditions."

"How is that possible?"

He shrugged. "The assemblers don't need it."

"The assemblers?" I said. "Are you telling me you've got molecular assemblers on this line?"

"Yes. Of course."

"Assemblers are doing your fabrication for you?"

"Of course. I thought you understood that."

"No, Ricky," I said, "I didn't understand that at all. And I don't like to be lied to."

He got a wounded look on his face. "I'm not lying."

But I was certain that he was.

One of the first things scientists learned about molecular manufacturing was how phenomenally difficult it was to carry out. In 1990, some IBM researchers pushed xenon atoms around on a nickel plate until they formed the letters "IBM" in the shape of the company logo. The entire logo was one ten-billionth of an inch long and could only be seen through an electron microscope. But it made a striking visual and it got a lot of publicity. IBM allowed people to think it was a proof of concept, the opening of a door to molecular manufacturing. But it was more of a stunt than anything else.

Because pushing individual atoms into a specific arrangement was slow, painstaking, and expensive work. It took the IBM researchers a whole day to move thirty-five atoms. Nobody believed you could create a whole new technology in this way. Instead, most people believed that nanoengineers would eventually find a way to build "assemblers"— miniature molecular machines that could turn out specific molecules the way a ball-bearing machine turned out ball bearings. The new technology would rely on molecular machines to make molecular products.

It was a nice concept, but the practical problems were daunting. Because assemblers were vastly more complicated than the molecules they made, attempts to design and build them had been difficult from the outset. To my knowledge, no laboratory anywhere in the world had actually done it. But now Ricky was telling me, quite casually, that Xymos could build molecular assemblers that were now turning out molecules for the company.

And I didn't believe him.

I had worked all my life in technology, and I had developed a feel for what was possible. This kind of giant leap forward just didn't happen. It never did. Technologies were a form of knowledge, and like all knowledge, technologies grew, evolved, matured. To believe otherwise was to believe that the Wright brothers could build a rocket and fly to the moon instead of flying three hundred feet over sand dunes at Kitty Hawk.

Nanotechnology was still at the Kitty Hawk stage.

"Come on, Ricky," I said. "How are you really doing this?"

"The technical details aren't that important, Jack."

"What fresh bullshit is this? Of course they're important."

"Jack," he said, giving me his most winning smile. "Do you really think I'm lying to you?"

"Yes, Ricky," I said. "I do."

I looked up at the octopus arms all around me. Surrounded by glass, I saw my own reflection dozens of times in the surfaces around me. It was confusing, disorienting. Trying to gather my thoughts, I looked down at my feet.

And I noticed that even though we had been walking on glass walkways, some sections of the ground floor were glass, as well. One section was nearby. I walked toward it. Through the glass I could see steel ducting and pipes below ground level. One set of pipes caught my eye, because they ran from the storage room to a nearby glass cube, at which point they emerged from the floor and headed upward, branching into the smaller tubes.

That, I assumed, was the feedstock—the slush of raw organic material that would be transformed on the assembly line into finished molecules.

Looking back down at the floor, I followed the pipes backward to the place where they entered from the adjacent room. This junction was glass, too. I could see the curved steel underbellies of the big kettles I'd noticed earlier. The tanks that I had thought were a microbrewery. Because that's certainly what it had looked like, a small brewery. Machinery for controlled fermentation, for controlled microbial growth.

And then I realized what it really was.

I said, "You son of a bitch."

Ricky smiled again, and shrugged. "Hey," he said. "It gets the job done."

Those kettles in the next room were indeed tanks for controlled microbial growth. But Ricky wasn't making beer—he was making microbes, and I had no doubt about the reason why. Unable to construct genuine nanoassemblers, Xymos was using bacteria to crank out their molecules. This was genetic engineering, not nanotechnology.

"Well, not exactly," Ricky said, when I told him what I thought. "But I admit we're using a hybrid technology. Not much of a surprise in any case, is it?"

That was true. For at least ten years, observers had been predicting that genetic engineering, computer programming, and nanotechnology would eventually merge. They were all involved with similar—and interconnected—activities. There wasn't that much difference between using a computer to decode part of a bacterial genome and using a computer to help you insert new genes into the bacteria, to make new proteins. And there wasn't much difference between creating a new bacteria to spit out, say, insulin molecules, and creating a man-made, micromechanical assembler to spit out new molecules. It was all happening at the molecular level. It was all the same challenge of imposing human design on extremely complex systems. And molecular design was nothing if not complicated.

You could think of a molecule as a series of atoms snapped together like Lego blocks, one after another. But the image was misleading. Because unlike a Lego set, atoms couldn't be snapped together in any arrangement you liked. An inserted atom was subject to powerful local forces—magnetic and chemical—with frequently undesirable results. The atom might be kicked out of its position. It might remain, but at an awkward angle. It might even fold the entire molecule up in knots.

As a result, molecular manufacturing was an exercise in the art of the possible, of substituting atoms and groups of atoms to make equivalent structures that would work in the desired way. In the face of all this difficulty, it was impossible to ignore the fact that there already existed proven molecular factories capable of turning out large numbers of molecules: they were called cells.

"Unfortunately, cellular manufacturing can take us only so far," Ricky said. "We harvest the substrate molecules—the raw materials—and then we build on them with nanoengineering procedures. So we do a little of both."

I pointed down at the tanks. "What cells are you growing?"

"Theta-d 5972," he said.

"Which is?"

"A strain of *E. coli*."

E. coli was a common bacterium, found pretty much everywhere in the natural environment, even in the human intestine. I said, "Did anyone think it might not be a good idea to use cells that can live inside human beings?"

"Not really," he said. "Frankly that wasn't a consideration. We just wanted a well-studied cell that was fully documented in the literature. We chose an industry standard."

"Uh-huh . . ."

"Anyway," Ricky continued, "I don't think it's a problem, Jack. It won't thrive in the human gut. Theta-d is optimized for a variety of nutrient sources—to make it cheap to grow in the laboratory. In fact, I think it can even grow on garbage."

"So that's how you get your molecules. Bacteria make them for you."

"Yes," he said, "that's how we get the *primary* molecules. We harvest twenty-seven primary molecules. They fit together in relatively high-temperature settings where the atoms are more active and mix quickly."

"That's why it's hot in here?"

"Yes. Reaction efficiency has a maxima at one hundred forty-seven degrees Fahrenheit, so we work there. That's where we get the fastest combination rate. But these molecules will combine at much lower temperatures. Even around thirty-five, forty degrees Fahrenheit, you'll get a certain amount of molecular combination."

"And you don't need other conditions," I said. "Vacuum? Pressure? High magnetic fields?"

Ricky shook his head. "No, Jack. We maintain those conditions to speed up assembly, but it's not strictly necessary. The design is really elegant. The component molecules go together quite easily."

"And these component molecules combine to form your final assembler?"

"Which then assembles the molecules we want. Yes."

It was a clever solution, creating his assemblers with bacteria. But Ricky was telling me the components assembled themselves almost automatically, with nothing required but high temperature. What, then, was this complex glass building used for?

"Efficiency, and process separation," Ricky said. "We can build as many as nine assemblers simultaneously, in the different arms."

"And where do the assemblers make the final molecules?"

"In this same structure. But first, we reapply them."

I shook my head. I wasn't familiar with the term. "Reapply?"

"It's a little refinement we developed here. We're patenting it. You see, our system worked perfectly right from the start—but our yields were extremely low. We were harvesting half a gram of finished molecules an hour. At that rate, it would take several days to make a single camera. We couldn't figure out what the problem was. The late assembly in the arms is done in gas phase. It turned out that the molecular assemblers were heavy, and tended to sink to the bottom. The bacteria settled on a layer above them, releasing component molecules that were lighter still, and floated higher. So the assemblers were making very little contact with the molecules they were meant to assemble. We tried mixing technologies but they didn't help."

"So you did what?"

"We modified the assembler design to provide a lipotrophic base that would attach to the surface of the bacteria. That brought the assemblers into better contact with the component molecules, and immediately our yields jumped five orders of magnitude."

"And now your assemblers sit on the bacteria?"

"Correct. They attach to the outer cell membrane."

At a nearby workstation, Ricky punched up the assembler design on the flat panel display. The assembler looked like a sort of pinwheel, a series of spiral arms going off in different directions, and a dense knot of atoms in the center. "It's fractal, as I said," he said. "So it looks sort of the same at smaller orders of magnitude." He laughed. "Like the old joke, turtles all the way down." He pressed more keys. "Anyway, here's the attached configuration."

The screen now showed the assembler adhering to a much larger pill-shaped object, like a pinwheel attached to a submarine. "That's the Theta-d bacterium," Ricky said. "With the assembler on it."

As I watched, several more pinwheels attached themselves. "And these assemblers make the actual camera units?"

"Correct." He typed again. I saw a new image. "This is our target micromachine, the final camera. You've seen the bloodstream version. This is the Pentagon version, quite a bit larger and designed to be airborne. What you're looking at is a molecular helicopter."

"Where's the propeller?" I said.

"Hasn't got one. The machine uses those little round protrusions you see there, stuck in at angles. Those're motors. The machines actually maneuver by climbing the viscosity of the air."

"Climbing the *what*?"

"Viscosity. Of the air." He smiled. "Micromachine level, remember? It's a whole new world, Jack."

However innovative the design, Ricky was still bound by the Pentagon's engineering specs for the product, and the product wasn't performing. Yes, they had built a camera that couldn't be shot down, and it transmitted images very well. Ricky explained it worked perfectly during tests indoors. But outside, even a modest breeze tended to blow it away like the cloud of dust it was.

The engineering team at Xymos was attempting to modify the units to increase mobility, but so far without success. Meanwhile the Department of Defense decided the design constraints were unbeatable, and had backed away from the whole nano concept; the Xymos contract had been canceled; DOD was going to pull funding in another six weeks.

I said, "That's why Julia was so desperate for venture capital, these last few weeks?"

"Right," Ricky said. "Frankly, this whole company could go belly up before Christmas."

"Unless you fix the units, so they can work in wind."

"Right, right."

I said, "Ricky, I'm a programmer. I can't help you with your agent mobility problems. That's an issue of molecular design. It's engineering. It's not my area."

"Um, I know that." He paused, frowned. "But actually, we think the program code may be involved in the solution."

"The code? Involved in the solution to what?"

"Jack, I have to be frank with you. We've made a mistake," he said. "But it's not our fault. I swear to you. It wasn't us. It was the contractors." He started down the stairs. "Come on, I'll show you."

Walking briskly, he led me to the far side of the facility, where I saw an open yellow elevator cage mounted on the wall. It was a small elevator, and I was uncomfortable because it was open; I averted my eyes. Ricky said, "Don't like heights?"

"Can't stand them."

"Well, it's better than walking." He pointed off to one side, where an iron ladder ran up the wall to the ceiling. "When the elevator goes out, we have to climb up that."

I shuddered. "Not me."

We rode the elevator all the way up to the ceiling, three stories above the ground. Hanging beneath the ceiling was a tangle of ducts and conduits, and a network of mesh walkways to enable workers to service them. I hated the mesh, because I could see through it to the floor far below. I tried not to look down. We had to duck repeatedly beneath the low-hanging pipes. Ricky shouted over the roar of the equipment.

"Everything's up here!" he yelled, pointing in various directions. "Air handlers over there! Water tank for the fire sprinkler system there! Electrical junction boxes there! This is really the center of everything!" Ricky continued down the walkway, finally stopping beside a big air vent, about three feet in diameter, that went into the outer wall.

"This is vent three," he said, leaning close to my ear. "It's one of four main vents that exhausts air to the outside. Now, you see those slots along the vent, and the square boxes that sit in the slots? Those are filter packs. We have microfilters arranged in successive layers, to prevent any external contamination from the facility."

"I see them . . ."

"You see them *now*," Ricky said. "Unfortunately, the contractor forgot to install the filters in this particular vent. In fact, they didn't even cut the slots, so the building inspectors never realized anything was missing. They signed off on the building; we started working here. And we vented unfiltered air to the outside environment."

"For how long?"

Ricky bit his lip. "Three weeks."

"And you were at full production?"

He nodded. "We figure we vented approximately twenty-five kilos of contaminants."

"And what were the contaminants?"

"A little of everything. We're not sure of exactly what."

"So you vented *E. coli*, assemblers, finished molecules, everything?"

"Correct. But we don't know what proportions."

"Do the proportions matter?"

"They might. Yes."

Ricky was increasingly edgy as he told me all this, biting his lip, scratching his head, avoiding my eyes. I didn't get it. In the annals of industrial pollution, fifty pounds of contamination was trivial. Fifty pounds of material would fit comfortably in a gym bag. Unless it was highly toxic or radioactive—and it wasn't—such a small quantity simply didn't matter.

I said, "Ricky, so what? Those particles were scattered by the wind across hundreds of miles of desert. They'll decay from sunlight and cosmic radiation. They'll break up, decompose. In a few hours or days, they're gone. Right?"

Ricky shrugged. "Actually, Jack, that's not what—"

It was at that moment that the alarm went off.

It was a quiet alarm, just a soft, insistent pinging, but it made Ricky jump. He ran down the walkway, feet clanging on the metal, toward a computer workstation mounted on the wall. There was a status window in the corner of the monitor. It was flashing red: PV-90 ENTRY.

I said, "What does that mean?"

"Something set off the perimeter alarms." He unclipped his radio and said, "Vince, lock us down."

The radio crackled. "We're locked down, Ricky."

"Raise positive pressure."

"It's up five pounds above baseline. You want more?"

"No. Leave it there. Do we have visualization?"

"Not yet."

"Shit." Ricky stuck the radio back on his belt, began typing quickly. The workstation screen divided into a half-dozen small images from security cameras mounted all around the facility. Some showed the surrounding desert from high views, looking down from rooftops. Others were ground views. The cameras panned slowly.

I saw nothing. Just desert scrub and occasional clumps of cactus.

"False alarm?" I said.

Ricky shook his head. "I wish."

I said, "I don't see anything."

"It'll take a minute to find it."

"Find what?"

"*That.*"

He pointed to the monitor, and bit his lip.

I saw what appeared to be a small, swirling cloud of dark particles. It looked like a dust devil, one of those tiny tornado-like clusters that moved over the ground, spun by convection currents rising from the hot desert floor. Except that this cloud was black, and it had some definition—it seemed to be pinched in the middle, making it look a bit like an old-fashioned Coke bottle. But it didn't hold that shape consistently. The appearance kept shifting, transforming.

"Ricky," I said. "What are we looking at?"

"I was hoping you'd tell me."

"It looks like an agent swarm. Is that your camera swarm?"

"No. It's something else."

"How do you know?"

"Because we can't control it. It doesn't respond to our radio signals."

"You've tried?"

"Yes. We've tried to make contact with it for almost two weeks," he said. "It's generating an electrical field that we can measure, but for some reason we can't interact with it."

"So you have a runaway swarm."

"Yes."

"Acting autonomously."

"Yes."

"And this has been going on for . . ."

"Days. About ten days."

"Ten days?" I frowned. "How is that possible, Ricky? The swarm's a collection of micro-robotic machines. Why haven't they decayed, or run out of power? And why exactly can't you control them? Because if they have the ability to swarm, then there's some electrically mediated interaction among them. So you should be able to take control of the swarm—or at least disrupt it."

"All true," Ricky said. "Except we can't. And we've tried everything we can think of." He was focused on the screen, watching intently. "That cloud is independent of us. Period."

"And so you brought me out here . . ."

"To help us get the fucking thing back," Ricky said.

DAY 6
9:32 A.M.

It was, I thought, a problem no one had ever imagined before. In all the years that I had been programming agents, the focus had been on getting them to interact in a way that produced useful results. It never occurred to us that there might be a larger control issue, or a question of independence. Because it simply couldn't happen. Individual agents were too small to be self-powered; they had to get their energy from some external source, such as a supplied electrical or microwave field. All you had to do was turn off the field, and the agents died. The swarm was no more difficult to control than a household appliance, like a kitchen blender. Flip the power off and it went dead.

But Ricky was telling me this cloud had been self-sustaining for days. That just didn't make sense. "Where is it getting power?"

He sighed. "We built the units with a small piezo wafer to generate current from photons. It's only supplementary—we added it as an afterthought—but they seem to be managing with it alone."

"So the units are solar-powered," I said.

"Right."

"Whose idea was that?"

"The Pentagon asked for it."

"And you built in capacitance?"

"Yeah. They can store charge for three hours."

"Okay, fine," I said. Now we were getting somewhere. "So they have enough power for three hours. What happens at night?"

"At night, they presumably lose power after three hours of darkness."

"And then the cloud falls apart?"

"Yes."

"And the individual units drop to the ground?"

"Presumably, yes."

"Can't you take control of them then?"

"We could," Ricky said, "if we could find them. We go out every night, looking. But we can never find them."

"You've built in markers?"

"Yes, sure. Every single unit has a fluorescing module in the shell. They show up blue-green under UV light."

"So you go out at night looking for a patch of desert that glows blue-green."

"Right. And so far, we haven't found it."

That didn't really surprise me. If the cloud collapsed tightly, it would form a clump about six inches in diameter on the desert floor. And it was a big desert out there. They could easily miss it, night after night.

But as I thought about it, there was another aspect that didn't make sense. Once the cloud fell to the ground—once the individual units lost power—then the cloud had no organization. It could be scattered by wind, like so many dust particles, never to re-form. But evidently that didn't happen. The units didn't scatter. Instead, the cloud returned day after day. Why was that?

"We think," Ricky said, "that it may hide at night."

"Hide?"

"Yeah. We think it goes to some protected area, maybe an overhang, or a hole in the ground, something like that."

I pointed to the cloud as it swirled toward us. "You think that swarm is capable of *hiding*?"

"I think it's capable of adapting. In fact, I know it is." He sighed. "Anyway, it's more than just one swarm, Jack."

"There's more than one?"

"There's at least three. Maybe more, by now."

I felt a momentary blankness, a kind of sleepy gray confusion that washed over me. I suddenly couldn't think, I couldn't put it together. "What are you saying?"

"I'm saying it reproduces, Jack," he said. "The fucking swarm reproduces."

The camera now showed a ground-level view of the dust cloud as it swirled toward us. But as I watched, I realized it wasn't swirling like a dust devil. Instead, the particles were twisting one way, then another, in a kind of sinuous movement.

They were definitely swarming.

"Swarming" was a term for the behavior of certain social insects like ants or bees, which swarmed whenever the hive moved to a new site. A cloud of bees will fly in one direction and then another, forming a dark river in the air. The swarm might halt and cling to a tree for perhaps an hour, perhaps overnight, before continuing onward. Eventually the bees settled on a new location for their hive, and stopped swarming.

In recent years, programmers had written programs that modeled this insect behavior. Swarm-intelligence algorithms had become an important tool in computer programming. To programmers, a swarm meant a population of computer agents that acted together to solve a problem by distributed intelligence. Swarming became a popular way to organize agents to work together. There were professional organizations and conferences devoted entirely to swarm-intelligence programs. Lately it had become a kind of default solution—if you couldn't code anything more inventive, you made your agents swarm.

But as I watched, I could see this cloud was not swarming in any ordinary sense. The sinuous back-and-forth motion seemed to be only part of its movement. There was also a rhythmic expansion and contraction, a pulse, almost like breathing. And intermittently, the cloud seemed to thin out, and rise higher, then to collapse down, and become more squat. These changes occurred continuously, but in a repeating rhythm—or rather a series of superimposed rhythms.

"Shit," Ricky said. "I don't see the others. And I know it's not alone." He pressed the radio again. "Vince? You see any others?"

"No, Ricky."

"Where are the others? Guys? Speak to me."

Radios crackled all over the facility. Bobby Lembeck: "Ricky, it's alone."

"It can't be alone."

Mae Chang: "Ricky, nothing else is registering out there."

"Just one swarm, Ricky." That was David Brooks.

"It can't be alone!" Ricky was gripping the radio so tightly his fingers were white. He pressed the button. "Vince? Take the PPI up to seven."

"You sure?"

"Do it."

"Well, all right, if you really think—"

"Just skip the fucking commentary, and do it!"

Ricky was talking about increasing the positive pressure inside the building to seven pounds per square inch. All clean facilities maintained a positive pressure so that outside dust particles could not enter from any leak; they would be blown outward by the escaping air. But one or two pounds was enough to maintain that. Seven pounds of positive pressure was a lot. It was unnecessary to keep out passive particles.

But of course these particles weren't passive.

Watching the cloud swirl and undulate as it came closer, I saw that parts of it occasionally caught the sunlight in a way that turned it a shimmering, iridescent silver. Then the color faded, and the swarm became black again. That had to be the piezo panels catching the sun. But it clearly demonstrated that the individual microunits were highly mobile, since the entire cloud never turned silver at the same time, but only portions, or bands.

"I thought you said the Pentagon was giving up on you, because you couldn't control this swarm in wind."

"Right. We couldn't."

"But you must have had strong wind in the last few days."

"Of course. Usually comes up in late afternoon. We had ten knots yesterday."

"Why wasn't the swarm blown away?"

"Because it's figured that one out," Ricky said gloomily. "It's adapted to it."

"How?"

"Keep watching, you'll probably see it. Whenever the wind gusts, the swarm sinks, hangs near the ground. Then it rises up again once the wind dies down."

"This is emergent behavior?"

"Right. Nobody programmed it." He bit his lip. Was he lying again?

"So you're telling me it's learned . . ."

"Right, right."

"How can it learn? The agents have no memory."

"Uh . . . well, that's a long story," Ricky said.

"They have memory?"

"Yes, they have memory. Limited. We built it in." Ricky pressed the button on his radio. "Anybody hear anything?"

The answers came back, crackling in his handset.

"Not yet."

"Nothing."

"No sounds?"

"Not yet."

I said to Ricky, "It makes sounds?"

"We're not sure. Sometimes it seems like it. We've been trying to record it . . ." He flicked keys on the workstation, quickly shifting the monitor images, making them larger, one after another. He shook his head. "I don't like this. That thing can't be alone," he said. "I want to know where the others are."

"How do you know there are others?"

"Because there always are." He chewed his lip tensely as he looked at the monitor. "I wonder what it's up to now . . ."

We didn't have long to wait. In a few moments, the black swarm had come within a few yards of the building. Abruptly, it divided in two, and then divided again. Now there were three swarms, swirling side by side.

"Son of a bitch," Ricky said. "It was hiding the others inside itself." He pushed his button again. "Guys, we got all three. And they're close."

They were, in fact, too close to be seen by the ground-view camera. Ricky switched to the overhead views. I saw three black clouds, all moving laterally along the side of the building. The behavior seemed distinctly purposeful.

"What're they trying to do?" I said.

"Get inside," Ricky said.

"Why?"

"You'd have to ask them. But yesterday one of them—"

Suddenly, from a clump of cactus near the building, a cottontail rabbit sprinted away across the desert floor. Immediately, the three swarms turned and pursued it.

Ricky switched the monitor view. We now watched at ground level. The three clouds converged on the terrified bunny, which was moving fast, a whitish blur on the screen. The clouds swirled after it with surprising speed. The behavior was clear: *they were hunting*.

I felt a moment of irrational pride. PREDPREY was working perfectly! Those swarms might as well be lionesses chasing a gazelle, so purposeful was their behavior. The swarms turned sharply, then split up, cutting off the rabbit's escape to the left and right. The behavior of the three clouds clearly appeared coordinated. Now they were closing in.

And suddenly one of the swarms sank down, engulfing the rabbit. The other two swarms fell on it moments later. The resulting particle cloud was so dense, it was hard to see the rabbit anymore. Apparently it had flipped onto its back, because I saw its hind legs kicking spasmodically in the air, above the cloud itself.

I said, "They're killing it . . ."

"Yeah," Ricky said, nodding. "That's right."

"I thought this was a camera swarm."

"Yeah, well."

"How are they killing it?"

"We don't know, Jack. But it's fast."

I frowned. "So you've seen this before?"

Ricky hesitated, bit his lip. Didn't answer me, just stared at the screen.

I said, "Ricky, you've seen this before?"

He gave a long sigh. "Yeah. Well, the first time was yesterday. They killed a rattlesnake yesterday."

I thought, *they killed a rattlesnake yesterday*. I said, "Jesus, Ricky." I thought of the men in the helicopter, talking about all the dead animals. I wondered if Ricky was telling me all he knew.

"Yeah."

The rabbit no longer kicked. A single protruding foot trembled with small convulsions, and then was still. The cloud swirled low to the ground around the animal, rising and falling slightly. This continued for almost a minute.

I said, "What're they doing now?"

Ricky shook his head. "I'm not sure. But they did this before, too."

"It almost looks like they're eating it."

"I know," Ricky said.

Of course that was absurd. PREDPREY was just a biological analogy. As I watched the pulsing cloud, it occurred to me that this behavior might actually represent a program hang. I couldn't remember exactly what rules we had written for individual units after the goal was attained. Real predators, of course, would eat their prey, but there was no analogous behavior for these micro-robots. So perhaps the cloud was just swirling in confusion. If so, it should start moving again soon.

Usually, when a distributed-intelligence program stalled, it was a temporary phenomenon. Sooner or later, random environmental influences would cause enough units to act that they induced all the others to act, too. Then the program would start up again. The units would resume goal seeking.

This behavior was roughly what you saw in a lecture hall, after the lecture was over. The audience milled around for a while, stretching, talking to people close to them, or greeting friends, collecting coats and belongings. Only a few people left at once, and the main crowd ignored them. But after a certain percentage of the audience had gone, the remaining people would stop milling and begin to leave quickly. It was a kind of focus change.

If I was right, then I should see something similar in the behavior of the cloud. The swirls should lose their coordinated appearance; there should be ragged wisps of particles rising into the air. Only then would the main cloud move.

I glanced at the timeclock in the corner of the monitor. "How long has it been now?"

"About two minutes."

That wasn't particularly long for a stall, I thought. At one point when we were writing PREDPREY, we used the computer to simulate coordinated agent behavior. We always restarted after a hang, but finally we decided to wait and see if the program was really permanently stalled. We found that the program might hang for as long as twelve hours before suddenly kicking off, and coming back to life again. In fact, that behavior interested the neuroscientists because—

"They're starting," Ricky said.

And they were. The swarms were beginning to rise up from the dead rabbit. I saw at once that my theory was wrong. There was no raggedness, no rising wisps. The three clouds rose up together, smoothly. The behavior seemed entirely nonrandom and controlled. The clouds swirled separately for a moment, then merged into one. Sunlight flashed on shimmering silver. The rabbit lay motionless on its side.

And then the swarm moved swiftly away, whooshing off into the desert. It shrank toward the horizon. In moments, it was gone.

Ricky was watching me. "What do you think?"

"You've got a breakaway robotic nanoswarm. That some idiot made self-powered and self-sustaining."

"You think we can get it back?"

"No," I said. "From what I've seen, there's not a chance in hell."

Ricky sighed, and shook his head.

"But you can certainly get rid of it," I said. "You can kill it."

"We can?"

"Absolutely."

"Really?" His face brightened.

"Absolutely." And I meant it. I was convinced that Ricky was overstating the problem he faced. He hadn't thought it through. He hadn't done all he could do.

I was confident that I could destroy the runaway swarm quickly. I expected that I'd be done with the whole business by dawn tomorrow— at the very latest.

That was how little I understood my adversary.

DAY 6
10:11 A.M.

In retrospect, I was right about one thing: it was vitally important to know how the rabbit had died. Of course I know the reason now. I also know why the rabbit was attacked. But that first day at the laboratory, I didn't have the faintest notion of what had happened. And I could never have guessed the truth.

None of us could have, at that point.

Not even Ricky.

Not even Julia.

It was ten minutes after the swarms had gone and we were all standing in the storage room. The whole group had gathered there, tense and anxious. They watched me as I clipped a radio transmitter to my belt, and pulled a headset over my head. The headset included a video camera, mounted by my left ear. It took a while to get the video transmitter working right.

Ricky said, "You're really going out there?"

"I am," I said. "I want to know what happened to that rabbit." I turned to the others. "Who's coming with me?"

Nobody moved. Bobby Lembeck stared at the floor, hands in his pockets. David Brooks blinked rapidly, and looked away. Ricky was inspecting his fingernails. I caught Rosie Castro's eye. She shook her head. "No fucking way, Jack."

"Why not, Rosie?"

"You saw it yourself. They're hunting."

"Are they?"

"Sure as hell looked like it."

"Rosie," I said, "I trained you better than this. How can the swarms be hunting?"

"We all saw it." She stuck her chin out stubbornly. "All three of the swarms, hunting, coordinated."

"But how?" I said.

Now she frowned, looking confused. "What are you asking? There's no mystery. The agents can communicate. They can each generate an electrical signal."

"Right," I said. "How big a signal?"

"Well . . ." She shrugged.

"How big, Rosie? It can't be much, the agent is only a hundredth of the thickness of a human hair. Can't be generating much of a signal, right?"

"True . . ."

"And electromagnetic radiation decays according to the square of the radius, right?" Every school kid learned that fact in high school physics. As you moved away from the electromagnetic source, the strength faded fast—very fast.

And what that meant was the individual agents could only communicate with their immediate neighbors, with agents very close to them. Not to other swarms twenty or thirty yards away.

Rosie's frown deepened. The whole group was frowning now, looking at each other uneasily.

David Brooks coughed. "Then what did we see, Jack?"

"You saw an illusion," I said firmly. "You saw three swarms acting independently, and you thought they were coordinated. But they're not. And I'm pretty certain that other things you believe about these swarms aren't true, either."

*   *   *

There was a lot I didn't understand about the swarms—and a lot I didn't believe. I didn't believe, for example, that the swarms were reproducing. I thought Ricky and the others must be pretty unnerved even to imagine it. After all, the fifty pounds of material they'd exhausted into the environment could easily account for the three swarms I had seen—and dozens more besides. (I was guessing that each swarm consisted of three pounds of nanoparticles. That was roughly the weight of a large bee swarm.)

As for the fact that these swarms showed purposeful behavior, that was not in the least troubling; it was the intended result of low-level programming. And I didn't believe the swarms were coordinated. It simply wasn't possible, because the fields were too weak.

Nor did I believe the swarms had the adaptive powers that Ricky attributed to them. I'd seen too many demos of robots carrying out some task—like cooperating to push a box around the room—which was interpreted by observers as intelligent behavior, when in fact the robots were stupid, minimally programmed, and cooperating by accident. A lot of behavior looked smarter than it was. (As Charley Davenport used to say, "Ricky should thank God for that.")

And finally, I didn't really believe that the swarms were dangerous. I didn't think that a three-pound cloud of nanoparticles could represent much of a threat to anything, not even a rabbit. I wasn't at all sure it had been killed. I seemed to recall that rabbits were nervous creatures, prone to die of fright. Or the pursuing particles might have swarmed in through the nose and mouth, blocking the respiratory passages and choking the animal to death. If so, the death was accidental, not purposeful. Accidental death made more sense to me.

In short, I thought that Ricky and the others had consistently misinterpreted what they saw. They'd spooked themselves.

On the other hand, I had to admit that several unanswered questions nagged at me.

The first, and most obvious, was why the swarm had escaped their control. The original camera swarm was designed to be controlled by an RF transmitter beaming toward it. Now apparently the swarm ignored transmitted radio commands, and I didn't understand why. I suspected an error in manufacturing. The particles had probably been made incorrectly.

Second was the question of the swarm's longevity. The individual particles were extremely small, subject to damage from cosmic rays, photochemical decay, dehydration of their protein chains, and other environmental factors. In the harsh desert, all the swarms should have shriveled up and died of "old age" many days ago. But they hadn't. Why not?

Third, there was the problem of the swarm's apparent goal. According to Ricky, the swarms kept coming back to the main building. Ricky believed they were trying to get inside. But that didn't seem to be a reasonable agent goal, and I wanted to look at the program code to see what was causing it. Frankly, I suspected a bug in the code.

And finally, I wanted to know why they had pursued the rabbit. Because PREDPREY didn't program units to become literal predators. It merely used a predator model to keep the agents focused and goal-oriented. Somehow, that had changed, and the swarms now appeared to be actually hunting.

That, too, was probably a bug in the code.

To my mind, all these uncertainties came down to a single, central question—how had the rabbit died? I didn't think it had been killed. I suspected the rabbit's death was accidental, not purposeful.

But we needed to find out.

I adjusted my portable radio headset, with the sunglasses and the video camera mounted by the left eye. I picked up the plastic bag for the rabbit's body and turned to the others. "Anybody coming with me?"

There was an uncomfortable silence.

Ricky said, "What's the bag for?"

"To bring the rabbit back in."

"No fucking way," Ricky said. "You want to go out there, that's your business. But you're not bringing that rabbit back here."

"You've got to be kidding," I said.

"I'm not. We run a level-six clean environment here, Jack. That rabbit's *filthy*. Can't come in."

"All right, then, we can store it in Mae's lab and—"

"No way, Jack. Sorry. It's not coming through the first airlock."

I looked at the others. They were all nodding their heads in agreement.

"All right, then. I'll examine it out there."

"You're really going to go out?"

"Why not?" I looked at them, one after another. "I have to tell you guys, I think you've all got your knickers in a twist. The cloud's not dangerous. And yes, I'm going out." I turned to Mae. "Do you have a dissection kit of some kind that—"

"I'll come with you," she said quietly.

"Okay. Thanks." I was surprised that Mae was the first to come around to my way of seeing things. But as a field biologist, she was probably better than the others at assessing real-world risk. In any case, her decision seemed to break some tension in the room; the others visibly relaxed. Mae went off to get the dissecting tools and some lab equipment. That was when the phone rang. Vince answered it, and turned to me. "You know somebody named Dr. Ellen Forman?"

"Yes." It was my sister.

"She's on the line." Vince handed me the phone, and stepped back. I felt suddenly nervous. I glanced at my watch. It was eleven o'clock in the morning, time for Amanda's morning nap. She should be asleep in her crib by now. Then I remembered I had promised my sister I would call her at eleven to check in, to see how things were going.

I said, "Hello? Ellen? Is everything all right?"

"Sure. Fine." A long, long sigh. "It's fine. I don't know how you do it, is all."

"Tired?"

"About as tired as I've ever felt."

"Kids get off to school okay?"

Another sigh. "Yes. In the car, Eric hit Nicole on the back, and she punched him on the ear."

"You've got to interrupt them if they start that, Ellen."

"So I'm learning," she said wearily.

"And the baby? How's her rash?"

"Better. I'm using the ointment."

"Her movements okay?"

"Sure. She's well coordinated for her age. Is there a problem I should know about?"

"No, no," I said. I turned away from the group, lowered my voice. "I meant, is she pooping okay?"

Behind me, I heard Charley Davenport snicker.

"Copiously," Ellen said. "She's sleeping now. I took her to the park for a while. She was ready to go down. Everything's okay at the house. Except the pilot for the water heater went out, but the guy's coming to fix it."

"Good, good . . . Listen, Ellen, I'm in the middle of something here—"

"Jack? Julia called from the hospital a few minutes ago. She was looking for you."

"Uh-huh . . ."

"When I said you'd gone to Nevada, she got pretty upset."

"Is that right?"

"She said you didn't understand. And you were going to make it worse. Something like that. I think you better call her. She sounded agitated."

"Okay. I'll call."

"How are things going out there? You be back tonight?"

"Not tonight," I said. "Sometime tomorrow morning. Ellen, I have to go now—"

"Call the kids at dinnertime, if you can. They'd like to hear from you. Auntie Ellen is fine, but she's not Dad. You know what I mean."

"Okay. You'll eat at six?"

"About."

I told her I'd try to call, and I hung up.

*   *   *

Mae and I were standing by the double glass walls of the outer airlock, just inside the building entrance. Beyond the glass, I could see the solid-steel fire door that led outside. Ricky was standing beside us, gloomy and nervous, watching as we made our final preparations.

"You sure this is necessary? To go outside?"

"It's essential."

"Why don't you and Mae wait until nightfall, and go out then?"

"Because the rabbit won't be there," I said. "By nightfall, coyotes or hawks will have come and taken the carcass away."

"I don't know about that," Ricky said. "We haven't seen any coyotes around here for a while."

"Oh hell," I said impatiently, turning on my radio headset. "In the time we've spent arguing about this, we could have been out and back already. See you, Ricky."

I went through the glass door, and stood in the airlock. The door hissed shut behind me. The air handlers whooshed briefly in the now-familiar pattern, and then the far glass slid open. I walked toward the steel fire door. Looking back, I saw Mae stepping into the airlock.

I opened the fire door a crack. Harsh, glaring sunlight laid a burning strip on the floor. I felt hot air on my face. Over the intercom, Ricky said, "Good luck, guys."

I took a breath, pushed the door wider, and stepped out into the desert.

The wind had dropped, and the midmorning heat was stifling. Somewhere a bird chittered; otherwise it was silent. Standing by the door, I squinted in the glare of the sunlight. A shiver ran down my back. I took another deep breath.

I was certain that the swarms were not dangerous. But now that I was outside, my theoretical inferences seemed to lose force. I must have caught Ricky's tension, because I was feeling distinctly uneasy. Now that I was outside, the rabbit carcass looked much farther away than I had imagined. It was perhaps fifty yards from the door, half the length of a football field. The surrounding desert seemed barren and exposed. I scanned the shimmering horizon, looking for black shapes. I saw none.

The fire door opened behind me, and Mae said, "Ready when you are, Jack."

"Then let's do it."

We set off toward the rabbit, feet crunching on the desert sand. We moved away from the building. Almost immediately, my heart began to pound, and I started to sweat. I forced myself to breathe deeply and slowly, working to stay calm. The sun was hot on my face. I knew I had let Ricky spook me, but I couldn't seem to help it. I kept glancing toward the horizon.

Mae was a couple of steps behind me. I said, "How're you doing?"

"I'll be glad when it's over."

We were moving through a field of knee-high yellow cholla cactus. Their spines caught the sun. Here and there, a large barrel cactus stuck up from the floor like a bristling green thumb.

Some small, silent birds hopped on the ground, beneath the cholla. As we approached, they took to the air, wheeling specks against the blue. They landed a hundred yards away.

At last we came to the rabbit, surrounded by a buzzing black cloud. Startled, I hesitated a step.

"It's just flies," Mae said. She moved forward and crouched down beside the carcass, ignoring the flies. She pulled on a pair of rubber gloves, and handed me a pair to put on. She placed a square sheet of plastic on the ground, securing it with a rock at each corner. She lifted the rabbit and set it down in the center of the plastic. She unzipped a little dissection kit and laid it open. I saw steel instruments glinting in sunlight: forceps, scalpel, several kinds of scissors. She also laid out a syringe and several rubber-topped test tubes in a row. Her movements were quick, practiced. She had done this before.

I crouched down beside her. The carcass had no odor. Externally I could see no sign of what had caused the death. The staring eye looked pink and healthy.

Mae said, "Bobby? Are you recording me?"

Over the headset, I heard Bobby Lembeck say, "Move your camera down."

Mae touched the camera mounted on her sunglasses.

"Little more . . . little more . . . Good. That's enough."

"Okay," Mae said. She turned the rabbit's body over in her hands, inspecting it from all sides. She dictated swiftly: "On external examination the animal appears entirely normal. There is no sign of congenital anomaly or disease, the fur is thick and healthy in appearance. The nasal passages appear partially or entirely blocked. I note some fecal material excreted at the anus but presume that is normal evacuation at the time of death."

She flipped the animal onto its back and held the forepaws apart with her hands. "I need you, Jack." She wanted me to hold the paws for her. The carcass was still warm and had not begun to stiffen.

She took the scalpel and swiftly cut down the exposed midsection. A red gash opened; blood flowed. I saw bones of the rib cage, and pinkish coils of intestine. Mae spoke continuously as she cut, noting the tissue color and texture. She said to me "Hold here," and I moved my one hand down, to hold aside the slick intestine. With a single stroke of the scalpel she sliced opened the stomach. Muddy green liquid spilled out, and some pulpy material that seemed to be undigested fiber. The inner wall of the stomach appeared roughened, but Mae said that was normal. She ran her finger expertly around the stomach wall, then paused.

"Umm. Look there," she said.

"What?"

"There." She pointed. In several places the stomach was reddish, bleeding slightly as if it had been rubbed raw. I saw black patches in the midst of the bleeding. "That's not normal," Mae said. "That's pathology." She took a magnifying glass and peered closer, then dictated: "I observe dark areas approximately four to eight millimeters in diameter, which I presume to be clusters of nanoparticles present in the stomach lining," she said. "These clusters are found in association with mild bleeding of the villous wall."

"There are nanoparticles in the stomach?" I said. "How did they get there? Did the rabbit eat them? Swallow them involuntarily?"

"I doubt it. I would assume they entered actively."

I frowned. "You mean they crawled down the—"

"Esophagus. Yes. At least, I think so."

"Why would they do that?"

"I don't know."

She never paused in her swift dissection. She took scissors and cut upward through the breastbone, then pushed the rib cage open with her fingers. "Hold here." I moved my hands to hold the ribs open as she had done. The edges of bone were sharp. With my other hand, I held the hind legs open. Mae worked between my hands.

"The lungs are bright pink and firm, normal appearance." She cut one lobe with the scalpel, then again, and again. Finally she exposed the bronchial tube, and cut it open. It was dark black on the inside.

"Bronchi show heavy infestation with nanoparticles consistent with inhalation of swarm elements," she said, dictating. "You getting this, Bobby?"

"Getting it all. Video resolution is good."

She continued to cut upward. "Following the bronchial tree toward the throat . . ."

And she continued cutting, into the throat, and then from the nose back across the cheek, then opening the mouth . . . I had to turn away for a moment. But she continued calmly to dictate. "I am observing heavy infiltration of all the nasal passages and pharynx. This is suggestive of partial or full airway obstruction, which in turn may indicate the cause of death."

I looked back. "What?"

The rabbit's head was hardly recognizable any longer, she had cut the jaw free and was now peering down the throat. "Have a look for yourself," she said, "there seems to be dense particles closing the pharynx, and a response that looks something like an allergic reaction or—"

Then Ricky: "Say, are you guys going to stay out much longer?"

"As long as it takes," I said. I turned to Mae. "What kind of allergic reaction?"

"Well," she said, "you see this area of tissue, and how swollen it is, and you see how it's turned gray, which is suggestive—"

"You realize," Ricky said, "that you've been out there four minutes already."

"We're only out here because we can't bring the rabbit back," I said.

"That's right, you can't."

Mae was shaking her head as she listened to this. "Ricky, you're not helping here . . ."

Bobby said, "Don't shake your head, Mae. You're moving the camera back and forth."

"Sorry."

But I saw her raise her head, as if she was looking toward the horizon, and while she did so, she uncorked a test tube and slipped a slice of stomach lining into the glass. She put it in her pocket. Then looked back down. No one watching the video would have seen what she did. She said, "All right, we'll take blood samples now."

"Blood's all you're bringing in here, guys," Ricky said.

"Yes, Ricky. We know."

Mae reached for the syringe, stuck the needle into an artery, drew a blood sample, expelled it into a plastic tube, popped the needle off one-handed, put on another, and drew a second sample from a vein. Her pace never slowed.

I said, "I have the feeling you've done this before."

"This is nothing. In Sichuan, we were always working in heavy snow-storms, you can't see what you're doing, your hands are freezing, the animal's frozen solid, can't get a needle in . . ." She set the tubes of blood aside. "Now we will just take a few cultures, and we're done . . ." She flipped over her case, looked. "Oh, bad luck."

"What's that?" I said.

"The culture swabs aren't here."

"But you had them inside?"

"Yes, I'm sure of it."

I said, "Ricky, you see the swabs anywhere?"

"Yes. They're right here by the airlock."

"You want to bring them out to us?"

"Oh sure, guys." He laughed harshly. "No way I'm going out there in daylight. You want 'em, you come get 'em."

Mae said to me, "You want to go?"

"No," I said. I was already holding the animal open; my hands were in position. "I'll wait here. You go."

"Okay." She got to her feet. "Try and keep the flies off. We don't want any more contamination than necessary. I'll be back in a moment." She moved off at a light jog toward the door.

I heard her footsteps fade, then the clang of the metal door shutting behind her. Then silence. Attracted by the slit-open carcass, the flies came back in force, buzzing around my head, trying to land on the exposed guts. I released the rabbit's hind legs and swatted the flies away with one hand. I kept myself busy with the flies, so I wouldn't think about the fact that I was alone out here.

I kept glancing off in the distance, but I never saw anything. I kept brushing away the flies, and occasionally my hand touched against the rabbit's fur, and that was when I noticed that beneath the fur, the skin was bright red.

Bright red—exactly like a bad sunburn. Just seeing it made me shiver.

I spoke into my headset. "Bobby?"

Crackle. "Yes, Jack."

"Can you see the rabbit?"

"Yes, Jack."

"You see the redness of the skin? Are you picking that up?"

"Uh, just a minute."

I heard a soft whirr by my temple. Bobby was controlling the camera remotely, zooming in. The whirring stopped.

I said, "Can you see this? Through my camera?"

There was no answer.

"Bobby?"

I heard murmurs, whispers. Or maybe it was static.

"Bobby, are you there?"

Silence. I heard breathing.

"Uh, Jack?" Now it was the voice of David Brooks. "You better go in."

"Mae hasn't come back yet. Where is she?"

"Mae's inside."

"Well, I have to wait, she's going to do cultures—"

"No. Come in now, Jack."

I let go of the rabbit, and got to my feet. I looked around, scanned the horizon. "I don't see anything."

"They're on the other side of the building, Jack."

His voice was calm, but I felt a chill. "They are?"

"Come inside now, Jack."

I bent over, picked up Mae's samples, her dissection kit lying beside the rabbit carcass. The black leather of the kit was hot from the sun.

"Jack?"

"Just a minute . . ."

"Jack. Stop fucking around."

I started toward the steel door. My feet crunching on the desert floor. I didn't see anything at all.

But I heard something.

It was a peculiar low, thrumming sound. At first I thought I was hearing machinery, but the sound rose and fell, pulsing like a heartbeat. Other beats were superimposed, along with some kind of hissing, creating a strange, unworldly quality—like nothing I'd ever heard.

When I look back on it now, I think that more than anything else, it was the sound that made me afraid.

I walked faster. I said, "Where are they?"

"Coming."

"Where?"

"Jack? You better run."

"What?"

"*Run.*"

I still couldn't see anything, but the sound was building in intensity. I broke into a jog. The frequency of the sound was so low, I felt it as a vibration in my body. But I could hear it, too. The thumping, irregular pulse.

"Run, Jack."

I thought, Fuck it.

And I ran.

*   *   *

Swirling and glinting silver, the first swarm came around the corner of the building. The hissing vibration was coming from the cloud. Sliding along the side of the building, it moved toward me. It would reach the door long before I could.

I looked back to see a second swarm as it came around the far end of the building. It, too, moved toward me.

The headset crackled. I heard David Brooks: "Jack, you can't make it."

"I see that," I said. The first swarm had already reached the door, and was standing in front of it, blocking my way. I stopped, uncertain what to do. I saw a stick on the ground in front of me, a big one, four feet long. I picked it up, swung it in my hand.

The swarm pulsed, but did not move from the door.

The second swarm was still coming toward me.

It was time for a diversion. I was familiar with the PREDPREY code. I knew the swarms were programmed to pursue moving targets if they seemed to be fleeing from them. What would make a good target?

I cocked my arm, and threw the black dissection kit high into the air, in the general direction of the second swarm. The kit landed on edge, and tumbled across the ground for a moment.

Immediately, the second swarm began to go after it.

At the same moment, the first swarm moved away from the door, also pursuing the kit. It was just like a dog chasing a ball. I felt a moment of elation as I watched it go. It was, after all, just a programmed swarm. I thought: *This is child's play*. I hurried toward the door.

That was a mistake. Because apparently my hasty movement triggered the swarm, which immediately stopped, and swirled backward to the door again, blocking my path. There it remained, pulsing streaks of silver, like a blade glinting in the sun.

Blocking my path.

It took me a moment to realize the significance of that. My movement hadn't triggered the swarm to pursue me. The swarm hadn't chased me at all. Instead it had moved to block my way. It was anticipating my movement.

That wasn't in the code. The swarm was inventing new behavior, appropriate to the situation. Instead of pursuing me, it had fallen back and trapped me.

It had gone beyond its programming—way beyond. I couldn't see how that had happened. I thought it must be some kind of random reinforcement. Because the individual particles had very little memory. The intelligence of the swarm was necessarily limited. It shouldn't be that difficult to outsmart it.

I tried to feint to the left, then the right. The cloud went with me, but only for a moment. Then it dropped back to the door again. As if it knew that my goal was the door, and by staying there it would succeed.

That was far too clever. There had to be additional programming they hadn't told me about. I said into the headset, "What the hell have you guys done with these things?"

David: "It's not going to let you get past, Jack."

Just hearing him say that irritated me. "You think so? We'll see."

Because my next step was obvious. Close to the ground like this, the swarm was structurally vulnerable. It was a cluster of particles no larger than specks of dust. If I disrupted the cluster—if I broke up its structure—then the particles would have to reorganize themselves, just as a scattered flock of birds would re-form in the air. That would take at least a few seconds. And in that time I would be able to get through the door.

But how to disrupt it? I swung the stick in my hand, hearing it whoosh through the air, but it was clearly unsatisfactory. I needed something with a much bigger flat surface, like a paddle or a palm frond—something to create a large disrupting wind . . .

My mind was racing. I needed something.

Something.

Behind me, the second cloud was closing in. It moved toward me in an erratic zigzag pattern, to cut off any attempt I might make to run past it. I watched with a kind of horrified fascination. I knew that this, too, had never been coded in the program. This was self-organized, emergent behavior—and its purpose was only too clear. It was stalking me.

The pulsing sound grew louder as the swarm came closer and closer.

I had to disrupt it.

Turning in a circle, I looked at the ground all around me. I saw nothing I could use. The nearest juniper tree was too far away. The cholla cactuses were flimsy. I thought, of course there's nothing out here, it's the fucking desert. I scanned the exterior of the building, hoping someone had left out an implement, like a rake . . .

Nothing.

Nothing at all. I was out here with nothing but the shirt on my back, and there was nobody that could help me to—

Of course!

The headset crackled: "Jack, listen . . ."

But I didn't hear any more after that. As I pulled my shirt over my head, the headset came away, falling to the ground. And then, holding the shirt in my hand, I swung it in broad whooshing arcs through the air. And screaming like a banshee, I charged the swarm by the door.

The swarm vibrated with a deep thrumming sound. It flattened slightly as I ran toward it, and then I was in the midst of the particles, and plunged into an odd semidarkness, like being in a dust storm. I couldn't see anything—I couldn't see the door—I groped blindly for the doorknob—and my eyes stung from the particles, but I kept swinging my shirt in broad whooshing arcs, and in a moment the darkness began to fade. I was dispersing the cloud, sending particles spinning off in all directions. My vision was clearing, and my breathing was still okay, though my throat felt dry and painful. I began to feel thousands of tiny pinpricks all over my body, but they hardly hurt.

Now I could see the door in front of me. The doorknob was just to my left. I kept swinging my shirt, and suddenly the cloud seemed to clear entirely away, almost as if it was moving out of range of my disruption. In that instant I slipped through the door and slammed it shut behind me.

I blinked in sudden darkness. I could hardly see. I thought my eyes would adjust from the glare of sunlight, and I waited a moment, but my vision did not improve. Instead, it seemed to be getting worse. I could just make out the glass doors of the airlock directly ahead. I still felt the stinging pinpricks all over my skin. My throat was dry and my breathing was raspy. I coughed. My vision was dimming. I started to feel dizzy.

On the other side of the airlock, Ricky and Mae stood watching me. I heard Ricky shout, "Come on, Jack! Hurry!"

My eyes burned painfully. My dizziness grew rapidly worse. I leaned against the wall to keep from falling over. My throat felt thick. I was having difficulty breathing. Gasping, I waited for the glass doors to open, but they remained closed. I stared stupidly at the airlock.

"You have to stand in front of the doors! Stand!"

I felt like the world was in slow motion. All my strength was gone. My body felt weak and shaky. The stinging was worse. The room was getting darker. I didn't think I could stand up on my own.

"Stand! Jack!"

Somehow, I shoved away from the wall, and lurched toward the airlock. With a hiss, the glass doors slid open.

"Go, Jack! Now!"

I saw spots before my eyes. I was dizzy, and sick to my stomach. I stumbled into the airlock, banging against the glass as I stepped inside. With every second that passed it was harder to breathe. I knew I was suffocating.

Outside the building, I heard the low thrumming sound start up again. I turned slowly to look back.

The glass doors hissed shut.

I looked down at my body but could barely see it. My skin appeared black. I was covered in dust. My body ached. My shirt was black with dust, too. The spray stung me, and I closed my eyes. Then the air handlers started up, whooshing loudly. I saw the dust sucked off my shirt. My vision was clearer, but I still couldn't breathe. The shirt slipped from my hand, flattening against the grate at my feet. I bent to reach down for it. My body began to shake, tremble. I heard only the roar of the handlers.

I felt a wave of nausea. My knees buckled. I sagged against the wall.

I looked at Mae and Ricky through the second glass doors; they seemed far away. As I watched, they receded even farther, moving away into the distance. Soon they were too far away for me to worry any longer. I knew I was dying. As I closed my eyes, I fell to the ground, and the roar of the air handlers faded into cold and total silence.

DAY 6
11:12 A.M.

"Don't move."

Something icy-cold coursed through my veins. I shuddered.

"Jack. Don't move. Just for a second, okay?"

Something cold, a cold liquid running up my arm. I opened my eyes. The light was directly overhead, glaring, greenish-bright; I winced. My whole body ached. I felt like I'd been beaten. I was lying on my back on the black counter of Mae's biology lab. Squinting in the glare, I saw Mae standing beside me, bent over my left arm. She had an intravenous line in my elbow.

"What's going on?"

"Jack, please. Don't move. I've only done this on lab animals."

"That's reassuring." I lifted my head to see what she was doing. My temples throbbed. I groaned, and lay back.

Mae said, "Feel bad?"

"Terrible."

"I'll bet. I had to inject you three times."

"With what?"

"You were in anaphylactic shock, Jack. You had a severe allergic reaction. Your throat almost closed up."

"Allergic reaction," I said. "That's what it was?"

"Severe one."

"It was from the swarm?"

She hesitated for a moment, then: "Of course."

"Would nano-sized particles cause an allergic reaction like that?"

"They certainly could . . ."

I said, "But you don't think so."

"No, I don't. I think the nanoparticles are antigenically inert. I think you reacted to a coliform toxin."

"A coliform toxin . . ." My throbbing headache came in waves. I took a breath, let it out slowly. I tried to figure out what she was saying. My mind was slow; my head hurt. A coliform toxin.

"Right."

"A toxin from *E. coli* bacteria? Is that what you mean?"

"Right. Proteolytic toxin, probably."

"And where would a toxin like that come from?"

"From the swarm," she said.

That made no sense at all. According to Ricky the *E. coli* bacteria were only used to manufacture precursor molecules. "But bacteria wouldn't be present in the swarm itself," I said.

"I don't know, Jack. I think they could be."

Why was she so diffident? I wondered. It wasn't like her. Ordinarily, Mae was precise, sharp. "Well," I said, "somebody knows. The swarm's been *designed*. Bacteria's either been designed in, or not."

I heard her sigh, as if I just wasn't getting it.

But what wasn't I getting?

I said, "Did you salvage the particles that were blown off in the airlock? Did you keep the stuff from the airlock?"

"No. All the airlock particles were incinerated."

"Was that a smart—"

"It's built into the system, Jack. As a safety feature. We can't override it."

"Okay." Now it was my turn to sigh. So we didn't have any examples of swarm agents to study. I started to sit up, but she put a gentle hand on my chest, restraining me.

"Take it slowly, Jack."

She was right, because sitting up made my headache much worse. I swung my feet over the side of the table. "How long was I out?"

"Twelve minutes."

"I feel like I was beaten up." My ribs ached with every breath.

"You had a lot of trouble breathing."

"I still do." I reached for a Kleenex and blew my nose. A lot of black stuff came out, mixed with blood and dust from the desert. I had to blow my nose four or five times to clear it. I crumpled the Kleenex and started to throw it away. Mae held out her hand. "I'll take that."

"No, it's okay—"

"Give it to me, Jack."

She took the Kleenex and slipped it into a little plastic bag and sealed it. That was when I realized how stupidly my mind was working. Of course that Kleenex would contain exactly the particles I wanted to study. I closed my eyes, breathed deeply, and waited for the throbbing in my head to ease up a little. When I opened my eyes again the glare in the room was less bright. It almost looked normal.

"By the way," Mae said, "Julia just called. She said you can't call her back, something about some tests. But she wanted to talk to you."

"Uh-huh."

I watched Mae take the Kleenex bag and put it inside a sealed jar. She screwed down the lid tightly. "Mae," I said, "if there's *E. coli* in the swarm, we can find out by looking at that right now. Shouldn't we do that?"

"I can't right now. I will as soon as I can. I'm having a little trouble with one of the fermentation units, and I need the microscopes for that."

"What kind of trouble?"

"I'm not sure yet. But yields are falling in one tank." She shook her head. "It's probably nothing serious. These things happen all the time. This whole manufacturing process is incredibly delicate, Jack. Keeping it going is like juggling a hundred balls at once. I have my hands full."

I nodded. But I was starting to think that the real reason she wasn't looking at the Kleenex was that she already knew the swarm contained bacteria. She just didn't think it was her place to tell me that. And if that's what was going on, then she never would tell me.

"Mae," I said. "Somebody has to tell me what's going on here. Not Ricky. I want somebody to really tell me."

"Good," she said. "I think that's a very good idea."

*　　　*　　　*

That was how I found myself sitting in front of a computer workstation in one of those small rooms. The project engineer, David Brooks, sat beside me. As he talked, David continuously straightened his clothes— he smoothed his tie, shot his cuffs, snugged his collar, pulled up the creases in his trousers from his thighs. Then he'd cross one ankle over his knee, pull up his sock, cross the other ankle. Run his hands over his shoulders, brushing away imaginary dust. And then start over again. It was all unconscious, of course, and with my headache I might have found it irritating. But I didn't focus on it. Because with every piece of new information David gave me, my headache got worse and worse.

Unlike Ricky, David had a very organized mind, and he told me everything, starting from the beginning. Xymos had contracted to make a micro-robotic swarm that would function as an aerial camera. The particles were successfully manufactured, and worked indoors. But when they were tested outside, they lacked mobility in wind. The test swarm was blown away in a strong breeze. That was six weeks ago.

"You tested more swarms after that?" I said.

"Yes, many. Over the next four weeks, or so."

"None worked?"

"Right. None worked."

"So those original swarms are all gone—blown away by the wind?"

"Yes."

"Which means the runaway swarms that we see now have nothing to do with your original test swarms."

"Correct . . ."

"They are a result of contamination . . ."

David blinked rapidly. "What do you mean, contamination?"

"The twenty-five kilos of material that was blown by the exhaust fan into the environment because of a missing filter . . ."

"Who said it was twenty-five kilos?"

"Ricky did."

"Oh, no, Jack," David said. "We vented stuff *for days*. We must have vented five or six hundred kilos of contaminants—bacteria, molecules, assemblers."

So Ricky had been understating the situation again. But I didn't understand why he bothered to lie about this. After all, it was just a mistake. And as Ricky had said, it was the contractor's mistake. "Okay," I said. "And you saw the first of these desert swarms when?"

"Two weeks ago," David said, nodding and smoothing his tie.

He explained that at first, the swarm was so disorganized that when it first appeared, they thought it was a cloud of desert insects, gnats or something. "It showed up for a while, going here and there around the laboratory building, and then it was gone. It seemed like a random event."

A swarm appeared again a couple of days later, he said, and by then it was much better organized. "It displayed distinctive swarming behavior, that sort of swirling in the cloud that you've seen. So it was clear that it was our stuff."

"And what happened then?"

"The swarm swirled around the desert near the installation, like before. It came and went. For the next few days, we tried to gain control of it by radio, but we never could. And eventually—about a week after that—we found that none of the cars would start." He paused. "I went out there to have a look, and I found that all the onboard computers were dead. These days all automobiles have microprocessors built into them. They control everything from fuel injection to radios and door locks."

"But now the computers were not functioning?"

"Yeah. Actually, the processor chips themselves were fine. But the memory chips had eroded. They'd literally turned to dust."

I thought, *Oh shit.* I said, "Could you figure out why?"

"Sure. It wasn't any big mystery, Jack. The erosion had the characteristic signature of gamma assemblers. You know about that? No? Well, we have nine different assemblers involved in manufacturing. Each assembler has a different function. The gamma assemblers break down carbon material in silicate layers. They actually cut at the nano level—slicing out chunks of carbon substrate."

"So these assemblers cut the memory chips in the cars."

"Right, right, but . . ." David hesitated. He was acting as if I were missing the point. He tugged at his cuffs, fingered his collar. "The thing you have to keep in mind, Jack, is that these assemblers can work at room temperature. If anything, the desert heat's even better for them. Hotter is more efficient."

For a moment I didn't understand what he was talking about. What difference did it make about room temperature or desert heat? What did that have to do with memory chips in cars? And then suddenly, finally, the penny dropped.

"Holy shit," I said.

He nodded. "Yeah."

David was saying that a mixture of components had been vented into the desert, and that these components—which were designed to self-assemble in the fabrication structure—would also self-assemble in the outside world. Assembly could be carried out autonomously in the desert. And obviously, that's exactly what was happening.

I ticked the points off to make sure I had it right. "Basic assembly begins with the bacteria. They've been engineered to eat anything, even garbage, so they can find something in the desert to live off of."

"Right."

"Which means the bacteria multiply, and begin churning out molecules that self-combine, forming larger molecules. Pretty soon you have assemblers, and the assemblers begin to do the final work and turn out new microagents."

"Right, right."

"Which means that the swarms *are* reproducing."

"Yes. They are."

"And the individual agents have memory."

"Yes. A small amount."

"And they don't need much, that's the whole point of distributed intelligence. It's collective. So they have intelligence, and since they have memory, they can learn from experience."

"Yes."

"And the PREDPREY program means they can solve problems. And the program generates enough random elements to let them innovate."

"Right. Yes."

My head throbbed. I was seeing all the implications, now, and they weren't good.

"So," I said, "what you're telling me is this swarm reproduces, is self-sustaining, learns from experience, has collective intelligence, and can innovate to solve problems."

"Yes."

"Which means for all practical purposes, it's alive."

"Yes." David nodded. "At least, it behaves as if it is alive. *Functionally* it's alive, Jack."

I said, "This is very fucking bad news."

Brooks said, "Tell me."

"I'd like to know," I said, "why this thing wasn't destroyed a long time ago."

David said nothing. He just smoothed his tie, and looked uncomfortable.

"Because you realize," I said, "that you're talking about a mechanical plague. That's what you've got here. It's just like a bacterial plague, or a viral plague. Except it's mechanical organisms. You've got a fucking man-made plague."

He nodded. "Yes."

"That's evolving."

"Yes."

"And it's not limited by biological rates of evolution. It's probably evolving much faster."

He nodded. "It *is* evolving faster."

"How much faster, David?"

Brooks sighed. "Pretty damn fast. It'll be different this afternoon, when it comes back."

"Will it come back?"

"It always does."

"And why does it come back?" I said.

"It's trying to get inside."

"And why is that?"

David shifted uncomfortably. "We have only theories, Jack."

"Try me."

"One possibility is that it's a territorial thing. As you know, the original PREDPREY code includes a concept of a range, of a territory in which the predators will roam. And within that core range, it defines a sort of home base, which the swarm may consider to be the inside of this facility."

I said, "You believe that?"

"Not really, no." He hesitated. "Actually," he said, "most of us think that it comes back looking for your wife, Jack. It's looking for Julia."

DAY 6
11:42 A.M.

That was how, with a splitting headache, I found myself on the phone to the hospital in San Jose. "Julia Forman, please." I spelled the name for the operator.

"She's in the ICU," the operator said.

"Yes, that's right."

"I'm sorry but direct calls are not allowed."

"Then the nursing station."

"Thank you, please hold."

I waited. No one was answering the phone. I called back, went through the operator again, and finally got through to the ICU nursing station. The nurse told me Julia was in X-ray and didn't know when she would be back. I said Julia was supposed to be back by now. The nurse said rather testily that she was looking at Julia's bed right now, and she could assure me Julia wasn't in it.

I said I'd call back.

I shut the phone and turned to David. "What was Julia doing in all this?"

"Helping us, Jack."

"I'm sure. But how, exactly?"

"In the beginning, she was trying to coax it back," he said. "We needed the swarm close to the building to take control again by radio. So Julia helped us keep it close."

"How?"

"Well, she entertained it."

"She what?"

"I guess you'd call it that. It was very quickly obvious that the swarm had rudimentary intelligence. It was Julia's idea to treat it like a child. She went outside with bright blocks, toys. Things a kid would like. And the swarm seemed to be responding to her. She was very excited about it."

"The swarm was safe to be around at that time?"

"Yes, completely safe. It was just a particle cloud." David shrugged. "Anyway, after the first day or so, she decided to go a step further and formally test it. You know, test it like a child psychologist."

"You mean, teach it," I said.

"No. Her idea was to test it."

"David," I said. "That swarm's a distributed intelligence. It's a goddamn net. It'll learn from whatever you do. Testing *is* teaching. What exactly was she doing with it?"

"Just, you know, sort of games. She'd lay out three colored blocks on the ground, two blue and one yellow, see if it would choose the yellow. Then with squares and triangles. Stuff like that."

"But David," I said. "You all knew this was a runaway, evolving outside the laboratory. Didn't anybody think to just go out and destroy it?"

"Sure. We all wanted to. Julia wouldn't allow it."

"Why?"

"She wanted it kept alive."

"And nobody argued with her?"

"She's a vice president of the company, Jack. She kept saying the swarm was a lucky accident, that we had stumbled onto something really big, that it could eventually save the company and we mustn't destroy it. She was, I don't know, she was really taken with it. I mean, she was proud of it. Like it was her invention. All she wanted to do was 'rein it in.' Her words."

"Yeah. Well. How long ago did she say that?"

"Yesterday, Jack." David shrugged. "You know, she only left here yesterday afternoon."

It took me a moment to realize that he was right. Just a single day had passed since Julia had been here, and then had had her accident. And in that time, the swarms had already advanced enormously.

"How many swarms were there yesterday?"

"Three. But we only saw two. I guess one was hiding." He shook his head. "You know, one of the swarms had become like a pet to her. It was smaller than the others. It'd wait for her to come outside, and it always stuck close to her. Sometimes when she came out it swirled around her, like it was excited to see her. She'd talk to it, too, like it was a dog or something."

I pressed my throbbing temples. "She talked to it," I repeated. Jesus Christ. "Don't tell me the swarms have auditory sensors, too."

"No. They don't."

"So talking was a waste of time."

"Uh, well . . . we think the cloud was close enough that her breath deflected some of the particles. In a rhythmic pattern."

"So the whole cloud was one giant eardrum?"

"In a way, yeah."

"And it's a net, so it learned . . ."

"Yeah."

I sighed. "Are you going to tell me it talked back?"

"No, but it started making weird sounds."

I nodded. I'd heard those weird sounds. "How does it do that?"

"We're not sure. Bobby thinks it's the reverse of the auditory deflection that allows it to hear. The particles pulse in a coordinated front, and generate a sound wave. Sort of like an audio speaker."

It would have to be something like that, I thought. Even though it seemed unlikely that it could do it. The swarm was basically a dust cloud of miniature particles. The particles didn't have either the mass or the energy to generate a sound wave.

A thought occurred to me. "David," I said, "was Julia out there yesterday, with the swarms?"

"Yes, in the morning. No problem. It was a few hours later, after she left, that they killed the snake."

"And was anything killed before that?"

"Uh . . . possibly a coyote a few days ago, I'm not sure."

"So maybe the snake wasn't the first?"

"Maybe . . ."

"And today they killed a rabbit."

"Yeah. So it's progressing fast, now."

"Thank you, Julia," I said.

I was pretty sure the accelerated behavior of the swarms that we were seeing was a function of past learning. This was a characteristic of distributed systems—and for that matter a characteristic of evolution, which could be considered a kind of learning, if you wanted to think of it in those terms. In either case, it meant that systems experienced a long, slow starting period, followed by ever-increasing speed.

You could see that exact speedup in the evolution of life on earth. The first life shows up four billion years ago as single-cell creatures. Nothing changes for the next two billion years. Then nuclei appear in the cells. Things start to pick up. Only a few hundred million years later, multicellular organisms. A few hundred million years after that, explosive diversity of life. And more diversity. By a couple of hundred million years ago there are large plants and animals, complex creatures, dinosaurs. In all this, man's a latecomer: four million years ago, upright apes. Two million years ago, early human ancestors. Thirty-five thousand years ago, cave paintings.

The acceleration was dramatic. If you compressed the history of life on earth into twenty-four hours, then multicellular organisms appeared in the last twelve hours, dinosaurs in the last hour, the earliest men in the last forty seconds, and modern men less than one second ago.

It had taken two billion years for primitive cells to incorporate a nucleus, the first step toward complexity. But it had taken only 200 million years—one-tenth of the time—to evolve multicellular animals. And it took only four million years to go from small-brained apes with crude bone tools to modern man and genetic engineering. That was how fast the pace had increased.

This same pattern showed up in the behavior of agent-based systems. It took a long time for agents to "lay the groundwork" and to accomplish the early stuff, but once that was completed, subsequent progress could be swift. There was no way to skip the groundwork, just as there was no way for a human being to skip childhood. You had to do the preliminary work.

But at the same time, there was no way to avoid the subsequent acceleration. It was, so to speak, built into the system.

Teaching made the progression more efficient, and I was sure Julia's teaching had been an important factor in the behavior of the swarm now. Simply by interacting with it, she had introduced a selection pressure in an organism with emergent behavior that couldn't be predicted. It was a very foolish thing to do.

So the swarm—already developing rapidly—would develop even more rapidly in the future. And since it was a man-made organism, evolution was not taking place on a biological timescale. Instead, it was happening in a matter of hours.

Destroying the swarms would be more difficult with each passing hour.

"Okay," I said to David. "If the swarms are coming back, then we better get ready for them." I got to my feet, wincing at the headache, and headed for the door.

"What do you have in mind?" David said.

"What do you think I have in mind?" I said. "We've got to kill these things cold stone dead. We have to wipe them off the face of the planet. And we have to do it right now."

David shifted in his chair. "Fine with me," he said. "But I don't think Ricky's going to like it."

"Why not?"

David shrugged. "He's just not."

I waited, and said nothing.

David fidgeted in his chair, more and more uncomfortable. "The thing is, he and Julia are, uh, in agreement on this."

"They're in agreement."

"Yes. They see eye to eye. I mean, on this."

I said, "What are you trying to say to me, David?"

"Nothing. Just what I said. They agree the swarms should be kept alive. I think Ricky's going to oppose you, that's all."

I needed to talk to Mae again. I found her in the biology lab, hunched over a computer monitor, looking at images of white bacterial growth on dark red media. I said, "Mae, listen, I've talked to David and I need to— uh, Mae? Have you got a problem?" She was looking fixedly at the screen.

"I think I do," she said. "A problem with the feedstock."

"What kind of problem?"

"The latest Theta-d stocks aren't growing properly." She pointed to an image in the upper corner of the monitor, which showed bacteria growing in smooth white circles. "That's normal coliform growth," she said. "That's how it's supposed to look. But here . . ." She brought up another image in the center of the screen. The round forms appeared moth-eaten, ragged and misshapen. "That's not normal growth," she said, shaking her head. "I'm afraid it's phage contamination."

"You mean a virus?" I said. A phage was a virus that attacked bacteria.

"Yes," she said. "Coli are susceptible to a very large number of phages. T4 phage is of course the most common, but Theta-d was engineered to be T4-resistant. So I suspect it's a new phage that's doing this."

"A new phage? You mean it's newly evolved?"

"Yes. Probably a mutant of an existing strain, that somehow gets around the engineered resistance. But it's bad news for manufacturing. If we have infected bacterial stocks, we'll have to shut down production. Otherwise we'll just be spewing viruses out."

"Frankly," I said, "shutting down production might be a good idea."

"I'll probably have to. I'll try to isolate it, but it looks aggressive. I may not be able to get rid of it without scrubbing the kettle. Starting over with fresh stock. Ricky's not going to like it."

"Have you told him about this?"

"Not yet." She shook her head. "I don't think he needs more bad news right now. And besides . . ." She stopped, as if she had thought better of what she was going to say.

"Besides what?"

"Ricky has a huge stake in the success of this company." She turned to face me. "Bobby heard him on the phone the other day, talking about his stock options. And sounding worried. I think Ricky sees Xymos as his last big chance to score. He's been here five years. If this doesn't work out, he'll be too senior to start over at a new company. He's got a wife and baby; he can't gamble another five years, waiting to see if the next company clicks. So he's really trying to make this happen, really driving himself. He's up all night, working, figuring. He isn't sleeping more than three or four hours. Frankly, I worry it's affecting his judgment."

"I can imagine," I said. "The pressure must be terrible."

"He's so sleep-deprived it makes him erratic," Mae said. "I'm never sure what he'll do, or how he'll respond. Sometimes I get the feeling he doesn't want to get rid of the swarms at all. Or maybe he's scared."

"Maybe," I said.

"Anyway, he's erratic. So if I were you I'd be careful," she said, "when you go after the swarms. Because that's what you're going to do, isn't it? Go after them?"

"Yes," I said. "That's what I'm going to do."

DAY 6
1:12 P.M.

They had all gathered in the lounge, with the video games and pinball machines. Nobody was playing them now. They were watching me with anxious eyes as I explained what we had to do. The plan was simple enough—the swarm itself was dictating what we had to do, although I was skipping that uncomfortable truth.

Basically, I told them we had a runaway swarm we couldn't control. And the swarm exhibited self-organizing behavior. "Whenever you have a high SO component, it means the swarm can reassemble itself after an injury or disruption. Just as it did with me. So this swarm has to be totally, physically destroyed. That means subjecting the particles to heat, cold, acid, or high magnetic fields. And from what I've seen of its behavior, I'd say our best chance to destroy it is at night when the swarm loses energy and sinks to the ground."

Ricky whined, "But we already told you, Jack, we can't find it at night—"

"That's right, you can't," I said. "Because you didn't tag it. Look, it's a big desert out there. If you want to trace it back to its hiding place, you've got to tag it with something so strong you can follow its trail wherever it goes."

"Tag it with what?"

"That's my next question," I said. "What kind of tagging agents have we got around here?" I was greeted with blank looks. "Come on, guys.

This is an industrial facility. You must have *something* that will coat the particles and leave a trail we can follow. I'm talking about a substance that fluoresces intensely, or a pheromone with a characteristic chemical signature, or something radioactive . . . No?"

More blank looks. Shaking their heads.

"Well," Mae said, "of course, we have radioisotopes."

"All right, fine." Now we were getting somewhere.

"We use them to check for leaks in the system. The helicopter brings them out once a week."

"What isotopes do you have?"

"Selenium-72 and Rhenium-186. Sometimes Xenon-133 as well. I'm not sure what we've got on hand right now."

"What kind of half-lives are we talking about?" Certain isotopes lost radioactivity very rapidly, in a matter of hours or minutes. If so, they wouldn't be useful to me.

"Half-life averages about a week," Mae said. "Selenium's eight days. Rhenium's four days. Xenon-133 is five days. Five and a quarter."

"Okay. Any of them should do fine for our purposes," I said. "We only need the radioactivity to last for one night, after we tag the swarm."

Mae said, "We usually put the isotopes in FDG. It's a liquid glucose base. You could spray it."

"That should be fine," I said. "Where are the isotopes now?"

Mae smiled bleakly. "In the storage unit," she said.

"Where is that?"

"Outside. Next to the parked cars."

"Okay," I said. "Then let's go out and get them."

"Oh, for Christ's sake," Ricky said, throwing up his hands. "Are you out of your mind? You nearly died out there this morning, Jack. You can't go back out."

"There isn't any choice," I said.

"Sure there is. Wait until nightfall."

"No," I said. "Because that means we can't spray them until tomorrow. And we can't trace and destroy them until tomorrow night. That means we wait thirty-six hours with an organism that is evolving fast. We can't risk it."

"Risk it? Jack, if you go out now, you'll never survive. You're fucking crazy even to consider it."

Charley Davenport had been staring at the monitor. Now he turned to the group. "No, Jack's not crazy." He grinned at me. "And I'm going with him." Charley began to hum: "Born to Be Wild."

"I'm going, too," Mae said. "I know where the isotopes are stored."

I said, "It's not really necessary, Mae, you can tell me—"

"No. I'm coming."

"We'll need to improvise a spray apparatus of some kind." David Brooks was rolling up his sleeves carefully. "Presumably, remotely controlled. That's Rosie's specialty."

"Okay, I'll come, too," Rosie Castro said, looking at David.

"You're all going?" Ricky stared from one to another of us, shaking his head. "This is extremely risky," he said. "*Extremely* risky."

Nobody said anything. We all just stared at him.

Then Ricky said, "Charley, *will you shut the fuck up?*" He turned to me. "I don't think I can allow this, Jack . . ."

"I don't think you have a choice," I said.

"I'm in charge here."

"Not now," I said. I felt a burst of annoyance. I felt like telling him he'd screwed the pooch by allowing a swarm to evolve in the environment. But I didn't know how many critical decisions Julia had made. In the end, Ricky was obsequious to management, trying to please them like a child pleasing a parent. He did it charmingly; that was how he had moved ahead in life. That was also his greatest weakness.

But now Ricky stuck out his chin stubbornly. "You just can't do it, Jack," he said. "You guys can't go out there and survive."

"Sure we can, Ricky," Charley Davenport said. He pointed to the monitor. "Look for yourself."

The monitor showed the desert outside. The early afternoon sun was shining on scrubby cactus. One stunted juniper in the distance, dark against the sun. For a moment I didn't understand what Charley was talking about. Then I saw the sand blowing low on the ground. And I noticed the juniper was bent to one side.

"That's right, folks," Charley Davenport said. "We got a high wind out there. High wind, no swarms—remember? They have to hug the ground." He headed toward the passageway leading to the power station. "Time's a-wasting. Let's do it, guys."

Everybody filed out. I was the last to leave. To my astonishment, Ricky pulled me aside, blocked the door with his body. "I'm sorry, Jack, I didn't want to embarrass you in front of the others. But I just can't let you do this."

"Would you rather have somebody else do it?" I said.

He frowned. "What do you mean?"

"You better face facts, Ricky. This is already a disaster. And if we can't get it under control right away, then we have to call for help."

"Help? What do you mean?"

"I mean, call the Pentagon. Call the Army. We have to call somebody to get these swarms under control."

"Jesus, Jack. We can't do that."

"We have no choice."

"But it would destroy the company. We'd never get funding again."

"That wouldn't bother me one bit," I said. I was feeling angry about what had happened in the desert. A chain of bad decisions, errors and fuckups extending over weeks and months. It seemed as if everyone at Xymos was doing short-term solutions, patch-and-fix, quick and dirty. No one was paying attention to the long-term consequences.

"Look," I said, "you've got a runaway swarm that's apparently lethal. You can't screw around with this anymore."

"But, Julia—"

"Julia isn't here."

"But she said—"

"I don't care what she said, Ricky."

"But the company—"

"Fuck the company. Ricky." I grabbed him by the shoulders, shook him once hard. "Don't you get it? *You won't go outside*. You're *afraid* of this thing, Ricky. We have to kill it. And if we can't kill it soon, we have to call for help."

"*No.*"

"Yes, Ricky."

"*We'll see about that*," he snarled. His body tensed, his eyes flared. He grabbed my shirt collar. I just stood there, staring at him. I didn't move. Ricky glared at me for a moment, and then released his grip. He patted me on the shoulder and smoothed out my collar. "Ah hell, Jack," he said. "What am I doing?" And he gave me his self-deprecating surfer grin. "I'm sorry. I think the pressure must be getting to me. You're right. You're absolutely right. Fuck the company. We have to do this. We have to destroy those things right away."

"Yes," I said, still staring at him. "We do."

He paused. He took his hand away from my collar. "You think I'm acting weird, don't you? Mary thinks I'm acting weird, too. She said so, the other day. Am I acting weird?"

"Well . . ."

"You can tell me."

"Maybe on edge . . . You getting any sleep?"

"Not much. Couple of hours."

"Maybe you should take a pill."

"I did. Doesn't seem to help. It's the damn pressure. I've been here a week now. This place gets to you."

"I imagine it must."

"Yeah. Well, anyway." He turned away, as if suddenly embarrassed. "Look, I'll be on the radio," he said. "I'll be with you every step of the way. I'm very grateful to you, Jack. You've brought sanity and order here. Just . . . just be careful out there, okay?"

"I will."

Ricky stepped aside.

I went out the door past him.

Going down the hallway to the power station, with the air conditioners roaring full blast, Mae fell into step beside me. I said to her, "You really don't need to go out there, Mae. You could tell me over the radio how to handle the isotopes."

"It's not the isotopes I'm concerned with," she said, her voice low, so it would be buried in the roar. "It's the rabbit."

I wasn't sure I'd heard her. "The what?"

"The rabbit. I need to examine the rabbit again."

"Why?"

"You remember that tissue sample I cut from the stomach? Well, I looked at it under the microscope a few minutes ago."

"And?"

"I'm afraid we have big problems, Jack."

DAY 6
2:52 P.M.

I was the first one out the door, squinting in the desert sunlight. Even though it was almost three o'clock, the sun seemed as bright and hot as ever. A hot wind ruffled my trousers and shirt. I pulled my headset mouthpiece closer to my lips and said, "Bobby, you reading?"

"I read you, Jack."

"Got an image?"

"Yes, Jack."

Charley Davenport came out and laughed. He said, "You know, Ricky, you really are a stupid shmuck. You know that?"

Over my headset, I heard Ricky say, "Save it. You know I don't like compliments. Just get on with it."

Mae came through the door next. She had a backpack slung over one shoulder. She said to me, "For the isotopes."

"Are they heavy?"

"The containers are."

Then David Brooks came out, with Rosie close behind him. She made a face as she stepped onto the sand. "Jesus, it's hot," she said.

"Yeah, I think you'll find deserts tend to be that way," Charley said.

"No shit, Charley."

"I wouldn't shit you, Rosie." He belched.

I was busy scanning the horizon, but I saw nothing. The cars were parked under a shed about fifty yards away. The shed ended in a square white concrete building with narrow windows. That was the storage unit.

We started toward it. Rosie said, "Is that place air-conditioned?"

"Yes," Mae said. "But it's still hot. It's poorly insulated."

"Is it airtight?" I said.

"Not really."

"That means no," Davenport said, laughing. He spoke into his headset. "Bobby, what wind do we have?"

"Seventeen knots," Bobby Lembeck said. "Good strong wind."

"And how long until the wind dies? Sunset?"

"Probably, yeah. Another three hours."

I said, "That'll be plenty of time."

I noticed that David Brooks was not saying anything. He just trudged toward the building. Rosie followed close behind him.

"But you never know," Davenport said. "We could all be toast. Any minute now." He laughed again, in his irritating way.

Ricky said, "Charley, why don't you shut the fuck up?"

"Why don't you come out and make me, big boy?" Charley said. "What's the matter, your veins clogged with chicken shit?"

I said, "Let's stay focused, Charley."

"Hey, I'm focused. I'm focused."

The wind was blowing sand, creating a brownish blur just above the ground. Mae walked beside me. She looked across the desert and said abruptly, "I want to have a look at the rabbit. You all go ahead if you want."

She headed off to the right, toward the carcass. I went with her. And the others turned in a group and followed us. It seemed everybody wanted to stay together. The wind was still strong.

Charley said, "Why do you want to see it, Mae?"

"I want to check something." She was pulling on gloves as she walked.

The headset crackled. Ricky said, "Would somebody please tell me what the hell is going on?"

"We're going to see the rabbit," Charley said.

"What for?"

"Mae wants to see it."

"She saw it before. Guys, you're very exposed out there. I wouldn't be waltzing around."

"Nobody's waltzing around, Ricky."

By now I could see the rabbit in the distance, partially obscured by the blowing sand. In a few moments, we were all standing over the carcass. The wind had blown the body over on its side. Mae crouched down, turned it on its back, laid open the carcass.

"Jeez," Rosie said.

I was startled to see that the exposed flesh was no longer smooth and pink. Instead, it was roughened everywhere, and in a few places looked as if it had been scraped. And it was covered by a milky white coating.

"Looks like it was dipped in acid," Charley said.

"Yes, it does," Mae said. She sounded grim.

I glanced at my watch. All this had occurred in two hours. "What happened to it?"

Mae had taken out her magnifying glass and was bent close to the animal. She looked here and there, moving the glass quickly. Then she said, "It's been partially eaten."

"Eaten? By what?"

"Bacteria."

"Wait a minute," Charley Davenport said. "You think this is caused by Theta-d? You think the *E. coli* is eating it?"

"We'll know soon enough," she said. She reached into a pouch, and pulled out several glass tubes containing sterile swabs.

"But it's only been dead a short time."

"Long enough," Mae said. "And high temperatures accelerate growth." She daubed the animal with one swab after another, replacing each in a glass tube.

"Then the Theta-d must be multiplying very aggressively."

"Bacteria will do that if you give them a good nutrient source. You shift into log phase growth where they're doubling every two or three minutes. I think that's what's happening here."

I said, "But if that's true, it means the swarm—"

"I don't know what it means, Jack," she said quickly. She looked at me and gave a slight shake of the head. The meaning was clear: *not now*.

But the others weren't put off. "Mae, Mae, Mae," Charley Davenport said. "You're telling us that the swarms killed the rabbit in order to eat it? In order to grow more coli? And make more nanoswarms?"

"I didn't say that, Charley." Her voice was calm, almost soothing.

"But that's what you *think*," Charley continued. "You think the swarms consume mammalian tissue in order to reproduce—"

"Yes. That's what I think, Charley." Mae put her swabs away carefully, and got to her feet. "But I've taken cultures, now. We'll run them in Luria and agerose, and we'll see what we see."

"I bet if we come back in another hour, this white stuff will be gone, and we'll see black forming all over the body. New black nanoparticles. And eventually there'll be enough for a new swarm."

She nodded. "Yes. I think so, too."

"And that's why the wildlife around here has disappeared?" David Brooks said.

"Yes." She brushed a strand of hair back with her hand. "This has been going on for a while."

There was a moment of silence. We all stood around the rabbit carcass, our backs to the blowing wind. The carcass was being consumed so quickly, I imagined I could almost see it happening right before my eyes, in real time.

"We better get rid of those fucking swarms," Charley said.

We all turned, and set off for the shed.

Nobody spoke.

There was nothing to say.

As we walked ahead, some of those small birds that hopped around the desert floor under the cholla cactus suddenly took to the air, chittering and wheeling before us.

I said to Mae, "So there's no wildlife, but the birds are here?"

"Seems to be that way."

The flock wheeled and came back, then settled to the ground a hundred yards away.

"Maybe they're too small for the swarms to bother with," Mae said. "Not enough flesh on their bodies."

"Maybe." I was thinking there might be another answer. But to be sure, I would have to check the code.

I stepped from the sun into the shade of the corrugated shed, and moved along the line of cars toward the door of the storage unit. The door was plastered with warning symbols—for nuclear radiation, biohazard, microwaves, high explosives, laser radiation. Charley said, "You can see why we keep this shit outside."

As I came to the door, Vince said, "Jack, you have a call. I'll patch it." My cell phone rang. It was probably Julia. I flipped it open. "Hello?"

"Dad." It was Eric. With that emphatic tone that he got when he was upset.

I sighed. "Yes, Eric."

"When are you coming back?"

"I'm not sure, son."

"Will you be here for dinner?"

"I'm afraid not. Why? What's the problem?"

"She is *such* an asshole."

"Eric, just tell me what the problem—"

"Aunt Ellen sticks up for her all the time. It's not fair."

"I'm kind of busy now, Eric, so just tell me—"

"Why? What are you doing?"

"Just tell me what's wrong, son."

"Never mind," he said, turning sulky, "if you're not coming home, it doesn't matter. Where are you, anyway? Are you in the desert?"

"Yes. How did you know that?"

"I talked to Mom. Aunt Ellen made us go to the hospital to see her. It's not fair. I didn't want to go. She made me anyway."

"Uh-huh. How is Mom?"

"She's checking out of the hospital."

"She's finished all her tests?"

"The doctors wanted her to stay," Eric said. "But she wants to get out. She has a cast on her arm, that's all. She says everything else is fine. Dad? Why do I always have to do what Aunt Ellen says? It's not fair."

"Let me talk to Ellen."

"She isn't here. She took Nicole to buy a new dress for her play."

"Who's with you at the house?"

"Maria."

"Okay," I said. "Have you done your homework?"

"Not yet."

"Well, get busy, son. I want your homework done before dinner." It was amazing how these lines just popped out of a parent's mouth.

By now I had reached the storage room door. I stared at all the warning signs. There were several I didn't know, like a diamond made up of four different colored squares inside, each with a number. Mae unlocked the door and went in.

"Dad?" Eric started to cry. "When are you coming home?"

"I don't know," I said. "I hope by tomorrow."

"Okay. Promise?"

"I promise."

I could hear him sniffling, and then through the phone a long *snarff* sound as he wiped his nose on his shirt. I told him he could call me later if he wanted to. He seemed better, and said okay, and then said good-bye.

I hung up, and entered the storage building.

The interior was divided into two large storage rooms, with shelves on all four walls, and freestanding shelves in the middle of the rooms. Concrete walls, concrete floor. There was another door in the second room, and a corrugated rollup door for truck deliveries. Hot sunlight came in through wood-frame windows. The air-conditioning rumbled noisily but, as Mae had said, the rooms were still hot. I closed the door behind me, and looked at the seal. It was just ordinary weather stripping. The shed was definitely not airtight.

I walked along the shelves, stacked with bins of spare parts for the fabrication machinery, and the labs. The second room had more mundane items: cleaning supplies, toilet paper, bars of soap, boxes of cereal, and a couple of refrigerators filled with food.

I turned to Mae. "Where are the isotopes?"

"Over here." She led me around a set of shelves, to a steel lid set in the concrete floor. The lid was about three feet in diameter. It looked like a buried garbage can, except for the glowing LED and keypad in the center. Mae dropped to one knee, and punched in a code quickly.

The lid lifted with a hiss.

I saw a ladder that led down into a circular steel chamber. The isotopes were stored in metal containers of different sizes. Apparently Mae could tell which they were just by looking, because she said, "We have Selenium-172. Shall we use that?"

"Sure."

Mae started to climb down into the chamber.

"Will you fucking *cut it out*?" In a corner of the room, David Brooks jumped back from Charley Davenport. Charley was holding a big spray bottle of Windex cleaner. He was testing the squeeze trigger mechanism, and in the process spraying streaks of water on David. It didn't look accidental. "Give me that damn thing," David said, snatching the bottle away.

"I think it might work," Charley said blandly. "But we'd need a remote mechanism."

From the first room, Rosie said, "Would this work?" She held up a shiny cylinder, with wires dangling from it. "Isn't this a solenoid relay?"

"Yes," David said. "But I doubt it can exert enough force to squeeze this bottle. Has it got a rating? We need something bigger."

"And don't forget, you also need a remote controller," Charley said. "Unless you want to stand there and spray the fucker yourself."

Mae came up from below, carrying a heavy metal tube. She walked to the sink, and reached for a bottle of straw-colored liquid. She pulled on heavy rubber-coated gloves, and started to mix the isotope into the liquid. A radiation counter over the sink was chattering.

Over the headset, Ricky said, "Aren't you guys forgetting something? Even if you have a remote, how are you going to get the cloud to come to it? Because I don't think the swarm will just come over and stand there while you hose it down."

"We'll find something to attract them," I said.

"Like what?"

"They were attracted to the rabbit."

"We don't have any rabbits."

Charley said, "You know, Ricky, you are a very negative person."

"I'm just telling you the facts."

"Thank you for sharing," Charley said.

Like Mae, Charley was seeing it, too: Ricky had dragged his feet every step of the way. It was as if Ricky wanted to keep the swarms alive. Which made no sense at all. But that's how he was behaving.

I would have said something to Charley about Ricky, but over our headsets everybody heard everything. The downside of modern communications: everybody can listen in.

"Hey guys?" It was Bobby Lembeck. "How's it coming?"

"We're getting there. Why?"

"The wind's dropping."

"What is it now?" I said.

"Fifteen knots. Down from eighteen."

"That's still strong," I said. "We're okay."

"I know. I'm just telling you."

From the next room, Rosie said, "What's thermite?" In her hand she held a plastic tray filled with thumb-sized metal tubes.

"Careful with that," David said. "It must be left over from construction. I guess they did thermite welding."

"But what is it?"

"Thermite is aluminum and iron oxide," David said. "It burns very hot—three thousand degrees—and so bright you can't look directly at it. And it'll melt steel for welding."

"How much of that have we got?" I said to Rosie. "Because we can use it tonight."

"There's four boxes back there." She plucked one tube from the box. "So how do you set 'em off?"

"Be careful, Rosie. That's a magnesium wrapper. Any decent heat source will ignite it."

"Even matches?"

"If you want to lose your hand. Better use road flares, something with a fuse."

"I'll see," she said, and she disappeared around the corner.

The radiation counter was still clicking. I turned to the sink. Mae had capped the isotope tube. She was now pouring the straw-colored liquid into a Windex bottle.

"Hey, guys?" It was Bobby Lembeck again. "I'm picking up some instability. Wind's fluctuating at twelve knots."

"Okay," I said. "We don't need to hear every little change, Bobby."

"I'm seeing some instability, is all."

"I think we're okay for the moment, Bobby."

Mae was going to be another few minutes, in any case. I went over to a computer workstation and turned it on. The screen glowed; there was a menu of options. Aloud, I said, "Ricky, can I put up the swarm code on this monitor?"

"The code?" Ricky said. He sounded alarmed. "What do you want the code for?"

"I want to see what you guys have done."

"Why?"

"Ricky, for Christ's sake, can I see it or not?"

"Sure, of course you can. All the code revisions are in the directory slash code. It's passworded."

I was typing. I found the directory. But I wasn't being allowed to enter it. "And the password is?"

"It's l-a-n-g-t-o-n, all lowercase."

"Okay."

I entered the password. I was now in the directory, looking at a list of program modifications, each with file size and date. The document sizes were large, which meant that these were all programs for other aspects of the swarm mechanism. Because the code for the particles themselves would be small—just a few lines, maybe eight, ten kilobytes, no more.

"Ricky."

"Yes, Jack."

"Where's the particle code?"

"Isn't it there?"

"God damn it, Ricky. Stop screwing around."

"Hey, Jack, I'm not responsible for the archiving—"

"Ricky, these are workfiles, not archives," I said. "Tell me *where*."

A brief pause. "There should be a subdirectory slash C-D-N. It's kept there."

I scrolled down. "I see it."

Within this directory, I found a list of files, all very small. The modification dates started about six weeks ago. There was nothing new from the last two weeks.

"Ricky. You haven't changed the code for two weeks?"

"Yeah, about that."

I clicked on the most recent document. "You got high-level summaries?" When these guys had worked for me, I always insisted that they write natural language summaries of the program structure. It was faster to review than documentation within the code itself. And they often solved logic problems when they had to write it out briefly.

"Should be there," Ricky said.

On the screen, I saw:

```
/*Initialize*/
For j=1 to L x V do
Sj = 0 /*set initial demand to 0/
End For
For i=l to z do
  For j = 1 to L x V do
  ∂ij = (state (x,y,z)) /*agent threshold param*/
  Ø ij = (intent (Cj,Hj)) /*agent intention fill*/
  Response = 0 /* begin agent response*/
  Zone = z(i) /* intitial zone unlearned by agent*/
  Sweep =1 /* activate agent travel*/
  End For
End For
/*Main*/
For kl=1 to RVd do
  For tm=1 to nv do
    For ∂ = l to j do /* tracking surrounds*/
```

```
Ø ij = (intent (Cj,Hj)) /*agent intention fill*/
∂ij <> (state (x,y,z)) /*agent is in motion*/
∂ikl = (filed (x,y,z)) /*track nearest agents */
```

I scanned it for a while, looking for how they had changed it. Then I scrolled down into the actual code, to see the implementation. But the important code wasn't there. The entire set of particle behaviors was marked as an object call to a something titled "compstat_do."

"Ricky," I said, "what's 'compstat_do'? Where is it?"

"Should be there."

"It's not."

"I don't know. Maybe it's compiled."

"Well that isn't going to do me any good, is it?" You couldn't read compiled code. "Ricky, I want to see that damn module. What is the problem?"

"No problem. I have to look for it, is all."

"Okay . . ."

"I'll do it when you get back."

I glanced over at Mae. "Have you gone through the code?"

She shook her head. Her expression seemed to say it was never going to happen, that Ricky would make up more excuses and keep putting me off. I didn't understand why. I was there to advise them on the code, after all. That was my area of expertise.

In the next room, Rosie and David were poking through the shelves of supplies, looking for radio relays. They weren't having any success. Across the room, Charley Davenport farted loudly and cried, "Bingo!"

"Jesus, Charley," Rosie said.

"You shouldn't hold things in," Charley said. "It makes you sick."

"*You* make me sick." Rosie said.

"Oh, sorry." Charley held up his hand, showing a shiny metal contraption. "Then I guess you don't want this remote-controlled compression valve."

"What?" Rosie said, turning.

"Are you kidding?" David said, going over to look.

"And it's got a pressure rating of ADC twenty pi."

"That should work fine," David said.

"If you don't fuck it up," Charley said.

They took the valve and went to the sink, where Mae was still pouring, wearing her heavy gloves. She said, "Let me finish . . ."

"Will I glow in the dark?" Charley said, grinning at her.

"Just your farts," Rosie said.

"Hey, they already do that. 'Specially when you light 'em."

"Jesus, Charley."

"Farts are methane, you know. Burns with a hard blue gemlike flame." And he laughed.

"I'm glad you appreciate yourself," Rosie said. "Because nobody else does."

"Ouch, ouch," Charley said, clutching his breast. "I die, I die . . ."

"Don't get our hopes up."

My headset crackled. "Hey guys?" It was Bobby Lembeck again. "Wind's just dropped to six knots."

I said, "Okay." I turned to the others. "Let's finish up, guys."

David said, "We're waiting for Mae. Then we'll fit this valve."

"Let's fit it back in the lab," I said.

"Well, I just want to make sure—"

"Back at the lab," I said. "Pack it up, guys."

I went to the window and looked out. The wind was still ruffling the juniper bushes, but there was no longer a layer of sand blowing across the ground.

Ricky came on the headset: "Jack, get your fucking team out of there."

"We're doing it now," I said.

David Brooks said in a formal tone, "Guys, there's no point in leaving until we have a valve that we know fits this bottle—"

"I think we better go," Mae said. "Finished or not."

"What good would that do?" David said.

"Pack up," I said. "Stop talking and pack it up *now*."

Over the headset, Bobby said, "Four knots and falling. Fast."

"Let's go, everybody," I said. I was herding them toward the door.

Then Ricky came on. "*No.*"

"What?"

"You can't leave now."

"Why not?"

"Because it's too late. They're here."

DAY 6
3:12 P.M.

Everyone went to the window; we banged heads trying to look out in all directions. As far as I could see, the horizon was clear. I saw nothing at all. "Where are they?" I said.

"Coming from the south. We have them on the monitors."

"How many?" Charley said.

"Four."

"Four!"

"Yeah, four."

The main building was south of us. There were no windows in the south wall of the shed.

David said, "We don't see anything. How fast are they coming?"

"Fast."

"Do we have time to run for it?"

"I don't think so."

David frowned. "He doesn't *think* so. Jesus."

And before I could say anything, David had bolted for the far door, opened it, and stepped out into the sunlight. Through the rectangle of the open door we saw him look to the south, shading his eyes with his hand. We all spoke at once:

"David!"

"David, what the fuck are you doing?"

"David, you asshole!"

"I'm trying to see . . ."

"Get back here!"

"You stupid bastard!"

But Brooks remained where he was, hands over his eyes. "I don't see anything yet," he said. "And I don't hear anything. Listen, I think maybe we can make a run for—uh, no we can't." He sprinted back inside, stumbled on the door frame, fell, scrambled to his feet, and slammed the door shut, pulled it tight behind him, tugging on the doorknob.

"Where are they?"

"Coming," he said. "They're coming." His voice shook with tension. "Oh Jesus, they're coming." He pulled back on the doorknob with both hands, using his whole body weight. He muttered over and over, "Coming . . . they're coming . . ."

"Oh great," Charley said. "The fucking guy's cracked."

I went over to David, and put my hand on his shoulder. He was pulling on the doorknob, breathing in ragged gasps. "David," I said quietly. "Let's take it easy now. Let's take a deep breath."

"I just—I have to keep—have to keep them—" He was sweating, his whole body tense, his shoulder shaking under my hand. It was pure panic.

"David," I said. "Let's take a deep breath, okay?"

"I have to—have to—have—have—have—"

"Big breath, David . . ." I took one, demonstrating. "That feels better. Come on now. Big breath . . ."

David was nodding, trying to hear me. He took a short breath. Then resumed his quick gasps.

"That's good, David, now another one . . ."

Another breath. His breathing slowed slightly. He stopped shaking.

"Okay, David, that's good . . ."

Behind me, Charley said, "I always knew that guy was fucked up. Look at him, talking to him like a fucking baby."

I glanced back, and shot Charley a look. He just shrugged. "Hey, I'm fucking right."

Mae said, "It's not helping, Charley."

"Fuck helping."

Rosie said, "Charley, just shut up for a while, okay?"

I turned back to David. I kept my voice even. "All right, David . . . That's good, breathe . . . okay now, let go of the doorknob."

David shook his head, refusing, but he seemed confused now, uncertain of what he was doing. He blinked his eyes rapidly. It was as if he was coming out of a trance.

I said softly, "Let go of the doorknob. It's not doing any good."

Finally, he let go, and sat back on the ground. He began to cry, head in hands.

"Oh Jesus," Charley said. "That's all we need."

"Shut up, Charley."

Rosie went to the refrigerator and came back with a bottle of water. She gave it to David, who drank as he cried. She helped him to his feet, nodded to me that she'd take it from here.

I went back to the center of the room, where the others were standing by the workstation screen. On the screen, the lines of code had been replaced by a monitor view of the north face of the main building. Four swarms were there, glinting silver as they moved up and down the length of the building.

"What're they doing?" I said.

"Trying to get in."

I said, "Why do they do that?"

"We're not sure," Mae said.

We watched for a moment in silence. Once again I was struck by the purposefulness of their behavior. They reminded me of bears trying to break into a trailer to get food. They paused at every doorway and closed window, hovering there, moving up and down along the seals, until finally moving on to the next opening.

I said, "And do they always try the doors like that?"

"Yes. Why?"

"Because it looks like they don't remember that the doors are sealed."

"No," Charley said. "They don't remember."

"Because they don't have enough memory?"

"Either that," he said, "or this is another generation."

"You mean these are new swarms since noon?"

"Yes."

I looked at my watch. "There's a new generation every three hours?"

Charley shrugged. "I couldn't say. We never found where they reproduce. I'm just guessing."

The possibility that new generations were coming that fast meant that whatever evolutionary mechanism was built into the code was progressing fast, too. Ordinarily, genetic algorithms—which modeled reproduction to arrive at solutions—ordinarily, they ran between 500 and 5,000 generations to arrive at an optimization. If these swarms were reproducing every three hours, it meant they had turned over something like 100 generations in the last two weeks. And with 100 generations, the behavior would be much sharper.

Mae watched them on the monitor and said, "At least they're staying by the main building. It seems like they don't know we're here."

"How would they know?" I said.

"They wouldn't," Charley said. "Their main sensory modality is vision. They may have picked up a little auditory over the generations, but it's still primarily vision. If they don't see it, it doesn't exist for them."

Rosie came over with David. He said, "I'm really sorry, guys."

"No problem."

"It's okay, David."

"I don't know what happened. I just couldn't stand it."

Charley said, "Don't worry, David. We understand. You're a psycho and you cracked. We get the picture. No problem."

Rosie put her arm around David, who blew his nose loudly. She stared at the monitor. "What's happening with them now?" Rosie said.

"They don't seem to know we're here."

"Okay . . ."

"We're hoping it stays that way."

"Uh-huh. And if it doesn't?" Rosie said.

I had been thinking about that. "If it doesn't, we rely on the holes in the PREDPREY assumptions. We exploit the weaknesses in the programming."

"Which means?"

"We flock," I said.

Charley gave a horse laugh. "Yeah, right, we flock—and pray like hell!"

"I'm serious," I said.

Over the last thirty years, scientists had studied predator-prey interactions in everything from the lion to the hyena to the warrior ant. There was now a much better understanding of how prey defended themselves. Animals like zebras and caribou didn't live in herds because they were sociable; herding was a defense against predation. Large numbers of animals provided increased vigilance. And attacking predators were often confused when the herd fled in all directions. Sometimes they literally stopped cold. Show a predator too many moving targets and it often chased none.

The same thing was true of flocking birds and schooling fish—those coordinated group movements made it harder for predators to pick out a single individual. Predators were drawn to attack an animal that was distinctive in some way. That was one reason why they attacked infants so often—not only because they were easier prey, but because they looked different. In the same way, predators killed more males than females because nondominant males tended to hang on the outskirts of the herd, where they were more noticeable.

In fact, thirty years ago when Hans Kruuk studied hyenas in the Serengeti, he found that putting paint on an animal guaranteed it would be killed in the next attack. That was the power of difference.

So the message was simple. Stay together. Stay the same.

That was our best chance.

But I hoped it wouldn't come to that.

The swarms disappeared for a while. They had gone around to the other side of the laboratory building. We waited tensely. Eventually they reappeared. They once again moved along the side of the building, trying openings one after another.

We all watched the monitor. David Brooks was sweating profusely. He wiped his forehead with his sleeve. "How long are they going to keep doing that?"

"As long as they fucking want," Charley said.

Mae said, "At least until the wind kicks up again. And it doesn't look like that's going to happen soon."

"Jesus," David said. "I don't know how you guys can stand it."

He was pale; sweat had dripped from his eyebrows onto his glasses. He looked like he was going to pass out. I said, "David. Do you want to sit down?"

"Maybe I better."

"Okay."

"Come on, David," Rosie said. She took him across the room to the sink, and sat him on the floor. He hugged his knees, put his head down. She put cold water on a paper towel and placed it on the back of his neck. Her gestures were tender.

"That fucking guy," Charley said, shaking his head. "That's all we need right now."

"Charley," Mae said, "you're not helping . . ."

"So what? We're trapped in this fucking shed, it's not fucking airtight, there's nothing we can do, no place we can go, and he's fucking cracking up, makes everything worse."

"Yes," she said quietly, "that's all true. And you're not helping it."

Charley gave her a look, and began to hum the theme from *The Twilight Zone*.

"Charley," I said. "Pay attention." I was watching the swarms. Their behavior had subtly changed. They no longer stayed close to the building. Instead, they now moved in a zigzag pattern away from the wall into the desert, and then back again. They were all doing it, in a kind of fluid dance.

Mae saw it, too. "New behavior . . ."

"Yes," I said. "Their strategy isn't working, so they're trying something else."

"Not going to do shit for them," Charley said. "They can zigzag all they want, it won't open any doors."

Even so, I was fascinated to see this emergent behavior. The zigzags were becoming more exaggerated; the swarms were moving farther and farther away from the buildings. Their strategy was shifting progressively. It was evolving as we watched. "It's really amazing," I said.

"Little fuckers," Charley said.

One of the swarms was now quite close to the rabbit carcass. It approached within a few yards, and swirled away again, heading back to the main building. A thought occurred to me. "How well do the swarms see?"

The headset clicked. It was Ricky. "They see fabulously," he said. "It's what they were made to do, after all. Eyesight's twenty-oh-five," he said. "Fantastic resolution. Better than any human."

I said, "And how do they do the imaging?" Because they were just a series of individual particles. Like the rods and cones in the eye, central processing was required to form a picture from all the inputs. How was that processing accomplished?

Ricky coughed. "Uh . . . not sure."

Charley said, "It showed up in later generations."

"You mean they evolved vision on their own?"

"Yeah."

"And we don't know how they do it . . ."

"No. We just know they just do."

We watched as the swarm angled away from the wall, moved back near the rabbit, then returned to the wall once more. The other swarms were farther down the building, doing the same thing. Swirling out into the desert, then swirling back again.

Over the headset, Ricky said, "Why do you ask?"

"Because."

"You think they'll find the rabbit?"

"I'm not worried about the rabbit," I said. "Anyway, it looks like they already missed it."

"Then what?"

"Uh-oh," Mae said.

"Shit," Charley said, and he gave a long sigh.

We were looking at the nearest swarm, the one that had just bypassed the rabbit. That swarm had moved out into the desert again, perhaps ten yards away from the rabbit. But instead of turning back in its usual pattern, it had paused in the desert. It didn't move, but the silvery column rose and fell.

"Why is it doing that?" I said. "That up and down thing?"

"Something to do with imaging? Focusing?"

"No," I said. "I mean, why did it stop?"

"Program stall?"

I shook my head. "I doubt it."

"Then what?"

"I think it sees something."

"Like what?" Charley said.

I was afraid I knew the answer. The swarm represented an extremely high-resolution camera combined with a distributed intelligence network. And one thing distributed networks did particularly well was detect patterns. That was why distributed network programs were used to recognize faces for security systems, or to assemble the shattered fragments of archaeological pottery. The networks could find patterns in data better than the human eye.

"What patterns?" Charley said, when I told him. "There's nothing out there to detect except sand and cactus thorns."

Mae said, "And footprints."

"What? You mean *our* footprints? From us walking over here? Shit, Mae, the sand's been blowing for the last fifteen minutes. There's no footprints left to find."

We watched the swarm hang there, rising and falling like it was breathing. The cloud had turned mostly black now, with just an occasional glint of silver. It had remained at the same spot for ten or fifteen seconds, pulsing up and down. The other swarms were continuing in their zigzag course, but this one stayed where it was.

Charley bit his lip. "You really think it sees something?"

"I don't know," I said. "Maybe."

Suddenly, the swarm rose up, and began to move again. But it wasn't coming toward us. Instead, it moved on a diagonal over the desert, heading back toward the door in the power building. When it came to the door, it stopped, and swirled in place.

"What the hell?" Charley said.

I knew what it was. So did Mae. "It just tracked us," she said. "Backward."

The swarm had followed the path we had originally taken from the door to the rabbit. The question was, what would it do next?

The next five minutes were tense. The swarm retraced its path, going back to the rabbit. It swirled around the rabbit for a while, moving in slow semicircles back and forth. Then once again it retraced the route back to the power station door. It stayed at the door for a while, then returned to the rabbit.

The swarm repeated this sequence three times. Meanwhile, the other swarms had continued their zigzagging around the building, and were now out of sight. The solitary swarm returned to the door, then headed back to the rabbit again.

"It's stuck in a loop," Charley said. "It just does the same thing over and over again."

"Lucky for us," I said. I was waiting to see if the swarm would modify its behavior. So far it hadn't. And if it had very little memory, then it might be like an Alzheimer's patient, unable to remember it had done all this before.

Now it was going around the rabbit, moving in semicircles.

"Definitely stuck in a loop," Charley said.

I waited.

I hadn't been able to review all the changes they'd made to PRED-PREY, because the central module was missing. But the original program had a randomizing element built into it, to handle situations exactly like this. Whenever PREDPREY failed to attain its goal, and there were no specific environmental inputs to provoke new action, then its behavior was randomly modified. This was a well-known solution. For example, psychologists now believed a certain amount of random behavior was necessary for innovation. You couldn't be creative without striking out in new directions, and those directions were likely to be random—

"Uh-oh," Mae said.

The behavior had changed.

The swarm moved in larger circles, going around and around the rabbit. And almost immediately, it came across another path. It paused a moment, and then suddenly rose up, and began to move directly toward us. It was following exactly the same path we had taken, walking to the shed.

"Shit," Charley said. "I think we're fucked."

Mae and Charley rushed across the room to look out the window. David and Rosie stood and peered out the window above the sink. And I started to shout: "No, no! Get away from the windows!"

"What?"

"It's visual, remember? Get away from the windows!"

There was no good place to hide in the storage room, not really. Rosie and David crawled under the sink. Charley pushed in beside them, ignoring their protests. Mae slipped into the shadows of one corner of the room, easing herself into the space where two shelves didn't quite meet. She could only be seen from the west window, and then not easily.

The radio crackled. "Hey guys?" It was Ricky. "One's heading for you. And uh . . . No . . . two others are joining it."

"Ricky," I said. "Go off air."

"What?"

"No more radio contact."

"Why?"

"Off, Ricky."

I dropped down on my knees behind a cardboard carton of supplies in the main room. The carton wasn't large enough to hide me entirely—my feet stuck out—but like Mae, I wasn't easily seen. Someone outside would have to look at an angle through the north window to see me. In any case, it was the best I could do.

From my crouched position, I could just see the others huddled beneath the sink. I couldn't see Mae at all, unless I really stuck my head around the corner of the carton. When I did, she looked quiet, composed. I ducked back and waited.

I heard nothing but the hum of the air conditioner.

Ten or fifteen seconds passed. I could see the sunlight streaming in through the north window above the sink. It made a white rectangle on the floor to my left.

My headset crackled. "Why no contact?"

"Jesus fucking A," Charley muttered.

I put my finger to my lips, and shook my head.

"Ricky," I said, "don't these things have auditory capacity?"

"Sure, maybe a little, but—"

"Be quiet and stay off."

"But—"

I reached for the transmitter at my belt, and clicked it off. I signaled the others beneath the sink. They each turned their transmitters off.

Charley mouthed something to me. I thought he mouthed, "That fucking guy wants us killed."

But I couldn't be sure.

We waited.

It couldn't have been more than two or three minutes, but it seemed forever. My knees began to hurt on the hard concrete floor. Trying to get more comfortable, I shifted my position cautiously; by now I was sure the first swarm was in our vicinity. It hadn't appeared at the windows yet, and I wondered what was taking so long. Perhaps as it followed our path it had paused to inspect the cars. I wondered what swarm intelligence would make of an automobile. How puzzling it must look to that high-resolution eye. But maybe because the cars were inanimate, the swarm would ignore them as some sort of large, brightly colored boulders.

But still . . . What was taking so long?

My knees hurt more with every passing second. I changed my position, putting weight on my hands and raising my knees like a runner at the blocks. I had a moment of temporary relief. I was so focused on my pain that I didn't notice at first that the glaring white rectangle on the floor was turning darker at the center, and spreading out to the sides. In a moment the entire rectangle turned dull gray.

The swarm was here.

I wasn't certain, but I fancied that beneath the hum of the air conditioner was a deep thrumming sound. From my position behind the crate, I saw the window above the sink grow progressively darker from swirling black particles. It was as if there was a dust storm right outside. Inside the shed it was dark. Surprisingly dark.

Underneath the sink, David Brooks began to moan. Charley clapped his hand over his mouth. They looked upward, even though the sink blocked their view of the window above them.

And then the swarm vanished from the window, as quickly as it had come. Sunlight poured in again.

Nobody moved.

We waited.

Moments later, the window in the west wall turned dark, in the same way. I wondered why the swarm didn't enter. The window wasn't airtight. The nanoparticles could slide through the cracks without difficulty. But they didn't even seem to try.

Perhaps this was an instance where network learning was on our side. Perhaps the swarms had been trained by their experience at the lab to think doors and windows were impermeable. Maybe that's why they weren't trying.

The thought gave me a hopeful feeling that helped counteract the pain in my knees.

The west window was still dark, when the north window over the sink turned dark again. Now two swarms were looking in at the same time. Ricky had said there were three coming toward the building. He hadn't mentioned the fourth. I wondered where the third swarm was. A moment later, I knew.

Like a silent black mist, nanoparticles began to come into the room underneath the west door. Soon more particles entered, all around the door frame. Inside the room, the particles appeared to spin and swirl aimlessly, but I knew they would self-organize in a few moments.

Then at the north window, I saw more particles flooding through the cracks. Through the air-conditioning vents in the ceiling, still more particles rushed downward.

There was no point in waiting any longer. I got to my feet and stepped from my hiding place. I shouted for everybody to come out of hiding. "Form up in two rows!"

Charley grabbed the Windex spray bottle and fell into line, grumbling, "What do you think our fucking chances are?"

"The best they'll ever get," I said. "Reynolds rules! Form up and stay with me! Let's go—now!"

If we weren't so frightened, we might have felt ridiculous, shuffling back and forth across the room in a tight cluster, trying to coordinate our movements—trying to imitate a flock of birds. My heart was pounding in my chest. I heard a roaring sound in my ears. It was hard to focus on our steps. I knew we were awkward, but we got better quickly. When we came to a wall, we wheeled and headed back again, moving in unison. I started swinging my arms and clapping with each step. The others did the same. It helped our coordination. And we each fought our terror. As Mae said later, "It was step aerobics from hell."

And all the time, we watched the black nanoparticles as they came hissing into the room through cracks in doors and windows. It seemed to go on for a long time, but it was probably only thirty or forty seconds. Soon a kind of undifferentiated fog filled the room. I felt pinpricks all over my body, and I was sure the others felt it, too. David started moaning again, but Rosie was right beside him, encouraging him, urging him to keep it together.

Suddenly, with shocking speed the fog cleared, the particles coalescing into two fully formed columns that now stood directly before us, rising and falling in dark ripples.

Seen this close, the swarms exuded an unmistakable sense of menace, almost malevolence. Their deep thrumming sound was clearly audible, but intermittently I heard an angry hiss, like a snake.

But they did not attack us. Just as I had hoped, the programming deficits worked for us. Confronted by a cluster of coordinated prey, these predators were stymied. They did nothing at all.

At least for now.

Between claps, Charley said, "Do you believe—this fucking shit—it's working!"

I said, "Yes but maybe—not for long." I was worried about how long David could control his anxiety. And I was worried about the swarms. I didn't know how long they'd just stand there before they innovated new behavior. I said, "I suggest we—move toward that—back door behind us—and get the hell out."

As we wheeled away from the wall, I angled slightly toward the rear room. Clapping and stepping in unison, our group moved away from the swarms, which thrummed deeply and followed.

"And if we get outside, then what?" David whined. He was having trouble staying in sync with the rest of us. In his panic, he kept stumbling. He was sweating and blinking rapidly.

"We continue this way—flocking this way—back to the lab—and get inside—are you willing to try?"

"Oh jeez," he moaned. "It's so far . . . I don't know if . . ." He stumbled again, nearly lost his balance. And he wasn't clapping with the rest of us. I could almost feel his terror, his overwhelming urge to flee.

"David you stay with us—if you go on your own—you'll never make it—are you listening?"

David moaned, "I don't know . . . Jack . . . I don't know if I can . . ." He stumbled again, bumped into Rosie, who fell against Charley, who caught her and pulled her back to her feet. But our flock was knocked into momentary disarray, our coordination gone.

Immediately, the swarms turned dense black, coiled and tightened, as if ready to spring. I heard Charley whisper "Oh fuck," under his breath, and indeed, for a moment I thought he was right, and that it was all over.

But then we regained our rhythm, and immediately the swarms rose up, returned to normal. Their dense blackness faded. They resumed their steady pulsing. They followed us into the next room. But still they did not attack. We were now about twenty feet from the back door, the same door we had come in. I started to feel optimistic. For the first time, I thought it was possible we really might make it.

And then, in an instant, everything went to hell.

*   *   *

David Brooks bolted.

We were well into the back room, and about to work our way around the freestanding shelves in the center of the room, when he ran straight between the swarms and past them, heading for the far door.

The swarms instantly spun and chased him.

Rosie was screaming for him to come back, but David was focused on the door. The swarms pursued him with surprising speed. David had almost reached the door—his hand was reaching for the doorknob—when one swarm sank low, and spread itself across the floor ahead of him, turning it black.

The moment David Brooks reached the black surface, his feet shot out from under him, as if he had stepped on ice. He howled in pain as he slammed onto the concrete, and immediately tried to scramble to his feet again, but he couldn't get up; he kept slipping and falling, again and again. His eyeglasses shattered; the frames cut his nose. His lips were coated with swirling black residue. He started to have trouble breathing.

Rosie was still screaming as the second swarm descended on David, and the black spread across his face, onto his eyes, into his hair. His movements became increasingly frantic, he moaned pitifully like an animal, yet somehow, as he slid and tumbled on hands and knees, he managed to make his way toward the door. At last he lunged upward, grabbed the doorknob, and managed to pull himself to his knees. With a final desperate movement, he twisted the knob, and kicked the door open as he fell.

Hot sunlight flared into the shed—and the third swarm swirled in from outside.

Rosie cried, "We've got to do something!" I grabbed her arm as she ran past me toward David. She struggled in my grip. "We have to help him! We have to help him!"

"There's nothing we can do."

"We have to help him!"

"Rosie. *There's nothing we can do.*"

David was now rolling on the ground, black from head to toe. The third swarm had enveloped him. It was difficult to see through the dancing particles. It looked as though David's mouth was a dark hole, his eyeballs completely black. I thought he might be blind. His breath came in ragged gasps, with little choking sounds. The swarm was flowing into his mouth like a black river.

His body began to shudder. He clutched at his neck. His feet drummed on the floor. I was sure he was dying.

"Come on, Jack," Charley said. "Let's get the fuck out of here."

"You can't leave him!" Rosie shouted. "You can't, you can't!"

David was sliding out the door, into the sunlight. His movements were less vigorous now; his mouth was moving, but we heard only gasps.

Rosie struggled to get free.

Charley grabbed her shoulder and said, "God damn it, Rosie—"

"Fuck you!" She wrenched free from his grip, she stamped on my foot and in my moment of surprise I let go, and she sprinted across the shed into the next room, shouting "David! *David!*"

His hand, black as a miner's, stretched toward her. She grabbed his wrist. And in the same moment she fell, slipping on the black floor just as he had done. She kept saying his name, until she began to cough, and a black rim appeared on her lips.

Charley said, "Let's go, for Christ's sake. I can't watch."

I felt unable to move my feet, unable to leave. I turned to Mae. Tears were running down her cheeks. She said: "Go."

Rosie was still calling out David's name as she hugged him, pulled his body to her chest. But he didn't seem to be moving on his own anymore.

Charley leaned close to me and said, "*It's not your fucking fault.*"

I nodded slowly. I knew what he was saying was true.

"Hell, this is your first day on the job." Charley reached down to my belt, flicked my headset on. "Let's go."

I turned toward the door behind me.

And we went outside.

DAY 6
4:12 P.M.

Beneath the corrugated roof, the air was hot and still. The line of cars stretched away from us. I heard the whirr of a video camera motor up by the roof. Ricky must have seen us coming out on the monitors. Static hissed in my headset. Ricky said, "What the hell's going on?"

"Nothing good," I said. Beyond the line of shade, the afternoon sun was still bright.

"Where are the others?" Ricky said. "Is everybody okay?"

"No. Everybody is not."

"Well tell me—"

"Not now." In retrospect, we were all numb from what had happened. We didn't have any reaction except to try and get to safety.

The lab building stood across the desert a hundred yards to our right. We could reach the power station door in thirty or forty seconds. We set off toward it at a brisk jog. Ricky was still talking, but we didn't answer him. We were all thinking about the same thing: in another half a minute we would reach the door, and safety.

But we had forgotten the fourth swarm.

"Oh fuck," Charley said.

The fourth swarm swirled out from the side of the lab building, and started straight toward us. We stopped, confused. "What do we do?" Mae said, "Flock?"

"No." I shook my head. "There's only three of us." We were too small a group to confuse a predator. But I couldn't think of any other strategy to try. All the predator-prey studies I had ever read began to play back in my head. Those studies agreed on one thing. Whether you modeled warrior ants or Serengeti lions, the studies confirmed one major dynamic: left to their own devices, predators would kill all the prey until none remained—unless there was a prey refuge. In real life the prey refuge might be a nest in a tree, or an underground den, or a deep pool in a river. If the prey had a refuge, they'd survive. Without a refuge, the predators would kill them all.

"I think we're fucked," Charley said.

We needed a refuge. The swarm was bearing down on us. I could almost feel the pinpricks on my skin, and taste the dry ashen taste in my mouth. We had to find some kind of shelter before the swarm reached us. I turned full circle, looking in all directions, but there was nothing I could see, except—

"Are the cars locked?"

My headset crackled. "No, they shouldn't be."

We turned and ran.

The nearest car was a blue Ford sedan. I opened the driver's door, and Mae opened the passenger side. The swarm was right behind us. I could hear the thrumming sound as I slammed the door shut, as Mae slammed hers. Charley, still holding the Windex spray, was trying to open the rear passenger door, but it was locked. Mae twisted in the seat to unlock the door, but Charley had already turned to the next car, a Land Cruiser, and climbed inside. And slammed the door.

"Yow!" he said. "Fucking hot!"

"I know," I said. The inside of the car was like an oven. Mae and I were both sweating. The swarm rushed toward us, and swirled over the front windshield, pulsating, shifting back and forth.

Over the headset, a panicked Ricky said, "Guys? Where are you? Guys?"

"We're in the cars."

"Which cars?"

"What fucking difference does it make?" Charley said. "We're in two of the fucking cars, Ricky."

The black swarm moved away from our sedan over to the Toyota. We watched as it slid from one window to another, trying to get in. Charley grinned at me through the glass. "It's not like the shed. These cars are airtight. So . . . fuck 'em."

"What about the air vents?" I said.

"I shut mine."

"But they aren't airtight, are they?"

"No," he said. "But you'd have to go under the hood to begin to get in. Or maybe through the trunk. And I'm betting this overbred buzzball can't figure that out."

Inside our car, Mae was snapping closed the dashboard air ducts one after another. She opened the glove compartment, glanced inside, shut it again.

I said, "You find any keys?"

She shook her head, no.

Over the headset, Ricky said, "Guys? You got more company."

I turned to see two additional swarms coming around the shed. They immediately swirled over our car, front and back. I felt like we were in a dust storm. I looked at Mae. She was sitting very still, stony-faced, just watching.

The two new clouds finished circling the car, then came to the front. One was positioned just outside Mae's passenger door window. It pulsed, glinting silver. The other was on the hood of the car, moving back and forth from Mae to me. From time to time, it would rush the windshield, and disperse itself over the glass. Then it would coalesce again, back away down the hood, and rush again.

Charley cackled gleefully. "Trying to get in. I told you: they can't do it."

I wasn't so sure. I noticed that with each charge, the swarm would move farther back down the hood, taking a longer run. Soon it would back itself up to the front grill. And if it started inspecting the grill, it could find the opening to the air vents. And then it would be over.

Mae was rummaging in the utility compartment between the seats.

She came up with a roll of tape and a box of plastic sandwich baggies. She said, "Maybe we can tape the vents . . ."

I shook my head. "There's no point," I said. "They're nanoparticles. They're small enough to pass right through a membrane."

"You mean they'd come *through* the plastic?"

"Or around, through small cracks. You can't seal it well enough to keep them out."

"Then we just sit here?"

"Basically, yes."

"And hope they don't figure it out."

I nodded. "That's right."

Over the headset, Bobby Lembeck said, "Wind's starting to pick up again. Six knots."

It sounded like he was trying to be encouraging, but six knots wasn't anywhere near enough force. The swarms outside the windshield moved effortlessly around the car.

Charley said, "Jack? I just lost my buzzball. Where is it?"

I looked over at Charley's car, and saw that the third swarm had slid down to the front tire well, where it was swirling in circles and moving in and out through the holes in the hubcap.

"Checking your hubcaps, Charley," I said.

"Umm." He sounded unhappy, and with good reason. If the swarm started exploring the car thoroughly, it might stumble on a way in. He said, "I guess the question is, how big is their SO component, really?"

"That's right," I said.

Mae said, "In English?"

I explained. The swarms had no leader, and no central intelligence. Their intelligence was the sum of the individual particles. Those particles self-organized into a swarm, and their self-organizing tendency had unpredictable results. You really didn't know what they would do. The swarms might continue to be ineffective, as they were now. They might come upon the solution by chance. Or they might start searching in an organized way.

But they hadn't done that so far.

My clothes were heavy, soaked in sweat. Sweat was dripping from my nose and chin. I wiped my forehead with the back of my arm. I looked at Mae. She was sweating, too.

Ricky said, "Hey, Jack?"

"What."

"Julia called a while ago. She's checked out of the hospital and—"

"Not now, Ricky."

"She's coming out here tonight."

"We'll talk later, Ricky."

"I just thought you'd want to know."

"Jesus," Charley said, exploding. "Someone tell this asshole to shut up. We're *busy*!"

Bobby Lembeck said, "Eight knots of wind now. No, sorry . . . seven."

Charley said, "Jesus, the suspense is killing me. Where's my swarm now, Jack?"

"Under the car. I can't see what it's doing . . . No, wait . . . It's coming up behind you, Charley. Looks like it's checking out your taillights."

"Some kind of car freak," he said. "Well, it can check away."

I was looking over my shoulder at Charley's swarm when Mae said, "Jack. *Look*."

The swarm outside her window on the passenger side had changed. It was almost entirely silver now, shimmering but pretty stable, and on this silver surface I saw Mae's head and shoulders reflected back. The reflection wasn't perfect, because her eyes and mouth were slightly blurred, but basically it was accurate.

I frowned. "It's a mirror . . ."

"No," she said. "It's not." She turned away from the window to look at me. Her image on the silver surface did not change. The face continued to stare into the car. Then, after a moment or two, the image shivered, dissolved and re-formed to show the back of her head.

"What does that mean?" Mae said.

"I've got a pretty good idea, but—"

The swarm on the front hood was doing the same thing, except that its silver surface showed the two of us sitting side by side in the car, looking very frightened. Again, the image was somewhat blurred. And now it was clear to me that the swarm was not a literal mirror. The swarm itself was generating the image by the precise positioning of individual particles, which meant—

"Bad news," Charley said.

"I know," I said. "They're innovating."

"What do you figure, is it one of the presets?"

"Basically, yes. I assume it's imitation."

Mae shook her head, not understanding.

"The program presets certain strategies to help attain goals. The strategies model what real predators do. So one preset strategy is to freeze where you are and wait, to ambush. Another is to random-walk until you stumble on your prey, and then pursue. A third is to camouflage yourself by taking on some element of the environment, so you blend in. And a fourth is to mimic the prey's behavior—to imitate it."

She said, "You think this is imitation?"

"I think this is a form of imitation, yes."

"It's trying to make itself appear like us?"

"Yes."

"This is emergent behavior? It's evolved on its own?"

"Yes," I said.

"Bad news," Charley said mournfully. "Bad, bad news."

Sitting in the car, I started to get angry. Because what the mirror imaging meant to me was that I didn't know the real structure of the nanoparticles. I'd been told there was a piezo wafer that would reflect light. So it wasn't surprising that the swarm occasionally flashed silver in the sun. That didn't call for sophisticated orientation of the particles. In fact, you would expect that sort of silvery ripple as a random effect, just the way heavily trafficked highways will clog up and then flow freely again. The congestion was caused by random speed changes from one or two motorists, but the effect rippled down the entire highway. The same would be true of the swarms. A chance effect would pass like a wave down the swarm. And that's what we had seen.

But this mirroring behavior was something entirely different. The swarms were now producing images in color, and holding them fairly stable. Such complexity wasn't possible from the simple nanoparticle I'd been shown. I doubted you could generate a full spectrum from a silver layer. It was theoretically possible that the silver could be precisely tilted to produce prismatic colors, but that implied enormous sophistication of movement.

It was more logical to imagine that the particles had another method to create colors. And that meant I hadn't been told the truth about the particles, either. Ricky had lied to me yet again. So I was angry.

I had already concluded something was wrong with Ricky, and in retrospect, the problem lay with me, not him. Even after the debacle in the storage shed, I still failed to grasp that the swarms were evolving faster than our ability to keep pace with them. I should have realized what I was up against when the swarms demonstrated a new strategy—making the floor slippery to disable their prey, and to move them. Among ants, that would be called collective transport; the phenomenon was well known. But for these swarms, it was unprecedented, newly evolved behavior. Yet at the time I was too horrified to recognize its true significance. Now, sitting in the hot car, it wasn't useful to blame Ricky, but I was scared, and tired, and I wasn't thinking clearly.

"Jack." Mae nudged my shoulder, and pointed to Charley's car.

Her face was grim.

The swarm by the taillight of Charley's car was now a black stream that curved high in the air, and then disappeared in the seam where the red plastic joined the metal.

Over the headset I said, "Hey, Charley . . . I think it's found a way."

"Yeah, I see it. Fuck a duck."

Charley was scrambling into the backseat. Already particles were beginning to fill the inside of the car, making a gray fog that rapidly darkened. Charley coughed. I couldn't see what he was doing, he was down below the window. He coughed again.

"Charley?"

He didn't answer. But I heard him swearing.

"Charley, you better get out."

"Fuck these guys."

And then there was an odd sound, which at first I couldn't place. I turned to Mae, who was pressing her headset to her ear. It was a strange, rhythmic rasping. She looked at me questioningly.

"Charley?"

"I'm—spray these little bastards. Let's see how they do when they're wet."

Mae said, "You're spraying the isotope?"

He didn't answer. But a moment later he appeared in the window again, spraying in all directions with the Windex bottle. Liquid streaked across the glass, and dripped down. The interior of the car was growing darker as more and more particles entered. Soon we couldn't see him at all. His hand emerged from the black, pressed against the glass, then disappeared again. He was coughing continuously. A dry cough.

"Charley," I said, "run for it."

"Ah fuck. What's the point?"

Bobby Lembeck said, "Wind's ten knots. Go for it."

Ten knots wasn't enough but it was better than nothing.

"Charley? You hear?"

We heard his voice from the black interior. "Yeah, okay . . . I'm looking—can't find—fucking door handle, can't feel . . . Where's the goddamn door handle on this—" He broke into a spasm of coughing.

Over the headset, I heard voices inside the lab, all speaking rapidly. Ricky said, "He's in the Toyota. Where's the handle in the Toyota?"

Bobby Lembeck: "I don't know, it's not my car."

"Whose car is it? Vince?"

Vince: "No, no. It's that guy with the bad eyes."

"Who?"

"The engineer. The guy who blinks all the time."

"David Brooks?"

"Yeah. Him."

Ricky said, "Guys? We think it's David's car."

I said, "That's not going to do us any—"

And then I broke off, because Mae was pointing behind her to the backseat of our car. From the seam where the seat cushion met the back, particles were hissing into the car like black smoke.

I looked closer, and saw a blanket on the floor of the backseat. Mae saw it, too, and threw herself bodily into the back, diving between the seats. She kicked me in the head as she went, but she had the blanket and began stuffing it into the crack. My headset came off, and caught on the steering wheel as I tried to climb back to help her. It was cramped in the car. I heard a tinny voice from the earpieces.

"Come on," Mae said. "Come on."

I was bigger than she was; there wasn't room for me back there; my body jackknifed over the driver's seat as I grabbed the blanket and helped her stuff it.

I was vaguely aware that the passenger door banged open on the Toyota, and I saw Charley's foot emerge from the black. He was going to try his luck outside. Maybe we should, too, I thought, as I helped her with the blanket. The blanket wouldn't do any good, it was just a delaying tactic. Already I sensed the particles were sifting right through the cloth; the car was continuing to fill. The air was getting darker and darker. I felt the pinpricks all over my skin.

"Mae, let's run."

She didn't answer, she just kept pushing the blanket harder into the cracks. Probably she knew we'd never make it if we went outside. The swarms would run us down, get in our path, make us slip and fall. And once we fell, they would suffocate us. Just as they did to the others.

The air was thicker. I started to cough. In the semidarkness I kept hearing a tinny voice from the headsets. I couldn't tell where it was coming from. Mae's headset had fallen off, too, and I thought I had seen it on the front seat, but now it was becoming too dark to see. My eyes burned. I coughed continuously. Mae was coughing, too. I didn't know if she was still stuffing the blanket. She was just a shadow in the fog.

I squeezed my eyes against the sharp pain. My throat was tightening, and my cough was dry. I felt dizzy again. I knew we couldn't survive more than a minute or so, perhaps less. I looked back at Mae, but couldn't see her. I heard her coughing. I waved my hand, trying to clear the fog so I could see her. It didn't work. I waved my hand in front of the windshield, and it cleared momentarily.

Despite my fit of coughing, I saw the lab in the distance. The sun was shining. Everything looked normal. It was infuriating that it should appear so normal and peaceful while we coughed ourselves to death. I couldn't see what happened to Charley. He wasn't in front of me anywhere. In fact— I waved my hand again—all I saw was—

Blowing sand.

Jesus, *blowing sand*.

The wind was back up.

"Mae." I coughed. "Mae. The door."

I don't know if she heard me. She was coughing hard. I reached for the driver's side door, fumbling for the handle. I felt confused and disoriented. I was coughing continuously. I touched hot metal, jerked it down.

The door swung open beside me. Hot desert air rushed in, swirling the fog. The wind had definitely come up. "Mae."

She was racked with coughing. Perhaps she couldn't move. I lunged for the passenger door opposite me. My ribs banged on the gearshift. The fog was thinner now, and I saw the handle, twisted it, and shoved the door open. It banged shut in the wind. I pushed forward, twisted, shoved it open again, holding it open with my hand.

Wind blew through the car.

The black cloud vanished in a few seconds. The backseat was still dark. I crawled forward, out the passenger door, and opened the back door. She reached to me, and I hauled her out. We were both coughing hard. Her legs buckled. I threw her arm over my shoulder and half carried her out into the open desert.

Even now, I don't know how I made it back to the laboratory building. The swarms had vanished; the wind was blowing hard. Mae was a dead weight on my shoulders, her body limp, her feet dragging over the sand. I had no energy. I was racked with spasms of coughing, which often forced me to stop. I couldn't get my breath. I was dizzy, disoriented. The glare of the sun had a greenish tinge and I saw spots before my eyes. Mae was coughing weakly; her breaths shallow. I had the feeling she wouldn't survive. I trudged on, putting one foot ahead of the other.

Somehow the door loomed in front of me, and I got it open. I brought Mae into the black outer room. On the other side of the glass airlock, Ricky and Bobby Lembeck were waiting. They were cheering us on, but I couldn't hear them. My headset was back in the car.

The airlock doors hissed open, and I got Mae inside. She managed to stand, though she was doubled over coughing. I stepped away. The wind began to blow her clean. I leaned against the wall, out of breath, dizzy.

I thought, Haven't I done this before?

I looked at my watch. It was just three hours since I had narrowly escaped the last attack. I bent over and put my hands on my knees. I stared at the floor and waited for the airlock to become free. I glanced over at Ricky and Bobby. They were yelling, pointing to their ears. I shook my head.

Couldn't they see I didn't have a headset?

I said, "Where's Charley?"

They answered, but I couldn't hear them.

"Did he make it? Where's Charley?"

I winced at a harsh electronic squeal, and then over the intercom Ricky said, "—not much you can do."

"Is he here?" I said. "Did he make it?"

"No."

"Where is he?"

"Back at the car," Ricky said. "He never got out of the car. Didn't you know?"

"I was busy," I said. "So he's back there?"

"Yeah."

"Is he dead?"

"No, no. He's alive."

I was still breathing hard, still dizzy. "What?"

"It's hard to tell on the video monitor, but it looks like he is alive . . ."

"Then why the fuck don't you guys go get him?"

Ricky's voice was calm. "We can't, Jack. We have to take care of Mae."

"Someone here could go."

"We don't have anyone to spare."

"I can't go," I said. "I'm in no shape to go."

"Of course not," Ricky said, turning on his soothing voice. The undertaker's voice. "All this must be a terrible shock to you, Jack, all you've gone through—"

"Just . . . tell me . . . who's going to get him, Ricky?"

"To be brutally honest," Ricky said, "I don't think there's any point. He had a convulsion. A bad one. I don't think he has much left."

I said, "Nobody's going?"

"I'm afraid there's no point, Jack."

Inside the airlock, Bobby was helping Mae out and leading her down the corridor. Ricky was standing there. Watching me through the glass.

"Your turn, Jack. Come on in."

I didn't move. I stayed leaning against the wall. I said, "Somebody has to go get him."

"Not right now. The wind isn't stable, Jack. It'll fall again any minute."

"But he's alive."

"Not for long."

"Somebody has to go," I said.

"Jack, you know as well as I do what we're up against," Ricky said. He was doing the voice of reason now, calm and logical. "We've had terrible losses. We can't risk anybody else. By the time somebody gets to Charley, he'll be dead. He may be dead already. Come on and get in the airlock."

I was taking stock of my body, feeling my breathing, my chest, my deep fatigue. I couldn't go back out right now. Not in the condition I was in.

So I got into the airlock.

*   *   *

With a roar, the blowers flattened my hair, fluttered my clothes, and cleaned the black particles from my clothes and skin. My vision improved almost immediately. I breathed easier. Now they were blowing upward. I held out my hand and saw it turn from black to pale gray, then to normal flesh color again.

Now the blowers came from the sides. I took a deep breath. The pinpricks were no longer so painful on my skin. Either I was feeling them less, or they were being blown off my skin. My head cleared a little. I took another breath. I didn't feel good. But I felt better.

The glass doors opened. Ricky held out his arms. "Jack. Thank God you're safe."

I didn't answer him. I just turned around, and went back the way I had come.

"Jack . . ."

The glass doors whished shut, and locked with a thunk. "I'm not leaving him out there," I said.

"What're you going to do? You can't carry him, he's too big. What're you going to do?"

"I don't know. But I'm not leaving him behind, Ricky."

And I went back outside.

Of course I was doing exactly what Ricky wanted—exactly what he expected me to do—but I didn't realize it at the time. And even if somebody had told me, I wouldn't have credited Ricky with that degree of psychological sophistication. Ricky was pretty obvious in the way he managed people. But this time, he got me.

DAY 6
4:22 P.M.

The wind was blowing briskly. There was no sign of the swarms, and I crossed to the shed without incident. I didn't have a headset so I was spared Ricky's commentary.

The back passenger door of the Toyota was open. I found Charley lying on his back, motionless. It took me a moment to see he was still breathing, although shallowly. With an effort, I managed to pull him into a sitting position. He stared at me with dull eyes. His lips were blue and his skin was chalky gray. A tear ran down his cheek. His mouth moved.

"Don't try to talk," I said. "Save your energy." Grunting, I pulled him over to the edge of the seat, by the door, and swung his legs around so he was facing out. Charley was a big guy, six feet tall and at least twenty pounds heavier than I was. I knew I couldn't carry him back. But behind the backseat of the Toyota I saw the fat tires of a dirt bike. That might work.

"Charley, can you hear me?"

An almost imperceptible nod.

"Can you stand up?"

Nothing. No reaction. He wasn't looking at me; he was staring into space.

"Charley," I said, "do you think you can stand?"

He nodded again, then straightened his body so he slid off the seat, and landed on the ground. He stood shakily for a moment, his legs trembling, and then he collapsed against me, clutching me to hold himself up. I sagged under his weight.

"Okay, Charley . . ." I eased him back to the car, and sat him down on the running board. "Just stay there, okay?"

I let go of him, and he remained sitting. He still stared into space, unfocused.

"I'll be right back."

I went around to the back of the Land Cruiser, and popped the trunk. There was a dirt bike, all right—the cleanest dirt bike I had ever seen. It was encased in a heavy Mylar bag. And it had been wiped down after it was used. That would be David's way, I thought. He was always so clean, so organized.

I pulled the bike out of the car and set it on the ground. There was no key in the ignition. I went to the front of the Toyota, and opened the passenger door. The front seats were spotless and carefully ordered. David had one of those suction cup notepads on the dashboard, a cradle for his cell phone, and a telephone headset mounted on a little hook. I opened his glove box and saw that the interior was neatly arranged, too. Registration papers in an envelope, beneath a small plastic tray divided into compartments containing lip balm, Kleenex, Band-Aids. No keys. Then I noticed that between the seats there was a storage box for the CD player, and beneath it was a locked tray. It had the same kind of lock as the ignition. It probably opened with the ignition key.

I banged the tray with the heel of my hand, and heard something metallic rattle inside. It might have been a small key. Like a dirt bike key. Anyway, something metal.

Where were David's keys? I wondered if Vince had taken David's keys away on arrival, as he had taken mine. If so, then the keys were in the lab. That wouldn't do me any good.

I looked toward the lab building, wondering if I should go back to get them. That was when I noticed that the wind was blowing less strongly. There was still a layer of sand blowing along the ground, but it was less vigorous.

Great, I thought. That's all I need now.

Feeling new urgency, I decided to give up on the dirt bike and its missing key. Perhaps there was something in the storage shed that I could use
to move Charley back to the lab. I didn't remember anything, but I went
into the shed to check, anyway. I entered cautiously, hearing a banging
sound. It turned out to be the far door, banging open and shut in the
wind. Rosie's body lay just inside the door, alternately light and dark as the
door banged. She had the same milky coating on her skin that the rabbit
had had. But I didn't go over to look closely. I hastily searched the shelves,
opened the utility closet, looked behind stacked boxes. I found a furniture
dolly made of wooden slats with small rollers. But it would be useless in
sand.

I went back outside under the corrugated shed, and hurried to the
Toyota. There was nothing to do but try to carry Charley across to the
lab building. I might be able to manage it if he could support part of his
own weight. Maybe by now he was feeling better, I thought. Maybe he
was stronger.

But one look at his face told me he wasn't. If anything, he appeared
weaker.

"Shit, Charley, what am I going to do with you?"

He didn't answer.

"I can't carry you. And David didn't leave any keys in his car, so we're
out of luck—"

I stopped.

What if David were locked out of his car? He was an engineer, he
thought of contingencies like that. Even if it was unlikely to happen,
David would never be caught unprepared. He'd never be flagging down
cars asking if they had a wire hanger he could borrow. No, no.

David would have hidden a key. Probably in one of those magnetic
key boxes. I started to lie down on my back to look underneath the car
when it occurred to me that David would never get his clothes dirty just
to retrieve a key. He'd hide it cleverly, but within easy reach.

With that in mind, I ran my fingers along the inside of the front
bumpers. Nothing. I went to the back bumper, did the same. Nothing.
I felt under the running boards on both sides of the car. Nothing. No

magnetic box, no key. I couldn't believe it, so I got down and looked under the car, to see if there was a brace or a strut I had somehow missed with my fingers.

No, there wasn't. I felt no key.

I shook my head, puzzled. The hiding place needed to be steel for the magnetic box. And it needed to be protected from the elements. That was why almost everybody hid their keys inside the car bumpers.

David hadn't done that.

Where else could you hide a key?

I walked around the car again, looking at the smooth lines of the metal. I ran my fingers around the front grill opening, and under the back license plate indentation.

No key.

I started to sweat. It wasn't only the tension: by now I could definitely feel the drop in the wind. I went back to Charley, who was still sitting on the sideboard.

"How you doing, Charley?"

He didn't answer, just gave a little shrug. I took his headset off, and put it on. I heard static, and voices talking softly. It sounded like Ricky and Bobby, and it sounded like an argument. I pulled the mouthpiece near my lips and said, "Guys? Speak to me."

A pause. Bobby, surprised: "Jack?"

"That's right . . ."

"Jack, you can't stay there. The wind's been falling steadily for the last few minutes. It's only ten knots now."

"Okay . . ."

"Jack, you've got to come back in."

"I can't just yet."

"Below seven knots, the swarms can move."

"Okay . . ."

Ricky: "What do you mean, okay? Jesus, Jack, are you coming in or not?"

"I can't carry Charley."

"You knew that when you went out."

"Uh-huh."

"Jack. What the hell are you doing?"

I heard the whirr of the video monitor in the corner of the shed. I looked over the roof of the car and saw the lens rotate as they zoomed in on me. The Toyota was such a big car, it almost blocked my view of the camera. And the ski rack on top made it even higher. I vaguely wondered why David had a ski rack, because he didn't ski; he always hated cold. The rack must have come with the car as standard equipment and—

I swore. It was so obvious.

There was only one place I hadn't checked. I jumped up on the running board and looked at the roof of the car. I ran my fingers over the ski rack, and along the parallel tracks bolted to the roof. My fingers touched black tape against the black rack. I pulled the tape away, and saw a silver key.

"Jack? Nine knots."

"Okay."

I dropped back down to the ground, and climbed in the driver's seat. I put the key in the lock box and twisted it. The box opened. Inside I found a small yellow key.

"Jack? What're you doing?"

I hurried around to the back of the car. I fitted the yellow key in the ignition. I straddled the bike and started it up. The motor rumbled loudly under the corrugated shed.

"Jack?"

I walked the bike around the side of the car to where Charley was sitting. That was going to be the tricky part. The bike didn't have a kickstand; I moved as close to Charley as I could and then tried to support him enough that he could climb onto the backseat while I still sat on the bike and kept it upright. Fortunately, he seemed to understand what I was doing; I got him in place and told him to hold on to me.

Bobby Lembeck: "Jack? They're here."

"Where?"

"South side. Coming toward you."

"Okay."

I gunned the motor, and pulled the passenger door shut. And I stayed exactly where I was.

"Jack?"

Ricky: "What's the matter with him? He knows what the danger is."

Bobby: "I know."

"He's just sitting there."

Charley had his hands around my waist. His head was on my shoulder. I could hear his raspy breathing. I said, "Hold tight, Charley." He nodded.

Ricky: "Jack? What're you doing?"

Then at my ear, in a voice just above a whisper, Charley said, "Fucking idiot."

"Yes." I nodded. I waited. I could see the swarms now, coming around the building. This time there were nine swarms, and they headed straight for me in a V formation. Their own flocking behavior.

Nine swarms, I thought. Soon there would be thirty swarms, and then two hundred . . .

Bobby: "Jack, do you see them?"

"I see them." Of course I saw them.

And of course they were different from before. They were denser now, the columns thicker and more substantial. Those swarms didn't weigh three pounds anymore. I sensed they were closer to ten or twenty pounds. Maybe even more than that. Maybe thirty pounds. They would have real weight now, and real substance.

I waited. I stayed where I was. Some detached part of my brain was wondering what the formation would do when it reached me. Would they circle me? Would some of the swarms hang back and wait? What did they make of the noisy bike?

Nothing—they came right for me, flattening the V into a line, then into a kind of inverted V. I could hear the deep vibrating hum. With so many swarms it was much louder.

The swirling columns were twenty yards away from me, then ten. Were they able to move faster now, or was it my imagination? I waited until they were almost upon me before I twisted the throttle and raced forward. I passed straight through the lead swarm, into the blackness and out again, and then I was gunning for the power station door, bouncing over the desert, not daring to look back over my shoulder. It was a wild ride, and it only lasted a few seconds. As we reached the power station, I dropped the bike, put my shoulder under Charley's arm, and staggered the final step or two to the door.

The swarms were still fifty yards away from the door when I managed to turn the knob, pull, get one foot in the crack, and kick the door open the rest of the way. When I did that I lost my balance, and Charley and I more or less fell through the door onto the concrete. The door came swinging shut, and whanged into our legs, which hung outside. I felt a sharp pain in my ankles—but worse, the door was still open, kept ajar by our legs. Through the opening I could see the swarms approaching.

I scrambled to my feet and dragged Charley's inert body into the room. The door shut, but I knew it was a fire door, and it wasn't airtight. Nanoparticles could come right in. I had to get both of us into the airlock. We wouldn't be safe until the first set of glass doors had hissed shut.

Grunting and sweating, I hauled Charley into the airlock. I got him into a sitting position, propped up against the side blowers. That cleared his feet of the glass doors. And because only one person could be in the airlock at a time, I stepped back outside. And I waited for the doors to close.

But they didn't close.

I looked on the side wall for some sort of button, but I didn't see anything. The lights were on inside the airlock, so it was getting power. But the doors didn't close.

And I knew the swarms were fast approaching.

Bobby Lembeck and Mae came running into the far room. I saw them through the second set of glass doors. They were waving their arms, making big gestures, apparently indicating for me to come back into the airlock. But that didn't make sense. Into my headset, I said, "I thought you had to go one at a time."

They didn't have headsets, and couldn't hear me. They were waving frantically, come in, come in.

I held up two fingers questioningly.

They shook their heads. They seemed to be indicating I was missing the point.

At my feet, I saw the nanoparticles begin to come into the room like black steam. They were coming through the edges of the fire door. I had only five or ten seconds now.

I stepped back in the airlock. Bobby and Mae were nodding, approving. But the doors did not close. Now they were making other gestures, lifting.

"You want me to lift Charley?"

They did. I shook my head. Charley was slumped there in a sitting position, a dead weight on the ground. I looked back at the anteroom, and saw it was filling with black particles, starting to form a grayish mist in the air. The grayish mist was coming into the airlock as well. I felt the first tiny pinpricks on my skin.

I looked at Bobby and Mae, on the other side of the glass. They could see what was happening; they knew only seconds remained. They were again making gestures: lift Charley up. I bent over him, got my hands under his armpits. I tried to haul him to his feet, but he didn't budge.

"Charley, for God's sake, help." Groaning, I tried again. Charley kicked his legs and pushed with his arms and I got him a couple of feet off the ground. Then he slid back down. "Charley, come on, once more . . ." I pulled up as hard as I could, and this time he helped a lot and we got his legs back under him and with a final heave, got him standing. I kept my hands under his armpits; we were in a kind of crazy lovers' clench. Charley was wheezing. I looked back to the glass doors.

The doors didn't close.

The air was getting blacker all the time. I looked to Mae and Bobby, and they were frantic, holding up two fingers, shaking them at me. I didn't get it. "Yes, there's two of us . . ." What was wrong with the damned doors? Finally Mae bent over, and very deliberately pointed with one finger of each hand to her two shoes. I saw her mouth, "Two shoes." And point to Charley.

"Yeah, so, we have two shoes. He's standing on two shoes."

Mae shook her head.

She held up four fingers.

"Four shoes?"

The pinpricks were irritating, making it difficult to think. I felt the old confusion begin to seep over me. My brain felt sluggish. What did she mean, four shoes?

It was beginning to get dark in the airlock. It was becoming harder to see Mae and Bobby. They were pantomiming something else, but I didn't get it. They began to feel distant to me, distant and trivial. I was without energy, and without care.

Two shoes, four shoes.

And then I got it. I turned my back to Charley, leaned against him, and said, "Put your hands around my neck." He did, and I grabbed his legs and lifted his feet off the floor.

Instantly, the door hissed shut.

That was it, I thought.

The blowers began to blast down on us. The air rapidly cleared. I strained to hold Charley up and I managed until I saw the second set of doors unlock and slide open. Mae and Bobby hurried into the airlock.

And I just fell down. Charley landed on top of me. I think it was Bobby who dragged him off me. I'm not sure. From that point on, I don't remember much at all.

NEST

DAY 6
6:18 P.M.

I woke up in my bed in the residential module. The air handlers were roaring so loudly the room sounded like an airport. Bleary-eyed, I staggered over to the door. The door was locked.

I pounded on it for a while but nobody answered, even when I yelled. I went to the little workstation on the desk and clicked it on. A menu came up and I searched for some kind of intercom. I didn't see anything like that, although I poked around the interface for a while. I must have set something off, because a window opened and Ricky appeared, smiling at me. He said, "So, you're awake. How do you feel?"

"Unlock the goddamn door."

"Is your door locked?"

"Unlock it, damn it."

"It was only for your own protection."

"Ricky," I said, "open the damn door."

"I already did. It's open, Jack."

I walked to the door. He was right, it opened immediately. I looked at the latch. There was an extra bolt, some kind of remote locking mechanism. I'd have to remember to tape over that.

On the monitor, Ricky said, "You might want to take a shower."

"Yeah, I would. Why is the air so loud?"

"We turned on full venting in your room," Ricky said. "In case there were any extra particles."

I rummaged in my bag for clothes. "Where's the shower?"

"Do you want some help?"

"No, I do not want some help. Just tell me where the goddamn shower is."

"You sound angry."

"Fuck you, Ricky."

The shower helped. I stood under it for about twenty minutes, letting the steaming hot water run over my aching body. I seemed to have a lot of bruises—on my chest, my thigh—but I couldn't remember how I had gotten them.

When I came out, I found Ricky there, sitting on a bench. "Jack, I'm very concerned."

"How's Charley?"

"He seems to be okay. He's sleeping."

"Did you lock his room, too?"

"Jack. I know you've been through an ordeal, and I want you to know we're all very grateful for what you've done—I mean, the company is grateful, and—"

"Fuck the company."

"Jack, I understand how you might be angry."

"Cut the crap, Ricky. I got no goddamn help at all. Not from you, and not from anybody else in this place."

"I'm sure it must feel that way . . ."

"It *is* that way, Ricky. No help is no help."

"Jack, Jack. Please. I'm trying to tell you that I'm sorry for everything that happened. I feel terrible about it. I really do. If there were any way to go back and change it, believe me, I would."

I looked at him. "I don't believe you, Ricky."

He gave a winning little smile. "I hope in time that will change."

"It won't."

"You know that I always valued our friendship, Jack. It was always the most important thing to me."

I just stared at him. Ricky wasn't listening at all. He just had that silly smile-and-everything-will-be-fine look on his face. I thought, Is he on drugs? He was certainly acting bizarrely.

"Well, anyway." He took a breath, changed the subject. "Julia's coming out, that's good news. She should be here sometime this evening."

"Uh-huh. Why is she coming out?"

"Well, I'm sure because she's worried about these runaway swarms."

"How worried is she?" I said. "Because these swarms could have been killed off weeks ago, when the evolutionary patterns first appeared. But that didn't happen."

"Yes. Well. The thing is, back then nobody really understood—"

"I think they did."

"Well, no." He managed to appear unjustly accused, and slightly offended. But I was getting tired of his game.

"Ricky," I said, "I came out here on the helicopter with a bunch of PR guys. Who notified them there's a PR problem here?"

"I don't know about any PR guys."

"They'd been told not to get out of the helicopter. That it was dangerous here."

He shook his head. "I have no idea . . . I don't know what you're talking about."

I threw up my hands, and walked out of the bathroom.

"I don't!" Ricky called after me, protesting. "I swear, I don't know a thing about it!"

Half an hour later, as a kind of peace offering, Ricky brought me the missing code I had been asking for. It was brief, just a sheet of paper.

"Sorry about that," he said. "Took me a while to find it. Rosie took a whole subdirectory offline a few days ago to work on one section. I guess she forgot to put it back. That's why it wasn't in the main directory."

"Uh-huh." I scanned the sheet. "What was she working on?"

Ricky shrugged. "Beats me. One of the other files."

```
/*Mod Compstat_do*/
Exec (move{Ø ij (Cx1, Cy1, Cz1)} )/*init */
{∂ij (x1, y1, z1)} /*state*/
{∂ikl (x1,y1,z1) (x2,y2,z2) } /*track*/
Push {z(i)} /*store*/
React <advan> /*ref state*/
        ß1 {(dx(i, j, k)} {(place(Cj,Hj)}
        ß2 {(fx,(a,q)}
Place {z(q)} /*store*/
Intent <advan> /*ref intent*/
        ßijk {(dx(i, j, k)} {(place(Cj,Hj)}
        ßx {(fx,(a,q)}
Load {z(i)} /*store*/
Exec (move{Ø ij (Cx1, Cy1, Cz1)} )
Exec (pre{Ø ij (Hx1, Hy1, Hz1)} )
Exec (post{Ø ij (Hx1, Hy1, Hz1)} )
Push {∂ij (x1, y1, z1)}
        {∂ikl (x1,y1,z1) move (x2,y2,z2) } /*track*/
{0,1,0,01)
```

"Ricky," I said, "this code looks almost the same as the original."

"Yeah, I think so. The changes are all minor. I don't know why it's such an issue." He shrugged. "I mean, as soon as we lost control of the swarm, the precise code seemed a little beside the point to me. You couldn't change it, anyway."

"And how did you lose control? There's no evolutionary algorithm in this code here."

He spread his hands. "Jack," he said, "if we knew that, we'd know everything. We wouldn't be in this mess."

"But I was asked to come here and check problems with the code my team had written, Ricky. I was told the agents were losing track of their goals . . ."

"I'd say breaking free of radio control is losing track of goals."

"But the code's not changed."

"Yeah well, nobody really cared about the code itself, Jack. It's the implications of the code. It's the behavior that emerges from the code. That's what we wanted you to help us with. Because I mean, it *is* your code, right?"

"Yeah, and it's your swarm."

"True enough, Jack."

He shrugged in his self-deprecating way, and left the room. I stared at the paper for a while, and then wondered why he'd printed it out for me. It meant I couldn't check the electronic document. Maybe Ricky was glossing over yet another problem. Maybe the code really had been changed, but he wasn't showing me. Or maybe—

The hell with it, I thought. I crumpled up the sheet of paper, and tossed it in the wastebasket. However this problem got solved, it wasn't going to be with computer code. That much was clear.

Mae was in the biology lab, peering at her monitor, hand cupped under her chin. I said, "You feel okay?"

"Yes." She smiled. "How about you?"

"Just tired. And my headache's back."

"I have one, too. But I think mine's from this phage." She pointed to the monitor screen. There was a scanning electron microscope image of a virus in black and white. The phage looked like a mortar shell—bulbous pointed head, attached to a narrower tail.

I said, "That's the new mutant you were talking about before?"

"Yes. I've already taken one fermentation tank offline. Production is now at only sixty percent capacity. Not that it matters, I suppose."

"And what're you doing with that offline tank?"

"I'm testing anti-viral reagents," she said. "I have a limited number of them here. We're not really set up to analyze contaminants. Protocol is just to go offline and scrub any tank that goes bad."

"Why haven't you done that?"

"I probably will, eventually. But since this is a new mutant, I thought I better try and find a counteragent. Because they'll need it for future production. I mean, the virus will be back."

"You mean it will reappear again? Re-evolve?"

"Yes. Perhaps more or less virulent, but essentially the same."

I nodded. I knew about this from work with genetic algorithms—programs that were specifically designed to mimic evolution. Most people imagined evolution to be a one-time-only process, a confluence of chance events. If plants hadn't started making oxygen, animal life would never have evolved. If an asteroid hadn't wiped out the dinosaurs, mammals would never have taken over. If some fish hadn't come onto land, we'd all still be in the water. And so on.

All that was true enough, but there was another side of evolution, too. Certain forms, and certain ways of life, kept appearing again and again. For example, parasitism—one animal living off another—had evolved independently many times in the course of evolution. Parasitism was a reliable way for life-forms to interact; and it kept reemerging.

A similar phenomenon occurred with genetic programs. They tended to move toward certain tried-and-true solutions. The programmers talked about it in terms of peaks on a fitness landscape; they could model it as three-dimensional false-color mountain range. But the fact was that evolution had its stable side, too.

And one thing you could count on was that any big, hot broth of bacteria was likely to get contaminated by a virus, and if that virus couldn't infect the bacteria, it would mutate to a form that could. You could count on that the way you could count on finding ants in your sugar bowl if you left it out on the counter too long.

Considering that evolution has been studied for a hundred and fifty years, it was surprising how little we knew about it. The old ideas about survival of the fittest had gone out of fashion long ago. Those views were too simpleminded. Nineteenth-century thinkers saw evolution as "nature red in tooth and claw," envisioning a world where strong animals killed weaker ones. They didn't take into account that the weaker ones would inevitably get stronger, or fight back in some other way. Which of course they always do.

The new ideas emphasized interactions among continuously evolving forms. Some people talked of evolution as an arms race, by which they meant an ever-escalating interaction. A plant attacked by a pest evolves a pesticide in its leaves. The pest evolves to tolerate the pesticide, so the plant evolves a stronger pesticide. And so on.

Others talked about this pattern as coevolution, in which two or more life-forms evolved simultaneously to tolerate each other. Thus a plant attacked by ants evolves to tolerate the ants, and even begins to make special food for them on the surface of its leaves. In return the resident ants protect the plant, stinging any animal that tries to eat the leaves. Pretty soon neither the plant nor the ant species can survive without the other.

This pattern was so fundamental that many people thought it was the real core of evolution. Parasitism and symbiosis were the true basis for evolutionary change. These processes lay at the heart of all evolution, and had been present from the very beginning. Lynn Margulies was famous for demonstrating that bacteria had originally developed nuclei by swallowing other bacteria.

By the twenty-first century, it was clear that coevolution wasn't limited to paired creatures in some isolated spinning dance. There were coevolutionary patterns with three, ten, or n life-forms, where n could be any number at all. A cornfield contained many kinds of plants, was attacked by many pests, and evolved many defenses. The plants competed with weeds; the pests competed with other pests; larger animals ate both the plants and the pests. The outcome of this complex interaction was always changing, always evolving.

And it was inherently unpredictable.

That was, in the end, why I was so angry with Ricky.

He should have known the dangers, when he found he couldn't control the swarms. It was insanity to sit back and allow them to evolve on their own. Ricky was bright; he knew about genetic algorithms; he knew the biological background for current trends in programming.

He knew that self-organization was inevitable.

He knew that emergent forms were unpredictable.

He knew that evolution involved interaction with n forms.

He knew all that, and he did it anyway.

He did, or Julia did.

*   *   *

I checked on Charley. He was still asleep in his room, sprawled out on the bed. Bobby Lembeck walked by. "How long has he been asleep?"

"Since you got back. Three hours or so."

"Do you think we should wake him up, check on him?"

"Nah, let him sleep. We'll check him after dinner."

"When is that?"

"Half an hour." Bobby Lembeck laughed. "I'm cooking."

That reminded me I was supposed to call home around dinnertime, so I went into my room and dialed.

Ellen answered the phone. "Hello? What is it!" She sounded harried. I heard Amanda crying and Eric yelling at Nicole in the background. Ellen said, "Nicole, do *not* do that to your brother!"

I said, "Hi, Ellen."

"Oh, *thank God*," she said. "You have to speak to your daughter."

"What's going on?"

"Just a minute. Nicole, it's your father." I could tell she was holding out the phone to her.

A pause, then, "Hi, Dad."

"What's going on, Nic?"

"Nothing. Eric is being a brat." Matter-of-factly.

"Nic, I want to know what you did to your brother."

"Dad." She lowered her voice to a whisper. I knew she was cupping her hand over the phone. "Aunt Ellen is not very nice."

"I heard that," Ellen said, in the background. But at least the baby had stopped crying; she'd been picked up.

"Nicole," I said. "You're the oldest child, I'm counting on you to help keep things together while I'm gone."

"I'm trying, Dad. But he is a majorly turkey butt."

From the background: "I am not! Up yours, weasel poop!"

"Dad. You see what I'm up against."

Eric: "Up your hole with a ten-foot pole!"

I looked at the monitor in front of me. It showed views of the desert outside, rotating images from all the security cameras. One camera showed my dirt bike, lying on its side, near the door to the power station. Another camera showed the outside of the storage shed, with the door swinging open and shut, revealing the outline of Rosie's body inside. Two people had died today. I had almost died. And now my family, which yesterday had been the most important thing in my life, seemed distant and petty.

"It's very simple, Dad," Nicole was saying in her most reasonable grown-up voice. "I came home with Aunt Ellen from the store, I got a very nice blouse for the show, and then Eric came into my room and knocked all my books on the floor. So I told him to pick them up. He said no and called me the b-word, so I kicked him in the butt, *not* very hard, and took his G.I. Joe and hid it. That's all."

I said, "You took *his G.I. Joe?*" G.I. Joe was Eric's most important possession. He talked to G.I. Joe. He slept with G.I. Joe on the pillow beside him.

"He can have it back," she said, "as soon as he cleans up my books."

"Nic . . ."

"Dad, he called me the b-word."

"Give him his G.I. Joe."

The images on the screen were rotating through the various cameras. Each image only stayed on screen for a second or two. I waited for the image of the shed to come back up. I had a nagging feeling about it. Something bothered me.

"Dad, this is humiliating."

"Nic, you're not the mother—"

"Oh yeah, and she was here for maybe five seconds."

"She was at the house? Mom was there?"

"But then, big surprise, she had to go. She had a plane to catch."

"Uh-huh. Nicole, you need to listen to Ellen—"

"Dad, I told you she's being—"

"Because she's in charge until I get back. So if she says to do something, you do it."

"Dad. I feel this is unreasonable." Her members-of-the-jury voice.

"Well, honey, that's how it is."

"But my problem—"

"Nicole. *That's how it is.* Until I get back."

"When are you coming home?"

"Probably tomorrow."

"Okay."

"So. We understand each other?"

"Yes, Dad. I'll probably have a nervous breakdown here . . ."

"Then I promise I'll visit you in the mental hospital, as soon as I get back."

"Very funny."

"Let me speak to Eric."

I had a short conversation with Eric, who told me several times that it was not fair. I told him to put Nicole's books back. He said he didn't knock them down, it was an accident. I said to put them back anyway. Then I talked to Ellen briefly. I encouraged her as best I could.

Sometime during this conversation, the security camera showing the outside of the shed came up again. And I again saw the swinging door, and the outside of the shed. In this elevation the shed was slightly above grade; there were four wooden steps leading from the door down to ground level. But it all looked the way it should. I did not know what had bothered me.

Then I realized.

David's body wasn't there. It wasn't in the frame. Earlier in the day, I had seen his body slide out the door and disappear from view, so it should be lying outside. Given the slight grade, it might have rolled a few yards from the door, but not more than that.

No body.

But perhaps I was mistaken. Or perhaps there were coyotes. In any case the camera image had now changed. I'd have to sit through another cycle to see it again. I decided not to wait. If David's body was gone, there was nothing I could do about it now.

It was about seven o'clock when we sat down to eat dinner in the little kitchen of the residential module. Bobby brought out plates of ravioli with tomato sauce, and mixed vegetables. I had been a stay-at-home dad long enough to recognize the brands of frozen food he was using. "I really think that Contadina is better ravioli."

Bobby shrugged. "I go to the fridge, I find what's there."

I was surprisingly hungry. I ate everything on my plate.

"Couldn't have been that bad," Bobby said.

Mae was silent as she ate, as usual. Beside her, Vince ate noisily. Ricky was at the far end of the table, away from me, looking down at his food and not meeting my eyes. It was all right with me. Nobody wanted to talk about Rosie and David, but the empty stools around the table were pretty obvious. Bobby said to me, "So, you're going to go out tonight?"

"Yes," I said. "When is it dark?"

"Sunset should be around seven-twenty," Bobby said. He flicked on a monitor on the wall. "I'll get you the exact time."

I said, "So we can go out three hours after that. Sometime after ten."

Bobby said, "And you think you can track the swarm?"

"We should. Charley sprayed one swarm pretty thoroughly."

"As a result of which, I glow in the dark," Charley said, laughing. He came into the room and sat down.

Everyone greeted him enthusiastically. If nothing else, it felt better to have another body at the table. I asked him how he felt.

"Okay. A little weak. And I have a fucking headache from hell."

"I know. Me too."

"And me," Mae said.

"It's worse than the headache Ricky gives me," Charley said, looking down the table. "Lasts longer, too."

Ricky said nothing. Just continued eating.

"Do you suppose these things get into your brain?" Charley said. "I mean, they're nanoparticles. They can get inhaled, cross the blood-brain barrier . . . and go into the brain?"

Bobby pushed a plate of pasta in front of Charley. He immediately ground pepper all over it.

"Don't you want to taste it?"

"No offense. But I'm sure it needs it." He started to eat.

"I mean," he continued, "that's what everybody's worried about nano-technology polluting the environment, right? Nanoparticles are small enough to get places nobody's ever had to worry about before. They can get into the synapses between neurons. They can get into the cytoplasm of cardiac cells. They can get into cell nuclei. They're small enough to go anywhere inside the body. So maybe we're infected, Jack."

"You don't seem that worried about it," Ricky said.

"Hey, what can I do about it now? Hope I give it to you, is about all. Hey, this spaghetti's not bad."

"Ravioli," Bobby said.

"Whatever. Just needs a little pepper." He ground some more over the top.

"Sundown is seven-twenty-seven," Bobby said, reading the time off the monitor. He went back to eating. "And it does not need pepper."

"Fucking does."

"I already put in pepper."

"Needs more."

I said, "Guys? Are we missing anybody?"

"I don't think so, why?"

I pointed to the monitor. "Who's that standing out in the desert?"

DAY 6
7:12 P.M.

"Oh shit," Bobby said. He jumped up from the table and ran out of the room. Everyone else did, too. I followed the others.

Ricky was holding his radio as he went: "Vince, lock us down. Vince?"

"We're locked down," Vince said. "Pressure is five plus."

"Why didn't the alarm go off?"

"Can't say. Maybe they've learned to get past that, too."

I followed everybody into the utility room, where there were large wall-mounted liquid crystal displays showing the outside video cameras. Views of the desert from all angles.

The sun was already below the horizon, but the sky was a bright orange, fading into purple and then dark blue. Silhouetted against this sky was a young man with short hair. He was wearing jeans and a white T-shirt and looked like a surfer. I couldn't see his face clearly in the failing light, but even so, watching the way he moved, I thought there was something familiar about him.

"We got any floodlights out there?" Charley said. He was walking around, holding his bowl of pasta, still eating.

"Lights coming up," Bobby said, and a moment later the young man stood in glaring light. Now I could see him clearly—

And then it hit me. It looked like the same kid who had been in Julia's car last night after dinner, when she drove away, just before her accident. The same blond surfer kid who, now that I saw him again, looked like—

"Jesus, Ricky," Bobby said. "He looks like *you*."

"You're right," Mae said. "It's Ricky. Even the T-shirt."

Ricky was getting a soft drink out of the dispensing machine. He turned toward the display screen. "What're you guys talking about?"

"He looks like you," Mae said. "He even has your T-shirt with I Am Root on the front."

Ricky looked at his own T-shirt, then back at the screen. He was silent for a moment. "I'll be damned."

I said, "You've never been out of the building, Ricky. How come it's you?"

"Fucking beats me," Ricky said. He shrugged casually. Too casually?

Mae said, "I can't make out the face very well. I mean the features."

Charley moved closer to the largest of the screens and squinted at the image. "The reason you can't see features," he said, "is because there aren't any."

"Oh, come on."

"Charley, it's a resolution artifact, that's all."

"It's not," Charley said. "There're no fucking features. Zoom it in and see for yourself."

Bobby zoomed. The image of the blond head enlarged. The figure was moving back and forth, in and out of the frame, but it was immediately clear that Charley was right. There were no features. There was an oval patch of pale skin beneath the blond hairline; and there was the suggestion of a nose and brow ridges, and a sort of mound where the lips should be. But there were no actual features.

It was as if a sculptor had started to carve a face, and had stopped before he was finished. It was an unfinished face.

Except that the eyebrows moved, from time to time. A sort of wiggle, or flutter. Or perhaps that was an artifact.

"You know what we're looking at here, don't you?" Charley said. He sounded worried. "Pan down. Let's see the rest of him." Bobby panned down, and we saw white sneakers moving over the desert dirt. Except the sneakers didn't seem to be touching the ground, but rather hovering just above it. And the sneakers themselves were sort of blurry. There was a hint of shoelaces, and a streak where a Nike logo would be. But it was like a sketch, rather than an actual sneaker.

"This is very weird," Mae said.

"Not weird at all," Charley said. "It's a calculated approximation for density. The swarm doesn't have enough agents to make high-resolution shoes. So it's approximating."

"Or else," I said, "it's the best it can do with the materials at hand. It must be generating all these colors by tilting its photovoltaic surface at slight angles, catching the light. It's like those flash cards the crowd holds up in football stadiums to make a picture."

"In which case," Charley said, "its behavior is quite sophisticated."

"More sophisticated than what we saw earlier," I said.

"Oh, for Christ's sake," Ricky said irritably. "You're acting like this swarm is Einstein."

"Obviously not," Charley said, "'cause if it's modeling you, it's certainly no Einstein."

"Give it a rest, Charley."

"I would, Ricky, but you're such an asshole I get provoked over and over."

Bobby said, "Why don't you both give it a rest?"

Mae turned to me and said, "Why is the swarm doing this? Imitating the prey?"

"Basically, yes," I said.

"I hate to think of us as prey," Ricky said.

Mae said, "You mean it's been coded to, literally, physically imitate the prey?"

"No," I said. "The program instruction is more generalized than that. It simply directs the agents to attain the goal. So we are seeing one possible emergent solution. Which is more advanced than the previous version. Before, it had trouble making a stable 2-D image. Now it's modeling in three dimensions."

I glanced at the programmers. They had stricken looks on their faces. They knew exactly how big an advance they were witnessing. The transition to three dimensions meant that not only was the swarm now imitating our external appearance, it was also imitating our behavior. Our walks, our gestures. Which implied a far more complicated internal model.

Mae said, "And the swarm decided this on its own?"

"Yes," I said. "Although I'm not sure 'decided' is the right term. The emergent behavior is the sum of individual agent behaviors. There isn't anybody there to 'decide' anything. There's no brain, no higher control in that swarm."

"Group mind?" Mae said. "Hive mind?"

"In a way," I said. "The point is, there is no central control."

"But it *looks* so controlled," she said. "It looks like a defined, purposeful organism."

"Yeah, well, so do we," Charley said, with a harsh laugh.

Nobody else laughed with him.

If you want to think of it that way, a human being is actually a giant swarm. Or more precisely, it's a swarm of swarms, because each organ—blood, liver, kidneys—is a separate swarm. What we refer to as a "body" is really the combination of all these organ swarms.

We think our bodies are solid, but that's only because we can't see what is going on at the cellular level. If you could enlarge the human body, blow it up to a vast size, you would see that it was literally nothing but a swirling mass of cells and atoms, clustered together into smaller swirls of cells and atoms.

Who cares? Well, it turns out a lot of processing occurs at the level of the organs. Human behavior is determined in many places. The control of our behavior is not located in our brains. It's all over our bodies.

So you could argue that "swarm intelligence" rules human beings, too. Balance is controlled by the cerebellar swarm, and rarely comes to consciousness. Other processing occurs in the spinal cord, the stomach, the intestine. A lot of vision takes place in the eyeballs, long before the brain is involved.

And for that matter, a lot of sophisticated brain processing occurs beneath awareness, too. An easy proof is object avoidance. A mobile robot has to devote a tremendous amount of processing time simply to avoid obstacles in the environment. Human beings do, too, but they're never aware of it—until the lights go out. Then they learn painfully just how much processing is really required.

So there's an argument that the whole structure of consciousness, and the human sense of self-control and purposefulness, is a user illusion. We don't have conscious control over ourselves at all. We just think we do.

Just because human beings went around thinking of themselves as "I" didn't mean that it was true. And for all we knew, this damned swarm had some sort of rudimentary sense of itself as an entity. Or, if it didn't, it might very soon start to.

Watching the faceless man on the monitor, we saw that the image was now becoming unstable. The swarm had trouble keeping the appearance solid. Instead it fluctuated: at moments, the face and shoulders seemed to dissolve into dust, then reemerge as solid again. It was strange to watch it.

"Losing its grip?" Bobby said.

"No, I think it's getting tired," Charley said.

"You mean it's running out of power."

"Yeah, probably. It'd take a lot of extra juice to tilt all those particles into exact orientations."

Indeed, the swarm was reverting back to a cloud appearance again.

"So this is a low-power mode?" I said.

"Yeah. I'm sure they were optimized for power management."

"Or they are now," I said.

It was getting darker quickly, now. The orange was gone from the sky. The monitor was starting to lose definition.

The swarm turned, and swirled away.

"I'll be goddamned," Charley said.

I watched the swarm disappear into the horizon.

"Three hours," I said, "and they're history."

DAY 6
10:12 P.M.

Charley went back to bed right after dinner. He was still asleep at ten that night, when Mae and I were preparing to go out again. We were wearing down vests and jackets, because it was going to be cold. We needed a third person to go with us. Ricky said he had to wait for Julia, who was flying in any minute now; that was fine with me, I didn't want him anyway. Vince was off somewhere watching TV and drinking beer. That left Bobby.

Bobby didn't want to go, but Mae shamed him into coming. There was a question about how the three of us would get around, since it was possible the swarm hiding place might be some distance away, perhaps even several miles. We still had David's dirt bike, but that could only sit two. It turned out Vince had an ATV in the shed. I went to see him in the power unit to ask him for the key.

"Don't need a key," he said. He was sitting on a couch, watching *Who Wants to Be a Millionaire*. I heard Regis say, "Final answer?"

"I said, What do you mean?"

"Key's in it," Vince said. "Always there."

"Wait a minute," I said. "You mean there was a vehicle in the shed with keys in it all the time?"

"Sure." On the TV, I heard, "For four thousand dollars, what is the name of the smallest state in Europe?"

"Why didn't anybody tell me?" I said, starting to get mad.

Vince shrugged. "Couldn't say. Nobody asked me."

I stalked back to the main unit. "Where the hell is Ricky?"

"He's on the phone," Bobby said. "Talking to the brass back in the Valley."

Mae said, "Take it easy."

"I'm taking it easy," I said. "Which phone? In the main unit?"

"Jack." She put her hands on my shoulders, stopped me. "It's after ten o'clock. Forget it."

"Forget it? He could have gotten us killed."

"And right now we have work to do."

I looked at her calm face, her steady expression. I thought of the swift way she had eviscerated the rabbit.

"You're right," I said.

"Good," she said, turning away. "Now I think as soon as we get some backpacks, we'll be ready to go."

There was a reason, I thought, why Mae never lost an argument. I went to the storage cupboard and got out three packs. I threw one to Bobby.

"Let's hit the road," I said.

It was a clear night, filled with stars. We walked in darkness toward the storage shed, a dark outline against the dark sky. I pushed the dirt bike along. None of us talked for a while. Finally, Bobby said, "We're going to need lights."

"We're going to need a lot of things," Mae said. "I made a list."

We came to the storage shed, and pushed open the door. I saw Bobby hang back in the darkness. I went in, and fumbled for the lights. I flicked them on.

The interior of the storage shed appeared just as we had left it. Mae unzipped her backpack and began walking down the row of shelves. "We need portable lights . . . ignition fuses . . . flares . . . oxygen . . ."

Bobby said, "Oxygen? Really?"

"If this site is underground, yes, we may . . . and we need thermite."

I said, "Rosie had it. Maybe she set it down when she . . . I'll look."

I went into the next room. The box of thermite tubes lay overturned on the floor, the tubes nearby. Rosie must have dropped it when she ran. I wondered if she had had any in her hand. I looked over at her body by the door.

Rosie's body was gone.

"Jesus."

Bobby came running in. "What is it? What's wrong?"

I pointed to the door. "Rosie's gone."

"What do you mean, gone?"

I looked at him. "Gone, Bobby. The body was here before and now it's gone."

"How can that be? An animal?"

"I don't know." I went over and crouched down at the spot where her body had been. When I had last seen her, five or six hours ago, her body had been covered with a milky secretion. Some of that secretion covered the floor, too. It looked exactly like thick, dried milk. Up where her head had been, the secretion was smooth and undisturbed. But closer to the door, it appeared to have been scraped. There were streaks in the coating.

"It looks like she was dragged out," Bobby said.

"Yes."

I peered closely at the secretion, looking for footprints. A coyote alone couldn't have dragged her; a pack of animals would be needed to pull her out the door. They would surely leave marks. I saw none.

I got up and walked to the door. Bobby stood beside me, looking out into the darkness.

"You see anything?" he said.

"No."

I returned to Mae. She had found everything. She had coiled magnesium fuse. She had flare guns. She had portable halogen flashlights. She had head-mounted lamps with big elastic bands. She had small binoculars and night-vision goggles. She had a field radio. And she had oxygen bottles and clear-plastic gas masks. I was uneasy when I recognized that these were the same plastic masks I had seen on the men in the SSVT van back in California last night, except they weren't silvered.

And then I thought, Was it only last night? It was. Hardly twenty-four hours had passed.

It felt to me like a month.

Mae was dividing everything into the three backpacks. Watching her, I realized that she was the only one of us with actual field experience. In comparison, we were all stay-at-homes, theoreticians. I was surprised how dependent on her I felt tonight.

Bobby hefted the nearest pack and grunted. "You really think we need all this stuff, Mae?"

"It's not like you have to carry it; we're driving. And yes, better safe than sorry."

"Okay, fine, but I mean—a field radio?"

"You never know."

"Who you gonna call?"

"The thing is, Bobby," she said, "if it turns out you need any of this stuff, you *really* need it."

"Yeah, but it's—"

Mae picked up the second backpack, and slung it over her shoulder. She handled the weight easily. She looked at Bobby. "You were saying?"

"Never mind."

I picked up the third backpack. It wasn't bad. Bobby was complaining because he was scared. It was true that the oxygen bottle was a little larger and heavier than I would have liked, and it fitted awkwardly into the backpack. But Mae insisted we have extra oxygen.

Bobby said nervously, "Extra oxygen? How big do you guys think this hiding place is?"

"I have no idea," Mae said. "But the most recent swarms are much larger."

She went to the sink, and picked up the radiation counter. But when she unplugged it from the wall, she saw the battery was dead. We had to hunt for a new battery, unscrew the case, replace the battery. I was worried the replacement would be dead, too. If it was, we were finished.

Mae said, "We better be careful with the night-vision goggles, too. I don't know how good any of the batteries are for the stuff we have."

But the counter clicked loudly. The battery indicator glowed. "Full power," she said. "It'll last four hours."

"Let's get started," I said.

It was 10:43 P.M.

The radiation counter went crazy when we came to the Toyota, clicking so rapidly the sound was continuous. Holding the wand in front of her, Mae left the car, walked into the desert. She turned west and the clicks diminished. She went east and they picked up again. But as she continued east, the clicks slowed. She turned north, and they increased.

"North," she said.

I got on the bike, gunned the engine.

Bobby rumbled out of the shed on the All-Terrain Vehicle, with its fat rear tires and bicycle handlebars. The ATV looked ungainly but I knew it was probably better suited to night travel in the desert.

Mae got on the back of my bike, leaned over to hold the wand near the ground, and said, "Okay. Let's go."

We started off into the desert, under a cloudless night sky.

The headlight on the bike bounced up and down, jerking the shadows on the terrain ahead, making it difficult to see what was coming. The desert that had looked so flat and featureless in daylight was now revealed to have sandy dips, rock-filled beds, and deep arroyos that came up without warning. It took all my attention to keep the bike upright—particularly since Mae was continuously calling to me, "Go left . . . now right . . . now right . . . okay, too much, left . . ." Sometimes we had to make a full circle until she could be certain of the right path.

If anybody followed our track in daylight, they'd think the driver must be drunk, it twisted and turned so much. The bike jumped and swerved on rough ground. We were now several miles from the lab, and I was starting to worry. I could hear the counter clicks, and they were becoming less frequent. It was getting hard to distinguish the swarm trail from the background radiation. I didn't understand why that should happen but there was no question it was. If we didn't locate the swarm hiding place soon, we'd lose the trail entirely.

Mae was worried, too. She kept bending over closer and closer to the ground, with one hand on the wand and one hand around my waist. And I had to go slower, because the trail was becoming so faint. We lost the trail, found it, went off it again. Under the black canopy of stars, we backtracked, turned in circles. I caught myself holding my breath.

And at last I was going around and around in the same spot, trying not to feel desperate. I made the circle three times, then four, but to no avail: the counter in Mae's hand just clicked randomly. And suddenly it was clear to us that the trail was truly lost.

We were out here in the middle of nowhere, driving in circles.

We had lost the trail.

Exhaustion hit me suddenly, and hard. I had been running on adrenaline all day and now that I was finally defeated a deep weariness came over my body. My eyes drooped. I felt as if I could go to sleep standing on the bike.

Behind me, Mae sat up and said, "Don't worry, okay?"

"What do you mean?" I said wearily. "My plan has totally failed, Mae."

"Maybe not yet," she said.

Bobby pulled up close to us. "You guys look behind you?" he said. "Why?"

"Look back," he said. "Look how far we've come."

I turned and looked over my shoulder. To the south, I saw the bright lights of the fabrication building, surprisingly close. We couldn't be more than a mile or two away. We must have traveled in a big semicircle, eventually turning back toward our starting point.

"That's weird."

Mae had got off the bike, and stepped in front of the headlamp. She and was looking at the LCD readout on the counter. She said, "Hmmm."

Bobby said hopefully, "So, what do you say, Mae? Time to go back?"

"No," Mae said. "It's not time to go back. Take a look at this."

Bobby leaned over, and we both looked at the LCD readout. It showed a graph of radiation intensity, stepping progressively downward, and finally dropping quickly. Bobby frowned. "And this is?"

"Time course of tonight's readings," she said. "The machine's showing us that ever since we started, the intensity of the radiation has declined arithmetically—it's a straight-line decrease, a staircase, see there? And it's stayed arithmetic until the last minute or so, when the decrease suddenly became exponential. It just fell to zero."

"So?" Bobby looked puzzled. "That means what? I don't get it."

"I do." She turned to me, climbed back on the bike. "I think I know what happened. Go forward—slowly."

I let out the clutch, and rumbled forward. My bouncing headlight showed a slight rise in the desert, scrubby cactus ahead . . .

"No. Slower, Jack."

I slowed. Now we were practically going at a walk. I yawned. There was no point in questioning her; she was intense, focused. I was just tired and defeated. We continued up the desert rise until it flattened, and then the bike began to tilt downward—

"*Stop.*"

I stopped.

Directly ahead, the desert floor abruptly ended. I saw blackness beyond.

"Is that a cliff?"

"No. Just a high ridge."

I edged the bike forward. The land definitely fell away. Soon we were at the edge and I could get my bearings. We were at the crest of a ridge fifteen feet high, which formed one side of a very wide streambed. Directly beneath me I saw smooth river rocks, with occasional boulders and clumps of scraggly brush that stretched about fifty yards away, to the far side of the riverbed. Beyond the distant bank, the desert was flat again.

"I understand now," I said. "The swarm jumped."

"Yes," she said, "it became airborne. And we lost the trail."

"But then it must have landed somewhere down there," Bobby said, pointing to the streambed.

"Maybe," I said. "And maybe not."

I was thinking it would take us many minutes to find a safe route down. Then we would spend a long time searching among the bushes and rocks of the streambed, before picking up the trail again. It might take hours. We might not find it at all. From our position up here on top of the ridge, we saw the daunting expanse of desert stretching out before us.

I said, "The swarm could have touched down in the streambed. Or it could have come down just beyond the bed. Or it could have gone quarter mile beyond."

Mae was not discouraged. "Bobby, you stay here," she said. "You'll mark the position where it jumped. Jack and I will find a path down, go out into that plain, and run in a straight line east-west until we pick up the trail again. Sooner or later, we'll find it."

"Okay," Bobby said. "Got you."

"Okay," I said. We might as well do it. We had nothing to lose. But I had very little confidence we would succeed.

Bobby leaned forward over his ATV. "What's *that*?"

"What?"

"An animal. I saw glowing eyes."

"Where?"

"In that brush over there." He pointed to the center of the streambed.

I frowned. We both had our headlights trained down the ridge. We were lighting a fairly large arc of desert. I didn't see any animals.

"There!" Mae said.

"I don't see anything."

She pointed. "It just went behind that juniper bush. See the bush that looks like a pyramid? That has the dead branches on one side?"

"I see it," I said. "But . . ." I didn't see an animal.

"It's moving left to right. Wait a minute and it'll come out again."

We waited, and then I saw a pair of bright green, glowing spots. Close to the ground, moving right. I saw a flash of pale white. And almost immediately I knew that something was wrong.

So did Bobby. He twisted his handlebars, moving his headlamp to point directly to the spot. He reached for binoculars.

"That's not an animal . . ." he said.

Moving among the low bushes, we saw more white—flesh white. But we saw only glimpses. And then I saw a flat white surface that I realized with a shock was a human hand, dragging along the ground. A hand with outstretched fingers.

"Jesus," Bobby said, staring through the binoculars.

"What? What is it?"

"It's a body being dragged," he said. And then, in a funny voice, he said, "It's Rosie."

DAY 6
10:58 P.M.

Gunning the bike, I took off with Mae, running along the edge of the ridge until it sloped down toward the streambed floor. Bobby stayed where he was, watching Rosie's body. In a few minutes I had crossed the streambed to the other bank, and was moving back toward his light on the hill.

Mae said, "Let's slow down, Jack."

So I slowed down, leaning forward over my handlebars, trying to see the ground far ahead. Suddenly the radiation counter began to chatter again.

"Good sign," I said.

We moved ahead. Now we were directly across from Bobby on the ridge above. His headlamp cast a faint light on the ground all around us, sort of like moonlight. I waved for him to come down. He turned his vehicle and headed west. Without his light, the ground was suddenly darker, more mysterious.

And then we saw Rosie Castro.

Rosie lay on her back, her head tilted so she appeared to be looking backward, directly at me, her eyes wide, her arm outstretched toward me, her pale hand open. There was an expression of pleading—or terror—on her face. Rigor mortis had set in, and her body jerked stiffly as it moved over low shrubs and desert cactus.

She was being dragged away—but no animal was dragging her.

"I think you should turn your light off," Mae said.

"But I don't see what's doing it . . . there's like a shadow underneath her . . ."

"That's not a shadow," Mae said. "It's *them*."

"They're dragging her?"

She nodded. "Turn your light off."

I flicked off the headlamp. We stood in darkness. I said, "I thought swarms couldn't maintain power more than three hours."

"That's what Ricky said."

"He's lying again?"

"Or they've overcome that limitation in the wild."

The implications were unsettling. If the swarms could now sustain power through the night, then they might be active when we reached their hiding place. I was counting on finding them collapsed, the particles spread on the ground. I intended to kill them in their sleep, so to speak. Now it seemed they weren't sleeping.

We stood there in the cool dark air, thinking things over. Finally Mae said, "Aren't these swarms modeled on insect behavior?"

"Not really," I said. "The programming model was predator-prey. But because the swarm is a population of interacting particles, to some degree it will behave like any population of interacting particles, such as insects. Why?"

"Insects can execute plans that take longer than the lifespan of a single generation. They can build nests that require many generations. Isn't that true?"

"I think so . . ."

"So maybe one swarm carried the body for a while, and then another took over. Maybe there have been three or four swarms so far. That way none of them has to go three hours at night."

I didn't like the implications of that idea any better. "That would mean the swarms are working together," I said. "It would mean they're coordinated."

"They clearly are, by now."

"Except that's not possible," I said to her. "Because they don't have the signaling capability."

"It wasn't possible a few generations ago," Mae said. "Now it is. Remember the V formation that came toward you? They were coordinated."

That was true. I just hadn't realized it at the time. Standing there in the desert night, I wondered what else I hadn't realized. I squinted into the darkness, trying to see ahead.

"Where are they taking her?" I said.

Mae unzipped my backpack, and pulled out a set of night goggles. "Try these."

I was about to help her get hers, but she'd deftly taken her pack off, opened it, and pulled out her own goggles. Her movements were quick, sure.

I slipped on the headset, adjusted the strap, and flipped the lenses down over my eyes. These were the new GEN 4 goggles that showed images in muted color. Almost immediately, I saw Rosie in the desert. Her body was disappearing behind the scrub as she moved farther and farther away.

"Okay, so where are they taking her?" I said again. Even as I spoke, I raised the goggles higher, and at once I saw where they were taking her.

From a distance it looked like a natural formation—a mound of dark earth about fifteen feet wide and six feet high. Erosion had carved deep, vertical clefts so that the mound looked a little like a huge gear turned on edge. It would be easy to overlook this formation as natural.

But it wasn't natural. And erosion hadn't produced its sculpted look. On the contrary, I was seeing an artificial construction, similar to the nests made by African termites and other social insects.

Wearing the second pair of goggles, Mae looked for a while in silence, then said, "Are you going to tell me that is the product of self-organized behavior? That the behavior to make it just emerged all by itself?"

"Actually, yes," I said. "That's exactly what happened."

"Hard to believe."

"I know."

Mae was a good biologist, but she was a primate biologist. She was accustomed to studying small populations of highly intelligent animals that had dominance hierarchies and group leaders. She understood complex behavior to be the result of complex intelligence. And she had trouble grasping the sheer power of self-organized behavior within a very large population of dumb animals.

In any case, this was a deep human prejudice. Human beings expected to find a central command in any organization. States had governments. Corporations had CEOs. Schools had principals. Armies had generals. Human beings tended to believe that without central command, chaos would overwhelm the organization and nothing significant could be accomplished.

From this standpoint, it was difficult to believe that extremely stupid creatures with brains smaller than pinheads were capable of construction projects more complicated than any human project. But in fact, they were.

African termites were a classic example. These insects made earthen castlelike mounds a hundred feet in diameter and thrusting spires twenty feet into the air. To appreciate their accomplishment, you had to imagine that if termites were the size of people, these mounds would be skyscrapers one mile high and five miles in diameter. And like a skyscraper, the termite mound had an intricate internal architecture to provide fresh air, remove excess CO_2 and heat, and so on. Inside the structure were gardens to grow food, residences for royalty, and living space for as many as two million termites. No two mounds were exactly the same; each was individually constructed to suit the requirements and advantages of a particular site.

All this was accomplished with no architect, no foreman, no central authority. Nor was a blueprint for construction encoded in the termite genes. Instead these huge creations were the result of relatively simple rules that the individual termites followed in relation to one another. (Rules like, "If you smell that another termite has been here, put a dirt pellet on this spot.") Yet the outcome was arguably more complex than any human creation.

Now we were seeing a new construction made by a new creature, and it was again difficult to conceive how it might have been made. How could a swarm make a mound, anyway? But I was beginning to realize that out here in the desert, asking how something happened was a fool's errand. The swarms were changing fast, almost minute to minute. The natural human impulse to figure it out was a waste of time. By the time you figured it out, things would have changed.

Bobby rumbled up in his ATV, and cut his light. We all stood there under the stars. Bobby said, "What do we do now?"

"Follow Rosie," I said.

"Looks like Rosie is going into that mound," he said. "You mean we follow her there?"

"Yes," I said.

At Mae's suggestion, we walked the rest of the way. Lugging our backpacks, it took us the better part of ten minutes to reach the vicinity of the mound. We paused about fifty feet away. There was a nauseating smell in the air, a putrid odor of rotting and decay. It was so strong it made my stomach turn. Then too, a faint green glow seemed to be emanating from inside the mound.

Bobby whispered, "You really want to go in *there*?"

"Not yet," Mae whispered. She pointed off to one side. Rosie's body was moving up the slope of the mound. As she came to the rim, her rigid legs pointed into the air for a moment. Then her body toppled over, and she fell into the interior. But she stopped before she disappeared entirely; for several seconds, her head remained above the rim, her arm outstretched, as if she were reaching for air. Then, slowly, she slid the rest of the way down, and vanished.

Bobby shivered.

Mae whispered, "Okay. Let's go."

She started forward in her usual noiseless way. Following her, I tried to be as quiet as I could. Bobby crunched and crackled his way along the ground. Mae paused, and gave him a hard look.

Bobby held up his hands as if to say, what can I do?

She whispered, "*Watch where you put your feet.*"

He whispered, "I am."

"You're *not.*"

"It's dark, I can't see."

"You can *if you try.*"

I couldn't recall ever seeing Mae show irritation before, but we were all under pressure now. And the stench was terrible. Mae turned and once again moved forward silently. Bobby followed, making just as much noise as before. We had only gone a few steps before Mae turned, held up her hand, and signaled for him to stay where he was.

He shook his head, no. He clearly didn't want to be left alone.

She gripped his shoulder, pointed firmly to the ground, and whispered, "You stay here."

"No . . ."

She whispered, "You'll get us all killed."

He whispered, "I promise."

She shook her head, pointed to the ground. Sit.

Finally, Bobby sat down.

Mae looked at me. I nodded. We set out again. By now we were twenty feet from the mound itself. The smell was almost overpowering. My stomach churned; I was afraid I might be sick. And this close, we began to hear the deep thrumming sound. More than anything it was that sound that made me want to run away. But Mae kept going.

We crouched down as we climbed the mound, and then lay flat along the rim. I could see Mae's face in the green glow coming from inside. For some reason the stench didn't bother me anymore. Probably because I was too frightened.

Mae reached into the side pouch of her pack, and withdrew a small thumb-sized camera on a thin telescoping stick. She brought out a tiny LCD screen and set it on the ground between us. Then she slid the stick over the rim.

On the screen, we saw a green interior of smooth undulating walls. Nothing seemed to be moving. She turned the camera this way and that. All we saw were green walls. There was no sign of Rosie.

Mae looked at me, pointed to her eyes. Want to take a look now?
I nodded.
We inched forward slowly, until we could look over the rim.

It wasn't what I expected at all.

The mound simply narrowed an existing opening that was huge—twenty feet wide or more, revealing a rock slide that sloped downward from the rim and ended at a gaping hole in the rock to our right. The green light was coming from somewhere inside this gaping hole.

What I was seeing was the entrance to a very large cave. From our position on the rim, we couldn't see into the cave itself, but the thrumming sound suggested activity within. Mae opened the telescoping stick to its full length, and gently lowered the camera into the hole. Soon we could see farther into the cave. It was undoubtedly natural, and large: perhaps eight feet high, ten feet wide. The rock walls were pale white, and appeared to be covered with the milky substance we'd seen on Rosie.

And Rosie's body was only a short distance inside. We could see her hand sticking out around a bend in the rock wall. But we could see nothing beyond the bend.

Mae signaled me: want to go down?

I nodded slowly. I didn't like how this felt, I didn't like that I had no idea what was beyond the bend. But we really had no choice.

She pointed back toward Bobby. Get him?

I shook my head, no. He wouldn't help us here.

She nodded, and started very slowly to slide out of her backpack, making no sound at all, when she suddenly froze. Literally froze: she didn't move a muscle.

I looked at the screen. And I froze, too.

A figure had walked from behind the bend, and now stood alertly at the entrance of the cave, looking around.

It was Ricky.

*   *   *

He was behaving as if he had heard a sound, or had been alerted for some other reason. The video camera still dangled down the rim of the mound. It was pretty small; I didn't know if he would see it.

I watched the screen tensely.

The camera didn't have good resolution and the screen was the size of my palm, but it was still clear that the figure was Ricky. I didn't understand what he was doing here—or even how he had gotten here. Then another man came around the bend.

He was also Ricky.

I glanced at Mae, but she remained utterly still, a statue. Only her eyes moved.

I squinted at the screen. Within the limits of video resolution, the two figures appeared to be identical in every respect. Same clothes, same movements, same gestures and shrugs. I couldn't see the faces well, but I had the impression they were more detailed than before.

They didn't seem to notice the camera.

They looked up at the sky, and then at the rock slide for a while, and then they turned their backs on us, and returned to the interior of the cave.

Still Mae did not move. She had been motionless for almost a minute already and in that time she hadn't even blinked. Now the men were gone, and—

Another figure came around the corner. It was David Brooks. He moved awkwardly, stiffly at first, but he quickly became more fluid. I had the feeling I was watching a puppeteer perfect his moves, animating the figure in a more lifelike way. Then David became Ricky. And then David again. And the David figure turned and went away.

Still Mae waited. She waited fully two more minutes, and then finally withdrew the camera. She jerked her thumb, indicating we should go back. Together, we crept away from the rim, back down the mound, and moved away silently into the desert night.

We gathered a hundred yards to the west, near our vehicles. Mae was rummaging in her backpack; she pulled out a clipboard with a felt marker. She flicked on her penlight and began to draw.

"This is what you're up against," she said. "The cave has an opening like this, which you saw. Past the bend, there's a big hole in the floor, and the cave spirals downward for maybe a hundred yards. That brings you into one large chamber that is maybe a hundred feet high, and a couple of hundred feet wide. Single big room, that's all. There are no passages leading off, at least none that I saw."

"That you saw?"

"I've been in there," she said, nodding.

"When?"

"A couple of weeks ago. Back when we first started looking for the swarm's hiding place. I found that cave and went in there in daylight. I didn't find any indication of a swarm then." She explained that the cave was filled with bats, the whole ceiling covered with them, packed together in a pink squirming mass, all the way out to the entrance.

"Ugh," Bobby said. "I hate bats."

"I didn't see any bats there tonight."

"You think they've been driven away?"

"Eaten, probably."

"Jesus, guys," Bobby said, shaking his head. "I'm just a programmer. I don't think I can do this. I don't think I can go in there."

Mae ignored him. She said to me, "If we go in," she said, "we'll have to set off thermite, and keep doing it all the way down to the chamber. I'm not sure we have enough thermite to do that."

"Maybe not," I said. I had a different concern. "We're wasting our time unless we destroy all the swarms, and all the assemblers that are making them. Right?"

They both nodded.

"I'm not sure that'll be possible," I said. "I thought the swarms would be powered down at night. I thought we could destroy them on the ground. But they're not powered down—at least not all of them. And if just one of them gets past us, if it escapes from the cave . . ." I shrugged. "Then this has all been a waste of time."

"Right," Bobby said, nodding. "That's right. It'd be a waste of time."

Mae said, "We need some way to trap them in the cave."

"There isn't any way," Bobby said. "I mean, they can just fly out, whenever they want."

Mae said, "There might be a way." She started rummaging in her backpack again, looking for something. "Meanwhile, the three of us better spread out."

"Why?" Bobby said, alarmed.

"Just do it," Mae said. "Now get moving."

I tightened my backpack, and adjusted the straps so it wouldn't rattle. I locked the night-vision goggles up on my forehead, and I started forward. I had gotten about halfway to the mound when I saw a dark figure climb out into the night.

I dropped down as quietly as I could. I was in a thick patch of sagebrush three feet high, so I was reasonably well concealed. I looked over my shoulder, but I didn't see either Mae or Bobby; they'd dropped to the ground, too. I didn't know if they'd separated yet. Cautiously, I pushed aside a plant in front of me, and looked toward the mound.

The legs of the figure were silhouetted against the faint green glow. The upper body was black against the night stars. I flipped down the goggles, and waited a moment while they flared blue, and then saw the image resolve.

This time it was Rosie. Walking around in the night, looking in all directions, her body vigilant and alert. Except that she didn't move like Rosie, she moved more like a man. Then after a moment, the silhouette changed into Ricky. And it moved like Ricky.

The figure crouched down, and appeared to be looking over the tops of the sage. I wondered what had brought it out of the mound. I didn't have to wait long to find out.

Behind the figure, a white light appeared on the western horizon. It grew rapidly in brilliance, and soon I heard the thumping of helicopter blades. That would be Julia coming from the Valley, I thought. I wondered what was so urgent that she had had to leave the hospital against orders, and fly out here in the middle of the night.

As the helicopter approached, it switched on its searchlight. I watched the circle of blue-white light as it rippled over the ground toward us. The Ricky figure watched, too, then slid down out of sight.

And then the helicopter roared over me, blinding me for a moment in the halogen light. Almost immediately it banked sharply, and circled back.

What the hell was going on?

The helicopter made a slow arc, passing over the mound but not stopping, then coming to a stop right above where I was hiding. I was caught in the blue glow. I rolled onto my back and waved to the helicopter, pointing repeatedly toward the lab. I mouthed "Go!" and pointed away.

The helicopter descended, and for a moment I thought it was going to land right beside me. Then it abruptly banked again, and moved away low to the ground, heading south toward the concrete pad. The sound faded.

I decided I had better change my position fast. I got to my knees and in a crouch, moved crabwise thirty yards to the left. Then I dropped down again.

When I looked back at the mound, I saw three—no, four figures coming out of the interior. They moved apart, each heading to a different area of the mound. They all looked like Ricky. I watched as they went down the slope of the mound, and moved out into the bush. My heart began to pound in my chest. One of the figures was coming in my direction. As it approached, I saw it veer off to the right. It was going to the place where I had been before. When it reached my last hiding place, it stopped, and turned in all directions.

It was not far from me at all. I could see through the goggles that this new Ricky figure now had a complete face, and the clothing was much more detailed. In addition, this figure moved with the sensation of real body weight. It might be an illusion, of course, but I guessed that the swarm had increased mass, and now weighed fifty pounds, maybe more. Maybe twice that. If so, then the swarm now had enough mass to jolt you with a physical impact. Even knock you off your feet.

Through the goggles I saw the figure's eyes move, and blink. The surface of the face now had the texture of skin. The hair appeared to be composed of individual strands. The lips moved, the tongue licked nervously. All in all this face looked very much like Ricky—disturbingly like Ricky. When the head turned in my direction, I felt that Ricky was staring right at me.

And I suppose it was, because the figure began to move directly toward me.

I was trapped. My heart was thumping in my chest. I hadn't planned for this; I had no protection, no sort of defense. I could get up and run, of course, but there was nowhere to go. I was surrounded by miles of desert, and the swarms would hunt me down. In a few moments I would be—

With a roar, the helicopter came back. The Ricky figure looked toward it as it came, and then turned and fled, literally flying over the ground, not bothering any longer to animate the legs and feet. It was creepy to see this human replica, suddenly floating over the desert.

But the other three Ricky figures were running, too. Running hard, conveying a distinct sense of panic. Did the swarms fear the helicopter? It seemed they did. And as I watched, I understood why. Even though the swarms were now heavier and more substantial, they were still vulnerable to strong winds. The helicopter was a hundred feet in the air but the downdraft was powerful enough to deform the running figures, flattening them partially as they fled. It was as if they were being hammered down.

The figures vanished into the mound.

I looked back at Mae. She was standing up in the streambed now, talking on her radio to the helicopter. She'd needed that radio, all right. She yelled to me, "Let's go!" and began running toward me. I was dimly aware of Bobby, running away from the mound, back to his ATV. But there was no time to worry about him. The helicopter hung poised right above the mound itself. Dust whipped up, stinging my eyes.

Then Mae was beside me. Removing our goggles, we pulled on our oxygen masks. She turned me, twisted the tank valve behind me. I did the same for her. Then we put the night goggles back on. It seemed like a lot of contraptions jiggling and rattling around my face. She clipped a halogen flashlight to my belt, and another to her own. She leaned close, shouted: "Ready?"

"I'm ready!"

"Okay, let's go!"

There was no time to think. It was better that way. The helicopter downdraft roared in my ears. Together we clawed our way up the slope of the mound, our clothes whipping around us. We arrived at the edge, barely visible in the thick swirling dust. We couldn't see anything beyond the rim. We couldn't see what was below.

Mae took my hand, and we jumped.

DAY 6
11:22 P.M.

I landed on loose stones, and half stumbled, half slid down the slope toward the cave entrance. The thumping of the helicopter blades above us was loud. Mae was right beside me, but I could hardly see her in the thick dust. There were no Ricky figures anywhere in sight. We came to the cave entrance and stopped. Mae pulled out the thermite capsules. She gave me the magnesium fuses. She tossed me a plastic cigarette lighter. I thought, that's what we're using? Her face was already partly clouded behind the mask. Her eyes were hidden behind the night-vision goggles.

She pointed to the interior of the cave. I nodded.

She tapped me on the shoulder, pointed to my goggles. I didn't understand, so she reached forward by my cheek and flicked a switch.

"—me now?" she said.

"Yes, I hear."

"Okay then, let's go."

We started into the cave. The green glow had vanished in the thick dust. We had only the infrared light mounted on top of our night-vision goggles. We saw no figures. We heard nothing but the thumping of the helicopter. But as we went deeper into the cave, the sound began to fade.

And as the sound faded, so did the wind.

Mae was focused. She said, "Bobby? Do you hear me?"

"Yes, I hear you."

"Get your ass in here."

"I'm trying to—"

"Don't try. Get in here, Bobby."

I shook my head. If I knew Bobby Lembeck, he was never coming into this pit. We rounded the bend, and saw nothing but suspended dust, the vague outlines of cave walls. The walls seemed smooth here, with no place to hide. Then from the gloom directly ahead I saw a Ricky figure emerge. He was expressionless, just walking toward us. Then another figure from the left, and another. The three formed a line. They marched toward us at a steady pace, their faces identical and expressionless.

"First lesson," Mae said, holding out the thermite cap.

"Let's hope they don't learn it," I said, and I lit the fuse. It sputtered white-hot sparks. She tossed the cap forward. It landed a few feet in front of the advancing group. They ignored it, staring forward at us.

Mae said, "It's a three count . . . two . . . one . . . and *turn away*."

I twisted away, ducking my head under my arm just as a sphere of blinding white filled the tunnel. Even though my eyes were closed, the glare was so strong that I saw spots when I opened my eyes again. I turned back.

Mae was already moving forward. The dust in the air had a slightly darker tint. I saw no sign of the three figures.

"Did they run?"

"No. Vaporized," she said. She sounded pleased.

"New situations," I said. I was feeling encouraged. If the programming assumptions still held, the swarms would be weak when reacting to genuinely new situations. In time they would learn; in time they would evolve strategies to deal with the new conditions. But initially their response would be disorganized, chaotic. That was a weakness of distributed intelligence. It was powerful, and it was flexible, but it was slow to respond to unprecedented events.

"We hope," Mae said.

We came to the gaping hole in the cave floor she had described. In the night goggles, I saw a sort of sloping ramp. Four or five figures were coming up toward us, and there seemed to be more behind. They all looked like Ricky, but many of them were not so well formed. And those in the rear were just swirling clouds. The thrumming sound was loud.

"Second lesson." Mae held out a cap. It sizzled white when I lit it. She rolled it gently down the ramp. The figures hesitated when they saw it.

"Damn," I said, but then it was time to duck away, and shield my eyes from the explosive flash. Inside the confined space, there was a roar of expanding gas. I felt a burst of intense heat on my back. When I looked again, most of the swarms beneath us had vanished. But a few hung back, apparently undamaged.

They were learning.

Fast.

"Next lesson," Mae said, holding two caps this time. I lit both and she rolled one, and threw the second one deeper down the ramp. The explosions roared simultaneously, and a huge gust of hot air rolled upward past us. My shirt caught fire. Mae pounded it out with the flat of her hand, smacking me with rapid strokes.

When we looked again, there were no figures in sight, and no dark swarms.

We went down the ramp, heading deeper into the cave.

We had started with twenty thermite caps. We had sixteen left, and we had gone only a short distance down the ramp toward the large room at the bottom. Mae moved quickly now—I had to hurry to catch up with her—but her instincts were good. The few swarms that materialized before us all quickly backed away at our approach.

We were herding them into the lower room.

Mae said, "Bobby, where are you?"

The headset crackled. "—trying—get—"

"Bobby, come on, damn it."

But all the while we were moving deeper into the cave, and soon we heard only static. Down here, dust hung suspended in the air, diffusing the infrared beams. We could see clearly the walls and ground directly ahead of us, but beyond that, there was total blackness. The sense of darkness and isolation was frightening. I couldn't tell what was on either side of me unless I turned my head, sweeping my beam back and forth. I began to smell that rotten odor again, sharp and nauseating.

We were coming to level ground. Mae stayed calm; when a half-dozen swarms buzzed before us, she held out another cap for me to light. Before I could light the fuse, the swarms backed off. She advanced at once.

"Sort of like lion taming," she said.

"So far," I said.

I didn't know how long we could keep this up. The cave was large, much larger than I had imagined. Sixteen caps didn't seem like enough to get us through it. I wondered if Mae was worried, too. She didn't seem to be. But probably she wouldn't show it.

Something was crunching underfoot. I looked down and saw the floor was carpeted with thousands of tiny, delicate yellow bones. Like bird bones. Except these were the bones of bats. Mae was right: they'd all been eaten.

In the upper corner of my night-vision image, a red light began to blink. It was some kind of warning, probably the battery. "Mae . . ." I began. Then the red light went out, as abruptly as it had begun.

"What?" she said. "What is it?"

"Never mind."

And then at last we came to the large central chamber—except there was no central chamber, at least, not anymore. Now the huge space was filled from floor to ceiling with an array of dark spheres, about two feet in diameter, and bristling with spiky protrusions. They looked like enormous sea urchins. They were stacked in large clusters. The arrangement was orderly.

Mae said, "Is this what I think it is?" Her voice was calm, detached. Almost scholarly.

"Yeah, I think so," I said. Unless I was wrong, these spiked clusters were an organic version of the fabrication plant that Xymos had built on the surface. "This is how they reproduce." I moved forward.

"I don't know if we should go in . . ." she said.

"We have to, Mae. Look at it: it's ordered."

"You think there's a center?"

"Maybe." And if there was, I wanted to drop thermite on it. I continued onward.

Moving among the clusters was an eerie sensation. Thick mucuslike liquid dripped from the tips of the spikes. And the spheres seemed to be coated with a kind of thick gel that quivered, making the whole cluster seem to be moving, alive. I paused to look more closely. Then I saw that the surface of the spheres really was alive; crawling within the gel were masses of twisting black worms. "Jesus . . ."

"They were here before," she said calmly.

"What?"

"The worms. They were living in the layer of guano on the cave floor, when I came here before. They eat organic material and excrete high-content phosphorus compounds."

"And now they're involved in swarm synthesis," I said. "That didn't take long, just a few days. Coevolution in action. The spheres probably provide food, and collect their excretions in some way."

"Or collect *them*," Mae said dryly.

"Yeah. Maybe." It wasn't inconceivable. Ants raised aphids the way we raised cows. Other insects grew fungus in gardens for food.

We moved deeper into the room. The swarms swirled on all sides of us, but they kept their distance. Probably another unprecedented event, I thought: intruders in the nest. They hadn't decided what to do. I moved carefully; the floor was now increasingly slippery in spots. There was a kind of thick muck on the ground. In a few places it glowed streaky green. The streaks seemed to go inward, toward the center. I had the sense that the floor sloped gently downward.

"How much farther?" Mae said. She still sounded calm, but I didn't think she was. I wasn't either; when I looked back I could no longer see the entrance to the chamber, hidden behind the clusters.

And then suddenly we reached the center of the room, because the clusters ended in an open space, and directly ahead I saw what looked like a miniature version of the mound outside. It was a mound about four feet high, perfectly circular, with flat vanes extending outward on all sides. It too was streaked with green. Pale smoke was coming off the vanes.

We moved closer.

"It's hot," she said. And it was. The heat was intense; that's why it was smoking. She said, "What do you think is in there?"

I looked at the floor. I could see now that the streaks of green were running from the clusters down to this central mound. I said, "Assemblers." The spiky urchins generated raw organic material. It flowed to the center, where the assemblers churned out the final molecules. This is where the final assembly occurred.

"Then this is the heart," Mae said.

"Yeah. You could say."

The swarms were all around us, hanging back by the clusters. Apparently, they wouldn't come into the center. But they were everywhere around us, waiting for us.

"How many you want?" she said quietly, taking the thermite from her pack.

I looked around at all the swarms.

"Five here," I said. "We'll need the rest to get out."

"We can't light five at once . . ."

"It's all right." I held out my hand. "Give them to me."

"But, Jack . . ."

"Come on, Mae."

She gave me five capsules. I moved closer and tossed them, unlit, into the central mound. The surrounding swarms buzzed, but still did not approach us.

"Okay," she said. She understood immediately what I was doing. She was already taking out more capsules.

"Now four," I said, looking back at the swarms. They were restless, moving back and forth. I didn't know how long they would stay there. "Three for you, one for me. You do the swarms."

"Right . . ." She gave me one capsule. I lit the others for her. She threw them back in the direction we had come. The swarms danced away.

She counted: "Three . . . two . . . one . . . *now!*"

We crouched, ducked away from the harsh blast of light. I heard a cracking sound; when I looked again, some of the clusters were breaking up, falling apart. Spikes were rolling on the ground. Without hesitating, I lit the next capsule, and as it spit white sparks, I tossed it into the central mound.

"Let's *go*!"

We ran for the entrance. The clusters were crumbling in front of us. Mae leapt easily over the falling spikes, and kept going. I followed her, counting in my mind . . . three . . . two . . . one . . .

Now.

There was a kind of high-pitched shriek, and then a terrific blast of hot gas, a booming detonation and stabbing pain in my ears. The shock wave knocked me flat on the ground, sent me skidding forward in the sludge. I felt the spikes sticking in my skin all over my body. My goggles were knocked away, and I was surrounded by blackness. *Blackness*. I could see nothing at all. I wiped the sludge from my face. I tried to get to my feet, slipped and fell.

"Mae," I said. "Mae . . ."

"There was an explosion," she said, in a surprised voice.

"Mae, where are you? I can't see."

Everything was pitch black. I could see nothing at all. I was deep in some damn cave full of spiky things and I couldn't see. I fought panic.

"It's all right," Mae said. In the darkness I felt her hand gripping my arm. Apparently she could see me. She said, "The flashlight's on your belt." She guided my hand.

I fumbled in the darkness, feeling for the clip. I found it, but I couldn't get it open. It was a spring clip and my fingers kept slipping off. I began to hear a thrumming sound, low at first, but starting to build. My hands were sweating. Finally the clip opened, and I flicked the flashlight on with a sigh of relief. I saw Mae in the cold halogen beam; she still had her goggles, and looked away. I swung the beam around the cave. It had been transformed by the explosion. Many of the clusters had broken apart and the spikes were all over the floor. Some substance on the floor was beginning to burn. Acrid, foul smoke was billowing up. The air was thick and dark. . . . I stepped backward, and felt something squishy.

I looked down and saw David Brooks's shirt. Then I realized I was standing on what was left of David's torso, which had turned into a kind of whitish jelly. My foot was right in his abdomen. His rib cage scraped against my shin, leaving a white streak on my pants. I looked back and saw David's face, ghostly white and eroded, his features eaten away until he looked as featureless as the faces on the swarms. I felt instant nausea, and tasted bile.

"Come on," Mae said, grabbing my arm, squeezing it hard. "Come *on*, Jack."

With a sucking sound, my foot pulled free of the body. I tried to scrape my shoe on the floor, to get clean of the white muck. I was not thinking anymore, I was just fighting nausea and an overpowering sense of horror. I wanted to run. Mae was talking to me but I didn't hear her. I saw only glimpses of the room around me, and was only dimly aware that the swarms were emerging all around us, swarm after swarm after swarm. They were buzzing everywhere.

"*I need you, Jack*," Mae said, holding out four caps, and somehow, fumbling with the flashlight, I managed to light them and she flung them in all directions. I threw my hands over my eyes as the hot spheres exploded around me. When I looked again, the swarms were gone. But in only a few moments, they began to reemerge. First one swarm, then three, then six, then ten—and then too many to count. They were converging, with an angry buzz, toward us.

"How many caps have we got left?" I said.

"Eight."

I knew then that we were not going to make it. We were too deep in the cave. We would never get out. I had no idea how many swarms were around us—my halogen beam swung back and forth across what seemed like an army.

"Jack . . ." Mae said, holding out her hand. She never seemed to lose confidence. I lit three more caps and Mae threw them, retracing her steps toward the entrance as she did so. I stayed close to her, but I knew our situation was hopeless. Each blast scattered the swarms for just a moment. Then they quickly regrouped. There were far too many swarms.

"Jack." More thermite in her hands.

Now I could see the entrance to the chamber, just a few yards ahead. My eyes were watering from all the acrid smoke. My halogen light was just a narrow beam cutting through the dust. The air was getting thicker and thicker.

A final series of white-hot blasts, and we came to the entrance. I saw the ramp leading back toward the surface. I never thought we'd get this far. But I wasn't thinking anymore, everything was impressions.

"How many left?" I said.

Mae didn't answer me. I heard the rumble of an engine from somewhere above us. Looking up I saw a wobbling white light in the cave higher up. The rumble became very loud—I heard an engine gunned—and then I saw the ATV poised on the ramp above. Bobby was up there, shouting "Get outtttttt!"

Mae turned and ran up the ramp, and I scrambled to follow her. I was vaguely aware of Bobby lighting something that burst into orange flame, and then Mae pushed me against the wall as the riderless ATV roared down the ramp toward the chamber below, with a flaming cloth hanging from its gas tank. It was a motorized Molotov cocktail.

As soon as it passed, Mae shoved me hard in the back. "Run!"

I sprinted the last few yards up the ramp. Bobby was reaching down for us, hauling us up over the lip to the level above. I fell and scraped my knee but hardly felt it as he dragged me onto my feet again. Then I was running hard toward the cave entrance and had almost reached the opening when a fiery blast knocked us off our feet, and I went tumbling through the air, and smashed against one of the cave walls. I got to my feet, head ringing. My flashlight was gone. I heard a kind of strange screaming sound from somewhere behind me, or thought I did.

I looked at Mae and Bobby. They were getting to their feet. With the helicopter still thumping above us, we clambered up the incline and collapsed over the lip of the mound, and tumbled down the slopes, out into the cool, black desert night.

The last thing I saw was Mae waving the helicopter away, gesturing for it to go, go, go—

And then the cave exploded.

The ground jumped beneath my feet, knocking me over. I fell to the ground just as the shock wave caused sharp pain in my ears. I heard the deep rumble of the explosion. From the mouth of the cave an enormous angry fireball billowed upward, orange laced in black. I felt a wave of heat rolling down toward me, and then it was gone, and everything was suddenly quiet, and the world around me was black.

How long I lay there beneath the stars I am not sure. I must have lost consciousness, because the next thing I remember was Bobby pushing me up into the backseat of the helicopter. Mae was already inside, and she leaned over to buckle me in. They were both looking at me with expressions of concern. I wondered dully if I had been injured. I didn't feel any pain. The door slammed beside me, and Bobby got in the front next to the pilot.

We had done it. We had succeeded.

I could hardly believe it was over.

The helicopter rose into the air and I saw the lights of the lab in the distance.

PREY

DAY 7
12:12 A.M.

"Jack."

Julia rushed toward me as I came down the corridor. In the overhead light her face looked beautiful in a lean, elegant way. She was in truth more beautiful than I remembered. Her ankle was bandaged and she had a cast on her wrist. She threw her arms around me and buried her head in my shoulder. Her hair smelled of lavender. "Oh, Jack, Jack. Thank God you're all right."

"Yeah," I said hoarsely. "I'm okay."

"I'm so glad . . . so glad."

I just stood there, feeling her hug me. Then I hugged her back. I didn't know how to react. She was so energized, but I was exhausted, flat.

"Are you all right, Jack?" she said, still hugging me.

"Yeah, Julia." I said, just above a whisper. "I am."

"What's wrong with your voice?" she said, pulling back to look at me. She scanned my face. "What's wrong?"

"He probably burned his vocal cords," Mae said. She was hoarse, too. Her face was blackened with soot. She had a cut on her cheek, and another on her forehead.

Julia embraced me again, her fingers touched my shirt. "Darling, you're hurt . . ."

"Just my shirt."

"Jack, are you sure you're not hurt? I think you're hurt . . ."

"No, I'm okay." I stepped away from her awkwardly.

"I can't tell you," she said, "how grateful I am for what you did tonight, Jack. What all of you did," she added, turning to the others. "You, Mae, and Bobby too. I'm only sorry I wasn't here to help. I know this is all my fault. But we're very grateful. The company is grateful."

I thought, The company? But all I said was, "Yeah, well, it had to be done."

"It did, yes, it certainly did. Quickly and decisively. And you did it, Jack. Thank God."

Ricky was standing in the background, head bobbing up and down. He was like one of those mechanical birds that drinks from a water glass. Bobbing up and down. I felt unreal, as if I was in a play.

"I think we should all have a drink to celebrate," Julia was saying, as we went down the corridor. "There must be some champagne around here. Ricky? Is there? Yes? I want to celebrate what you guys have done."

"I just want to sleep," I said.

"Oh, come on, just one glass."

It was typical Julia, I thought. Involved in her own world, not noticing how anyone around her was feeling. The last thing any of us wanted to do right now was drink champagne.

"Thanks anyway," Mae said, shaking her head.

"Are you sure? Really? It'd be fun. How about you, Bobby?"

"Maybe tomorrow," Bobby said.

"Oh well, okay, after all, you're the conquering heroes! We'll do it tomorrow, then."

I noticed how fast she was talking, how quick her body movements were. I remembered Ellen's comment about her taking drugs. It certainly seemed like she was on something. But I was so tired I just didn't give a damn.

"I've told the news to Larry Handler, the head of the company," she said, "and he's very grateful to you all."

"That's nice," I said. "Is he going to notify the Army?"

"Notify the Army? About what?"

"About the runaway experiment."

"Well, Jack, that's all taken care of now. You've taken care of it."

"I'm not sure we have," I said. "Some of the swarms might have escaped. Or there might be another nest out there. To be safe, I think we should call in the Army." I didn't really think we had missed anything, but I wanted to get outsiders in here. I was tired. I wanted somebody else to take over.

"The Army?" Julia's eyes flicked to Ricky, then back to me. "Jack, you're absolutely right," she said firmly. "This is an extremely serious situation. If there is the slightest chance something was missed, we must notify them at once."

"I mean tonight."

"Yes, I agree, Jack. Tonight. In fact, I'll do it right now."

I glanced back at Ricky. He was walking along, still nodding in that mechanical way. I didn't get it. What about Ricky's earlier panic? His fear that the experiment would be made public? Now it seemed he didn't care.

Julia said, "You three can get some sleep, and I'll call my contacts at the Pentagon."

"I'll go with you," I said.

"It's really not necessary."

"I want to," I said.

She glanced at me and smiled. "You don't trust me?"

"It's not that," I said. "But they might have questions I could answer for them."

"Okay, fine. Good idea. Excellent idea."

I felt sure that something was wrong. I felt as if I were in a play, and everyone was acting a part. Except I didn't know what the play was. I glanced over at Mae. She was frowning slightly. She must have sensed it, too.

We passed through the airlocks into the residential unit. Here the air felt uncomfortably cold to me; I shivered. We went into the kitchen and Julia reached for the phone.

"Let's make that call, Jack," she said.

I went to the refrigerator and got a ginger ale. Mae had an iced tea. Bobby had a beer. We were all thirsty. I noticed a bottle of champagne sitting in the fridge, waiting. I touched it; it was cold. There were six glasses in there, too, being chilled. She'd already planned the party.

Julia pushed the speakerphone button. We heard a dial tone. She punched in a number. But the call didn't go through. The line just went dead.

"Huh," she said. "Let's try that again . . ."

She dialed a second time. Again, the call failed to go through.

"That's funny. Ricky, I'm not getting an outside line."

"Try one more time," Ricky said.

I sipped my ginger ale and watched them. There was no question that this was all an act, a performance for our benefit. Julia dutifully dialed a third time. I wondered what number she was calling. Or did she know the number for the Pentagon by heart?

"Huh," she said. "Nothing."

Ricky picked up the phone, looked at the base, put it down again. "Should be okay," he said, acting puzzled.

"Oh for Christ's sake," I said. "Let me guess. Something has happened and we can't dial out."

"No, no, we can," Ricky said.

"I was just calling a few minutes ago," Julia said. "Just before you got back."

Ricky pushed away from the table. "I'll check the comm lines."

"You do that," I said, glowering.

Julia was staring at me. "Jack," she said, "I'm worried about you."

"Uh-huh."

"You're angry."

"I'm being fucked with."

"I promise you," she said quietly, meeting my eyes. "You're not."

Mae got up from the table, saying she was going to take a shower. Bobby wandered into the lounge to play a video game, his usual way to unwind. Soon I heard the sound of machine-gun fire, and the cries of dead bad guys. Julia and I were alone in the kitchen.

She leaned over the table toward me. She spoke in a low, earnest voice. "Jack," she said, "I think I owe you an explanation."

"No," I said. "You don't."

"I mean, for my behavior. My decisions these past days."

"It doesn't matter."

"It does to me."

"Maybe later, Julia."

"I need to tell you now. You see, the thing is, I just wanted to save the company, Jack. That's all. The camera failed and we couldn't fix it, we lost our contract, and the company was falling apart. I've never lost a company before. I never had one shot out from underneath me, and I didn't want Xymos to be the first. I was invested, I had a stake, and I guess I had my pride. I wanted to save it. I know I didn't use good judgment. I was desperate. It's nobody else's fault. They all wanted to stop it. I pushed them to go on. It was . . . it was my crusade." She shrugged. "And it was all for nothing. The company's going to fold in a matter of days. I've lost it." She leaned closer. "But I don't want to lose you, too. I don't want to lose my family. I don't want to lose *us*."

She dropped her voice lower, and stretched her hand across the table to cover mine. "I want to make amends, Jack. I want to make things right, and get us back on track again." She paused. "I hope you do, too."

I said, "I'm not sure how I feel."

"You're tired."

"Yes. But I'm not sure, anymore."

"You mean, about us?"

I said, "I hate this fucking conversation." And I did. I hated that she would start this when I was exhausted, when I had just gone through an ordeal that nearly got me killed and that was, ultimately, all her doing. I hated that she dismissed her involvement as "bad judgment" when it was considerably worse than that.

"Oh Jack, let's go back to the way we were," she said, and suddenly she leaned the rest of the way across the table and tried to kiss me on the lips. I pulled back, turned my head away. She stared at me, eyes pleading. "Jack, please."

"This is not the time or the place, Julia," I said.

A pause. She didn't know what to say. Finally: "The kids miss you."

"I'm sure they do. I miss them, too."

She burst into tears. "*And they don't miss me* . . ." she sobbed. "They don't even care about me . . . about their mother . . ." She reached for my hand again. I let her hold it. I tried to take stock of my feelings. I just felt tired, and very uncomfortable. I wanted her to stop crying.

"Julia . . ."

The intercom clicked. I heard Ricky's voice, amplified. "Hey, guys? We have a problem with the comm lines. You better come here right away."

The comm room consisted of a large closet in one corner of the maintenance room. It was sealed with a heavy security door, with a small tempered glass window set in the upper half. Through this window, I could see all the wiring panels and switch racks for the telecommunications in the lab. I also saw that great chunks of wiring had been yanked out. And slumped in a corner of the closet I saw Charley Davenport. He appeared to be dead. His mouth hung open, his eyes stared into space. His skin was purple-gray. A black buzzing swarm swirled around his head.

"I can't imagine how this happened," Ricky was saying. "He was fast asleep when I checked on him . . ."

"When was that?" I said.

"Maybe half an hour ago."

"And the swarm? How'd it get there?"

"I can't imagine," Ricky said. "He must have carried it with him, from outside."

"How?" I said. "He went through all the airlocks."

"I know, but . . ."

"But what, Ricky? How's it possible?"

"Maybe . . . I don't know, maybe it was in his throat or something."

"In his throat?" I said. "You mean, just hanging out between his tonsils? These things kill you, you know."

"Yeah, I know. Of course I know." He shrugged. "Beats me."

I stared at Ricky, trying to understand his demeanor. He had just discovered that his lab was invaded by a lethal nanoswarm, and he didn't appear to be upset at all. He was taking it all very casually.

Mae came hurrying into the room. She took in the situation with a glance. "Did anyone check the video playback?"

"We can't," Ricky said. He pointed to the closet. "The controls are disabled—in there."

"So you don't know how he got in there?"

"No. But he evidently didn't want us calling out. At least . . . that's how it looks."

Mae said, "Why would Charley go in there?"

I shook my head. I had no idea.

Julia said, "It's airtight. Maybe he knew he was infected and wanted to seal himself off. I mean, he locked the door from the inside."

I said, "He did? How do you know that?"

Julia said, "Um . . . I just assumed . . . uh . . ." She peered through the glass. "And, uh, you can see the lock reflected in that chrome fitting . . . see that one there?"

I didn't bother to look. But Mae did, and I heard her say, "Oh yes, Julia, you're right. Good observation. I missed that myself." It sounded very phony, but Julia didn't seem to react.

So everybody was playacting, now. Everything was staged. And I didn't understand why. But as I watched Mae with Julia, I noticed that she was being extremely careful with my wife. Almost as if she was afraid of her, or at least afraid of offending her.

That was odd.

And a little alarming.

I said to Ricky, "Is there a way to unlock the door?"

"I think so. Vince probably has a skeleton key. But nobody's unlocking that door now, Jack. Not as long as that swarm is in there."

"So we can't call anywhere?" I said. "We're stuck here? Incommunicado?"

"Until tomorrow, yes. Helicopter will be back tomorrow morning, on its regular run." Ricky peered in through the glass at the destruction. "Jeez. Charley really did a job on those switching panels."

I said, "Why do you think he would do that?"

Ricky shook his head. "Charley was a little crazy, you know. I mean he was colorful. But all that farting and humming . . . he was a few fries short of a Happy Meal, Jack."

"I never thought so."

"Just my opinion," he said.

I stood beside Ricky and looked through the glass. The swarm was buzzing around Charley's head, and I was starting to see the milky coating form on his body. The usual pattern.

I said, "What about pumping liquid nitrogen in there? Freezing the swarm?"

"We could probably do that," Ricky said, "but I'm afraid we'd damage the equipment."

"Can you turn the air handlers up enough to suck the particles out?"

"Handlers are going full-bore now."

"And you wouldn't want to use a fire extinguisher . . ."

He shook his head. "Extinguishers are Halon. Won't affect the particles."

"So we're effectively kept out of that room."

"Far as I can tell, yes."

"Cell phones?"

He shook his head. "Antennas route through that room. Every form of communication we have—cells, Internet, high-speed data trunks—everything goes through that room."

Julia said, "Charley knew that room was airtight. I bet he went there to protect the rest of us. It was a selfless act. A courageous act."

She was developing her theory about Charley, fleshing it out, adding details. It was a little distracting, considering the main problem was still unanswered—how to unlock the door, and disable the swarm. I said, "Is there another window in that closet?"

"No."

"This window in the door is the only one?"

"Yes."

"Okay, then," I said, "let's black out the window, and turn the lights out in there. And wait a few hours, until the swarm loses power."

"Jeez, I don't know," Ricky said doubtfully.

"What do you mean, Ricky?" Julia said. "I think it's a great idea. It's certainly worth a try. Let's do it *right now*."

"Okay, fine," Ricky said, immediately deferring to her. "But you're going to have to wait six hours."

I said, "I thought it was three hours."

"It is, but I want extra hours before I open that door. If that swarm gets loose in here, we've all had it."

In the end, that was what we decided to do. We got black cloth and taped it over the window, and put black cardboard over that. We turned out the lights and taped the light switch in the OFF position. At the end of that time, exhaustion hit me again. I looked at my watch. It was one o'clock in the morning. I said, "I have to go to bed."

"We should all get some sleep," Julia said. "We can revisit this in the morning."

We all headed off toward the residence module. Mae sidled up alongside me. "How are you feeling?" she said.

"Okay. My back's starting to hurt a little."

She nodded. "You better let me take a look at it."

"Why?"

"Just let me take a look, before you go to bed."

"Oh, Jack, darling," Julia cried. "You poor baby."

"What is it?"

I was sitting on the kitchen table with my shirt off. Julia and Mae were behind me, clucking.

"What is it?" I said again.

"There's some blistering," Mae said.

"Blistering?" Julia said. "His whole back is covered—"

"I think we have dressings," Mae said, interrupting her, reaching for the first-aid kit beneath the sink.

"Yes, I hope so." Julia smiled at me. "Jack, I can't tell you how sorry I am, that you had to go through this."

"This may sting a little," Mae said.

I knew that Mae wanted to talk to me alone, but there was no opportunity. Julia was not going to leave us alone for a minute. She had always been jealous of Mae, even years ago when I first hired Mae in my company, and now she was competing with her for my attention.

I wasn't flattered.

The dressings were cool at first, as Mae applied them, but within moments they stung bitterly. I winced.

"I don't know what painkillers we have," Mae said. "You've got a good area of second-degree burns."

Julia rummaged frantically through the first-aid kit, tossing contents out right and left. Tubes and canisters clattered to the floor. "There's morphine," she said at last, holding up a bottle. She smiled at me brightly. "That should do it!"

"I don't want morphine," I said. What I really wanted to say was that I wanted her to go to bed. Julia was annoying me. Her frantic edge was getting on my nerves. And I wanted to talk to Mae alone.

"There's nothing else," Julia said, "except aspirin."

"Aspirin is fine."

"I'm worried it won't be—"

"*Aspirin is fine.*"

"You don't have to bite my head off."

"I'm sorry. I don't feel well."

"Well, I'm only trying to help." Julia stepped back. "I mean, if you two want to be alone, you should just say so."

"No," I said, "we do not want to be alone."

"Well, I'm only trying to help." She turned back to the medicine kit. "Maybe there is something else . . ." Containers of tape and plastic bottles of antibiotics fell to the floor.

"Julia," I said. "Please stop."

"What am I doing? What am I doing that is so awful?"

"Just stop."

"I'm only trying to help."

"I know that."

Behind me, Mae said, "Okay. All finished now. That should hold you until tomorrow." She yawned. "And now, if you don't mind, I'm going to bed."

I thanked her, and watched her leave the room. When I turned back, Julia was holding a glass of water and two aspirins for me.

"Thank you," I said.

"I never liked that woman," she said.

"Let's get some sleep," I said.

"There's only single beds here."

"I know."

She moved closer. "I'd like to be with you, Jack."

"I'm really tired. I'll see you in the morning, Julia."

I went back to my room and looked at the bed. I didn't bother taking off my clothes.

I don't remember my head touching the pillow.

DAY 7
4:42 A.M.

I slept restlessly, with constant and terrible dreams. I dreamed that I was back in Monterey, marrying Julia again, and I was standing in front of the minister when she came up alongside me in her bridal gown, and when she lifted the veil I was shocked by how beautiful and young and slender she was. She smiled at me, and I smiled back, trying to conceal my uneasiness. Because now I saw she was more than slender, her face was thin, almost emaciated. Almost a skull.

Then I turned to the minister in front of us, but it was Mae, and she was pouring colored liquids back and forth in test tubes. When I looked back at Julia she was very angry, and said she never liked that woman. Somehow it was my fault. I was to blame.

I woke up briefly, sweating. The pillow was soaked. I turned it over, and went back to sleep. I saw myself sleeping on the bed, and I looked up and saw that the door to my room was open. Light came in from the hallway outside. A shadow fell across my bed. Ricky came into the room and looked down at me. His face was backlit and dark, I couldn't see his expression, but he said, "I always loved you, Jack." He leaned over to whisper something in my ear, and I realized as his head came down that he was going to kiss me instead. He was going to kiss me on the lips, passionately. His mouth was open. His tongue licked his lips. I was very upset, I didn't know what to do, but at that moment Julia came in and said, "What's going on?" and Ricky hastily pulled away, and made some kind of evasive comment. Julia was very angry and said, "Not now, you fool," and Ricky made another evasive comment. And then Julia said, "This is completely unnecessary, it will take care of itself." And Ricky said, "There are constriction coefficients for deterministic algorithms if you do interval global optimization." And she said, *"It won't hurt you if you don't fight it."* She turned on the light in the room and walked out.

Then I was suddenly back in my Monterey wedding, Julia was standing beside me in white, and I turned to look back at the audience, and I saw my three kids sitting in the first row, smiling and happy. And as I watched a black line appeared around their mouths, and swept down their bodies, until they were cloaked in black. They continued to smile, but I was horrified. I ran to them, but I couldn't rub the black cloak off. And Nicole said calmly, "Don't forget the sprinklers, Dad."

I woke up, tangled up in the sheets, drenched in sweat. The door to my room was open. A rectangle of light fell across my bed from the hallway outside. I looked over at the workstation monitor. It said "4:55 A.M." I closed my eyes and lay there for a while, but I couldn't go back to sleep. I was wet and uncomfortable. I decided to take a shower.

Shortly before five in the morning, I got out of bed.

The hallway was silent. I walked down the corridor to the bathrooms. The doors to all the bedrooms were open, which seemed strange. I could see everybody sleeping as I walked past. And the lights were on in all the bedrooms. I saw Ricky asleep, and I saw Bobby, and I saw Julia, and Vince. Mae's bed was empty. And of course Charley's bed was empty.

I stopped in the kitchen to get a ginger ale from the refrigerator. I was very thirsty, my throat painful and parched. And my stomach felt a little queasy. I looked at the champagne bottle. I suddenly had a funny feeling about it, as if it might have been tampered with. I took it out and looked closely at the cap, at the metal foil that covered the cork. It looked entirely normal. No tampering, no needle marks, no nothing.

Just a bottle of champagne.

I put it back and closed the refrigerator door.

I began to wonder if I had been unfair to Julia. Maybe she really did believe she'd made a mistake and wanted to put things right. Maybe she just wanted to show her gratitude. Maybe I was being too tough on her. Too unforgiving.

Because when you thought about it, what had she done that was suspicious or wrong? She'd been glad to see me, even if she was over the top. She'd accepted responsibility for the experiment, and she'd apologized for it. She'd immediately agreed to make the call to the Army. She'd agreed with my plan to kill the swarm in the comm room. She'd done everything she could do to show she supported me, and was on my side.

But I still was uneasy.

And of course there was the matter of Charley and his swarm. Ricky's idea that Charley had somehow been carrying the swarm inside his body, in his mouth or under his armpit or something, didn't make a lot of sense to me. Those swarms killed within seconds. So it left a question—how *did* the swarm get into the comm room with Charley? Did it get in from outside? Why hadn't it attacked Julia and Ricky and Vince?

I forgot about my shower.

I decided to go down to the utility room, and look around outside the comm room door. Maybe there was something I had missed. Julia had been talking a lot, interrupting my train of thought. Almost as if she hadn't wanted me to figure something out . . .

There I was again, being hard on Julia.

I went through the airlock, down the corridor, through another airlock. When you were tired, it was annoying to have that wind blowing on you. I came out into the utility area, and went toward the comm room door. I didn't notice anything.

I heard the sound of a clicking keyboard, and looked into the biology lab. Mae was there, at her workstation.

I said, "What are you doing?"

"Checking the video playback."

"I thought we couldn't do that, because Charley pulled the wires."

"That's what Ricky said. But it isn't true."

I started to come around the lab bench, to look over her shoulder. She held up her hand.

"Jack," she said. "Maybe you don't want to look at this."

"What? Why not?"

"It's, uh . . . maybe you don't want to deal with this. Not right now. Maybe tomorrow."

But of course after that, I practically ran around the table to see what was on her monitor. And I stopped. What I saw on her screen was an image of an empty corridor. With a time code at the bottom of the picture. "Is this it?" I said. "Is this what I shouldn't deal with?"

"No." She turned in her chair. "Look, Jack, you have to go through all the security cameras in sequence, and each one only records ten frames a minute, so it's very difficult to be sure of what we're—"

"Just show me, Mae."

"I have to go back a bit . . ." She pressed the BACK button in the corner of the keyboard repeatedly. Like many new control systems, the Xymos system was modeled on Internet browser technology. You could go backward in work, retracing your steps.

The frames jumped backward until she came to the place she wanted. Then she ran it forward, the security images jumping from one camera to the next in rapid succession. A corridor. The main plant. Another angle on the plant. An airlock. Another corridor. The utility room. A corridor. The kitchen. The lounge. The residence hallway. An exterior view, looking down at the floodlit desert. Corridor. The power room. The outside, ground level. Another corridor.

I blinked. "How long have you been doing this?"

"About an hour."

"Jesus."

Next I saw a corridor. Ricky moving down it. Power station. Outside, looking down on Julia stepping into the floodlight. A corridor. Julia and Ricky together, embracing, and then a corridor, and—

"Wait," I said.

Mae hit a button. She looked at me, said nothing. She pressed another key, flicked the images forward slowly. She stopped on the camera that showed Ricky and Julia.

"Ten frames."

The movement was blurred and jerky. Ricky and Julia moved toward each other. They embraced. There was a clear sense of ease, of familiarity between them. And then they kissed passionately.

"Aw, shit," I said, turning away from the screen. "Shit, shit, shit."

"I'm sorry, Jack," Mae said. "I don't know what to say."

I felt a wave of dizziness, almost as if I might collapse. I sat down on the table. I kept my body turned away from the screen. I just couldn't look. I took a deep breath. Mae was saying something more, but I didn't hear her words. I took another breath. I ran my hand through my hair.

I said, "Did you know about this?"

"No. Not until a few minutes ago."

"Did anybody?"

"No. We used to joke about it sometimes, that they had a relationship, but none of us believed it."

"Jesus." I ran my hand through my hair again. "Tell me the truth, Mae. I need to hear the truth. Did you know about this or not?"

"No, Jack. I didn't."

Silence. I took a breath. I tried to take stock of my feelings. "You know what's funny?" I said. "What's funny is that I've suspected this for a while now. I mean, I was pretty sure it was happening, I just didn't know who . . . I mean . . . Even though I expected it, it's still kind of a shock."

"I'm sure."

"I never would have figured Ricky," I said. "He's such a . . . I don't know . . . smarmy kind of guy. And he's not a big power guy. Somehow I would have thought she'd pick someone more important, I guess." As I said it, I remembered my conversation with Ellen after dinner.

Are you so sure about Julia's style?

That was after I'd seen the guy in the car. The guy whose face I couldn't really make out . . .

Ellen: *It's called denial, Jack.*

"Jesus," I said, shaking my head. I felt angry, embarrassed, confused, furious. It kept changing every second.

Mae waited. She didn't move or speak. She was completely still. Finally she said, "Do you want to see any more?"

"Is there more?"

"Yes."

"I don't know if I, uh . . . No, I don't want to see any more."

"Maybe you better."

"No."

"I mean, it might make you feel better."

"I don't think so," I said. "I don't think I can take it."

She said, "It may not be what you think, Jack. At least, it may not be exactly what you think."

It's called denial, Jack.

"Sorry, Mae," I said, "but I don't want to pretend anymore. I saw it. I know what it is."

I thought I'd be with Julia forever. I thought we loved the kids together, we had a family, a house, a life together. And Ricky had a new baby of his own. It just was weird. It didn't make sense to me. But then, things never turn out the way you think they will.

I heard Mae typing quickly on the keyboard. I turned so I could see her, but not the screen. "What're you doing?"

"Trying to find Charley. See if I can track what happened to him over the last few hours."

She continued typing. I took a breath. She was right. Whatever was going on in my personal life was already well advanced. There was nothing I could do about it, at least not right now.

I turned all the way around and faced the screen.

"Okay," I said. "Let's look for Charley."

It was disorienting to watch the camera images flash by, repeating in sequence. People popped in and out of images. I saw Julia in the kitchen. The next time I saw her and Ricky in the kitchen. The refrigerator door was open, then shut. I saw Vince in the main plant room, then he popped out. I saw him in a corridor, then gone.

"I don't see Charley."

"Maybe he's still asleep," Mae said.

"Can you see in the bedrooms?"

"Yes, there are cameras there, but I'd have to change security cycle. Ordinary cycle doesn't go into the bedrooms."

"How big a deal is it to change the security cycle?"

"I'm not sure. This is really Ricky's area. The system here is pretty complicated. Ricky's the only one who really knows how to work it. Let's see if we find Charley in the regular cycle."

So that's what we did, waiting to see if he appeared in any of the standard camera images. We searched for about ten minutes more. From time to time, I had to look away from the images, though it never seemed to bother Mae. But sure enough, we saw him in the residential hallway, walking down the corridor, rubbing his face. He'd just woken up.

"Okay," Mae said. "We got him."

"What's the time?"

She froze the image, so we could read it. It was 12:10 A.M.

I said, "That's only about half an hour before we got back."

"Yes." She ran the images forward. Charley disappeared from the hallway, but we saw him briefly, heading into the bathroom. Then we saw Ricky and Julia in the kitchen. I felt my body tense. But they were just talking. Then Julia put the champagne in the refrigerator, and Ricky started handing her glasses to put in beside the bottle.

It was difficult to be sure what happened next, because of the frame rate. Ten frames a second of video meant that you only got an image every six seconds, so events appeared blurred and jumpy when things moved fast, because too much happened between the frames.

But this is what I thought happened:

Charley showed up, and began talking to the two of them. He was smiling, cheerful. He pointed to the glasses. Julia and Ricky put the glasses away while they talked to him. Then he held up his hand, to stop.

He pointed to a glass that Julia was holding in her hand before she put it in the refrigerator. He said something.

Julia shook her head, and put the glass in the refrigerator.

Charley seemed puzzled. He pointed again to another glass. Julia shook her head. Then Charley hunched his shoulders and thrust out his chin, as if he were getting angry. He poked the table repeatedly with his finger, making a point.

Ricky stepped forward between Julia and Charley. He acted like someone interrupting an argument. He held his hands up soothingly to Charley: take it easy.

Charley wasn't taking it easy. He was pointing to the sink, heaped with unwashed dishes.

Ricky shook his head, and put his hand on Charley's shoulder.

Charley brushed it off.

The two men began to argue. Meanwhile, Julia calmly put the rest of the glasses into the refrigerator. She seemed indifferent to the argument a few feet from her, almost as if she didn't hear it. Charley was trying to get around Ricky to the refrigerator, but Ricky kept moving to block him, and held his hands up each time.

Ricky's whole demeanor suggested that he did not regard Charley as rational. He was treating Charley in that careful way you do when someone's out of control.

Mae said, "Is Charley being affected by the swarm? Is that why he's acting that way?"

"I can't tell." I looked closer at the screen. "I don't see any swarm."

"No," she said. "But he's pretty angry."

"What does he want them to do?" I said.

Mae shook her head. "Put the glasses back? Wash them? Use different glasses? I can't tell."

I said, "Charley doesn't care about that stuff. He'd eat out of a dirty plate somebody else had used." I smiled. "I've seen him do it."

Suddenly, Charley stepped several paces back. For a moment, he was completely still, as if he had discovered something that stunned him. Ricky said something to him. Charley began pointing and shouting at both of them. Ricky tried to approach him.

Charley kept backing away, and then he turned to the phone, mounted on the wall. He lifted the receiver. Ricky came forward, very quickly, his body a blur, and slammed the phone down. He shoved Charley back—hard. Ricky's strength was surprising. Charley was a big guy, but he went down to the floor, and skidded backward a few feet.

Charley got to his feet, continued to yell, then he turned and ran out of the room.

Julia and Ricky exchanged a glance. Julia said something to him.

Immediately, Ricky ran after Charley.

Julia ran after Ricky.

"Where are they going?" I said.

Mae released the HOLD button, and the screen flashed "Updating Time," and then we started seeing images from all the cameras again, in sequence. We saw Charley running down a corridor, and we saw Ricky start after him. We waited impatiently for the next cycle. But nobody was visible there.

Another cycle. Then we saw Charley in the utility room, dialing the phone. He glanced over his shoulder. A moment later, Ricky came in, and Charley hung up the phone. They argued, circling around each other.

Charley picked up a shovel, and swung it at Ricky. The first time Ricky dodged away. The second time it caught him on the shoulder and knocked him to the floor. Charley swung the shovel over his head, and slammed it down on Ricky's head. The gesture was brutal, the intention clearly murderous. Ricky managed to duck back just as the shovel smashed onto the concrete.

"My God . . ." Mae said.

Ricky was getting to his feet, when Charley turned and saw Julia enter the room. Julia held out her hand, pleading with Charley (to put down the shovel?). Charley looked from one of them to the other. And then Vince entered the room, too. Now that they were all in the room, he seemed to lose his urge to fight. They were circling him, closing in.

Suddenly Charley dashed for the comm room, stepped inside, and tried to shut the door behind him. Ricky was on him in a flash. He had his foot in the door and Charley couldn't get it closed. Charley's face looked angry through the glass. Vince came right alongside Ricky. With both of them at the door, I couldn't see what was happening. Julia seemed to be giving orders. I thought I saw her reach her hand through the crack in the door, but it was difficult to be sure.

In any case, the door opened, and both Vince and Ricky entered the room. The action that came next was swift, blurred on the video, but apparently the three men were fighting, and Ricky managed to get behind Charley, and get him in a hammerlock; Vince pulled Charley's arm behind his back, and together the two men subdued Charley. He stopped fighting. The image was less blurred.

"What's happening?" Mae said. "They never told us any of this."

Ricky and Vince were holding Charley from behind. Charley was panting, his chest heaving, but he no longer struggled. Julia came into the room. She looked at Charley, and had some conversation with him.

And then Julia walked up to Charley, and kissed him full and long on the lips.

Charley struggled, tried to wrench away. Vince grabbed a fistful of Charley's hair and tried to hold his head steady. Julia continued to kiss him. Then she stepped away, and as she did I saw a river of black between her mouth and Charley's. It was only there for a moment, and then it faded.

"Oh my God," Mae said.

Julia wiped her lips, and smiled.

Charley sagged, dropped to the ground. He appeared dazed. A black cloud came out of his mouth, and swirled around his head. Vince patted him on the head and left the room.

Ricky went over to the panels—and pulled out wiring by the handful. He literally ripped the panels apart. Then he turned back to Charley, said something else, and walked out of the comm room.

At once Charley sprang to his feet, closed the door, and locked it. But Ricky and Julia just laughed, as if this was a futile gesture. Charley sagged again, and from then on he was out of sight.

Ricky threw his arm around Julia's shoulder, and they walked out of the room together.

"Well, you two are certainly up bright and early!"

I turned.

Julia was standing in the doorway.

DAY 7
5:12 A.M.

She came forward into the room, smiling. "You know, Jack," she said, "if I didn't trust you so completely, I'd think there was something going on between the two of you."

"Really," I said. I stepped away from Mae a little, while she typed quickly. I felt tremendously uneasy. "Why would you think that?"

"Well, you had your heads together about *something*," she said, as she came toward us. "You looked quite fascinated by what you were seeing on the screen. What're you looking at, anyway?"

"It's ah, technical."

"May I see? I'm interested in technical things. Didn't Ricky tell you I had a new technical interest? I do. I'm fascinated by this technology. It's a new world, isn't it? The twenty-first century has arrived. Don't get up, Mae. I'll just look over your shoulder."

By now she had walked around the bench, and could see the screen. She frowned at the image, which showed bacterial cultures on a red growth medium. White circles within red circles. "What's this?"

Mae said, "Bacterial colonies. We've got some contamination of the coli stock. I had to take one tank offline. We're trying to figure out what's wrong."

"Probably phage, don't you think?" Julia said. "Isn't that what it usually is with bacterial stocks—a virus?" She sighed. "Everything about molecular manufacturing is so *delicate*. Things go wrong so easily, and so often. You have to keep alert for trouble." She glanced at me, and at Mae. "But surely this isn't what you've been looking at all this time . . ."

"Actually, it is," I said.

"What? Pictures of mold?"

"Bacteria."

"Yes, bacteria. You've been looking at this the whole time, Mae?"

She shrugged, nodded. "Yes, Julia. It's my job."

"And I don't question your dedication for a moment," Julia said. "But do you mind?" Her hand darted forward and hit the BACK key in the corner of the keyboard.

The previous screen showed more pictures of bacterial growth.

The next screen showed a virus electron micrograph.

And then a table of growth data over the last twelve hours.

Julia continued to hit the BACK key half a dozen times more, but all she saw were images of bacteria and viruses, graphs, and data tables. She took her hand away from the keyboard. "You seem to be devoting a lot of time to this. Is it really so important?"

"Well, it's a contaminant," Mae said. "If we don't control it, we'll have to shut down the entire system."

"Then by all means keep at it." She turned to me. "Want to have breakfast? I'd imagine you must be starving."

"Sounds great," I said.

"Come with me," Julia said. "We'll make it together."

"Okay," I said. I glanced at Mae. "I'll see you later. Let me know if I can do anything to help."

I left with Julia. We started down the corridor to the residences.

"I don't know why," Julia said, "but that woman bothers me."

"I don't know why either. She's very good. Very thoughtful, very conscientious."

"And very pretty."

"Julia . . ."

"Is that why you won't kiss me? Because you're involved with her?"

"Julia, for Christ's sake."

She stared at me, waiting.

"Look," I said. "It's been a rough couple of weeks for everybody. Frankly, you've been difficult to live with."

"I'm sure I have."

"And frankly, I've been pretty angry with you."

"With good reason, I know. I'm sorry for what I put you through." She leaned over, kissed me on the cheek. "But it feels so distant now. I don't like the tension between us. What do you say we kiss and make up?"

"Maybe later," I said. "We have a lot to do now."

She got playful, puckering her lips, kissing air. "Oooh, come on, sweetie, just a little smooch . . . come on, it won't kill you . . ."

"Later," I said.

She sighed, and gave up. We continued down the corridor in silence for a while. Then she said, in a serious voice, "You're avoiding me, Jack. And I want to know why."

I didn't answer her, I just gave a long-suffering sigh and kept walking, acting like what she'd said was beneath response. In fact, I was badly worried.

I couldn't keep refusing to kiss her forever; sooner or later she'd figure out what I knew. Maybe she already had. Because even when Julia was acting girlish, she seemed sharper, more alert than she'd ever been before. I had the feeling she didn't miss anything. And I had the same feeling about Ricky. It was as if they were tuned up, ultra-aware.

And I was worried about what I'd seen on Mae's monitor. The black cloud that seemed to come from Julia's mouth. Had it really been there, on the video? Because as far as I knew, swarms killed their prey on contact. They were merciless. Now Julia seemed to be harboring a swarm. How could that be? Did she have some sort of immunity? Or was the swarm tolerating her, not killing her for some reason? And what about Ricky and Vince? Did they have immunity, too?

One thing was clear: Julia and Ricky did not want us to call anybody. They had deliberately isolated us in the desert, knowing that they would have only a few hours until the helicopter arrived. So apparently, that's all the time they needed. To do what? Kill us? Or just infect us? What?

Walking down the corridor next to my wife, I felt as if I was walking with a stranger. With somebody I didn't know anymore. Somebody who was immensely dangerous.

I glanced at my watch. The helicopter would be here in less than two hours, now.

Julia smiled. "Got an appointment?"

"No. Just thinking it's time for breakfast."

"Jack," she said. "Why won't you be honest with me?"

"I'm being honest . . ."

"No. You were wondering how long until the helicopter comes."

I shrugged.

"Two hours," she said. And she added, "I'll bet you'll be glad to get out of here, won't you?"

"Yes," I said. "But I'm not leaving until everything is done."

"Why? What's left to be done?"

By now we had reached the residential unit. I could smell bacon and eggs cooking. Ricky came around the corner. He smiled heartily when he saw me. "Hey, Jack. How'd you sleep?"

"I slept okay."

"Really? 'Cause you look a little tired."

"I had bad dreams," I said.

"Oh yes? Bad dreams? Bummer."

"It happens sometimes," I said.

We all went into the kitchen. Bobby was making breakfast. "Scrambled eggs with chives and cream cheese," he said cheerfully. "What kind of toast do you guys want?"

Julia wanted wheat toast. Ricky wanted English muffin. I said I didn't want anything. I was looking at Ricky, noticing again how strong he appeared. Beneath his T-shirt, the muscles were well defined, cut. He caught me staring at him. "Something wrong?"

"No. Just admiring your butch look." I tried to be light, but the truth was that I felt incredibly uncomfortable in the kitchen with all of them around me. I kept thinking of Charley, and how swiftly they had attacked him. I wasn't hungry; I just wanted to get out of there. But I couldn't see how to do it without arousing suspicion.

Julia went to the refrigerator, opened the door. The champagne was in there. "You guys ready to celebrate now?"

"Sure," Bobby said. "Sounds great, a little mimosa in the morning . . ."

"Absolutely not," I said. "Julia, I'm going to insist you take this situation seriously. We're not out of the woods yet. We have to get the Army in here, and we haven't been able to call. It's not time to break out the champagne."

She pouted. "Oh, you're such a spoilsport . . ."

"Spoilsport hell. You're being ridiculous."

"Oooh, baby, don't get mad, just kiss me, kiss me." She puckered her lips again, and leaned across the table.

But it seemed like getting angry was the only move I had. "God damn it, Julia," I said, raising my voice, "the only reason we are in this mess is because you didn't take it seriously in the first place. You had a runaway swarm out there in the desert for what—two weeks? And instead of eradicating it, you played with it. You fooled around until it got out of control, and as a result three people are dead. This is not a goddamn celebration, Julia. It's a disaster. And I am not drinking any fucking champagne while I am here and neither is anyone else." I took the bottle to the sink and smashed it. I turned back to her. "Got it?"

Stony-faced, she said, "That was completely unnecessary."

I saw Ricky looking at me thoughtfully. As if he was trying to decide something. Bobby turned his back while he cooked, as if he was embarrassed by a marital spat. Had they gotten to Bobby? I thought I saw a thin black line at his neck, but I couldn't be sure, and I didn't dare stare.

"Unnecessary?" I said, full of outrage. "Those people were my friends. And they were your friends, Ricky. And yours, Bobby. And I don't want to hear this celebration shit anymore!" I turned and stomped out of the room. As I left, Vince was coming in.

"Better take it easy, pal," Vince said. "You'll give yourself a stroke."

"Fuck off," I said.

Vince raised his eyebrows. I brushed past him.

"You're not fooling anybody, Jack!" Julia called after me. "I know what you're really up to!"

My stomach flipped. But I kept walking.

"I can see right through you, Jack. I know you're going back to *her*."

"Damn right!" I said.

Was that what Julia really thought? I didn't believe it for a moment. She was just trying to mislead me, to keep me off guard until . . . what? What were they going to do?

There were four of them. And only two of us—at least, there were two if they hadn't already gotten to Mae.

Mae wasn't in the biology laboratory. I looked around and saw that a side door was ajar, leading downstairs to the underground level where the fermentation chambers were installed. Up close, they were much larger than I had realized, giant stainless spheres about six feet across. They were surrounded by a maze of pipes and valves and temperature control units. It was warm here, and very noisy.

Mae was standing by the third unit, making notes on a clipboard and shutting a valve. She had a rack of test tubes at her feet. I went down and stood beside her. She looked at me, then shot a glance toward the ceiling, where a security camera was mounted. She walked around to the other side of the tank, and I followed her. Over here, the tank blocked the camera.

She said, "They slept with the lights on."

I nodded. I knew what it meant, now.

"They're all infected," she said.

"Yes."

"And it's not killing them."

"Yes," I said, "but I don't understand why."

"It must have evolved," she said, "to tolerate them."

"That fast?"

"Evolution can happen fast," she said. "You know the Ewald studies."

I did. Paul Ewald had studied cholera. What he found was that the cholera organism would quickly change to sustain an epidemic. In places where there were no sanitary water supplies but perhaps a ditch running through a village, the cholera was virulent, prostrating the victim and killing him where he fell from massive overwhelming diarrhea. The diarrhea contained millions of cholera organisms; it would run into the water supply and infect others in the village. In this way the cholera reproduced, and the epidemic continued.

But when there was sanitary water supply, the virulent strain could not reproduce. The victim would die where he fell but his diarrhea would not enter the water supply. Others would not be infected, and the epidemic would fade. Under those circumstances, the epidemic evolved to a milder form, enabling the victim to walk around and spread the milder organisms by contact, dirty linens, and so on.

Mae was suggesting that the same thing had happened to the swarms. They had evolved to a milder form, which could be transmitted from one person to another.

"It's creepy," I said.

She nodded. "But what can we do about it?"

And then she began to cry silently, tears running down her cheeks. Mae was always so strong. Seeing her upset unnerved me now. She was shaking her head. "Jack, there's nothing we can do. There's four of them. They're stronger than we are. They're going to kill us the way they killed Charley."

She pressed her head against my shoulder. I put my arm around her. But I couldn't comfort her. Because I knew she was right.

There was no way out.

Winston Churchill once said that being shot at focused the mind wonderfully. My mind was going very fast now. I was thinking that I had made a mistake and I had to fix it. Even though it was a typically human mistake.

Considering that we live in an era of evolutionary everything—

evolutionary biology, evolutionary medicine, evolutionary ecology, evolutionary psychology, evolutionary economics, evolutionary computing—it was surprising how rarely people thought in evolutionary terms. It was a human blind spot. We looked at the world around us as a snapshot when it was really a movie, constantly changing. Of course we knew it was changing but we behaved as if it wasn't. We denied the reality of change. So change always surprised us. Parents were even surprised by the maturing of their own children. They treated them as younger than they really were.

And I had been surprised by the change in the evolution of the swarms. There was no reason why the swarms shouldn't evolve in two directions at the same time. Or three, or four, or ten directions, for that matter. I should have anticipated that. I should have looked for it, expected it. If I had, I might be better prepared to deal with the situation now.

But instead I had treated the swarm as one problem—a problem out there, in the desert—and I had ignored other possibilities.

It's called denial, Jack.

I started to wonder what else I was denying now. What else I had failed to see. Where did I go wrong? What was the first clue I had missed? Probably the fact that my initial contact with a swarm had produced an allergic reaction—a reaction that almost killed me. Mae had called it a coliform reaction. Caused by a toxin from the bacteria in the swarm. That toxin was obviously the result of an evolutionary change in the *E. coli* that made up the swarm. Well, for that matter, the very presence of phage in the tank was an evolutionary change, a viral response to the bacteria that—

"Mae," I said. "Wait a minute."

"What?"

I said, "There might be something we can do to stop them."

She was skeptical; I could see it in her face. But she wiped her eyes and listened.

I said, "The swarm consists of particles and bacteria, is that right?"

"Yes . . ."

"The bacteria provide the raw ingredients for the particles to reproduce themselves. Right? Okay. So if the bacteria die, the swarm dies too?"

"Probably." She frowned. "Are you thinking of an antibiotic? Giving everyone an antibiotic? Because you need a lot of antibiotics to clear an *E. coli* infection, they'd have to take drugs for several days, and I don't—"

"No. I'm not thinking of antibiotics." I tapped the tank in front of me. "I'm thinking of this."

"Phage?"

"Why not?"

"I don't know if it will work," she said. She frowned. "It might. Except . . . how're you going to get the phage into them? They won't just drink it down, you know."

"Then we'll fill the atmosphere with it," I said. "They'll breathe it in and they'll never know."

"Uh-huh. How do we fill the atmosphere?"

"Easy. Don't shut down this tank. Feed the bacteria into the system. I want the assembly line to start making virus—a lot of virus. Then we release into the air."

Mae sighed. "It won't work, Jack," she said.

"Why not?"

"Because the assembly line won't make a lot of virus."

"Why not?"

"Because of the way the virus reproduces. You know—the virus floats around, attaches to a cell wall, and injects itself into the cell. Then it takes over the cell's own RNA, and converts it to making more viruses. The cell ceases all its normal metabolic functions, and just cranks out viruses. Pretty soon the cell is packed with viruses, and it bursts like a balloon. All the viruses are released, they float to other cells, and the process starts all over."

"Yes . . . so?"

"If I introduce phage into the assembly lines, the virus will reproduce rapidly—for a while. But it will rupture a lot of cell membranes, leaving behind all those membranes as a lipid crud. The crud will clog the intermediate filters. After about an hour or two, the assembly lines will start to overheat, the safety systems will kick in, and shut everything down. The whole production line will just stop. No virus."

"Can the safety systems be turned off?"

"Yes. But I don't know how."

"Who does?"

"Only Ricky."

I shook my head. "That won't do us any good. Are you sure you can't figure out—"

"There's a code," she said. "Ricky's the only one who knows it."

"Oh."

"Anyway, Jack, it'd be too dangerous to turn off the safeties. Parts of that system operate at high temperature, and high voltages. And there's a lot of ketones and methane produced in the arms. It's continuously monitored and drawn off to keep the levels below a certain concentration. But if it isn't drawn off, and you start high voltage sparking . . ." She paused, shrugged.

"What're you saying? It could explode?"

"No, Jack. I'm saying it *will* explode. In a matter of minutes after the safeties are shut off. Six, maybe eight minutes at most. And you wouldn't want to be there when that happens. So you can't use the system to produce a lot of virus. Safeties on or safeties off, it just won't work."

Silence.

Frustration.

I looked around the room. I looked at the steel tank, curving upward over my head. I looked at the rack of test tubes at Mae's feet. I looked in the corner, where I saw a mop, a bucket, and a one-gallon plastic bottle of water. And I looked at Mae, frightened, still on the verge of tears, but somehow holding it together.

And I had a plan.

"Okay. Do it anyway. Release the virus into the system."

"What's the point of that?"

"Just do it."

"Jack," she said. "Why are we doing this? I'm afraid they know that we know. We can't fool them. They're too clever. If we try to do this, they'll be onto us in a minute."

"Yes," I said. "They probably will."

"And it won't work, anyway. The system won't make viruses. So why, Jack? What good will it do?"

Mae had been a good friend through all this, and now I had a plan and I wasn't going to tell her. I hated to do it this way, but I had to make a distraction for the others. I had to fool them. And she had to help me do it—which meant she had to believe in a different plan.

I said, "Mae, we have to distract them, to fool them. I want you to release the virus into the assembly line. Let them focus on that. Let them worry about that. Meanwhile, I'll take some virus up to the maintenance area beneath the roof, and dump it into the sprinkler reservoir."

"And then set the sprinklers off?"

"Yes."

She nodded. "And they'll be soaked in virus. Everybody in this facility. Drenched."

"Right."

She said, "It just might work, Jack."

"I can't think of anything better," I said. "Now open one of those valves, and let's draw off some test tubes of virus. And I want you to put some virus into that gallon jug over there."

She hesitated. "The valve is on the other side of the tank. The security camera will see us."

"That's okay," I said. "It can't be helped now. You just have to buy me a little time."

"And how do I do that?"

I told her. She made a face. "You're kidding! They'll never do that!"

"Of course not. I just need a little time."

*   *   *

We went around the tank. She filled the test tubes. The liquid that came out was a thick brown slop. It smelled fecal. It looked fecal. Mae said to me, "Are you sure about this?"

"Got to do it," I said. "There's no choice."

"You first."

I picked up the test tube, took a breath, and swallowed it whole. It was disgusting. My stomach heaved. I thought I would vomit, but I didn't. I took another breath, swallowed some water from the gallon jug, and looked at Mae.

"Awful, huh?" she said.

"Awful."

She picked up a test tube, held her nose, and swallowed. I waited through her coughing fit. She managed not to vomit. I gave her the gallon jug, she drank, and poured the rest out onto the floor. Then she filled it with brown slop.

The last thing she did was twist the handle of a big flow valve. "There," she said. "It's going into the system now."

"Okay," I said. I took two test tubes and stuck them in my shirt pocket. I took the gallon jug. It said ARROWHEAD PURE WATER on the label. "See you later." And I hurried off.

As I went down the hallway, I figured there was one chance in a hundred that I would succeed. Maybe only one chance in a thousand.

But I had a chance.

Later on, I watched the entire scene on the security camera, so I knew what happened to Mae. She walked into the kitchen, carrying her rack of brown test tubes. The others were all there, eating. Julia gave her a frosty look. Vince ignored her. Ricky said, "What've you got there, Mae?"

"Phage," she said.

"What for?"

Now Julia looked over. Mae said, "It's from the fermentation tank."

"Ew, no wonder it stinks."

"Jack just drank one. He made me drink one."

Ricky snorted. "What'd you do that for? Jeez, I'm surprised you didn't puke."

"I almost did. Jack wants all of you to drink one, too."

Bobby laughed. "Yeah? What for?"

"To make sure none of you is infected."

Ricky frowned. "Infected? What do you mean, infected?"

"Jack says that Charley was harboring the swarm inside his body, so maybe the rest of us are, too. Or some of us. So you drink this virus, and it'll kill the bacteria inside you, and kill the swarm."

Bobby said, "Are you serious? Drink that crap? No way, Mae!"

She turned to Vince.

"Smells like shit to me," Vince said. "Let someone else try it first."

Mae said, "Ricky? You want to be the first?"

Ricky shook his head. "I'm not drinking that. Why should I?"

"Well, for one thing, you'd be assured you weren't infected. And for another, we would be assured, too."

"What do you mean, it's a test?"

Mae shrugged. "That's what Jack thinks."

Julia frowned. She turned to Mae. "Where is Jack now?" she said.

"I don't know. The last time I saw him was by the fermentation chambers. I don't know where he is now."

"Yes, you do," Julia said coldly. "You know exactly where he is."

"I don't. He didn't tell me."

"He *did* tell you. He tells you everything," Julia said. "In fact, you and he planned this little interlude, didn't you? You couldn't seriously expect us to drink that stuff. *Where is Jack, Mae?*"

"I told you, I don't know."

Julia said to Bobby, "Check the monitors. Find him." She came around the table. "Now then, Mae." Her voice was calm, but full of menace. "I want you to answer me. And I want you to tell me the truth."

Mae backed away from her. Ricky and Vince were closing in on either side of her. Mae backed against the wall.

Julia advanced slowly. "Tell me now, Mae," she said. "It will be much better for you if you cooperate."

From the other side of the room, Bobby said, "I found him. He's going through the fab room. He's carrying a jug of the crap, looks like."

"Tell me, Mae," Julia said, leaning close to Mae. She was so close their lips were almost touching. Mae squeezed her eyes and her lips tightly shut. Her body was beginning to shake with fear. Julia caressed her hair. "Don't be afraid. There's nothing to be afraid of. Just tell me what he is doing with that jug," Julia said.

Mae began to sob hysterically. "I knew it wouldn't work. I told him you would find out."

"Of course we would," Julia said quietly. "Of course we would find out. Just tell now."

"He took the jug of virus," Mae said, "and he's putting it in the water sprinklers."

"Is he?" Julia said. "That's really very clever of him. Thank you, sweetie."

And she kissed Mae on the mouth. Mae squirmed, but her back was against the wall, and Julia held her head. When Julia finally stepped back, she said, "Try and stay calm. Just remember. It won't hurt you if you don't fight against it."

And she walked out of the room.

Things happened faster than I expected. I could hear them running toward me down the corridor. I hastily hid the jug, then ran back and continued crossing the fabrication room. That was when they all came after me. I started to run. Vince tackled me, and I hit the concrete floor hard. Ricky threw himself on top of me after I was down. He knocked the wind out of me. Then Vince kicked me in the ribs a couple of times, and together they dragged me to my feet to face Julia.

"Hi, Jack," she said, smiling. "How's it going?"

"It's been better."

"We've had a nice talk with Mae," Julia said. "So there's no point in beating around the bush." She looked around the floor nearby. "Where is the jug?"

"What jug?"

"Jack." She shook her head sadly. "Why do you bother? Where is the jug of phage you were going to put in the sprinkler system?"

"I don't have any jug."

She stepped close to me. I could feel her breath on my face. "Jack . . . I know that look on your face, Jack. You have a plan, don't you? Now tell me where the jug is."

"What jug?"

Her lips brushed mine. I just stood there, still as a statue. "Jack darling," she whispered, "you know better than to play with dangerous things. I want the jug."

I stood there.

"Jack . . . just one kiss . . ." She was close, seductive.

Ricky said, "Forget it, Julia. He's not afraid of you. He drank the virus and he thinks it'll protect him."

"Will it?" Julia said, stepping back.

"Maybe," Ricky said, "but I bet he's afraid to die."

And then he and Vince began dragging me across the fabrication room. They were taking me to the high mag field room. I began to struggle.

"That's right," Ricky said. "You know what's coming, don't you?"

This was not in my plan. I hadn't expected it; I didn't know what I could do now. I struggled harder, kicking and twisting, but they were both immensely strong. They just dragged me forward. Julia opened the heavy steel door to the mag room. Inside, I saw the circular drum of the magnet, six feet in diameter.

They shoved me in roughly. I sprawled on the ground in the room. My head banged against the steel shielding. I heard the door click and lock.

I got to my feet.

I heard the rumble of the cooling pumps as they started up. The intercom clicked. I heard Ricky's voice. "Ever wonder why these walls are made out of steel, Jack? Pulsed magnets are dangerous. Run them continuously, and they blow apart. Get ripped apart by the field they generate. We got a one-minute load time. So you've got one minute to think it over."

I had been in this room before, when Ricky showed me around. I remembered there was a knee plate, a safety cutoff. I hit it with my knee.

"Won't work, Jack," Ricky said laconically. "I inverted the switching. Now it turns the magnet on, instead of off. Thought you'd like to know."

The rumbling was louder. The room began to vibrate slightly. The air grew swiftly colder. In a moment I could see my breath.

"Sorry if you're uncomfortable, but that's only temporary," Ricky said. "Once the pulses get going, the room'll heat up fast. Uh, let's see. Forty-seven seconds."

The sound was a rapid *chunk-chunk-chunk*, like a muffled jackhammer. It was loud, and getting louder. I could hardly hear Ricky over the intercom.

"Now Jack," he said. "You have a family. A family that needs you. So think about your choices very carefully."

I said, "Let me speak to Julia."

"No, Jack. She doesn't want to talk to you right now. She's very disappointed in you, Jack."

"Let me speak to her."

"Jack, aren't you listening to me? She says no. Not until you tell her where the virus is."

Chunk-chunk-chunk. The room was starting to get warmer. I could hear the gurgle of the coolant as it went through the piping. I kicked the safety plate with my knee.

"I told you, Jack. It'll only turn the magnet on. Are you having trouble hearing me?"

"Yes," I yelled. "I am."

"Well that's too bad," Ricky said. "I'm sorry to hear that."

At least, I thought that's what he was saying. The *chunk-chunk-chunk* seemed to fill the room, to make the very air vibrate. It sounded like an enormous MRI, those giant pumps. My head hurt. I stared at the magnet, at the heavy bolts that held the plates together. Those bolts would soon become missiles.

"We're not fucking around, Jack," Ricky said. "We'd hate to lose you. Twenty seconds."

The load time was the time it took to charge the magnet capacitors, so that millisecond pulses of electricity could be delivered. I wondered how long after loading it would take for the pulses to blow the magnet apart. Probably a few seconds at most. So time was running out for me. I didn't know what to do. Everything had gone horribly wrong. And the worst part was that I had lost the only advantage I ever had, because they now recognized the importance of the virus. Earlier they hadn't focused on it as a threat. But now they understood, and were demanding I hand it over. Soon they would think to destroy the fermentation tank. They would eradicate the virus very thoroughly, I felt sure.

And there was nothing I could do about it. Not now.

I wondered how Mae was, and whether they had hurt her. I wondered if she was still alive. I felt detached, indifferent. I was sitting in an over-sized MRI, that was all. This big terrifying sound, it must have been how Amanda felt, when she was in the MRI . . . My mind drifted, uncaring.

"Ten seconds," Ricky said. "Come on, Jack. Don't be a hero. It's not your style. Tell us where it is. Six seconds. Five. Jack, come on . . ."

The *chunk-chunk-chunk* stopped, and there was a *whang!* and a scream of rending metal. The magnet had switched on, for a few milliseconds.

"First pulse," Ricky said. "Don't be an asshole, Jack."

Another *whang! Whang! Whang!* The pulses were coming faster and faster. I saw the jacketing on the coolant beginning to indent with each pulse. They were coming too fast.

Whang! Whang!

I couldn't take it anymore. I shouted, "Okay! Ricky! I'll tell you!"

Whang! "Go ahead, Jack!" *Whang!* "I'm waiting."

"No! Turn it off first. And I only tell Julia."

Whang! Whang! "Very unreasonable of you, Jack. You're in no position to bargain." *Whang!*

"You want the virus, or you want it to be a surprise?"

Whang! Whang! Whang!

And then abruptly, silence. Nothing but the low swoosh of the coolant flowing through the jacketing. The magnet was hot to the touch. But at least the MRI sound had stopped.

The MRI . . .

I stood in the room, and waited for Julia to come in. And then, thinking it over, I sat down.

I heard the door unlock. Julia walked in.

"Jack. You're not hurt, are you?"

"No," I said. "Just my nerves are shot."

"I don't know why you put yourself through it," she said. "It was totally unnecessary. But guess what? I have good news. The helicopter just arrived."

"It did?"

"Yes, it's early today. Just think, wouldn't it be nice to be on it now, going home? Back to your house, back to your family? Wouldn't that feel great?"

I sat there with my back against the wall, looking up at her. "Are you saying I can go?"

"Of course, Jack. There's no reason for you to stay here. Just give me the bottle of virus, and go home."

I didn't believe her for a second. I was seeing the friendly Julia, the seductive Julia. But I didn't believe her. "Where is Mae?"

"She's resting."

"You've hurt her."

"No. No, no, no. Why would I do that?" She shook her head. "You really don't understand, do you? I don't want to hurt anybody, Jack. Not you, not Mae, not anybody. I especially don't want to hurt you."

"Try telling that to Ricky."

"Jack. Please. Let's put emotion aside and be logical for a moment. You're doing all this to yourself. Why can't you accept the new situation?" She held out her hand to me. I took it, and she pulled me up. She was strong. Stronger than I ever remembered her being. "After all," she said, "you're an integral part of this. You killed the wild type for us, Jack."

"So the benign type could flourish . . ."

"Exactly, Jack. So the benign type could flourish. And create a new synergy with human beings."

"The synergy that you have now, for example."

"That's right, Jack." She smiled. It was a creepy smile.

"You are, what? Coexisting? Coevolving?"

"Symbiotic." She was still smiling.

"Julia, this is all bullshit," I said. "This is a disease."

"Well of course you would say that. Because you don't know any better, yet. You haven't experienced it." She came forward and hugged me. I let her do it. "You have no idea what's ahead of you."

"Story of my life," I said.

"Stop being so stubborn, for once. Just go along with it. You look tired, Jack."

I sighed. "I am tired," I said. And I was. I was feeling distinctly weak in her arms. I was sure she could sense it.

"Then why don't you just relax. Embrace me, Jack."

"I don't know. Maybe you're right."

"Yes, I am." She smiled again, ruffled my hair with her hand. "Oh, Jack . . . I really have missed you."

"Me too," I said. "I missed you." I gave her a hug, squeezed her, held her close. Our faces were close. She looked beautiful, her lips parted, her eyes staring up at me, soft, inviting. I felt her relax. Then I said, "Just tell me one thing, Julia. It's been bothering me."

"Sure, Jack."

"Why did you refuse to have an MRI in the hospital?"

She frowned, leaned back to look at me. "What? What do you mean?"

"Are you like Amanda?"

"Amanda?"

"Our baby daughter . . . you remember her. She was cured by the MRI. Instantly."

"What are you talking about?"

"Julia, does the swarm have some problem with magnetic fields?"

Her eyes widened. She began to struggle in my grip. "Let go of me! Ricky! Ricky!"

"Sorry, hon," I said. I kicked the plate with my knee. And there was a loud *whang!* as the magnet pulsed.

Julia screamed.

Her mouth was open as she screamed, a steady continuous sound, her face rigid with tension. I held her hard. The skin of her face began to shiver, vibrating rapidly. And then her features seemed to grow, to swell as she screamed. I thought her eyes looked frightened. The swelling continued, and began to break up into rivulets, and streams.

And then in a sudden rush Julia literally disintegrated before my eyes.

The skin of her swollen face and body blew away from her in streams of particles, like sand blown off a sand dune. The particles curved away in the arc of the magnetic field toward the sides of the room.

I felt her body growing lighter and lighter in my arms. Still the particles continued to flow away, with a kind of whooshing sound, to all corners of the room. And when it was finished, what was left behind—what I still held in my arms—was a pale and cadaverous form. Julia's eyes were sunk deep in her cheeks. Her mouth was thin and cracked, her skin translucent. Her hair was colorless, brittle. Her collarbones protruded from her bony neck. She looked like she was dying of cancer. Her mouth worked. I heard faint words, hardly more than breathing. I leaned in, turned my ear to her mouth to hear.

"Jack," she whispered. "It's eating me."

I said, "I know."

Her voice was just a whisper. "You have to do something."

"I know."

"Jack . . . the children . . ."

"Okay."

She whispered, "I . . . kissed them . . ."

I said nothing. I just closed my eyes.

"Jack . . . Save my babies . . . Jack . . ."

"Okay," I said.

I glanced up at the walls and saw, all around me, Julia's face and body stretched and fitted to the room. The particles retained her appearance, but were now flattened onto the walls. And they were still moving, coordinating with the movement of her lips, the blink of her eyes. As I watched, they began to drift back from the walls toward her in a flesh-colored haze.

Outside the room, I heard Ricky shouting, "Julia! Julia!" He kicked the door a couple of times, but he didn't come in. I knew he wouldn't dare. I had waited a full minute so the capacitors were charged. He couldn't stop me from pulsing the magnet now. I could do it at will—at least, until the charge ran out. I didn't know how long that would be.

"Jack . . ."

I looked at her. Her eyes were sad, pleading.

"Jack," she said. "I didn't know . . ."

"It's all right," I said. The particles were drifting back, reassembling her face before my eyes. Julia was becoming solid, and beautiful again.

I kicked the knee plate.

Whang!

The particles shot away, flying back to the walls, though not so swiftly this time. And I had the cadaverous Julia in my arms again, her deep-set eyes pleading with me.

I reached into my pocket, and pulled out one of the vials of phage. "I want you to drink this," I said.

"No . . . no . . ." She was agitated. "Too late . . . for . . ."

"Try," I said. I held the vial to her lips. "Come on, darling. I want you to try."

"No . . . please . . . Not important . . ."

Ricky was yelling: "Julia! Julia!" He pounded on the door. "Julia, are you all right?"

The cadaver eyes rolled toward the door. Her mouth worked. Her skeleton fingers plucked at my shirt, scratching the cloth. She wanted to tell me something. I turned my head again, so I could hear.

She breathed shallowly, weakly. I couldn't catch the words. And then suddenly they were clear.

She said, *"They have to kill you now."*

"I know," I said.

"Don't let them . . . Children . . ."

"I won't."

Her bony hand touched my cheek. She whispered, "You know I always loved you, Jack. I would never hurt you."

"I know, Julia. I know."

The particles on the walls were drifting free once more. Now they seemed to telescope back, returning to her face and body. I kicked the knee plate once again, hoping for more time with her, but there was only a dull mechanical thunk.

The capacitor was drained.

And suddenly, in a *whoosh*, all the particles returned, and Julia was full and beautiful and strong as before, and she pushed me away from her with a contemptuous look and said in a loud, firm voice, "I'm sorry you had to see that, Jack."

"So am I," I said.

"But it can't be helped. We're wasting time. I want the bottle of virus, Jack. And I want it right now."

In a way it made everything easier. Because I understood I wasn't dealing with Julia anymore. I didn't have to worry about what might happen to her. I just had to worry about Mae—assuming she was still alive—and me.

And assuming I could stay alive for the next few minutes.

DAY 7
7:12 A.M.

"Okay," I said to her. "Okay. I'll get you the virus."

She frowned. "You've got that look on your face again . . ."

"No," I said. "I'm done. I'll take you."

"Good. We'll start with those vials in your pocket."

"What, these here?" I said. I reached into my pocket for them as I went through the door. Outside, Ricky and Vince were waiting for me.

"Very fucking funny," Ricky said. "You know you could have killed her. You could have killed your own wife."

"How about that," I said.

I was still fumbling in my pocket, as if the test tubes were stuck in the cloth. They didn't know what I was doing, so they grabbed me again, Vince on one side and Ricky on the other.

"Guys," I said, "I can't do this if you—"

"Let him go," Julia said, coming out of the room.

"Like hell," Vince said. "He'll pull something."

I was still struggling, trying to bring the tubes out. Finally I had them in my hand. While we struggled, I threw one onto the ground. It smashed on the concrete floor, and brown sludge spattered up.

"Jesus!" They all jumped away, releasing me. They stared at the floor, and bent over to look at their feet, making sure none of it had touched them.

And in that moment, I ran.

*　　*　　*

I grabbed the jug from its hiding place, and kept going across the fabrication room. I had to get all the way across the room to the elevator, and ride it up to the ceiling level, where all the basic system equipment was located. Up there, where the air handlers were, and the electrical junction boxes—and the tank for the sprinkler system. If I could reach the elevator and ride it just seven or eight feet in the air, then they couldn't touch me.

If I could do that, then my plan would work.

The elevator was a hundred and fifty feet away.

I ran hard, vaulting over the lowest arms of the octopus, ducking beneath the chest-high sections. I glanced back and couldn't see them through the maze of arms and machinery. But I heard the three of them shouting, and I heard running feet. I heard Julia say, "He's going for the sprinklers!" Ahead, I saw the yellow open cage of the elevator.

I was going to make it, after all.

At that moment, I stumbled over one of the arms and went sprawling. The jug skidded across the floor, came to rest against a support beam. I scrambled quickly to my feet again, and retrieved the jug. I knew they were right behind me. I didn't dare look back now.

I ran for the elevator, ducking beneath one final pipe, but when I looked again, Vince was already there. He must have known a shortcut through the octopus arms; somehow he had beaten me. Now he stood in the open cage, grinning. I looked back and saw Ricky just a few yards behind me, closing fast.

Julia called, "Give it up, Jack! It's no good."

She was right about that, it was no good at all. I couldn't get past Vince. And I couldn't outrun Ricky now, he was much too close. I jumped over a pipe, stepped around a standing electrical box, and ducked down. As Ricky jumped the pipe, I slammed my elbow upward between his legs. He howled and went down, rolling on the floor in agony. I stopped and kicked him in the head as hard as I could. That was for Charley.

I ran.

At the elevator, Vince stood in a half-crouch, fists bunched. He was relishing a fight. I ran straight toward him and he grinned broadly in anticipation.

And at the last moment, I swerved left. I jumped.

And started climbing the ladder on the wall.

Julia screamed, "Stop him! Stop him!"

It was difficult climbing, because I had my thumb hooked through the jug; the bottle kept banging painfully against the back of my right hand as I went up. I focused on the pain. I panic at heights and I didn't want to look down. And so I couldn't see what was dragging at my legs, pulling me back toward the floor. I kicked, but whatever it was held on to me.

Finally, I turned to look. I was ten feet above the ground, and two rungs beneath me, Ricky had his free arm locked around my legs, his hand clutching my ankle. He jerked at my feet, and yanked them off the rung. I slid for an instant and then felt a burst of searing pain in my hands. But I held on.

Ricky was smiling grimly. I kicked my legs backward, trying to hit his face, but to no avail, he had both legs locked tight against his chest. He was immensely strong. I kept trying until I realized that I could pull one leg up and free. I did, and stomped down on his hand that was holding on to the rung. He yelled, and released my legs to hold on to the ladder with his other hand. I stomped again—and kicked straight back, catching him right under the chin. He slid down five rungs, then caught himself. He hung there, near the bottom of the ladder.

I climbed again.

Julia was running across the floor. "Stop him!"

I heard the elevator grind as Vince rode up past me, heading toward the top. He would wait for me there.

I climbed.

I was fifteen feet above the floor, then twenty. I looked down to see Ricky pursuing me but he was far behind, I didn't think he could catch me, and then Julia came swirling up through the air toward me, spiraling like a corkscrew—and grabbed the ladder right alongside me. Except she wasn't Julia, she was the swarm, and for a moment the swarm was disorganized enough that I could see right through her in places; I could see the swirling particles that composed her. I looked down and saw the real Julia, deathly pale, standing and looking up at me, her face a skull. By now the swarm alongside me became solid-appearing, as I had seen it become solid before. It looked like Julia. The mouth moved and I heard a strange voice say "Sorry, Jack." And the swarm shrank, becoming denser still, collapsing into a small Julia, about four feet tall.

I turned to climb again.

The small Julia swung back, and slammed hard against my body. I felt like I was hit by a sack of cement, the wind knocked out of me. My grip loosened from the ladder, and I barely managed to hang on, as the Julia swarm smashed against me again. I ducked and dodged, grunting in pain, and kept going despite the impacts. The swarm had enough mass to hurt me, but not enough to knock me off the ladder.

The swarm must have realized it, too, because now the small Julia swarm compressed itself into a sphere, and slid smoothly forward to envelop my head in a buzzing cloud. I was totally blind. I could see nothing at all. It was as if I was in a dust storm. I groped for the next rung on the ladder, and the next after that. Pinpricks stung my face and hands, the pain becoming more intense, sharper. Apparently the swarm was learning how to focus pain. But at least it hadn't learned to suffocate. The swarm did nothing to interfere with my breathing.

I kept on.

I climbed in darkness.

And then I felt Ricky pulling at my legs again. And in that moment, finally, I didn't see how I could go on.

I was twenty-five feet in the air, hanging on to a ladder for dear life, dragging a jug of brown sludge up with me, with Vince above waiting and Ricky below dragging, and a swarm buzzing around my head, blinding me and stinging me like hell. I was exhausted and defeated and I could feel my energy draining away. My fingers felt shaky on the rungs. I couldn't hold my grip much longer. I knew that all I had to do was release my grip and fall, and it would be over in an instant. I was finished, anyway.

I felt for the next rung, gripped it, and hauled my body up. But my shoulders burned. Ricky was pulling down fiercely. I knew he would win. They would all win. They were always going to win.

And then I thought of Julia, pale as a ghost and brittle thin, saying in a whisper "Save my babies." I thought of the kids, waiting for me to come back. I saw them sitting around the table waiting for dinner. And I knew I had to go on no matter what.

So I did.

It's not clear to me now what happened to Ricky. Somehow he pulled my legs off the rungs, and I hung in the air from my arms, kicking wildly, and I must have kicked him in the face and broken his nose.

Because in an instant Ricky let go of me, and I heard a thump-thump-thumping as his body went down the ladder, and he desperately tried to grab the rungs as he fell. I heard, "Ricky, no!" and the cloud vanished from my head, I was completely free again. I looked down and saw the Julia swarm alongside Ricky, who had caught himself about twelve feet above the floor. He looked up angrily. His mouth and nose were gushing blood. He started toward me but the Julia swarm said, "No, Ricky. No, you can't! Let Vince."

And then Ricky half climbed, half fell the rest of the way down the ladder to the ground, and the swarm reinhabited Julia's pale body, and the two of them stood there and watched me.

I turned away from them and looked up the ladder.

Vince was standing there, five feet above me.

His feet were on the top rungs, and he was leaning over, blocking my way. There was no possible way I could get past him. I paused to take stock, shifted my weight on the ladder, got one leg up to the next rung, hooked my free arm around the rung nearest my face. But as I raised my leg, I felt the lump in my pocket. I paused.

I had one more vial of phage.

I reached into my pocket, and drew it out to show him. I pulled out the cork with my teeth. "Hey, Vince," I said. "How about a shit shower?"

He didn't move. But his eyes narrowed.

I moved up another rung.

"Better get back, Vince," I said. I was panting so hard I couldn't manage the proper menace. "Get on back before you get wet . . ."

One more rung. I was only three rungs below him.

"It's your call, Vince." I held the vial in my other hand. "I can't hit your face from down here. But I'll sure as hell hit your legs and shoes. Do you care?"

One more rung.

Vince stayed where he was.

"Maybe not," I said. "You like to live dangerously?"

I paused. If I advanced another rung, he could kick me in the head. If I stayed where I was, he would have to come down to me, and I could get him. So I stayed.

"What do you say, Vince? Going to stay, or go?"

He frowned. His eyes flicked back and forth, from my face to the vial, and back again.

And then he stepped away from the ladder.

"Good boy, Vince."

I came up one rung.

He had stepped back so far that now I couldn't see where he was. I thought he was probably planning to rush me at the top. So I got ready to duck down, and swing laterally.

Last rung.

And now I saw him. He wasn't planning anything. Vince was shaking with panic, a cornered animal, huddled back in the dark recess of the walkway. I couldn't read his eyes, but I saw his body tremble.

"Okay, Vince," I said. "I'm coming up."

I stepped onto the mesh platform. I was right at the top of the stairs, surrounded by roaring machinery. Not twenty paces away, I saw the paired steel tanks for the sprinkler system. I glanced down and saw Ricky and Julia, staring up at me. I wondered if they realized how close I was to my goal.

I looked back at Vince, just in time to see him pull a translucent white plastic tarp off a corner box. He wrapped himself in the tarp like a shield, and then, with a guttural yell, he charged. I was right at the edge of the ladder. I had no time to get out of the way, I just turned sideways and braced myself against a big three-foot pipe against the coming impact.

Vince slammed into me.

The vial went flying out of my hand, shattering on the mesh. The jug was knocked from my other hand and tumbled along the walkway, coming to rest at the lip of the mesh path. Another few inches and it would go over. I moved toward it.

Still hiding behind the tarp, Vince smashed into me again. I was slammed back against the pipe. My head clanged on steel. I slipped on the brown sludge that dripped through holes in the mesh, barely kept my balance. Vince slammed me again.

In his panic he never realized I had lost my weapons. Or perhaps he couldn't see through the tarp. He just kept pounding me with his full body, and I finally slipped on the sludge and went down on my knees. I immediately scrambled toward the jug, which was about ten feet away. That odd behavior made Vince stop for a moment; he pulled down the tarp, saw the jug, and lunged for it, vaulting his whole body forward in the air.

But he was too late. I had my hand on the jug, and yanked it away, just as Vince landed, tarp and all, right where the jug had been. His head banged hard on the walkway lip. He was momentarily stunned, shaking his head to clear it.

And I grabbed the edge of the tarp, and yanked upward.

Vince yelled, and went over the side.

I watched as he hit the floor. His body didn't move. Then the swarm came off him, sliding into the air like his ghost. The ghost joined Ricky and Julia who were looking up at me. Then they turned away and hurried across the floor of the fabrication room, jumping over the octopus arms as they went. Their movements conveyed a clear sense of urgency. You might even think they were frightened.

Good, I thought.

I got to my feet and headed for the sprinkler tanks. The instructions were stenciled on the lower tank. It was easy to figure out the valves. I twisted the inflow, unscrewed the filler cap, waited for the pressurized nitrogen to hiss out, and then dumped in the jug of phage. I listened as it gurgled into the tank. Then I screwed the cap back on, twisted the valve, repressurized with nitrogen.

And I was done.

I took a deep breath.

I was going to win this thing, after all.

I rode the elevator down, feeling good for the first time all day.

DAY 7
8:12 A.M.

They were all clustered together on the other side of the room—Julia, Ricky, and now Bobby, as well. Vince was there, too, hovering in the background, but I could sometimes see through him, his swarm was slightly transparent. I wondered which of the others were only swarms now. I couldn't be sure. But it didn't matter now, anyway.

They were standing beside a bank of computer monitors that showed every parameter of the manufacturing process: graphs of temperature, output, God knows what else. But they had turned their backs to the monitors. They were watching me.

I walked calmly toward them, in measured steps. I was in no rush. Far from it. I must have taken a full two minutes to cross the fabrication room to where they were standing. They regarded me with puzzlement, and then with increasingly open amusement.

"Well, Jack," Julia said finally. "How's your day going?"

"Not bad," I said. "Things are looking up."

"You seem very confident."

I shrugged.

"You've got everything under control?" Julia said.

I shrugged again.

"By the way, where is Mae?"

"I don't know. Why?"

"Bobby's been looking for her. He can't find her anywhere."

"I have no idea," I said. "Why were you looking for her?"

"We thought we should all be together," Julia said, "when we finish our business here."

"Oh," I said. "Is that what happens now? We finish?"

She nodded slowly. "Yes, Jack. It is."

I couldn't risk looking at my watch, I had to try and gauge how much time had passed. I was guessing three or four minutes. I said, "So, what do you have in mind?"

Julia began to pace. "Well, Jack, I'm very disappointed in how things have gone with you. I really am. You know how much I care about you. I would never want anything to happen to you. But you're fighting us, Jack. And you won't stop fighting. And we can't have that."

"I see," I said.

"We just can't, Jack."

I reached in my pocket and brought out a plastic cigarette lighter. If Julia or the others noticed, they gave no sign.

She kept pacing. "Jack, you put me in a difficult position."

"How's that?"

"You've been privileged to witness the birth of something truly new, here. Something new and miraculous. But you are not sympathetic, Jack."

"No, I'm not."

"Birth is painful."

"So is death," I said.

She continued to pace. "Yes," she said. "So is death." She frowned at me.

"Something the matter?"

"Where is Mae?" she said again.

"I don't know. I don't have the faintest idea."

She continued to frown. "We have to find her, Jack."

"I'm sure you will."

"Yes, we will."

"So you don't need me," I said. "Just do it on your own. I mean, you're the future, if I remember right. Superior and unstoppable. I'm just a guy."

Julia started walking around me, looking at me from all sides. I could see she was puzzled by my behavior. Or appraising. Maybe I had over done it. Gone too far. She was picking up something. She suspected something. And that made me very nervous.

I turned the cigarette lighter over in my hands, nervously.

"Jack," she said. "You disappoint me."

"You said that already."

"Yes," she said. "But I am still not sure . . ."

As if on some unspoken cue the men all began to walk in circles. They were moving in concentric circles around me. Was this some kind of scanning procedure? Or did it mean something else?

I was trying to guess the time. I figured five minutes had elapsed.

"Come, Jack. I want to look more closely."

She put her arm on my shoulder and led me over to one of the big octopus arms. It was easily six feet across, and mirrored on its surface. I could see Julia standing next to me. Her arm over my shoulder.

"Don't we make a handsome couple? It's a shame. We could have such a future."

I said, "Yeah, well . . ."

And the moment I spoke, a river of pale particles streamed off Julia, curved in the air, and came down like a shower all over my body and into my mouth. I clamped my mouth shut, but it didn't matter, because in the mirror my body seemed to dissolve away, to be replaced by Julia's body. It was as if her skin had left her, flowed into the air, and slid down over me. Now there were two Julias standing side by side in front of the mirror.

I said, "Cut it out, Julia."

She laughed. "Why? I think it's fun."

"Stop it," I said. I sounded like myself, even though I looked like Julia. "Stop it."

"Don't you like it? I think it's amusing. You get to be me, for a while."

"I said, stop it."

"Jack, you're just no fun anymore."

I pulled at the Julia-image on my face, trying to tear it away like a mask. But I felt only my own skin beneath my fingertips. When I scratched at my cheek, the Julia-cheek showed scratches in the mirror.

I reached back and touched my own hair. In my panic, I dropped the cigarette lighter. It clattered on the concrete floor.

"Get it off me," I said. "Get it off."

I heard a *whoosh* in my ears, and the Julia-skin was gone, sweeping into the air, then descending onto Julia. Except that she now looked like me. Now there were two Jacks, side by side in the mirror.

"Is this better?" she said.

"I don't know what you are trying to prove." I took a breath.

I bent over and picked up the lighter.

"I'm not trying to prove anything," she said. "I'm just feeling you out, Jack. And you know what I found? You've got a secret, Jack. And you thought I wouldn't find it out."

"Yes?"

"But I did," she said.

I didn't know how to take her words. I wasn't sure where I was anymore, and the changes in appearance had so unnerved me that I had lost track of the time.

"You're worried about the time, aren't you, Jack," she said. "You needn't be. We have plenty of time. Everything is under control here. Are you going to tell us your secret? Or do we have to make you tell?"

Behind her, I could see the stacked monitor screens of the control station. The corner ones had a flashing bar along the top, with lettering that I couldn't read. I could see that some of the graphs were rising steeply, their lines turning from blue to yellow to red as they climbed.

I did nothing.

Julia turned to the men. "Okay," she said. "Make him tell."

The three men converged toward me. It was time to show them. It was time to spring my trap.

"No problem," I said. I raised my lighter, flicked the flame, and held it under the nearest sprinkler head.

The men stopped in their tracks. They watched me.

I held the lighter steady. The sprinkler head blackened with the smoke.

And nothing happened.

*　　　*　　　*

The flame was melting the soft metal tab beneath the sprinkler head. Splotches of silver were dripping on the ground at my feet. And still nothing happened. The sprinklers didn't come on.

"Oh shit," I said.

Julia was watching me thoughtfully. "It was a nice try. Very inventive, Jack. Good thinking. But you forgot one thing."

"What's that?"

"There's a safety system for the plant. And when we saw you going for the sprinklers, Ricky turned the system off. Safeties off, sprinklers off." She shrugged. "Guess you're out of luck, Jack."

I flicked the lighter off. There was nothing for me to do. I just stood there, feeling foolish. I thought I smelled a faint odor in the room. A kind of sweetish, nauseating odor. But I couldn't be sure.

"It was a nice try, though," Julia said. "But enough is enough."

She turned to the men, and jerked her head. The three of them walked toward me. I said, "Hey guys, come on . . ." They didn't react. Their faces were impassive. They grabbed me and I started to struggle. "Hey, come on now . . ." I pulled free of them. "Hey!"

Ricky said, "Don't make it any harder for us, Jack," and I said, "Fuck you, Ricky," and I spit in his face just as they threw me to the floor. I was hoping the virus would get in his mouth. I was hoping I would delay him, that we would have a fight. Anything for a delay. But they threw me to the floor, and then they all fell on me and began to strangle me. I could feel their hands on my neck. Bobby had his hands over my mouth and nose. I tried to bite him. He just kept his hands firmly in place and stared at me. Ricky smiled distantly at me. It was as if he didn't know me, had no feeling for me. They were all strangers, killing me efficiently and quickly. I pounded on them with my fists, until Ricky got his knee on one of my arms, pinning it down, and Bobby got the other arm. Now I couldn't move at all. I tried to kick my legs, but Julia was sitting on my legs. Helping them out. I saw the world start to turn misty before my eyes. A faint and misty gray.

Then there was a faint popping sound, almost like popcorn, or glass cracking, and then Julia screamed, *"What is that?"*

The three men released me, and got to their feet. They walked away from me. I lay on the ground, coughing. I didn't even try to get up.

"What is that?'" Julia yelled.

The first of the octopus tubes burst open, high above us. Brown liquid steam hissed out. Another tube popped open, and another. The sound of hissing filled the room. The air was turning dark foggy brown, billowing brown.

Julia screamed "What *is* that?"

"It's the assembly line," Ricky said. "It's overheated. And it's blowing."

"How? How can that happen?"

I sat up, still coughing, and got to my feet. I said, "No safety systems, remember? You turned them off. Now it's blowing virus all through this room."

"Not for long," Julia said. "We'll have the safeties back in two seconds." Ricky was already standing at the control board, frantically hitting keys.

"Good thinking, Julia," I said. I lit my cigarette lighter, and held it under the sprinkler head.

Julia screamed, "Stop! Ricky, stop!"

Ricky stopped.

I said, "Damned if you do, damned if you don't."

Julia turned in fury and hissed, *"I hate you."*

Already her body was turning shades of gray, fading to a kind of monochrome. So was Ricky, the color washing out of him. It was the virus in the air, already affecting their swarms.

There was a brief crackle of sparks, from high in the octopus arms. Then another short lightning arc. Ricky saw it and yelled, "Forget it, Julia! We take our chances!" He hit the keys and turned the safety system back on. Alarms started to sound. The screens flashed red with the excess concentrations of methane and other gases. The main screen showed: SAFETY SYSTEMS ON.

And the sprinklers burst into cones of brown spray.

*   *   *

They screamed as the water touched them. They were writhing and beginning to shrink, to shrivel right before my eyes. Julia's face was contorted. She stared at me with pure hatred. But already she was starting to dissolve. She fell to her knees, and then onto her back. The others were all rolling on the floor, screaming in pain.

"Come on, Jack." Someone was tugging at my sleeve. It was Mae. "Come on," she said. "This room is full of methane. You have to go."

I hesitated, still looking at Julia. Then we turned and ran.

DAY 7
9:11 A.M.

The helicopter pilot pushed the doors open as we ran across the pad. We jumped in. Mae said, "Go!"

He said, "I'll have to insist you get your harnesses on before—"

"Fly this fucking thing!" I yelled.

"Sorry, it's a regulation, and it's not safe—"

Black smoke started to pour out of the power station door we had just come out of. It billowed into the blue desert sky.

The pilot saw it and said, "Hang on!"

We lifted off and headed north, swinging wide of the building. Now there was smoke coming from all the exhaust vents near the roof. A black haze was rising into the air.

Mae said, "Fire burns the nanoparticles and the bacteria, too. Don't worry."

The pilot said, "Where are we going?"

"Home."

He headed west, and within minutes we had left the building behind. It disappeared below the horizon. Mae was sitting back in her seat, eyes closed. I said to her, "I thought it was going to blow up. But they turned the safety system back on again. So I guess it won't."

She said nothing.

I said, "So what was the big rush to get out of there? And where were you, anyway? Nobody could find you."

She said, "I was outside, in the storage shed."

"Doing what?"

"Looking for more thermite."

"Find any?"

There was no sound. Just a flash of yellow light that spread across the desert horizon for an instant, and then faded. You could almost believe it never happened. But the helicopter rocked and jolted as the shock wave passed us.

The pilot said, "Holy Mother of God, what was that?"

"Industrial accident," I said. "Very unfortunate."

He reached for his radio. "I better report it."

"Yes," I said. "You better do that."

We flew west, and I saw the green line of the forest and the rolling foothills of the Sierras, as we crossed into California.

DAY 7
11:57 P.M.

It's late.

Almost midnight. The house is silent around me. I am not sure how this will turn out. The kids are all desperately sick, throwing up after I gave them the virus. I can hear my son and daughter retching in separate bathrooms. I went in to check on them a few minutes ago, to see what was coming up. Their faces were deathly pale. I can see they're afraid, because they know I'm afraid. I haven't told them about Julia yet. They haven't asked. They're too sick to ask right now.

I'm worried most about the baby, because I had to give her the virus, too. It was her only hope. Ellen's with her now, but Ellen is vomiting, too. The baby has yet to throw up. I don't know whether that's good or bad. Young kids react differently.

I think I'm okay, at least for the moment. I'm dead tired. I think I've been dozing off from time to time all night. Right now I'm sitting here looking out the back window, waiting for Mae. She hopped the fence at the end of my backyard, and is probably scrambling around in the brush on the slope that goes down behind the property, where the sprinklers are. She thought there was a faint green light coming from somewhere down the slope. I told her not to go down there alone, but I'm too tired to go get her. If she waits until tomorrow, the Army can come here with flame throwers and blast the hell out of whatever it is.

The Army is acting dumb about this whole thing, but I have Julia's computer here at home, and I have an email trail on her hard drive. I removed the hard drive, just to be safe. I duped it, and put the original in a safe deposit box in town. I'm not really worried about the Army. I'm worried about Larry Handler and the others at Xymos. They know they have horrific lawsuits on their hands. The company will declare bankruptcy sometime this week, but they're still liable for criminal charges. Larry especially. I wouldn't cry if he went to jail.

Mae and I have managed to put together most of the events of the past few days. My daughter's rash was caused by gamma assemblers—the micromachines that assembled finished molecules from component fragments. The gammas must have been on Julia's clothing when she came home from the lab. Julia worried about that possibility; that was why she took a shower as soon as she got home. The lab itself had good decontamination procedures, but Julia was interacting with the swarms outside the lab. She knew there was a danger.

Anyway, that night she accidentally let the gammas loose in the nursery. The gamma assemblers are designed to cut microfragments of silicon, but faced with a pliable substance like skin, they only pinch it. It's painful, and causes microtrauma of a sort that nobody had ever seen before. Or would ever have suspected. No wonder Amanda didn't have a fever. She didn't have an infection. She had a coating of biting particles on her skin. The magnetic field of the MRI cured her in an instant; all the assemblers were yanked away from her in the first pulse. (Apparently that is also what happened to the guy in the desert. He somehow came in contact with a batch of assemblers. He had been camping within a mile of the Xymos desert facility.)

Julia knew what was wrong with Amanda, but she didn't tell anybody. Instead she called the Xymos cleanup crew, which showed up in the middle of the night while I was at the hospital. Only Eric saw them, and now I know what he saw. Because the same crew arrived here a few hours ago to sweep my house. They were the same men I'd seen in the van on the road that night.

The lead man wears a silver bunny suit that's antimagnetic, and he does look ghostly. His silvered mask makes him appear faceless. He goes into the environment first to check it out. Then four other men in coveralls follow, to vacuum and clean up. I had told Eric he'd dreamed it, but he hadn't. The crew left behind one of their sensor cubes, under Amanda's bed. That was intentional, to check for residual gammas in case they'd missed any. It wasn't a surge suppressor; it was just constructed to look like one.

When I finally figured all this out, I was furious with Julia for not telling me what was going on. For making me worry. But of course, she was diseased. And there's no point in being angry with her now.

Eric's MP3 player was cut by gamma assemblers, the same way the cars in the desert were. And just as the MRI was. For some reason the gamma assemblers cut memory chips and leave central processors alone. I haven't heard an explanation why.

There *was* a swarm in the convertible with Julia that night. It had come back with her from the desert. I don't know whether she brought it intentionally or not. The swarm could collapse into nothing, which is why Eric didn't see anything when he went out to the car to look. And I wasn't sure of what I saw when she pulled away, which was reasonable enough. The swarm was probably catching the light in odd ways. In my memory, it looked a little like Ricky, but it was probably too soon for the swarm to be taking on appearances. It hadn't evolved that much, yet. Or maybe I just saw an indistinct shape, and in my jealousy I imagined it to be a person. I don't think I made it up, but maybe I did. Ellen thinks I might have.

After her car crashed, Julia called for the cleanup crews. That's why they were there on the road late that night. They were waiting to go down the hill and clean up the site. I don't know what caused the crash itself, whether it was something to do with the swarm or whether it was just an accident. There's no one to ask about it now.

The facility in the desert was entirely destroyed. There was enough methane in the main laboratory to produce a fireball in excess of two thousand degrees Fahrenheit. Any biological materials would have been incinerated. But I still worry. They never found any bodies in the ruins, not even skeletons.

*   *   *

Mae took the bacteriophage to her old lab in Palo Alto. I hope she made them understand how desperate the situation is. She's being very quiet about their reaction. I think they should put the phage into the water supply, but Mae says the chlorine will take it out. Maybe there should be a vaccine program. As far as we know, the phage works to kill the swarms.

Sometimes I have ringing in my ears, which is a worrisome sign. And I feel a vibrating in my chest and abdomen. I can't tell if I am just paranoid, or if something is really happening to me. I try to keep a brave face for the kids, but of course you can't fool kids. They know I'm frightened.

The last mystery to be cleared up was why the swarms always returned to the laboratory. It never made any sense to me. I kept worrying about it because it was such an unreasonable goal. It didn't fit the PREDPREY formulations. Why would a predator keep returning to a particular location?

Of course, in retrospect there was only one possible answer. The swarms were intentionally programmed to return. The goal was explicitly defined by the programmers themselves.

But why would anybody program in a goal like that?

I didn't know until a few hours ago.

The code that Ricky showed me wasn't the code they had actually used on the particles. He couldn't show me the real code, because I would have known immediately what had been done. Ricky didn't ever tell me. Nobody ever told me.

What bothers me most is an email I found on Julia's hard drive earlier today. It was from her to Ricky Morse, with a CC to Larry Handler, the head of Xymos, outlining the procedure to follow to get the camera swarm to work in high wind. The plan was to intentionally release a swarm into the environment.

And that's exactly what they did.

They pretended it was an accidental release, caused by missing air filters. That's why Ricky gave me that long guided tour, and the song and dance about the contractor and ventilation system. But none of what he told me was true. The release was planned.

It was intentional from the beginning.

When they couldn't make the swarm work in high wind, they tried to engineer a solution. They failed. The particles were just too small and light—and arguably too stupid, too. They had design flaws from the beginning and now they couldn't solve them. Their whole multimillion-dollar defense project was going down the drain, and they couldn't solve it.

So they decided to make the swarm solve it for them.

They reconfigured the nanoparticles to add solar power and memory. They rewrote the particle program to include a genetic algorithm. And they released the particles to reproduce and evolve, and see if the swarm could learn to survive on its own.

And they succeeded.

It was so dumb, it was breathtaking. I didn't understand how they could have embarked on this plan without recognizing the consequences. Like everything else I'd seen at Xymos, it was jerry-built, half-baked, concocted in a hurry to solve present problems and never a thought to the future. That might be typical corporate thinking when you were under the gun, but with technologies like these it was dangerous as hell.

But of course, the real truth was more complicated. The technology itself invited the behavior. Distributed agent systems ran by themselves. That was how they functioned. That was the whole point: you set them up and let them go. You got in the habit of doing that. You got in the habit of treating agent networks that way. Autonomy was the point of it all.

But it was one thing to release a population of virtual agents inside a computer's memory to solve a problem. It was another thing to set real agents free in the real world.

They just didn't see the difference. Or they didn't care to see it.

And they set the swarm free.

The technical term for this is "self-optimization." The swarm evolves on its own, the less successful agents die off, and the more successful agents reproduce the next generation. After ten or a hundred generations, the swarm evolves toward a best solution. An optimum solution.

This kind of thing is done all the time inside the computer. It's even used to generate new computer algorithms. Danny Hillis did one of the first of those runs years back, to optimize a sorting algorithm. To see if the computer could figure out how to make itself work better. The program found a new method. Other people quickly followed his lead.

But it hasn't been done with autonomous robots in the real world. As far as I know, this was the first time. Maybe it's already happened, and we just didn't hear about it. Anyway, I'm sure it'll happen again.

Probably soon.

It's two in the morning. The kids finally stopped vomiting. They've gone to sleep. They seem to be peaceful. The baby is asleep. Ellen is still pretty sick. I must have dozed off again. I don't know what woke me. I see Mae coming up the hill from behind my house. She's with the guy in the silver suit, and the rest of the SSVT team. She's walking toward me. I can see that she's smiling. I hope her news is good.

I could use some good news right now.

Julia's original email says, "We have nothing to lose." But in the end they lost everything—their company, their lives, everything. And the ironic thing is, the procedure worked. The swarm actually solved the problem they had set for it.

But then it kept going, kept evolving.
And they let it.
They didn't understand what they were doing.
I'm afraid that will be on the tombstone of the human race.
I hope it's not.
We might get lucky.

BIBLIOGRAPHY

This novel is entirely fictitious, but the underlying research programs are real. The following references may assist the interested reader to learn more about the growing convergence of genetics, nanotechnology, and distributed intelligence.

Adami, Christoph. *Introduction to Artificial Life*. New York: Springer-Verlag, 1998.

Bedau, Mark A., John S. McCaskill, Norman H. Packard, and Steen Rasmussen. *Artificial Life VII, Proceedings of the Seventh International Conference on Artificial Life*. Cambridge, Mass.: MIT Press, 2000.

Bentley, Peter, ed. *Evolutionary Design by Computers*. San Francisco: Morgan Kaufmann, 1999.

Bonabeau, Eric, Marco Dorigo, and Guy Theraulaz. *Swarm Intelligence: From Natural to Artificial Systems*. New York: Oxford Univ. Press, 1999.

Brams, Steven J. *Theory of Moves*. New York: Cambridge Univ. Press, 1994.

Brooks, Rodney A. *Cambrian Intelligence*. Cambridge, Mass.: MIT Press, 1999.

Camazine, Scott, Jean-Louis Deneubourg, Nigel R. Franks, James Sneyd, Guy Theraulaz, and Eric Bonabeau. *Self-Organization in Biological Systems*. Princeton, N.J.: Princeton, 2001. See especially chapter 19.

Caro, T. M., and Clare D. Fitzgibbon. "Large Carnivores and Their Prey." In Crawley, *Natural Enemies*, 1992.

Crandall, B. C. "Molecular Engineering," in B. C. Crandall, ed., *Nanotechnology*, Cambridge, Mass.: MIT Press, 1996.

Crawley, Michael J., ed. *Natural Enemies: The Population Biology of Predators, Parasites, and Diseases*. London: Blackwell, 1992.

Davenport, Guy, tran. *7 Greeks*. New York: New Directions, 1995.

BIBLIOGRAPHY

Dobson, Andrew P., Peter J. Hudson, and Annarie M. Lyles. "Macroparasites," from Crawley, *Natural Enemies*, 1992.

Drexler, K. Eric. *Nanosystems, Molecular Machinery, Manufacturing, and Computation*. New York: Wiley & Sons, 1992.

———. "Introduction to Nanotechnology," in Krummenacker and Lewis, *Prospects in Nanotechnology*.

Ewald, Paul W. *Evolution of Infectious Disease*. New York: Oxford Univ. Press, 1994.

Ferber, Jacques. *Multi-Agent Systems: An Introduction to Distributed Artificial Intelligence*. Reading, Mass.: Addison-Wesley, 1999.

Goldberg, David E. *Genetic Algorithms in Search, Optimization and Machine Learning*. Boston: Addison-Wesley, 1989.

Hassell, Michael P. *The Dynamics of Competition and Predation*. Institute of Biology, Studies in Biology No. 72, London: Edward Arnold, 1976.

Hassell, Michael P., and H. Charles J. Godfray. "The Population Biology of Insect Parasitoids," in Crawley, *Natural Enemies*, 1992.

Holland, John H. *Hidden Order: How Adaptation Builds Complexity*. Cambridge, Mass.: Perseus, 1996.

Koza, John R. "Artificial Life: Spontaneous Emergence of Self-Replicating and Evolutionary Self-Improving Computer Programs," in Langton, ed., *Artificial Life III*.

Kelly, Kevin. *Out of Control*. Cambridge, Mass.: Perseus, 1994.

Kennedy, James, and Russell C. Eberhart. *Swarm Intelligence*. San Diego: Academic Press, 2001.

Kohler, Timothy A., and George J. Gumerman. *Dynamics in Human and Primate Societies: Agent-Based Modeling of Social and Spatial Processes*. New York: Oxford Univ. Press, 2000.

Kortenkamp, David, R. Peter Bonasso, and Robin Murphy. *Artificial Intelligence and Mobile Robots*. Cambridge, Mass.: MIT Press, 1998.

Krummenacker, Markus, and James Lewis, eds. *Prospects in Nanotechnology: Toward Molecular Manufacturing*. New York: Wiley & Sons, 1995.

Kruuk, Hans. *The Spotted Hyena: A Study of Predation and Social Behavior*. Chicago: Univ. Chicago Press, 1972.

Langton, Christopher G., ed. *Artificial Life*. Santa Fe Institute Studies in the Sciences of Complexity, Proc. Vol. VI. Reading, Mass.: Addison-Wesley, 1989.

Langton, Christopher G., Charles Taylor, J. Doyne Farmer, and Steen Rasmussen, eds. *Artificial Life II*. Santa Fe Institute Studies in the Sciences of Complexity, Proc. Vol. X. Redwood City, Calif.: Addison-Wesley, 1992.

Langton, Christopher G., ed. *Artificial Life III*. Santa Fe Institute Studies in the Sciences of Complexity, Proc. Vol. XVII. Reading, Mass.: Addison-Wesley, 1994.

Levy, Steven. *Artificial Life*. New York: Pantheon, 1992.

Lyshevski, Sergey Edward. *Nano- and Microelectromechanical Systems: Fundamentals of Nano- and Microengineering*. New York: CRC Press, 2001.

Millonas, Mark M., "Swarms, Phase Transitions, and Collective Intelligence," in Langton, ed., *Artificial Life III*.

Mitchell, Melanie. *An Introduction to Genetic Algorithms*. Cambridge, Mass.: MIT Press, 1996.

Nishimura, Shin I. "Studying Attention Dynamics of a Predator in a Prey-Predator System," in Bedau et al., *Artificial Life VII*.

Nishimura, Shin I., and Takashi Ikegami. "Emergence of Collective Strategies in a Prey-Predator Game Model." *Artificial Life*, V. 3, no. 4, 1997, p. 423 ff.

Nolfi, Stefano. "Coevolving Predator and Prey Robots: Do 'Arms Races' Arise in Artificial Evolution?" *Artificial Life*, Fall 98, V. 4, 1998, p. 311 ff.

Nolfi, Stefano, and Dario Floreano. *Evolutionary Robotics: The Biology, Intelligence, and Technology of Self-Organizing Machines*. Cambridge, Mass.: MIT Press, 2000.

Reggia, James A., Reiner Schulz, Gerald S. Wilkinson, and Juan Uriagereka. "Conditions Enabling the Evolution of Inter-Agent Signaling in an Artificial World." *Artificial Life*, V. 7, 2001, p. 3.

Reynolds, Craig R. "An Evolved, Vision-Based Model of Obstacle Avoidance Behavior" in Langton, ed., *Artificial Life III*.

Schelling, Thomas C. *Micromotives and Macrobehavior*. New York: Norton, 1978.

Solem, Johndale C. "The Motility of Microrobots," in Langton, et al., *Artificial Life III*.

Wooldridge, Michael. *Reasoning About Rational Agents*. Cambridge, Mass.: MIT Press, 2000.

Yaeger, Larry. "Computational Genetics, Physiology, Metabolism, Neural Systems, Learning, Vision, and Behavior or PolyWorld: Life in a New Context," in Langton, ed., *Artificial Life III*.